SPRINTER

Bruce Jones

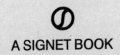

A SIGNET BOOK

SIGNET
Published by New American Library, a division of
Penguin Putnam Inc., 375 Hudson Street, New York, New York 10014, U.S.A.
Penguin Books Ltd, 27 Wrights Lane, London W8 5TZ, England
Penguin Books Australia Ltd, Ringwood, Victoria, Australia
Penguin Books Canada Ltd, 10 Alcorn Avenue, Toronto, Ontario, Canada M4V 3B2
Penguin Books (N.Z.) Ltd, 182–190 Wairau Road, Auckland 10, New Zealand

Penguin Books Ltd, Registered Offices:
Harmondsworth, Middlesex, England

Published by Signet, an imprint of New American Library, a division of Penguin Putnam Inc. This is an authorized reprint of a hardcover edition published by Doubleday,
a division of Bantam Doubleday Dell Publishing Group, Inc., 1540 Broadway, New
York, New York 10036.

First Signet Printing, August 1999
10 9 8 7 6 5 4 3 2 1

 REGISTERED TRADEMARK — MARCA REGISTRADA

Printed in the United States of America

PUBLISHER'S NOTE
This is a work of fiction. Names, characters, places, and incidents either are the product of the author's imagination or are used fictitiously, and any resemblance to actual
persons, living or dead, events, or locales is entirely coincidental.

to my agent
Harvey Klinger
for going the distance

"The FBI's internal computer system has as much security as the highest secrets the government has. We have a variety of protections . . . We have software protection, we have protection that relates to background investigations of our personnel . . . we have a lot of oversight, a lot of checks and balances. We have audit trails. We have periodic inquiries of those audit trails. We have a variety of surprise inspections, encryption. The list goes on and on . . ."

—David Nemecek,
FBI assistant director

"There is no security . . ."
—Allen Schweitzer,
indicted 1991 for penetrating the FBI's secret NCIC files

Prologue

Irv Bradford held the prickly specter of death within him. Held it close.

It was not death itself Bradford feared. Rather sudden oblivion, dying without warning, blindsided from this world without opportunity to put one's affairs in order, kiss loved ones good-bye, contemplate a final time the mysterious mosaic of life. It was the idea of being rent suddenly apart.

This paranoia was not lost on wife or confidants, the several confidants Bradford had left. In his position as head of a multibillion-dollar publishing empire there were but a trusted few, the two who might have understood and applauded his caution already dead.

The publisher ruminated daily in the furnace blast of the executive sauna, seeking to seep the fear from his pores, that sensation of something always just behind him. His own paper, the *Union,* had labeled his ongoing nemesis the Solobomber, a shadowy elusive force who'd slipped consistently—seemingly efffortlessly—through FBI fingers since last March when the first victims were targeted. The feds, in fact, were awash in flat-footed humiliation, flummoxed over everything from what kind of bomb the killer employed to exactly how he'd arranged the destruction of two other worldwide corporation heads, heads even bigger than Bradford's.

Irv Bradford, though, had not fought his way to the top of San Diego's most honored tabloid with timidity; he was a fighter, had fought cancer back in '86, fought the loss of his son to Vietnam, would fight this shadowy evil as well. In the noisy hive of offices shared with the *Union,* Bradford conducted business as usual unruffled and professional, answering last-minute queries from the afternoon shift, signing this, officiating that, and finally, toward day's end, calling in Manuel.

A refugee from Argentine guerrilla warfare who spoke little English but excelled in weaponry and explosive detection, Manuel would enter with his slender aluminum pole, the angled horseshoe hoop clicking, and sweep Bradford's cluttered office. Sweep under the desk, under the files, in the files, under the air conditioner . . . sweep the ceiling, walls, and even—which always made Bradford smile—a perfunctory sniff under the coffee machine. Satisfied, he would nod, and Bradford would ease—slightly more mollified now—into his swivel chair, lean back, and excuse Manuel. Bradford was always mildly surprised when the chair did not explode beneath him.

All packages, of course, all mails—even slender envelopes—were opened by others outside the office. Anything weighing more than a pound was carefully dismantled in the alley behind the building by a professional member of the San Diego bomb squad. When they were too busy—or out of patience—Bradford found his own people. He had specified emphatically to family and relatives *to not* under any circumstances have birthday or Father's Day presents delivered to the office.

After work, Bradford's ritual rarely varied. Manuel was waiting beside Bradford's shiny Lexus, metal detector in hand. It was Manuel who opened the locked car, Manuel who stepped inside first, sweeping his clicking metal hoop around the interior, including both trunk and hood. And, of course, a thorough search *beneath* the automobile, even though it was parked all day in a private stall, guarded by two beefy, expensive attendants. Bradford did not take chances. He had a wife and three kids dependent on him, and a fervent desire to live well past retirement, which, since he was CEO of the paper, would come at his discretion.

A quick stop-off at O'Toolie's for an unwinder, then down to the Embarcadero, 23 Soma Slip, and again to the faithful Manuel waiting dockside with his horseshoe metal detector beside the publisher's seventeen-foot powder-blue ketch. Usually the sweeping was all done, unless Bradford left work early, in which case he waited patiently beside the surf-slapped pilings for the dark-skinned bomb expert to comb galley, lazaret, the sole of the cabin, bulkheads, forecastle, binnacle, the bilge, and the keel. All carefully scrutinized and scoured, even though the boat had been rocking easily under constant guard from morning to eventide. Once Manuel gave his nod, publisher Irving Bradford would step gingerly aboard.

Tonight he'd stayed late. His feet hurt, a headache was beginning behind his left eye. He'd have just under two hours of leisure time to coast lazily about San Diego Harbor, wave at the tourists on Mission Beach, scout the peninsula between Coronado Island and the mainland, or prowl the navy yards, watch the shrouds and stays of the mighty steel-hulled *Star of India* blink on as twilight deepened to smog-tinged amber, then indigo. Then, pulled by guilt and Miranda's waiting supper, he'd point the blue ketch's bow back to the slip and home, two more gratefully sipped brandies already under his belt.

He opted for Coronado's seaward side this evening, scuttling past the majestic Hotel del Coronado and down the skinny finger of the Silver Strand. Not bothering to check the radio for weather, he drifted parallel to shore a few kilometers, dreaming—as always—of sailing on and on . . . right on over the border to Mexico, away from all strife and worry, deadlines and mad bombers. Always coming about instead, at the last moment, and heading back to the jaded safety of his Point Loma three-story and Miranda's good kitchen smells. Maybe his wife was right. Thus far the Solobomber had never struck this far south. Though, of course, Bradford knew something Miranda did not. Knew money and power were the least of the things that linked him to the two previous victims. He saw them, these victims, bloodied and torn in fitful dreams, in the swirling vortex of his shower's drain . . . sometimes numbering his own face among them. His real hope, of course, was that someone—feds, police, someone—would catch up with the bomber before the bomber caught up with him. A not overweening hope, but constantly there, a warm pulse at his left shoulder.

Tonight, however, the brandies did the warming, Irv Bradford nestled cozily under the red glow of the chart table lamp, hand-polished brass and leather glowing around him from years of tenderly applied oil. He loved his family but oh how he loved the little ketch. He reached for the bottle and felt the tension slip away.

A glance at his watch told him he would be even later than anticipated. Screw it. The day had been tedious, grueling, and he'd allowed himself to be lulled by the hull's rhythmic roll, the alcohol spreading warmth in his gut, pressing out the plucking fear. Miranda would be silently angry, but he could assuage this slightly by phoning—or better yet by using the newly installed Sprinter 9000 computer to fax her a brief love note. He grinned at his mind's picture of her pulling his clumsy apology from the bleeping machine in his study. Something brief, and overly sentimental. She'd still give him a cold shoulder over colder dinner, but she'd come alive in his arms later . . .

He set down his tinkling glass, made a mental note to restock the cabin's fridge with ice. He switched on the computer, felt its confident hum, reached for the keys, bulldog editions and mad bombers the furthest thing from his mind for the moment.

He rounded the inlet past the big jetty that would put him on course for the Embarcadero and his slip and home. Pacific Highway, parallel with the Embarcadero, was overlit tonight, he noticed, and bereft of normal evening traffic. A crowd gathered there flanking the street, some activity transpiring. He gave the crowd a short hello blast on the ketch's horn.

The Point Loma lighthouse winked at him coyly once on its evening's revolution. Irv placed his hands on the keyboard, forming words in his mind.

The explosion, when it came, was so vast, so purifyingly brilliant, he wasn't even sure of his final thoughts in this world . . . though he felt they might have been of her . . .

Chapter 1

Elvis was rounding Olive Street with her, climbing the high notes, as Jeni was climbing the first real hill. It was a good sign.

Presley was reaching high and smooth, sliding between stanzas of one of her favorites: "I Was the One." That way he had—his magical young voice had—of changing not only key but timbre and range to a nearly female falsetto always thrilled her to her toes.

She'd need it. She'd need it in her toes, her calves, and her tight, muscular runner's tendons if she were to win this race.

For the past fifteen minutes now, Jeni had been pumping rhythmically along the Embarcadero's closed Pacific Highway, blocked north and south with zebra-striped police sawhorses. She ran easily, unhurriedly, content for now with an even, graceful lope. She was somewhere in the middle of the other sixty or so runners, her bright orange safety shorts flapping, the big number 6 sign banging softly at her back. There was no question in her mind that she could beat all the others, beat them without even overly exerting herself. All the other runners with the possible exception of one.

A willowy black girl with endless legs, reedy frame, and a look about her vaguely aboriginal face that suggested incalculable reserve, *beaucoup* endurance, had caught Jeni's eye halfway through the race as she pulled up doggedly, smoothly, on her left. Like Jeni, this long-legged dark angel held back in midpack, waiting for the final yards of the race, waiting for the sprint.

For Jeni—assuming her calculations were correct—the final sprint would come at Jewel and Second Street, just this side of the turn into Sea Port Village. From there it was less than two hundred yards to the Naval Head-quarters Building and the fluttering yellow tape that meant victory or defeat for half a hundred chest-heaving competitors. Only one would claim it.

Looking over the restless competitors from the starting blocks, Jeni was pretty sure her chances were good, even excellent. And she wanted this trophy badly, needed it. Crouched there on her fingertips under the track gun, stereo earphones in place, tape loaded with Elvis fa-vorites, she basked in good vibes, in cautious confidence. There were two or three lean-muscled male runners that looked to have some staying power, but nothing she shouldn't be able to handle. When the gun fired, she let them, and half of the rest, surge ahead eagerly, foolishly, only a handful wise enough to hold back with her, pacing themselves. Of these, none possessed her natural grace, the power in the bulge of her hard, sexy thighs. If she could beat these, she could take the rest, take the trophy—and the prize money—home.

Then, rounding Rosecrans for the final mile, she'd seen a dark shadow sweep confidently into her peripheral vi-sion, a flat-chested, whippet-thin wonder with legs like a savanna cheetah. Everything about the black runner be-spoke wilderness cunning. She paced Jeni neatly, a syn-chronous ghost, physically her mirror opposite: dark, springy curls to Jeni's blond ponytail, shallow chest and

narrow buttocks to Jeni's curvy fuselage. Cheap, slapping
Keds to Jeni's overpriced Reeboks.

Still, Jeni thought she had a chance. Elvis had just
completed the sweet agonies of "I Was the One" through
her Sprinter 9000 Walkman, and was launching into the
plaintive peals of her all-time favorite: "I Want You, I
Need You, I Love You." If she could win a race with any
song in her head, it was that one. She felt the surge of
Scotty Moore's guitar intro, buckled down, gritted her
teeth, and picked up the pace. The black girl stayed even.

Most of the others had fallen behind now. Only two
desperately red-faced men pumped ahead, one bald and bespectacled with an almost feminine gait, the other fireplug-
sturdy, not built for the long haul: they would soon be eating
her dust. Hers and the dark, reedy black girl's, who seemed
now to be matching Jeni's every move, even anticipating it,
picking apart the blond, bouncing ponytail style without
ever once looking in her direction. Eerie.

Even so, Jeni felt confident. She had depleted none of
her reserve for the final sprint. And in a sprint, Jeni Starbuck was just damn hard to catch. Olive was coming up
fast on her left. She girded herself for the dash.

But as though anticipating it, the black girl spurted
ahead suddenly, so heart-jarringly abrupt, Jeni felt a stab
of adrenaline, saw an inner vision of the Roadrunner
powering past the coyote as though he was just standing
there.

Off guard, cursing under her breath, Jeni poured it on,
all the angrier because her tactic—to start her sprint at
Olive—had been foiled. It would be a longer sprint now,
one that would use every ounce of reserve. She found herself hating the black woman.

Fanned by this, she gained even ground with the dark,
whipping legs in seconds, tucked her chin, and let it all

out, not even hearing Elvis now, listening to naught but the desperate chug of her heart, the vibrating timpani of running shoes thwacking cement.

With this burst of speed, the black girl finally looked at her, and in the glance Jeni saw the specter of the other woman's defeat. Her heart hitched with victory. Her flashing legs inched ahead.

It would be close, but she could hold a dead sprint longer than anyone. The black girl began to fall behind . . .

Fifty yards from the fluttering finish banner, she heard a short horn blast to seaward, flicked an absent glance that way and—in the grip of victory—detected briefly the hull of a sleek, powder-blue sailing yacht rounding the jetty.

Twenty yards from the finish, and a full body length ahead of the black runner, Jeni felt the earth lurch beneath her (*quake!*) followed immediately by a wall of heat, the sudden backwash of a giant bird's wing pressing her off balance. Closest to shore, she took the full brunt of the blast, even partially shielded the black runner, the concussion, lagging just behind the heat, knocking the runners together in a tangle of legs and running shoes. Reedy or not, the dark-skinned girl was tall and solid. It was Jeni who went down.

She took the brunt on her right knee and upper leg— didn't feel the pain of torn flesh, didn't even hear the echo of the explosion in the bay, the startled cries of the spectators wrenching around to see. Didn't notice the other runners passing her.

She sat on the warm macadam on the heels of her bloodied hands, bathed in the orange glow of the explosion's climbing plume, and watched with hooded eyes as the black girl snapped the winner's ribbon gracefully and raced onward to glory.

* * *

Afterward, mired in defeat, Jeni limped to her rusty
Volvo, not daring to meet any spectators' eyes. No problem: they were all turned toward the remains of the yacht
smoldering in the bay. Jeni scrambled past the news cameras, waiting at the finish line and now suddenly agog
with a much bigger story, and managed to climb in and
drive to Harvey Wahlbanger's for a much needed drink.
She had not drunk once since training had begun two
months ago. As Dr. Keegie had reminded pointedly, psychiatric drugs and alcohol don't mix, unless you're looking for a suicide cocktail. The truth was she wasn't taking
her drugs on a regular basis anymore either, and she figured the chance was worth it. One drink wouldn't kill her.

She hadn't planned on stopping off—had planned on
winning—had not brought along proper attire for a noisy,
blue-collar bar. Well, screw that too. She was tired and
testy and needed a drink. Her knee was beginning to sting
badly now. She could dab brandy on it to protect against
infection.

She arrived in time for the six o'clock news on the
milky-screened Zenith above the bar, the same one that
had glowed there for the past four years, maybe longer for
all Jeni Starbuck knew.

She found an old familiar booth, ordered a bourbon
neat from a face she didn't recognize. None of the girls in
their tight red Wahlbanger T-shirts looked familiar, it had
been that long. Some of the regulars were familiar, however. Over there in his favorite place near the TV was
Harvey Spencer, the shortest, fastest cop on San Diego's
Finest. And there in a shadowed corner was Big Tim
Turner, a hulking veteran who had lost none of his steely
girth over the years, or so it seemed. Jeni didn't make eye
contact with either of them.

She sipped her drink when it came and watched the

dim screen, wondering if any news of the bay explosion had made it to the six o'clock spot in time. She supposed it was possible, if someone was fast on his feet. There had certainly been enough cameras covering the race.

Finally, after weather, sports, local human interest stories, and endless commercials, here it came: a last-minute spot on *"the apparent accidental explosion of a yacht in San Diego Harbor, not far from the legendary* Star of India *sailing vessel moored at the Embarcadero, and less than a hundred yards from the annual Race Against AIDS then in progress . . ."*

Hard information was sketchy, the silver-haired anchorman groping for adjectives, clearly rattled by being handed a last-minute bulletin, filling in the blank spaces by constantly repeating bare-bone facts about time and place while the engineer rolled and rerolled the only quick shot of the explosion. One quickly thinking cameraman had swung toward it just after the concussion. The scene began with the runners from a slightly high angle as if shot from the top of a news van, a distant shot in which Jeni could barely pick herself and the black girl out, lurching ahead of the others. The camera zoomed to a tight shot of the excited spectators, caught their startled expressions and the thud of the explosion, jiggled and panned raggedly right, finally settling on the greasy black pall rising above the bay. Jeni could see the stern of the blue yacht she'd glimpsed earlier slip under waves pocked with raining debris—then only dissipating smoke. Just keep it on the boat, she thought in her booth, gut tightening, just keep it on the boat, don't come back to the damn race . . .

But the camera did swing back, first to the milling, disrupted crowd, then to the now empty street—or nearly empty, but for Jeni squatting there on her haunches, gripping her bleeding knee. And oh Christ, *no,* now the damn camera was zooming in tighter still, until Jeni Starbuck's pretty, mystified countenance filled the bar's twenty-seven-inch Color Trak screen, for all of San Diego County to see. "Oh Jesus, give me a break!" It came out unbidden—too loudly—and people in the saloon were turning to look now, to put a face with the voice, match it with the face on the flickering screen above the bar.

Jeni looked down at her drink, cheeks flaming.

Great. Fine. Take a *good* look! It's been that kind of fucking day!

They rolled the tape twice more. Finally—merci-fully—switched back to the studio and the fumbling silver-haired anchor—more details on this incident as it develops, stay with Channel 7, etc.

"Hey."

She glanced up and found a stained T-shirt blocking the light, a muscular torso towering over her, ruddy face above it. It smiled with yellow teeth and bad dental work, a day's growth of beard and the reek of beer breath. "That you on the tube?"

She looked back at her drink. "No."

"Yeah? Looks like you." A beefy hand gestured toward the conspicuously empty seat across from her, dark eyes eager. Jeni actually considered it a moment; it might be easier just to let him sit, let him buy her a drink, and then make her excuses and get the hell out of there. But she was tired and sweaty and felt like taking nobody's shit tonight.

"I'm expecting someone," she told him.

The ruddy face was not dissuaded. "Yer knee's cut. Sure you're okay?"

She glanced down. The knee was indeed bleeding again, and hurting all of a sudden like hell. "I'm fine. Just a scratch. Thanks for asking."

But answering him at all was a mistake, politeness mistaken for interest; he was used to hard women, acid-tongued rejections. He stood there and grinned at Jeni until she had to look up. "Was there something else?"

"Runner, huh. Who you runnin' from, honey, yer old man?"

Jeni nearly smiled at the inadvertent irony.

"Name's Howie Cruthers."

"Hello, Howie. Will you excuse me now, please?"

"How about two lonely people share a drink?"

"Thanks, Howie, I'm not lonely."

From his private, shadowy corner, Big Tim Turner looked up to access the situation. Jeni might have seen him smile but it was hard to tell in this light.

The stained T-shirt sat down without being invited, leaned across the scarred table. "You sure look lonely to me! Just one little drink, how about it?"

"Howie, take a hike, huh?"

He answered by grinning beer breath on her. He wasn't going away. "I never met no runners before. How about we go somewhere and fuck?"

It just wasn't her day. "I'm a cop, Howie, you better peddle your papers elsewhere."

But Howie was determined to get laid tonight, and quickly, before he was too drunk. "How about *your* papers? You're a cop, prove it. Let's see some ID."

Jeni dragged in another sigh. "Look, I'm tired and I stink, okay?"

A ham-sized fist closed over her slim, white wrist. There was heat and vast power behind it.

Jeni, not resisting, leaned toward him with an air of resignation. "Okay, I'm not a cop. But I am tired. Exhausted. And you're in a hurry. Would a quick blow job satisfy you?"

Pleasant surprise on the stupid face, then the picket fence grin again. "Your place or mine?"

Jeni leaned closer, voice lowered. "There's a latch on the lady's room door. What do you say?"

Howie let go her wrist and they stood together. From his corner Big Tim Turner sat upright with his beer, one brow rising on the wide, craggy face. But he made no effort to intervene. She hadn't supposed he would. She snatched up her purse and led the ruddy-faced Howie to the back of the saloon.

Jeni entered the lady's room first, checked it quickly for occupants, held the door for Howie, turned, and latched it closed behind her. Turned again and cracked his left shin with a short, snapping kick of her right leg. The effort caused her to wince from the scrape incurred during the race.

Howie, shocked beyond thought, smacked the grimy sink with his butt. Jeni had considered the groin area as target, but rejected that as gratuitous. Anyway, once the legs go, the opponent goes.

Nonetheless, she added the safety measure of a chest kick, putting a day's worth of frustration and disappointment behind it. Less massive than he appeared, Howie Cruthers cracked the hinges off the toilet booth door in his backward retreat, arms pinwheeling, slammed hard against the plastic lid, a noise like the ringing from a well. Jeni rode the inertia, leapt astride his chest, whipping out a shiny Ruger, placed the bright muzzle under his nostrils, shoved hard, and gave him a piggy face. Fear brimmed Howie's eyes. She gave him a moment to think about it, then straightened, turned, and stepped on his nuts on the way out.

Back in her booth she finished her drink, barely breathing hard, a fact she noted with some satisfaction. Like riding a bike; you never really forget.

Big Tim Turner regarded her calmly from his shadowed corner, starting on another beer. This time she was pretty sure he smiled just a little.

There was another time, of course, when he might have assisted. When she was ATF. Before the Fall.

The roughhouse, however brief, only aggravated the weeping leg wound.

She was finally obliged to stop off at Las Flores Emergency and have it looked at. It was streaming by the time she got there. An intern who must have been ten years her junior rewarded her with seven deep stitches and deeper hurt; she sucked back pain twice and he apologized, chagrined. The wound, he announced, located at the upper left portion of the femur at the superpatellar bursa, was nowhere near the femoral artery and should, in fact, cause her little problem with her running, though it would remain tender to the touch.

Perched there on a cold, antiseptic metal table, all long, tapered legs and little red running shorts, Jeni discerned distant trembling in the young doctor's otherwise sure hands—found herself taken aback when, in cow-eyed terror, he asked her for a date. She declined. Took a prescription for codeine from him and left.

Limping through the parking lot, visions of the cow eyes accompanying every painful step, she managed a secret smile for the young doctor: the day, it seemed, not a total loss . . .

Chapter 2

The tall man stepped from Dulles International into bright Washington sunshine, an achingly beautiful day.

He had sat in the terminal an extra fifteen minutes waiting for a red Mazda from Avis. He favored red and this was to be a favored day, a celebratory day, around the axis of which his life—the lives of so many others—would surely turn.

He drove around the city for a while before heading for Pennsylvania Avenue and the Hoover Building.

He rolled down the windows of the rental car and let the wind rustle his hair, the sweet smell of cherry blossoms filling flared nostrils. He had arranged the day around cherry blossom season and the city was riotous with them. He spent ten minutes at the Lincoln monument alone. He wept a few traces of tears. The towering, seated figure with the wise, hooded eyes always brought tears to his own.

He loved Washington. It was so . . . white. Marble white. Bright with it. It almost hurt the eyes. If he stared at the bright marble icons long enough—the alabaster tombs and shrines—he would get a headache. He would not stare today; this was not a day for headaches. This was a day for elation.

He had lunch at the Windsor Hotel on Delmonte Street,

ordered clams on the half shell and Plaza Pudding. He drove around town some more, smiling. He was in no hurry. He relished each moment here, knowing it would be his last. Things were already set in motion, the mission already begun. Washington was just one last final check.

At just past midnight, he drove the rental car to E Street, to Hoover's Taj Mahal, the FBI headquarters building.

He walked to Pennsylvania Avenue. It was a long walk from the larger E Street entrance, but because it was such a lovely evening, he took it. Besides, the E Street entrance was for the unwashed masses, folks from Oklahoma on vacation, wanting the tour. Of the Bureau's 24,000 employees, more than 7,500 used the Pennsylvania doors.

He approached the sign-in desk, smiled at a plain-clothes agent seated there, and showed him a badge and his FBI ID. Both were real, but neither belonged to the tall man with the easy smile. He signed the register and asked the agent affably how things were going. How do they always go? the agent replied, and they both laughed companionably.

He left the desk and walked through a glass door, and another, to the agency's mainframe computer system, a room occupying the entire first floor, an area the size of a football field.

He walked across spotless tile floors, through rarefied, temperature-controlled air, past row after endless row of softly humming, cream-colored containers. On his left were banks of disks and tapes, stretching to infinity; on his right, shelf upon shelf of backup batteries. The latter were there in case the emergency generator should shut down, a vast improbability, but the Bureau was nothing if not prudent.

At this hour, the big room—alive with humming circuits—was void of human life.

He moved to the central control console at the far end. There was a day when the console would have been manned by a small team of technicians, twenty-four hours a day. Now machines could do it better than man. A sign of the times.

He sat down in the swivel chair and, hands over the keys, paused to reflect a moment. Beneath his fingers, deep within the workings of the huge matrix, lay a complex of interlinking systems and subsystems that contained countless millions of records. More records than any man could hope to read. They listed everything from the profound to the prosaic—from the deepest, darkest secrets of other world governments (secrets that could ruin them with the punch of a button) to the inane readout of a traffic ticket in Topeka, Kansas.

He held his fingers over the keys and felt their nascent power. Felt himself glow inwardly.

The massive headquarters mainframes, complex as they were, held two basic functions: the National Crime Information Center (NCIC), which provided a national criminal records system database for local, state, and federal agencies, plus the Royal Canadian Mounted Police, criminal justice agencies in Puerto Rico and the U.S. Virgin Islands; and secondly, the FBI's own internal network and its eleven subdivisions. The latter was used over two and a half million times a day. All of the agency's fifty-six field offices and five hundred auxiliary offices had access to it. It was the FBI's chief combatant against criminal technology. He who controlled the FBI mainframes held incalculable power. Before the system there was paper. Mountains of it. Tens of millions of three-by-five index cards and reference files, one and two inches thick, all stored in various field offices with no central access. Now there was the computer.

Fingers trembling—but not uncontrollably—he finally touched the keys. Two of them. A small green light on the console winked to life.

It was then he heard the sound across the room.

Hands frozen over the keys, the tall man listened. It was a crisp, chopping sound, coming somewhere behind him.

He punched a key and the green light winked out.

He swiveled around, left the chair, and walked calmly to the far end of the room, past the humming banks and shelves. He turned left before the first glass door and into a small, eight-by-eleven room containing a sink, a coffee machine, and a small executive refrigerator. The door of the refrigerator stood open, its contents blocked by a squat, beefy figure in gray slacks and white shirt, the sleeves rolled up. The figure was attacking the freezer unit with an ice pick, the tip of his balding head dripping sweat.

"Good evening," the tall man offered softly.

The man at the fridge, Agent George Lortz, turned about, red-faced with effort but not wholly alarmed. "Hey. Who're you?"

The tall man in the doorway smiled affably. "Console security. You?"

The squat man looked him up and down once. "Me too. I thought there was to be only one of us."

"That's what I thought."

Agent Lortz shook his head, sighed, went back to his hacking, huffing between breaths. "Another Bureau fuckup. It's the Schweitzer thing. Ever since the bastard was indicted the big boys have been paranoid. Like anyone could ever access that fucking nightmare out there."

"So this is your first night on the job?"

More hacking, soft cursing. "Pain in the ass. We're just goddamn tokens, pal, you and me. The frigging computer

can safeguard itself. It's all for show. Jesus, why doesn't
the Bureau sink a few bucks into a decent refrigerator!"
More hacking, a splintering of ice, then a miss, a harsher
curse.

"It's all in the wrist. Let me give you a hand."

"Hey, thanks!" Lortz grinned, relieved, extending a
hand. "George Lortz, moonlighting from UCO."

"Bill Smith, NCIC. What are you after, George, Scotch
on the rocks?"

"Well . . ."

"Your secret is safe with me, George."

Agent Lortz grinned. "Scotch would be fine. And make
one for yourself." He edged gratefully toward the door,
handing over the ice pick. "I'll just go back to the console
and pretend I'm guarding the nation's secrets."

"I won't be two minutes," the tall man assured him.

Two minutes later, Lortz turned from one of the three
console chairs to find a tinkling, amber glass being proffered him. "Hey, thanks, you're a gentleman and a
scholar. Mmm, Christ that's good."

Clutching—untouched—his own glass, the tall man
sat down beside Lortz.

Agent Lortz propped his feet on the console expan-
sively, sat back, and sipped contentment. "You got to
hand it to old Schweitzer, though. Only man to break the
FBI's NCIC system. Caught with his hand in the till. And
the bastard skates. How do you figure that?"

The tall man opposite Lortz was staring at the keys in
front of him. His fingers itched. The tinkling glass in his
hand was a cold and alien thing. "I think the Bureau was
reluctant to advertise its failings where Mr. Schweitzer
was concerned," he replied evenly. "He claims to have
penetrated not only NCIC but the Bureau's internal and
highly classified investigative files as well, you know."

"No shit."

The tall man set down the cold glass of tinkling ice, eyes still locked on the keys. His fingers were burning now. "Oh, yes. It was Schweitzer's contention that anything and everything can be had. Even the more sensitive things, intelligence matters, domestic intelligence and otherwise—anything. Schweitzer claimed that there is no true security at the Bureau."

Lortz offered feigned interest. "Hmph."

"Indeed. His theorem was that no security in the strictest sense existed so long as the Bureau remains a good-old-boy network. Most of the private eyes in this country are former law enforcement from some level—city, state, county, federal. It's like a membership card into an elite clique, George."

Agent Lortz, brows raised, not at all sure, suddenly, he should be privy to this, nodded uncomfortably.

"I suppose as long as it's allowed to exist like that and people look the other way, the information will continue to be open to illegitimate hackers. You know there was a former police officer in Arizona who persuaded his ex-colleagues to get NCIC data so he could use it to hunt down and murder his girlfriend."

"That a fact?"

His fingers on fire, hovering above the keys with a life of their own, the man beside Agent Lortz nodded. "Indeed. An NCIC operator in Pennsylvania conducted background searches for her drug dealer boyfriend. The man wanted to know if any of his potential clients were undercover officers. You want my opinion, George, this kind of thing happens more than we'd like to believe. Is that a red light on your monitor?"

Lortz sat up, mildly alarmed, turned his head. As he did, the man beside him, in a swift, nearly casual move,

slid four inches of the six-inch steel ice pick into Agent
Lortz's right ear. The perfect point, upon contact with the
brain, continued the remaining two inches until halted by
the wooden hilt.

Lortz experienced quick, exquisite pain during the
brief eruption of his eardrum, but—as the brain has no
nerve endings of its own—was not aware of anything
penetrating it.

Lortz stood, confused, brought a slow hand to the short
wooden handle extending from his ear, and said, "What
the hell is this—?" more curious than alarmed, his fear
not yet catching up to him. The tall man watched him
impassively.

Lortz's hand came away dripping. His eyes grew
owlish and now his fear found him. He offered the man
seated at the console his dripping palm and an almost
comically bewildered expression. "What's going on? . . ."

The tall man stood. "More than almost anyone knows,"
he replied, and drew the Browning from beneath his
jacket, a movement he had hoped the ice pick would
negate.

Lortz, past comprehending anything, turned away,
wove drunkenly across the immaculate floor as though
seeking answers from unseen powers, leaving a crimson
path of tiny explosions in his wake. The tall man took aim
at close range and fired into Lortz's back. His aim was
perfect.

The round—he noted with clinical detachment—
entered George Lortz above the lumbar region, traced a
slightly angular trajectory through the intercostal space
between the ribs, ripping the spine in half, destroying—at
this intimate distance—the paravertebral muscles. It exited through a considerable chunk of splintering sternum,
finding final rest in a wall just above a shelf of computer

disks, doing them no harm. Lortz's heart burst. He died before hitting the floor in a shower of red so profound, his body was nearly exsanguinated.

The man at the console replaced the gun, turned to the keys quickly, and made crisp, decisive movements with his fingers. The computer hummed beneath him, warming hands gone cold, spreading warmth all the way to his already calming chest.

After a while the tall man grunted satisfaction, sat back, having left with the computer what he'd brought to give it. Spent, warm all over now, he sagged in the swivel chair, sighed resonately.

Soon afterward, he went to the little custodial alcove beside the kitchenette, where he secured mop, pail, solvent, and other articles of cleansing. The round he dug easily from the wall with his nail, leaving a hole so insignificant it would not be spotted for perhaps months. He hummed softly while he worked, in accompaniment to the humming computers around him.

Chapter 3

She was having a dream about Molly. Together they tip-toed, barefoot, across slippery La Jolla beach rocks, searching the tidal pools for crabs, heads bent low over swirling eddies of green water. The sun was setting, the brightness eclipsed behind Molly's dark hair, making a nimbus of light, a halo glow, and Jeni looked up and smiled, squinting, the light growing brighter, and said, "You look just like an angel," and Molly laughed as she slowly began to fade, even as Jeni reached out to delicate hands that slipped right through hers—

The trill of the phone startled her from sleep. She fumbled it to her ear.

"Jeni, it's Helene. Don't forget your appointment at eleven."

"I won't, Helene, thanks."

"Hope I didn't wake you."

"No . . ." Jeni sighed. "I wasn't asleep."

She could hear the knowing smile in Helene's voice. Never could bullshit Helene. "Good. See you soon."

Dr. Keegie's office was in the federal building across from the V.A. Hospital.

There was always traffic here—the federal building flanked the first mile of San Diego's urban tourist attraction, Gas Lamp Quarter—and things could get testy on a hot day in slow-motion bumper-to-bumper.

At least this was what Jeni always assumed made her restless and slightly irritable during her monthly sojourns to Keegie's psychiatric care. Lately, though, she'd begun to believe it was less the snarled traffic and more the fact of Keegie himself. Or not so much Keegie the man, but the fact that she was seeing him at all.

And it bothered her because there was no reason to resent needing a doctor, mental or otherwise. One did what one needed to do. And she needed Keegie, needed his prescriptions, had since the day of Molly's death. Yet the resentment lingered.

Or was it guilt?

She always had the prescriptions filled . . . didn't always take them.

Helene Sharp, Keegie's assistant, had her business face on this morning. A pretty face, dark, sensibly cut hair, almond eyes, a pert, perfect nose with a light sprinkle of freckles. "It's been bobbed twice," she'd confided, smiling, to Jeni once, "the look from my Jewish Brooklyn mother was not to be forgotten. I was seeing a Catholic man at the time, going to Mass with him on occasion just to see the inside of that beautiful church in El Cajon. Ma never said poop about that . . . but the nose! Jesus."

She had Brubeck's staccato piano on the waiting room speakers this morning, even though Keegie had admonished her repeatedly for anything approaching discordant jazz. Montavoni was his choice: soothing. Helene rolled her eyes. "They keep listening to Monivani," she'd tell him, "and they'll *really* know clinical depression."

There was no one in the little waiting room this morning—Jeni the only patient—and she came to the small frosted sliding window, leaned down to chat with

Helene, who hardly looked up from a teetering mound of papers, fingers flashing over the keys of the office Sprinter. "Putting everything into the new computer. A pain in the ass, but once it's there I can halve these file folders. Anyway, that's how he wants it. He's moving, you know."

Jeni was surprised. "Dr. Keegie! Where?"

"Washington. Big promotion. He's all puffed up about it. You didn't notice the aura of regality when you walked in?"

"What about you?"

Helene shrugged, not looking up, fingers flying—clicking—even with those long, lacquered nails. "I stay right here in the warm California sun. You couldn't get me back East shoveling that ice-crusted shit for all the tea in Starbucks. You ever seen frozen snow after tires and dirt turn it the color of dung? Sure you have, you're from Texas. How's the knee?"

"It's okay. Helene, I'll miss you."

"What miss? We'll finally have lunch together instead of just talking about it. I'm ready for a few months retirement, let Jack carry the load awhile. Anyway, Dr. Landon will always take me back."

"Is that who he's recommending for me—Landon?"

"I would guess. Dr. Landon's great. Young. Even handsome in a bookish way. Good change for both of us. Want some tea, I've got jasmine."

But Keegie was poking his head through the door now, smiling at Jeni behind his perfectly cropped psychiatrist's beard. "Top of the morning!" He did look regal. Quite satisfied with himself. Mentioned nothing about the Brubeck to Helene.

"I understand you're abandoning me."

Keegie, scanning her file over morning coffee, smiled

vaguely, not looking up. "Dr. Landon has more stamina than I and nearly as much talent, though he's inordinately brutal on Freud. Besides, 'abandon'—your choice of words—indicates you've reached the transference stage . . . you're nearly cured anyway," and the smile broadened and he did look up now.

"The sober Dr. Keegie makes a joke. You must be very happy about this Washington move, cold weather and all."

"I am. It's a great opportunity for me. But let's talk about you. You look terrible."

"Never mind what I said before . . . you haven't changed."

"How're the mood swings?"

Jeni settled back on the couch; not the clichéd psychiatrist's lying-down kind of leather couch, but a comfortable cotton with warm maple armrests and Santa Fe upholstery. And a Chumash Indian blanket at her feet for carpet, lots of oak and earth colors around her, Keegie's inner office as cozy as the outer office was austere. She wondered how the wonderfully colorful western motif would do in a Washington office. And the Santa Fe style bookshelves heaped with Oliver Saks tomes. Was Saks in vogue back East? "The mood swings are swinging," she told him.

"Any suicidal ideation?"

Jeni looked down in embarrassment. "No . . ."

"Taking your medication?"

"Yes."

"How much Klonopin have we got you on . . ." and he fingered her file again.

"I lied. I haven't been taking it."

He closed the file, placed it in his lap, sighed. Gave her his patient look. "And why, pray?"

"I can't take that stuff and run at the same time. It makes me . . . it slows me down."

"A precise indication that it's working."

"I can't have anything dragging at me when I'm running. And don't tell me to stop the running, I need the running."

"I wasn't going to. Did you quit the coffee? Don't lie."

"The coffee perks me up."

"And slaps you right back down again. Jeni, I can't help you if you won't help yourself. Shall I make you come in every morning so I can watch you take your meds?"

Jeni blew out breath, regarded a print on the stucco wall, an abstract: hot shades of orange rising into a hotter rectangle of yellow . . . hot as September sun. She could imagine herself out in the hills somewhere, the chaparral. She alone under the ceaseless sun, amid miles and miles of nothing . . .

Next to it, smaller, nothing more than a sketch really, was a charcoal drawing of Dr. Keegie himself, immediately recognizable but more for the mood than the actual line work. His sternness, his slight arrogance, his pomposity, all captured in the eyes and mouth, stark black against white.

Jeni nodded to it. "Who did that?"

"A client did it for me."

"Talented client."

Dr. Keegie appraised her sternly. "Talk to me, Jeni."

"Talk? Why? You're not a client-centered psychiatrist. You don't delve into your patient's deeper psyche, you prescribe pills."

"You're pissed this morning. Why?"

She shifted restlessly on the couch. "I don't know."

"Yes you do."

"You tell me, you're the doctor."

"Jeni."

She shook her head. "I don't need all this crap. I don't need the Klonopin."

"All right. Why?"

"It isn't helping."

"It will if you'll take it."

"I've taken it. I don't need drugs. I'm not—"

Keegie watched her. "What? Not depressed?"

He had her there. It infuriated her. "I don't see why being depressed over your daughter's death should be such an inordinate thing."

"No one said it was. Losing a child, divorcing a spouse, both are two of the most traumatic things that can happen to an individual, and you have both in your history. But it's been more than a year."

"Do you allow smoking in here?" she asked suddenly.

Keegie frowned amusement. "If absolutely necessary. Why? You don't smoke."

Jeni shrugged, turned away. "Just curious."

Keegie placed her folder on an end table beside him. "Jeni, you're seeing me because you got stuck with me after your suicide attempt." Jeni winced. She instantly hated his cool, matter-of-fact approach. "And it's precisely because I am a medication-based psychiatrist that I'm able to prescribe for your moods. You don't need a psychic witch doctor, your problems are clear and discernible. The trick is dealing with the symptoms. We can do that with the drugs, with the Klonopin and with other medication, but not if you refuse to take them."

"I don't need them!"

"Jeni . . ." too patiently, "you had a psychotic break last

year. Your brain chemistry's not back to normal. Not to mention your overdose—"

"Why do you keep mentioning it, then?" Anger flooded her now, thinking back on the two weeks in the V.A. psych ward with the schizophrenics and psychotics . . . ex-husband Brian visiting her every day, face filled with disappointment, with pity . . .

As if reading her thoughts, Keegie reached out and put a large hand over hers. "Jeni, you have a great deal of perfectly justifiable resentment in your life right now, Brian included, I'm sure. It's reasonable that some of that should seep over into his associates, into me. For that reason I think my transfer to Washington—your seeing Dr. Landon—is probably a good thing. Or if Landon is a problem, let Helene suggest someone else to you, I know you trust her."

"No, Landon's okay." She nodded toward the print. "Do you know who painted that?"

Keegie followed her gaze. "Yes. It's a Rothko. It's called *Orange and Yellow.*"

"As opposed to purple and puce."

Keegie smiled. "Don't make fun. He was considered an important abstract expressionist."

Jeni cocked her head. "Well, I know next to nothing about art."

Keegie studied the print. "You don't have to know art to like it."

"What does it mean, all that orange and all that yellow and nothing else, no shapes, no subject matter?"

"A painting needn't be subjective to be art. Rothko was experimenting with the relationships between one color and another rather than what happens when individual brushstrokes represent a familiar shape or object. He began his career as a surrealist, but eventually segued to less associative imagery, big floating areas of color that seemed to hover over the canvas. His color was nearly . . . how should I say it?"

"Incandescent."

"Good. That's very insightful. You see, you know more about art than you thought. How does it make you feel, all that bright hot color?"

Jeni regarded the print. "Restful."

Keegie nodded. "Yes. We definitely have a budding artist in the room."

"Is that why you hang it in here, so your patients will feel restful?"

"So they'll feel at ease, yes."

Jeni turned from the print. "But the sketch of you makes me uncomfortable. How do you explain that?"

"You tell me."

"I'm uncomfortable being here, period. I haven't worked through my guilt about Molly?"

Keegie shrugged. "Or perhaps you haven't fully realized that Molly was not your fault. Not your fault nor Brian's fault. That neither of you failed her. That it simply happened."

"I need to forgive myself is what you're saying. Simple as that."

"As clear. Not simple. Your time's up, I fear . . ." and he placed her folder atop his desk.

As she stood, Keegie jotted another prescription, tore it free of its pad. "Here. And take it this time. I want to see you in two weeks."

"When's the big move to Washington?"

"End of the month. You'll do fine with Landon. He's a nice guy, ask Helene."

* * *

Home was a weather-beaten clapboard one-story rental in Ocean Beach, a section of San Diego's south side that sounded nicer than it was.

A hippie haven in the sixties, it had never quite outgrown that, though there had been subtle changes with time: tourist shops along Alvarado Street boasted hand-painted signs advertising surfing apparatus now instead of rainbow bongs and hash pipes. Still, there could be found remnants of that bygone age in the stubbornly garish colors of the storefronts, the single-screen neighborhood theater that refused to close or make way for multiscreen bunkers, the way the main avenue dipped right down into the gray sand and morning fog of Pacific swells. Poverty chic, the locals labeled it. You could dress beach-casual, live beach-crummy, and still retain a certain crude style. Mostly you got an ocean view for a third of what you'd pay on Point Loma, Coronado, or Mission Beach. After the divorce, that's exactly what Jeni Starbuck could afford.

She came into her little faded summer cottage bringing pungent sea breeze and cat food from Ralph's Market. She shut the paint-peeling door with her rump, reached back, and twisted the police lock. Poverty chic, but not burglarproof.

Pierre Cardin in his immaculate black suit collided perfectly with her ankles, began his twisting, delicately timed accompaniment with her strides to the kitchen table, his motor running. He sidestepped Jeni's footfalls magically. "Did we find any mice today, Poo-Poo?" Mice weren't nearly the problem sand fleas were. Twice she'd had to flea-bomb the apartment to rid them of the hopping bits of pepper. On the other hand, fleas, though ugly, were basically passive; mice were cute but darted around creepily at night, and left their pellets in her cupboards amid shreds of pasteboard cracker boxes. It had been weeks since Pierre had brought one to her, displaying its limp carcass proudly at her feet or pillow. Maybe he'd cleaned out the nest. Brian would have had a cow. But then, Brian would never have lived like this, flea market furniture, books shelved on planks and cinder blocks. And the photographs, which Jeni would not, could not, put away: Molly at the tidal pools, Molly on Brian's shoulders at Sea World, Molly as a baby, a preschooler, dipping her face in a chocolate birthday cake. And of course the family portrait, Brian, Jeni, and Molly, taken only days before it happened, all smiling, Molly's pink cheeks and auburn hair fairly glowing with life. No, Brian, she was sure, had stored the albums, even removed the pictures of her and Molly from their place on his desk. Of course he did . . . he had another picture album now. Another family.

Jeni scooped cat food into Pierre's dish, forcing herself not to think of her ex-husband, his handsome face, his probable reaction if he knew how much she thought about him, how often. Ten years of marriage, even under the circumstances of its demise, was difficult to just sweep under the rug. Nights were worst. Forgetting . . . reaching for him . . .

"Here, cat, and don't choke." She scraped the last of the food from the tin, Pierre lunging, gulping as always, as though it were his last meal. He had choked alarmingly several times, Jeni pounding his narrow back. She'd switched brands twice. It did no good. He was a glutton.

She leaned back against the table and watched him with a smile. A glutton and her only family. Now that Molly was gone.

She shrugged off the thought—the attendant pain—by moving to the sink to wash her hands, wash the thought away. By the time she turned back, toweling, the big Persian (part Persian anyway—Molly'd found him in the back alley, a scrawny kitten, rail-thin and mewling plaintively) was already finished, searching her eyes for the second helping he never got. "You'll bloat like a pig." And she smiled and hunkered to rub his broad skull, the delicate trough behind his ears, and finally—to get him to close his eyes in ecstasy—under the white tuft of his rippling throat. Molly herself, only eight, had named him Pierre Cardin after a fashion show she'd seen on MTV displayed a tuxedo with its black bow tie.

Jeni shook away the thought, found herself staring at the warped linoleum floor absently. It needed cleaning. Pierre Cardin had given up begging more food from her, was licking desultorily at the film of flavor lining his dish.

Jeni pushed from the sink with conviction and went to draw her bath. Enough of this. She thought too often of Molly. She'd been warned about it, about moribund ruminations. "You have to let her go," Dr. Keegie had told her gently. "Keep her memory, but let her go, do you understand what I mean, Jeni?" She'd nodded, of course. Sure she understood. That—and the prescribed Klonopin, for anxiety attacks—didn't stop the thoughts, though. Or alter the sleepless nights. Or worse, the nights when she did sleep and the dreams came, the three of them still together, laughing. Brian still very much in love with her. Molly still very much alive. Until the flames. Until the dreams became nightmares.

Chapter 4

At San Diego International terminal, the newspapers, he noticed, were filled with front-page headlines about the bay bombing. The tall man didn't bother to pick one up. Sight unseen, he already knew far more about the explosion than any cop, or any of the TV news anchors who always referred to that part of California as the Southland.

To leave no record of his arrival, he passed by the rent-a-car vendors and took a shuttle bus to Highland Avenue, which was as close to Ocean Beach as he could get. From there, from a pay phone, he took a cab to Alvarado Street, paid the cabby, and—single leather suitcase in tow—walked the palm-lined streets, smiling. He loved San Diego. He loved the way the ocean smelled.

He extracted a copy of the *Reader*—the local area paper—from a plastic street canopy, and sat at a small, undistinguished-looking coffee shop and read the lease ads. He was pleased with what he found on the first page.

TO LET
SINGLE ROOM NEAR BEACH
LOVELY VIEW
CLEAN AND QUIET

He opened the leather suitcase, withdrew a laptop PC, switched it on, and went to work. In five minutes he knew all he needed to know and considerably more. It elicited another smile.

He finished his coffee, folded the paper under his arm, and made his call from the pay phone in the back of the coffee shop. A Mrs. Grindle answered. Yes, she could show him the room tonight.

"It has a lovely view of the ocean," she told him under hand-sewn plum-purple drapes, frail, taloned fingers tugging fruitlessly at the single, weather-warped window.

"Here, let me do that." He smiled.

Mrs. Grindle, gray, weary, arthritically beaten, was clearly glad for the help, clearly relieved to have someone other than young people with loud music and odd smells appraising her home. She stepped aside graciously, an almost curtsylike movement, and let the tall man in the dark suit lift the sill with a single sure tug. He brought the odor of sea breeze and manly cologne to Mrs. Grindle, who suddenly felt inclined to be flexible with the rent. Here was a gentleman. The way men used to be.

The tall man seemed unconcerned with matters of rental money, however, or the plum drapes, the immaculate bureau and accompanying doily, the crisp new linens on the small neat bed, or the newly papered walls with the lovely pastel roses picked out and worried over for an hour at Robinson's. Private if polite, he hardly seemed to notice the antique hooked rug, beaten by the boy down the street until every speck of dust was out of it, and placed just so before the small bed. Nor did he acknowledge the fine walnut writing desk that had been in her family for generations, though her worries about someone mistreating it were gratefully assuaged as the tall man carefully laid his single suitcase atop it, snapped it open, and withdrew his things.

"What line of work are you in, Mr.— I don't believe I caught your name . . ."

"I'm in the extermination business," the tall man told her, withdrawing a box of large Glad trash bags from the case, carefully separating one plastic sheet from another along the perforated lines.

"Oh?" Mrs. Grindle frowned concern, imagining the acrid odor of antiseptics filling her pine-smelling rooms. Yet something in his gentle, confident demeanor was calming, even soothing . . . the determined way he tore apart the trash bags, his long, even delicate fingers strong, firm, but gentle. He was certainly a careful young man, certainly orderly.

The tall man carefully placed each of the separated squares of plastic upon the shiny hardwood floor, the layers of Johnson's wax Mrs. Grindle had labored decades over. He even covered the newly cleaned hooked rug. He certainly was a neat young man, whatever he was up to.

"Is it some kind of . . . laboratory work?" she ventured cautiously. "I'm afraid I couldn't tolerate any chemicals in the room. And, of course, I'll be requiring a security deposit."

The tall man smiled, stretching to lay down the last square of plastic. "You needn't concern yourself, dear lady, I assure you. How long since Mr. Grindle passed on is it?"

"Oh, some years now," the old woman told him enthusiastically, so long had it been since anyone had bothered to ask. The tall man smoothed each plastic corner in place. Why cover the floor unless one expects to spill something? she wondered absently.

"And your grandchildren, they come by on the week-

ends?" taping the plastic sheets together now along their
edges.

"Dear no. Anne and Phillip have been grown for years,
they both moved back East . . . I'm all alone. Except for
the boy down the street who helps with the cleaning occasionally, runs errands for me." She added this last under a
quickening sense of something not quite right, as if im-
plying the boy might show up at any moment looking for
something to clean.

The tall man straightened from his task, smiling. "Come
this way a moment." He took her arm gently and, under his
smile, she allowed herself to be guided to the center of the
six-by-eight squares of black plastic. "I know all about
loneliness, Agatha."

She started at the sound of her first name, not having
heard it in years, not remembering giving it to this man.

His smile was disarming, calming. "I know all about
you . . ."

When he drew her into his arms, Mrs. Grindle was surprised but not truly alarmed. He smiled warmly into her
eyes and she thought she had it then: this was one of her
son Kenny's shipmates, come to see her years and years
after the accident, to express his sorrow at her loss, to
make her feel like a mother again. When he kissed her—
full and deeply on the lips—she did not pull away, so tender was he, didn't struggle even when his tongue squirmed
into her mouth, bringing with it a sweet agony of memories, a sluggish rush of hormones she'd thought long de-
serted her.

The struggling began with his unrelinquishing grip,
tightening as he reached around and pinched closed her
nostrils.

She kicked once, their shared breath—sealed tight by
his urgent lips—sour now with her bile, her fear. She

made a muffled sound like a dog's moaning preamble to baying, the effort puffing out the man's cheeks. Her liver-spotted knuckles beat twice at his back.

At the last, her wide eyes silent with pleading, he might—as the pleading faded—have glimpsed a measure of gratitude there before they rolled back white. Then the stiff, gray burden in his arms became a sack in which bones had settled. A stench arose in the room and spattered dripping onto the protecting squares of plastic. The tall man let the old woman settle into this, draping the ends of the polyethylene around her. Later, the upstairs room would be as spotless as before he came. Whoever discovered the corpse would find an elderly woman—downstairs—dead of old age, still and at last at peace within her lonely rooms.

He came to the window, raised it all the way, letting ocean pungence suffuse the room.

He stood there at the sill, breeze in his hair, watching the sun bloody itself into flat ocean horizon, shocking all blue from the smog-filled sky. San Diego had the prettiest sunsets.

Chapter 5

Fat Frieda, fatter than fat, blacker than black, muscled her ponderous laundry basket as Jeni came through the clinic door. "Yer late," the massive black woman intoned without looking up.

"I know," Jeni sighed, "I'm sorry," unable to believe she was still apologizing to one of the staff. *She* was the clinic's director, dammit!

She had disliked Fat Frieda almost from the beginning.

A mountain of imposing flesh and surly attitude, the big broad-faced woman had appeared like a national monument before Jeni's scarred Woolworth's desk one morning last spring. "Where the director of this place?"

Jeni blinked. "I'm the director. May I help you?"

"*You* the director! Girl, you look like Doris Day!"

Jeni put down her pen. "Is that a fact? Is there something I can do for you?"

Fat Frieda was already pulling off her purse and tying on her apron. "I work from seven to four, then I got to get home to my own kids. I don't like workin' no weekends, I like to be with my kids, but if it an emergency—a *real* emergency—I reckon you can call. I don't do no windows or floors. I ain't no janitor." And with that she glanced about, found an empty laundry basket, and went about her business.

Jeni stood up from behind the desk. "Ma'am?"

Frieda turned impatiently, basket secure in tree-trunk arms.

"The interview's concluded, is it?" Jeni inquired peevishly.

"Far as I'm concerned it is." And she gave the new director her back.

Jeni had come that close to firing her every morning for the next two weeks. Then, one rainy Thursday afternoon, little Jimmy Bowlens had begun a terrible racking cough in ward 7, wrenching spasms that echoed the halls, spewed bright blood across his sheets and wall. Jeni came running, heart racing, the staff all backing away in horror in the opposite direction, blocking her way, as if fearful the infected blood might suddenly leap upon and attack them.

Jeni had paused in the child's doorway, appalled at the dripping walls (so *much* of it!), had stood there impotently watching the helpless boy writhe gasping for air. As she was preparing to step inside, a mountain of flesh shouldered easily past her, strode unflinchingly to and cradled the spasming child in huge black arms, held him rocking until the hacking subsided, crooning a low Baptist spiritual. Before the boy was done, they were both leopard-spotted with blood. Fifteen minutes later the child was sleeping soundly in a spotless room, and Frieda was back toting her laundry basket as if nothing had happened. Jeni had declined firing her.

"Who's the new recruit?" she asked now, pointing past the window at the shabby backyard of the clinic, an ancient dump where the kids sometimes played. A redheaded mulatto girl of six or so laughed happily there amid others, some with hair, some without. Compared to her playmates, the new girl was the picture of health.

Fat Frieda turned with her laundry. "Pretty thing,

ain't she? Gots no name. Gots no parents, but what else
is new? Patrol boys brung her 'round. You gonna sign
her in?"

"She looks so strong."

"Gots a T-cell count below thirty-five."

"God, you'd never know it." Jeni, entranced, moved
closer to the window. "Well, she must have a name, this
won't do."

"Why don't you name her?"

"Me?" She watched the burnished curls, the bronzed
smile. "Look at that hair. Color of red ocean coral . . ."

Frieda grunted. "Then Coral it is, I reckon." She
pushed through the laundry room door, turned to give
Jeni's back a doubtful look. "Hey! White girl!"

Jeni turned.

Frieda's chocolate eyes were admonishing. "Don't go
gettin' attached now. She just as sick as the rest of 'em."

"I'm aware of that, Frieda, thank you." But she
watched the pretty red-haired child through the window
anyway. Watched smiling behind her desk, most of the
morning.

At lunchtime she always went to see her own daughter.

Molly's grave was in Point Loma, down Alvarado
Street, which necessitated driving past shoreline pali-
sades, glinting bay, and a postcard view of Coronado
Island.

Jeni could not make this journey without glimpsing
bay marinas, the narrow strip of green Coronado isle (not
a real island at all, but a finger of land connected by the
thin necklace of Silver Strand beaches fattening south-
ward toward Mexico's border), the steel gray of the naval
yards with their grim, moored flattops, the rolling terra-
cotta roofs of charming 1920s cottages, the grand red

minarets of the Del Coronado Hotel (Marilyn Monroe had romped with Tony Curtis here in *Some Like It Hot*), and, of course, the gleaming blue arc of the Coronado Bay Bridge, a graceful metal umbilicus linking island and mainland San Diego. The bridge over which she'd recently dashed to humiliating defeat.

Nor could she resist attempting to spy—from the highway cliffs—the little stucco one-story once their own, the house they'd bought when they'd first moved here from Texas . . . a wartime bungalow fraught with personal memories, few of them pleasant considering her love for the little house, the smell of the sea, being home all day with Molly. Gone, all gone.

She'd never actually spotted the house from the cliff drive. Masked by trees, other structures, the rush of traffic on Orange, it always eluded her. But she could approximate its location, imagine it there.

One bright optimistic morning, she'd even found courage to actually drive by their old place. Had done this exactly once.

It had been a disappointment. Smaller than memory promised, it had been reinhabited by faceless someones she never saw, phantoms who'd abused her lush, trim lawn, let her carefully cultivated bougainvillea grow recklessly across side yards, painted delicate trim an ungodly pink, whitewashed the delightful sanguine curve of sidewalk out front. Once-familiar wood, brick, shingles, and mortar were now imbued with an alien patina, corpse-like, only the shell of their old house remaining, all personality fled.

Thinking of Coronado, the metaphor she had invented for her marriage to Brian, inevitably triggered other thoughts.

During their first months on the island, freed of agency

work, she'd spent the days combing the beach, exploring old neighborhoods, seated at the local library (Molly asleep in her lap) reading up on Coronado's history . . . an island—a place—she'd thought would serve as home forever more. Always the voracious reader, inveterate researcher (her greatest virtue and worst asset during agency days), Jeni'd discovered within a mound of spine-faded volumes that in the entire history of the state of California, only one community had seceded from a city: Coronado. In 1890, the island town broke free of San Diego to set up its own government, its own lifestyle. Immediately afterward, state laws were put into place making it difficult if not impossible for secession to succeed elsewhere. But Coronado had won, making it, in Jeni's Texas-born eyes—eyes raised under stoic, Anglo-German traditionalism—a place of great romantic rebellion and independence. A world unto itself.

Hence the metaphor with her marriage to Brian: rebellious, independent, a world unto itself.

Right up to the day he'd managed to secede from her.

She pulled onto I-5, smiling irony. Everyone was trying to secede these days, from Rancho Palos Verdes to the San Fernando Valley, long-festering suburban resentment leading communities to consider formation of their own county or city governments. And the fever had spread beyond California, become a national state of mind.

At its most benign, it represented the same old exodus of city dwellers to the imagined paradise of the suburbs. At its most disturbing, it conjured haunting images of Ruby Ridge, Waco, the Freemen . . . countless disillusioned others, wrapped in the flag of freedom, searching, searching for the utopian Eden they convinced themselves was slipping away with every oil spill, every depletion of ozone. The enemy? Faceless bureaucratic demigods staging an impossibly complex government conspiracy, headed by Jews housing aliens in desert airplane hangars and rioting blacks eroding all moral fiber, all sense of *cohesion and place*.

Jeni shook her head behind the wheel. As if America were a *place* somehow disenfranchised from the rest of the planet.

She and Brian had discussed it, scoffed at it, under dying Coronado sunlight, frothy surf licking their ankles. California—then at least—had seemed a beacon against such unreasoning prejudice and paranoia; like their marriage, light-years from provincial Texan mind-sets.

Then came the fires.

And the earthquakes, the riots . . . and finally the divorce. And one day Jeni and Brian found themselves—to their chagrin—among the statistics. Joined now with the wandering, searching others . . . groping outward for some new sense of *place*.

Brian's *place*—his new house in Point Loma—was bigger than their old island home. As his new bride was bigger than Jeni, broader through the hips and shoulders, with a magnificent mane of blond curls, lovely eyes, spoiled by too-quick birdlike movements, a nervous set to her that seemed always in motion, though—to Jeni—she never appeared to be going anywhere of consequence. Her two boys were cute, even handsome, something her first husband must have contributed: Jeni could only conjecture, having never met him.

Like the ugly new trim on their old place, Jeni could never resist, when in the area (a rare, deliberately masochistic move), casting a glance at Brian's new two-story as her car swept by—a quick glimpse of the kitchen window's yellow curtains for some mysteriously shadowed sign of life within. She had never been rewarded. He wouldn't be at home now anyway. He'd be at the field office if he wasn't still in China.

She had seen Brian with his new family only on two occasions, both times outside the neighborhood: once at the supermarket, once at the mall, Marcia—Brian's new bride—uncomfortably pleasant on both occasions, narrow eyes constantly drifting to Jeni's bosom, as if divining why Brian had been induced to leave such abundance. The two boys had been distracted and curious by turns, Marcia always tugging the youngest one from handfuls of grapes or apples. Brian was translucent, a nervous ghost whose real self, she presumed, would return only with Jeni's departure from their presence.

She rounded Hillside now, powered up the steep hill to the bluff's cemetery perched there.

The cliff afforded the living a peaceful, cycloramic view of the Pacific. A good idea that didn't work: on sunny days the ocean vista was so postcard-beautiful one could think only of being very much alive. On cloudy days the slate-gray sea was oppressive with melancholy. And it was always windy here, often chill.

She braked at a gravel drive, walked the few scant yards of grassy embankment to Molly's headstone, which was closer to the narrow road than Jeni would have wished but all they could find at the time. She never liked the stone. Brian had picked it out, Jeni exhausted to near collapsing under arduous, heartbreaking funeral preparations. The stone was off-putting—too angularly modern, like office-complex architecture—Molly having been neither angular nor remotely modern. Jeni sorely regretted she hadn't been collected enough to pick out the stone herself.

"Hello, my darling . . ." She always addressed the stone the same way, always felt both remotely foolish and abruptly hallow, as though the words, having been spoken, solidified a concept kept subconsciously remote. Yet the words needed to be spoken. Molly was gone.

And yet everywhere. There in the leaning grass, the ancient oak, the fishy mist from the sea. In Jeni's heart, deep inside—and far, far out *there* someplace, on a plane, a sphere, the earthbound can't fathom.

She always stayed exactly half an hour. Always talked to the stone, not once remembering later what she'd said. Not once hearing the stone talk back.

And after the cemetery she always made the same phone call to the hospice.

"Hi, it's me. Everything okay?"

"Everything's fine," was the answer from one of the aides. If Fat Frieda got to the phone first it was: "Why don't you get your white ass back here and see yerself?"

Today it was Clarice Henry, a black woman with considerably more decorum than Frieda. "Everything's fine. The new girl is cute."

"Isn't she darling! And so healthy-looking!"

"I hear you named her."

" 'Coral.' Do you like it, Clarice?"

A moment of silence. Then: "Don't get too close, honey. She's a sick little girl."

Stung, Jeni sighed into the receiver. "I *know* that, Clarice, does everyone think I don't know that?"

But driving home later, she felt the wisdom of the other woman's words. It had been Jeni's own credo when she'd opened the clinic: show them love—guard your heart.

Naked, hair undone and down for washing, Jeni had just dimpled the hot, steaming bathwater with her big toe, perfumed vapor enfolding her, when the bedroom phone chirped.

She hesitated, craning. But not long, turned back, stepping into the water with both feet. It was hot. Burning hot now, which meant it would be scalding on her scraped knee, her leg and hands, and just right for the rest of her in a couple of minutes. The phone chirped. All she wanted to do was settle deep into the steam's embrace, close her eyes for a minute, and let the world go away. But she was still standing there, dry from the ankles up, thinking about it, head cocked while the phone demanded again and yet again.

Disgusted with herself, yanking down a towel, she padded the hall to the bedroom, leaving dark footprints with a noticeable arch, a runner's arch. You never could resist a ringing phone, Jennifer.

She grabbed up the handset curtly. "Yes?"

"Is this Jennifer Starbuck?"

"Yes, it is," impatience unconcealed, certain now it was an ad, "how may I help you?"

"The Jennifer Starbuck with the ATF?"

"I'm no longer with that organization. Who is this, please?"

"You know about the explosion, the one in the Coronado bay?"

A little squirt of adrenaline. "Yes."

"Agent Paul Miller would like to see you immediately. Do you know where the county courthouse is on Paradise Street?"

"Yes."

"Can you be there in half an hour?"

"I guess I could, what's this all about?"

"Agent Miller will explain. You know about the annex?"

"Annex?"

"There's a blue bungalow, Annex A, directly behind

the courthouse. Blue clapboard with white trim. Use the front door. Come alone, is that understood?"

"Would you mind identifying yourself, please?"

"Please acknowledge that you understand the directions."

She felt herself tighten, like the drying skin around her ankles. "Blue annex behind the courthouse."

"The password is 'Game Boy.' "

"The what?"

"Half an hour. It's urgent."

It came to her then. "Is this one of the guys from the office? You guys have nothing better to do these days, now that the president is thinking about shutting down the organization?"

But the receiver was dead against her ear.

She lingered by it, swathed in towel. The call had sounded sharp and clear—local—not miles away from some drunken Eliot Ness. A close call, which ruled out one of her old crew in Texas. ATF agent or not, it had sounded officious, sounded real. What could they possibly want with her now, these days? She hadn't heard from the agency since the Trouble.

Jeni left the tub full, ran a hot washcloth under her arms, splashed herself with cologne, yanked down a simple green dress, patted Pierre on the rump, and turned at a knock on her front door.

Brian stood there, still dressed in his business suit. Handsome beyond her memory.

"Brian."

"Hi."

"Well." Her heart started tripping. It had been months since she'd seen him, and he'd never been to her house. "What . . . a surprise."

She lingered in the doorway, wondering about protocol

under current circumstances. Damn it to hell, he'd *naturally* show now, when she was in a rush. "To what do I owe this pleasant surprise?" And she was shocked at the sarcasm in her own voice. She only hated him when he was nearby.

Whatever softness lay behind his eyes, if any, vanished at her tone. "I saw you fall last night on the news. Are you all right?"

She stood there on the lintel, wanting to slam the door in the handsome face, wanting to yank him inside and kiss the handsome face. "Oh. That. I'm okay. I'm fine. Jesus, damn television."

"It looked like you took a pretty bad spill."

"No, I'm okay, really. Thanks for asking."

"I'm sorry you lost the race."

"Yeah, well, that's the breaks."

"Did you have many bets down?"

"A few."

Her ex nodded. Then dug into his wallet. "Well, here . . ."

She stayed his hand from the bills. "No. I couldn't. The court said—"

"This isn't alimony. I had some bets down on you too."

"Brian, I lost."

"Yeah, I bet you'd lose." He handed her a hundred-dollar bill.

Which she refused stiffly. "You bet *against* me?"

"Take the money."

"Go to hell."

She started to close the door and he caught it, shoving the bill at her. "For chrissake, Jeni, take it for the kids."

She hesitated. Snatched the bill from him. Softened. "Okay. All right. Thanks. We can use it."

He nodded, watched her. "How are things at the hospice?"

"Kids are dying, how do you think things are at an AIDS hospice?"

When he sighed, made as if to leave, she softened further. "I'm sorry. It's been rough. And I—the group—does appreciate the money."

"What about you? Are you getting along all right?" He was looking past her at the dingy living room.

"I'm fine."

"You look thin."

"I'm fine. How about you? How're Marcia and the kids?"

A moment's hesitation. "Fine."

"That's good." The breeze off the bay brought his aftershave close, killing her.

And there was suddenly nothing else to say. She couldn't invite him in. Probably he wouldn't come in anyway. Probably this whole trip was about his guilt. Probably the money *was* meant for her, not the hospice. Well, screw him. At least not being able to invite him in would prevent rejection.

"Well," he said. "I'd better be going."

"Yeah." Better be going back to her. To her kids. A family.

"See you, Jeni."

"Yeah. Thanks."

She watched him descend the steps. Took the time from her appointment to come back inside, move through the house, and watch through the window as he walked to his car. Not their old car, a new one. She had always loved the way he walked, always with his hands in his pockets, head slightly bowed, as if vaguely embarrassed by his handsomeness. She watched until he drove away, until his car was no longer there and the street was as before he came, as though he'd never come at all. Yeah. Thanks. Thanks a lot.

She drove the clanking Volvo to Paradise as instructed, nosed into a metered parking space before the San Diego Courthouse.

She strode up the sidewalk near the harbor and around the building's ancient stone facade to a perpetually green, manicured back lawn. Flanked by towering shrubs and eucalyptus, the little blue clapboard annex was there. The rest of the back lawn was conspicuously empty.

Jeni hopped up the white, recently painted wooden stairs, started to knock, then shrugged and tried the silver knob. The door opened under her hand.

She entered a long open cement-floored room with white wooden walls, neatly cleaned windows, and no furniture, as spartan and clean as an army dayroom. It was empty.

At the far end was another newly whitewashed door.

Jeni said, "Hello?" to no one.

Feeling mildly silly, she strode the cement floor to the only other door, shoes making an even, inordinately loud clicking with no furniture or drapes to soften them. She found the door at the opposite end locked. She knocked.

Silence.

"What do you want here?"

She spun, heart seizing up, trained right hand nearly going automatically for the weapon she carried.

A black man stood near the opposite door leaning on a mop handle, a steel bucket on casters at his feet. He was dressed in a gray jumpsuit and black belt like a janitor. His skin was so black it looked blue, his hair wiry iron gray. She had not heard him come in.

"I was told to come here," Jeni offered. She should have said "instructed."

"By whom?"

"Whom." The man had education, spoke eloquently without accent. "Someone who told me to meet an Agent Miller."

The man accessed her calmly. "There's nobody by that name here. Nobody here at all, as you can see."

Jeni felt her weariness descend again, verge on anger, something a professional ATF agent would no longer allow herself. Well, screw that. She wasn't an agent any longer, just a citizen, a tired citizen who wanted to take a bath and put an end to this day. "I was told to meet with an Agent Miller here. Told it was urgent."

"You'd better leave, I think." Not threatening, but even.

It was a long drive down, she started to say, but screw that too; maybe it was a practical joke. Anyway she was too bushed to stand around and find out. The next time somebody called demanding her services they could damn well come to her. She pushed away from the door and strode the cement floor past the man in gray coveralls. The bucket, she noticed curiously, was empty. The mop dry.

Jeni hesitated at the door, not turning around again. "The password is 'Game Boy,' " she told the door in front of her.

When she turned around, the man was already at the other end of the empty room, holding the locked door open for her. "Room 17. Upstairs."

Beyond the door was a narrow hall of perhaps twenty feet; beyond that another door and beyond that a wide, noisy room, filled with seated women and the erratic hum of a hundred, ancient black metal sewing machines. All of the women were poor Hispanics and none of them looked up when Jeni came in. She had the feeling not one of them spoke English.

At each table next to each pair of busy brown hands, was a large pile of golf caps of various size and color. The brown, usually scarred and bandaged fingers, snatched a cap from the pile, placed it deftly beneath the chattering needle, embroidered an appliqué of the Coronado Bridge and the bright cursive "Welcome to San Diego!," jerked the cap free, placed it on a pile opposite, reached automatically for the next one. As automatically as the machine that did the sewing. Jeni had seen sweatshops on the evening news, usually accompanied by an acid editorial. She never dreamed of finding herself in one.

She moved through the forest of bent, perspiring women, dour resigned expressions, to a metal staircase, the only other exit in the room. She climbed this amid mixed smells of machine oil and body odor.

At the top of the stairs, Jeni found herself on a steel catwalk, a gangway that led above the bent, silent figures below to another building, another hallway. She moved under sentinels of bright, bare bulbs hanging from long cords out of black-beamed ceilings. The odor here was of mildew and dust.

In the hallway, she moved down a row of faded, paint-peeling wooden doors, the old kind with once-good wood and cut-glass doorknobs, each sporting a window of rippled, translucent glass and an Art Deco numeral. At the far end, framed by a dusty window, she found the black man waiting for her, arms folded and patient. As she approached, he nodded silently at the door beside him, the Art Deco numeral 17.

There had been no reason he had not simply accompanied her to her destination except to see if she could find it on her own.

Jeni turned to the door. The black man reached in front of her, knocked once, and opened it for her.

She entered a smoke-filled office, twenty by twenty, filled with cheap sixties furniture, ancient, overhead hanging bowl fixtures, blank walls, and six blank faces all turned toward her. The black man in the janitor uniform smiled and shut the door behind her.

Jeni stared at the six men staring at her.

All of them appeared in their mid- to late forties. Two were balding. They sat leisurely about the room on couches or chairs, ties loosened, jackets open or off altogether. Cops. Or Bureau men. She could smell it a mile off. One of them sat at the only new piece of equipment in the room, a big, industrial computer, its screen blank. It squatted atop a battered wooden table beneath a large, faded map of San Diego County. When the man at the table turned and saw Jeni, he made a flurried motion, touched a key swiftly on the computer's pad, and donned a set of headphones nearby, not taking his eyes off her until apparently convinced she could hear no sound from the computer. Everyone else just stared silently, some of them openmouthed. A sound from behind her turned her in the direction of a somewhat younger man she had not noticed before, leveling a gun straight at her face, his face neutral.

"Who the hell are you?" the older man closest to her finally demanded, not friendly.

Jeni straightened with department-trained authority, gripped the purse strap at her shoulder. "Jeni Starbuck—"

And almost before she could complete it someone else interrupted: "How'd you get in here?"

Jeni turned to him. "I was . . . summoned here. To report to an Agent Miller."

They all stared at her.

"Where are you from?" someone else said, and before that could be addressed someone else blurted: "How in hell did you find this place?" and started to rise, face graven. He was held back by the man seated beside him. "All right, everybody. Chill. Did Dieter let you in, young lady?"

"The name is Starbuck. The janitor . . . the man in the uniform let me in."

"The hell he did!" someone else said, and two more of them rose to their feet. Jeni stepped back reflexively, found the hard door at her back. The man with the gun turned slightly to accommodate her movement, and she saw instantly that he would not hesitate to shoot it given the order.

"All right," the calm man said, beat the others to their feet, holding out a restraining arm. "Let's just take it easy, fellas, she can't get out of the building."

Jeni said nothing, felt the weight of the Ruger pulling at her purse.

The calm man, tall and smiling benignly, looked somewhat like a young Paul Newman, eyes clear and blue, intently probing. Probing Jeni's at the moment. Unlike the others, he appeared unrattled by her presence. "Now then. Someone contacted you, is that it? Told you to come here?"

Jeni nodded.

"I see. And who was that, please?"

"He didn't say. He told me it was urgent, that an Agent Miller was expecting me—"

"There's no one here by that name!" from someone behind Paul Newman.

"All right, all right, sit down, Frank," the tall man confronting Jeni said without looking behind him.

The man who had spoken, balding and now red-faced

from the couch, fumed alarm. "Jesus! No names! Remember! No names!"

The tall blond smiled easily. "Take it easy, Frank, I think it's pretty obvious who brought her to us, don't you?" The man named Frank sat back down, shaking his head as though a great, delicately arranged plan had just come unwoven.

Jeni frowned. "Maybe you'd like to let me in on it, fellas, because truthfully I have better things to do today than play footsies with the feds."

The man named Frank reared up. "How do *you* know we're FBI?"

Jeni smiled sarcasm. "Let me guess. The shoes?"

The Paul Newman ringer almost smiled. "Got ya, Frank." Frank grumbled, easing back in his chair. The tall blond man addressed the agent behind Jeni. "Put it away, Krawsky." Without another sound Krawsky holstered his gun and left the room.

Jeni'd had enough. "Is there an Agent Miller here or not?"

"I'm Agent Miller," the man before her said. "Who are you?"

"I told you. Jeni Starbuck."

"Yeah, but who *are* you?" from someone else.

"She's ATF," from someone across the room in brown Florsheims and tanned slacks, and everyone—as if on command—turned toward him. He sat tilted back in a wooden chair near the man at the computer, his arms folded, a look of serenity about him. "From Texas, right, Ms. Starbuck?"

Jeni swallowed. "That was a long time ago. I'm not with the agency anymore."

The man nodded. "Transferred here to San Diego after the Lubbock thing, right?"

Jeni looked away. "I quit the agency three years ago."

"Not the way I hear it. I hear you were more or less kicked out on your—"

"Roger!"

"—something to do with your last hostage negotiations, isn't that correct? Jumped the gun a bit there?"

Jeni felt bile in her throat, kept her face neutral. "Depends on who's telling the story."

The man named Roger smiled. "And what about your bigshot husband?"

"We're divorced," Jeni told him coolly. She turned to Paul. "May I ask what this is all about, please?"

"His name was Brian Starbuck, wasn't it? You had a little girl—"

"Can it, Roger," Miller intervened.

Jeni turned to go.

"Hey!" from the man under the headphones at the computer table. "He's back on-line!"

Everyone turned to the man at the console now. He was nodding rapidly, mumbling into the mouthpiece attached to the phones, Jeni not quite able to hear—sensing she wasn't intended to.

The man at the console nodded again, placed his hand over the mouthpiece, and looked up at Agent Miller. "He says he wants me to open the mike."

The others looked aghast.

Agent Miller pursed his lips, drew in a deep breath. He turned, glanced toward Jeni, then back to the man at the console. "All right, open it."

"Wait a second, Paul!" simultaneously from two of the others, faces tight. "With *her* here?"

Jeni looked at the tall blond man. She was thinking: Looks like Paul Newman and his name is Paul.

Miller waved them off. "He *brought* her here, obviously! Open the mike, Ted. Ms. Starbuck is clearly supposed to be in on this."

The man at the console pulled the phones from his ears, tapped a key on the computer's keyboard, and pushed his swivel chair back from the table resignedly.

The big computer with the blank screen spoke. "Afternoon, gentlemen."

Everyone but Jeni bore a resigned, indignant look.

"How goes the investigation?" There was confidence in the voice, Jeni noted, and mocking to be sure. But not overly so. A youngish voice. An otherwise pleasant voice.

"We have received a visitor," Agent Miller told the computer. He began to pace the small room. Jeni had the feeling Miller wished he had a cigarette. "Ms. Jeni Starbuck, previously of the Bureau of Alcohol, Tobacco and Firearms. Currently . . ." He looked up at Jeni.

Unemployed by the government, unpopular with the local police, Jeni thought. She responded with: "I run."

". . . currently running. Recently divorced. Would you care to have a word with her, Mr. Handle?"

"Indeed," from the blank-screened computer. "Good day to you, Ms. Starbuck."

Jeni stepped closer to the wooden table. "Hello."

"How's the leg?"

Everyone turned expectantly toward her. Jeni faltered.

"You had the race sewed up. I'd like to take this opportunity to apologize for losing it for you. Next time take the inside track. Were you hurt otherwise by the explosion?"

Jeni glanced at Agent Miller. "Only my pride."

Muffled laughter from the computer. The man at the table adjusted a knob on the big twin-reel recorder beside it. "Well, to be fair, the reedy black girl was a worthy opponent."

"I would have beat her," she answered the dark screen,

her voice relaxed. First rule of hostage negotiations—appear relaxed. Even if you aren't. Jeni excelled at this.

"Oh, I quite agree. You're fast, very fast. You should have won the L.A. Marathon as well."

Jeni raised a brow, trading another look with Agent Miller. "You get around, Mr. Handle."

"Assuredly. Even more quickly than you, my dear. What happened in L.A., by the way? You were doing so well."

Jeni glanced up at the big wall map of San Diego County. Was he somewhere on the tattered green map, or somewhere far removed from it? "I got a stitch in my left side. It threw off my timing. It's a chronic problem."

"Shame. Thought you had that one knocked."

"Me too."

"Where did you learn to sprint like that. Lubbock High?"

"You seem to know all about me, Mr. Handle. You have me at a disadvantage."

A patient chuckle. "I have the whole city at a disadvantage, isn't that so, Agent Miller?"

"For the moment," Miller told the air calmly. He looked to Jeni, motioned toward an empty chair. She shook her head no politely.

"And how's Brian these days?" the computer asked her. "How's the ex? Ever hear from him?"

Jeni forced down a swallow. "Not really."

"But you'd like to, wouldn't you?"

Jeni remained calm, but not calm enough to meet Agent Miller's eyes. "Is that what you think, Mr. Handle?"

"It's what you think, Jeni. You think he blames you for the child. I'd like to talk to you about that sometime."

Heart tripping, Jeni shrugged. "Certainly. Whenever you wish."

There was silence from the computer for a time.

Agent Miller sighed, paced. "What is it you want specifically, Handle?"

" 'Certainly,' " the computer said. "I tell Ms. Starbuck that I'd like to talk to her sometime about her dead child and she very collectedly chirps, 'Certainly.' Her only child, mind you, that meant more than anything in the world to her. More than her own life. And she replies, 'Certainly.' It's what made her ten times the agent any of your misanthropes will ever be. The ability to completely detach herself from anything but the problem at hand! Admirable! Tell me, Agent Miller, is she pretty?"

Miller was accessing the area wall map himself now. "Don't you know, Mr. Handle?"

"I was soliciting your private opinion."

Miller watched the map impassively. "She's very attractive, Handle."

"Yes. And you have a weakness for blondes. How is it, Ms. Starbuck, the ATF came to let such a pretty, intelligent young woman escape their clutches?"

"Why don't you ask them?" Miller replied.

Handle grunted over the mike. "Jeni? Are you still there?"

"Yes."

"May I call you Jeni?"

"You may."

"Thank you. Jeni, how fast can you run a mile?"

She felt the others' eyes on her. Truthfully, she didn't know the answer, had never concerned herself with actual running times. "I have no idea. I specialize in marathons."

"Yes, indeed. Though your real strength is in the final burst. You're a quarter horse, aren't you, Jeni? A sprinter."

Jeni said nothing.

"The reason I ask is that in just about that amount of

time there's going to be a rather significant concussion approximately four blocks from the annex you're standing in now."

Jeni jerked toward Miller. Two of the others stood. The computer operator sat bolt upright.

Miller pointed at one of the men, who hurried quickly—silently—from the room. Miller grabbed up a pen and pad. "What blocks would those be, exactly, Mr. Handle?"

"Pardon me, Agent Miller, I'm conversing with Ms. Starbuck at the moment."

Jeni might have seen a cloud of intensity pass over the handsome Paul Newman face—quick as a heartbeat—then the composure returned.

"So what do you think, Jeni? Could you cover four city blocks in under four minutes? Little under a block a minute? Could you get there fast enough to stop the bomb?"

Jeni glanced about the little smoke-drifting room; everyone was waiting for her. "I suppose I'd have to have specific information before I could answer that."

The computer chuckled. "But then, of course, I'd be revealing the bomb's location and our friend Agent Miller would have time to phone and evacuate, yes?"

Jeni felt the tingle. The one that always accompanied the beginning of a big race. She began unconsciously rocking on her toes to prevent any prerunning cramping of her calves. "That could be a problem," she replied.

Another metallic chuckle. "All right. Fine. Let's say the bomb will explode at the old Statler Building on Alameda in just under four minutes. Just for argument's sake let's say that. Do you think you could reach that location in time to prevent the blast?"

Miller was pointing a finger but one of the other men was already dashing from the office.

"If you know my background as well as you seem to,

Mr. Handle, you know that my knowledge does not extend to dismantling explosive devices. Even if I could make it to the site in time, I'd be helpless to stop the explosion."

Handle seemed to pause for a beat. "Perhaps we could make a trade-off, Jeni. You reach the site, I stop the explosion. The important thing is, do you think you could make the run?"

Jeni took measured steps around the room. "The real question is: would I risk my life? Would I sacrifice myself for the safety of others? Is that what you're asking, Mr. Handle?"

A pause from the computer. Then: "I think I'm going to like working with you, Jeni. I really do. Bye for now."

The man at the wooden desk turned quickly, tapped at the keys, adjusted a knob on the tape recorder, turned to Miller with a look of exasperation. The man shook his head.

Behind Jeni, the door flew open again, the man who'd just rushed out, sticking his head in, red-faced. Miller nodded to him. "It's all right, he's off the air."

The man looked relieved. "The Statler Building's under evacuation. One of the security guards there told me he saw them clear it once during a fire scare. It took over ten minutes."

Somebody said, "Shit."

Miller stopped pacing. Almost regretfully he turned his eyes to Jeni, who stopped her own pacing under them. Incredibly, she heard herself blurt, "I know that building. I could make it."

Agent Miller appraised her with an expression close to mild amusement. It looked as if he might actually smile for a moment. He turned away, began pacing again. "He didn't say where the bomb was, Ms. Starbuck. Or even if it was really there. 'For the sake of argument,' he said."

Jeni nodded impatiently. "I'm cognitive of that, Agent Miller."

She became aware for the first time of the loud ticking of a big, black-framed wall clock, one of the old circular kind they used to use in schoolrooms.

Consciously or otherwise, everyone else was staring at the blank computer screen.

"Who is he?" Jeni broke the silence.

Agent Miller turned. "We only know who he isn't. We also know he's smart. He may or may not be the guy who blew up the boat in the bay. He certainly knows all about it. The size of the concussion from the bomb was exactly the way he described it. He seems to know explosives. And computers, obviously; he was smart enough to find us here."

"You're saying he might be the Solobomber? The one who blew up Paxton Jenns in San Francisco, and that other guy in L.A., that International Oil tycoon?"

Miller smiled at her. "If you know we're FBI, then you know we're not saying anything at this point. And certainly not to an outsider."

"Hey, you're the one who brought me inside!"

"No. Handle called you. He's the one who brought you here."

She watched him blankly.

Miller fished for cigarettes. "Why, I don't know exactly. Except he seems determined to make you part of this . . . jigsaw puzzle he's orchestrating for us."

This time Jeni smiled. "Okay. Maybe you'd better explain to me exactly who 'us' is."

The others looked to Miller expectantly.

"FBI. Special task force out of Quantico, working covert in San Diego on the Solobomber case."

"Jesus," someone muttered, as though sacred oaths had again been blasphemed.

That brought a rueful smirk from Miller. "Clearly we're not as covert as we thought we were. Handle phoned us on the Sprinter 9000 immediately after the bay bombing, taking credit for it. Only an insider could possibly know our location."

"Well, that narrows the suspects at least."

Miller shook his head. "We're an extremely small organization, Ms. Starbuck. What you might call a sub-subbranch of the FBI. Under two dozen small, and everyone's been accounted for."

Jeni started to mention the possibility of a mole, a whistle-blower—but the thought stuck in her throat. As if reading her mind, Miller looked up at her again. They stared at each other.

To change the subject, Jeni said, "What does he want with me?"

Miller shook his head. "I was hoping you could tell us that. I'm guessing he's an ex-ATF agent like yourself, maybe even knew you. Was there anything familiar about his voice? Anyone you might have worked with in the past?"

"No. Except for the phone call this morning, I don't recognize it."

"Anyone you ever knew in the program who might be capable of something like this?" Miller pressed. "A disgruntled agent?"

"I suppose any one of them would be capable of it, if any of them had the brainpower. But no, no one I can think of right off the bat. Does this guy Handle claim to be the Solobomber?"

"He doesn't claim or refute. We'll get a complete list of the men you and your ex-husband worked with. Meanwhile, search your memory. Anyone who might be an even marginal candidate—no matter how outlandish it may seem." He turned at the sound of a wall phone nearby. One of the other men snatched it up, nodded, turned to Miller. "Statler Building's sixty percent evacuated."

Miller was looking at his watch.

The tension in the room was palpable, everyone attempting to pretend it wasn't, to be professional, secretly waiting for the distant thud of an explosion. At four blocks, it wouldn't be all that distant.

They waited.

Jeni stood on one foot, then the other, weary but self-conscious about taking a seat. She couldn't shake the feeling she was supposed to be doing something. Her legs wanted to run. Where? Down the street to the Statler Building to stop the bombing? That was insane.

She turned to the man on the couch who had spoken earlier of her profile. He was watching her now, curiously, Jeni met his eyes unflinchingly. "Do I know you?" she asked pointedly.

The man held her eyes a moment, then glanced Miller's way. Miller was fitting a cigarette to his mouth. He shrugged at the man. "May as well talk to her, Jack. She's practically one of us now."

That brought murmurs of disapproval from the others, which Miller ignored.

"Agent Jack Higgins," from the man on the couch, amiably. "I was called into the Waco thing after the holocaust to sift through the ashes. A couple of the Branch Davidians were from Lubbock and my job was to follow up on them. Routine. I was in Lubbock the day you made the front page . . ."

Jeni nodded quickly, suddenly knowing it was coming, wishing she hadn't asked now.

Apparently sensing this, Higgins didn't pursue the matter. He did offer, "Sorry about your little girl. That has to be rough."

Jeni nodded, looking away now as though that would end it. "It is rough."

She felt the rest of the room watching her now, suddenly had nowhere to place her eyes.

Agent Miller was opening his mouth to say something when the phone burred. He snatched it up. "Yeah."

Miller nodded. "Good." Hung up.

He turned to the group, consulting his watch. "The building's been evacuated. It's past the four-minute mark. Looks like our friend was yanking our chain on this one." He looked around the room at his men, clear relief on his face. "Palmer phoned it in as a standard crank threat. The San Diego bomb squad is moving in now."

The room eased with released tension. A host of hands moved in unison to light cigarettes. Foreplay, urgency, and the afterglow smoke, Jeni thought, squinting annoyance as the upper levels of the room became a blue cloud bank, defying the air conditioner's pull.

Despite the ease of tension, Miller continued the short, elliptical path of his pacing. "We'll give the bomb experts a few minutes with their metal detectors, then wait for Palmer to phone us with the all-clear. Shouldn't take more than twenty minutes. Those guys know their stuff."

Another twenty minutes, Jeni thought. Her feet were killing her.

She found herself looking at the blank screen of the Sprinter 9000 computer. "May I ask a question?"

Agent Miller looked up. "Of course."

"According to my watch, the suspect was on the phone—
the computer—for more than two minutes that last time.
Why didn't you get a trace?"

That made everyone smile. Agent Miller regarded
her with admiration. "That's a very good question, Ms.
Starbuck."

"Tracing a call is pretty common knowledge," she
replied patiently.

Agent Miller was still smiling at her with his clear blue
eyes. "The old system of tracing may have been fairly
common knowledge. But not everyone knows that the
new fiber optics require less time to trace." He studied her
a moment. Jeni thought for an awful second he was going
to pursue Lubbock here in front of everybody. But he
didn't. "Yes, normally we would have nailed his location
after the first transmission. He stayed on-line for over five
minutes that time. But our boy has apparently found a
way to block a fiber-optic trace. We have no idea how. But
he certainly knows his computers."

Agent Miller nodded at the blank-faced terminal atop
the scarred wood table. "That's a brand-new Sprinter
9000 A, government issue. Do you know computers, Ms.
Starbuck?"

"I was ATF, Agent Miller. Mine wasn't a fancy new
Sprinter, of course, not in those days."

Miller smiled. "The department model here has a few
extra bells and whistles not found in the home version."
He strode to the table, indicated the keypad. "Now, the
typical owner of this computer can make a video phone
call anywhere in the continental United States and either
transmit a crystal-clear digital picture of himself or black
out the screen by depressing this discretion key. If you
just got out of the shower, you're having a bad hair day,
don't wish to be seen but still want to take the call, you

simply activate the key and the video chip is overridden, your morning face is hidden from the caller. With the department Sprinter, however, we can override the override and watch a caller whether he wants to be watched or not."

Another disapproving grumble from the others. "Dammit, Paul, that's top secret!" someone started.

Miller regarded the team with narrowed eyes. "I'm not going to repeat this again. We're going to be entertaining Ms. Starbuck for some time, I'm guessing, and I don't plan to spend the government's money dancing around technicalities with an ex-agent. Particularly an obviously intelligent ex-agent. Is that clear to everyone?"

Jeni felt herself color slightly at the flattery, endured more vague hostility from the others.

Agent Miller's face softened as he turned back to her. "As I was saying, our boy knows computers. Even secret government-issue computers. All the more reason we have to suspect he's been in some branch of the department before . . . or still is, for that matter. That and the fact that he has an inordinate interest in you. You're absolutely sure nothing about his voice sounded familiar? I can have Ted play it back for you."

Jeni shook her head. "No. I listened carefully. I've been searching my mind. I'm sorry."

Miller nodded. "That's all right. You just keep searching. We'll find the bastard. He may be smart but we've got people in Research and Development who're smarter. If we can't trace his calls because he's found some way to block the computer, then we'll find another way to get to him. Sooner or later he'll do something—say something—stupid, give himself away. And we'll move in."

The trick is to do that before any bombs go off, Jeni thought, knowing everyone else was thinking it too.

Fifteen minutes later, she had finally accepted a grudg-
ingly offered folding chair (invited to sit, but not too
close) and a Styrofoam cup of coffee to sip when the
phone burred again. Agent Miller was there. "Yeah?"

He hung up smiling. "San Diego's bomb squad has
combed the Statler Building floor-to-floor. No bomb.
They guarantee it."

The relief inside the room deepened another notch; ties
loosened, jokes made.

"So what now, boss?" Agent Higgins asked, easing
back into the sofa with his coffee.

Miller finally relinquished his pacing, took the time to
pour a cup of his own. "The ball's in his court. We'll wait
to see if he bothers to explain why he was bluffing. He's
got the cards right now and he knows it. We'll let him
play them for a while. Meantime, we work at cracking
whatever code he's using to block our trace." He looked
to Jeni. "Thanks for your help."

Jeni made an indifferent gesture. "I didn't do much."

"You did your job." He smiled.

She shrugged, thinking: My former job.

"You're free to go. But needless to say, I'd appreciate
your not leaving town for now. Agent Higgins will see
you out. Jack?"

"I can find my way," Jeni told him.

At the door, she was stopped by Miller's concerned
tone. "We'll send a black-and-white around every hour or
so just to check on you, if that's all right."

Disappointed, she turned to him. "I was an ATF agent
for twelve years, Mr. Miller. I still carry a licensed
weapon."

"We'll send someone anyway," Miller told her. He was
patting his pockets, finally accepted a cigarette from one
of the balding men. "I'm sure you're capable of taking

care of yourself, Jeni, but until we know what this joker wants, I'd appreciate your letting me nursemaid for now. I know it's an inconvenience. I'm sorry. Thankfully you don't—" and he caught himself.

He'd been about to say, "Thankfully you don't have a family," Jeni knew. As did the rest of the room. Miller covered the faux pas. "Thankfully you're not completely unfamiliar with this type of procedure."

Jeni lingered at the door, searching for an excuse to look back at the handsome face again. He made it easier for her. "Handle's not done with you, I can almost guarantee it. I'd like to send a couple of agents around to make sure you're okay. In the meantime, you might want to acquaint yourself with Sprinter literature." He reached out as one of the lesser agents handed him a huge sheaf of printed material. "I'll see what I can do about getting you a state-of-the-art Sprinter, but they're pretty hard to come by right now—demand is unbelievable."

Jeni nodded. "Whenever."

"Thanks again for coming down, Jeni."

She let herself out. Glad he was finally using her first name.

Chapter 6

The tall man lay on his back in Mrs. Grindle's small, uncomfortable bed staring at a gold-framed, sepia photo of Mr. and Mrs. Grindle on their wedding day.

Dressed for the occasion, the young Mr. Grindle was stern in his dark Sunday best, his new bride wan by comparison in flowing alabaster; both nervous, callow, uncertain about a future they both assumed would go on forever.

Mr. Grindle—probably twenty-one—had thick, close-cropped hair and the kind of pale blue eyes that always went translucent in old movies and tintypes. He was not unhandsome. Mrs. Grindle, though well defined of feature in later life, was surprisingly plain in youth. It seemed inconceivable that a young man like Grindle would marry this vaporous willow. The tall man could not imagine fucking her, her knowing how to fuck, or liking it. He *could* imagine that she came from money, however, that the young man endured much to this end, that when that end came—handsome face gone hard—he was tired of the money as well as the unreciprocal sex, and glad to be ridden with cancer, or heart disease or whatever immutable force had finally robbed him of youth and life. Mrs. Grindle, alone with her money, her memories, grateful the untidy fucking was no longer required of her, had been no less anxious to go; the tall man had seen it in her eyes.

He turned on the bed to the softly ticking grandfather clock in the shadowed corner, could see by these shadows, cast by moonlight, it was time to go; could see this without consulting the clock's face or his own watch; could sense it, the way he sensed the too-soft mattress under his back, the way he sensed the sweet coastal air pressing around him. He threw his legs over the mattress and reached for his suitcase. From this, he withdrew a small black attaché. This he took with him into the night, locking Mrs. Grindle's door behind him. The Sprinter 9000 laptop PC, he left on the nightstand table. It had told him everything he needed to know about his destination, about who waited at the end of it.

Chapter 7

She woke to the off-key ring of the doorbell.

Logy and distracted, Jeni searched for the nightstand clock. She saw, with a surge of adrenaline, that it was past noon. She'd slept the morning away. Then she remembered. She'd been unable to sleep again last night, had taken an extra Klonopin. It had put her away; they did that sometimes.

The doorbell was insistent.

Jeni pushed up, grabbed her robe, flicked at her hair in the hall mirror, shrugged at her morning face, paced the hall, and pulled back the door.

A dumpy young man in tan delivery uniform and cap stood there, a large cardboard box at his feet. The uniform was in need of pressing. He held a clipboard, sported a sprinkle of postadolescent pimples, ungainly posture. A nerd, Jeni thought absently, rubbing her eyes. "Yes?"

"Jennifer Starbuck?"

"Yes."

"Got a package here from an Agent Miller, needs your signature." He extended the clipboard. Jeni scanned the delivery slip, spotted: *One (1) Sprinter 9000 PC Model #66421.*

"A computer?"

"Yes ma'am." The pimply face smiled. "Brand-new

model. A beauty. Free installation too. Have you up and
running in fifteen minutes!" He handed her a Bic pen.

Jeni hesitated, blinking more sleep from her eyes. Took
the pen, finally, and scrawled her name on the bottom line.

"You're lucky, ma'am. Wish *I* had a brand-new Sprinter
9000."

It didn't take her long to realize—watching him install
it—that she knew as much as he did about the basic setup.
Once you knew the basics it was easy to extrapolate from
there. For her, at least. As she'd often been told, easy for
her was not necessarily easy for the majority. She always
thought she'd retain a certain humility about this, even
when an eighteen-year-old delivery boy's every movement emphasized his own convictions about women, especially concerning the intricacies of this brave new
computer world.

"Sprinter, of course, comes automatically on-line the
moment you type in the registration code," the young
man was patient to point out. Immediately the computer
zipped into high drive. The speed with which it accomplished this amazed even Jeni. The young man grinned
beneath his cap. "Forty-five Mgh of memory built in.
Wish I could afford one. Course you got the Cadillac
model—most of them aren't quite this powerful. Enjoy!"

She made coffee when he'd gone, stood drinking it by
the sink, far away from the kitchen table and the metal
beast squatting ominously atop it, watching her with a
single, baleful eye.

The young man with the cap and pimples had left her a
fat white instruction book. She glanced through it once:
Dick and Jane mentality compared to the opus Miller had
assigned her. She put the book on the sink and poured
more coffee.

Still, trial and error had always been her forte when it

came to electronics. A quick perusal of the first chapter
and she was on her way . . .

She rubbed her eyes and glanced at the kitchen clock. Two
hours had passed like two minutes. Caught in the cyber-
world, she'd lost track of time. It had just turned four.

Jeni blinked. A heartbeat of premonition passed like a
cloud. Four o'clock.

The big hand moved just past the 12, thin sweep-
second chasing it . . .

The earthquake that followed vibrated the floor beneath her bare feet and rattled the dishes in the cupboard.
Pierre Cardin sought her lap, clawing. Jeni gripped the
countertop in a flush of adrenaline and reminded herself
not to panic. The freight train roar trailed, ended.

Silence. A dog commenced barking somewhere.

Even before the phone started ringing beside her, she
realized who it was. That it hadn't been an earthquake
at all.

She was suddenly very wide awake indeed.

By the time she reached the blast site, fog and darkness
had settled over the city.

Agent Miller had phoned her from the office, wondered if she'd mind meeting him there, maybe she could
be of some help, who knew. There had been the diminishing congestion of rush-hour traffic to contend with,
further crowding streets already jammed with excited
rubberneckers, curiosity seekers.

The concussion, having taken place somewhere in the
Statler Building's lower levels, collapsed the first seven
stories like a house of cards, leaving only a skeletal husk,
one remaining wall of dripping debris in the back of the
structure and two forward columns to support the remain-

ing ten floors. The building, against amber sunset, looked like a layer cake out of which an enormous mouthful had been taken. The blast had fanned outward in a nearly perfect V across Broadway and Second, overturning cars, lampposts, and pedestrians with a wall of mortar, steel, and furnace heat. All the windows of the storefronts and office buildings across the street were either blown out or spiderwebbed, but amazingly, considering the Saturday street traffic, no casualties were yet reported from that sector.

Jeni stood in hastily donned beige sweater and jeans (she should have brought a coat), arms wrapped around herself against coolly descending Southern California night. She stared blankly at the destruction.

She kept thinking about Oklahoma, couldn't seem to get those TV news and magazine images out of her mind, though there was probably that much devastation right here in front of her, perhaps more. She could not shake the feeling she was somehow responsible, that she'd blown it again somehow . . .

FBI Agent Miller, plastic ID badge out in plain sight now over his breast pocket, scouted the perimeter with detectives from the San Diego bomb squad and Sheriff's Department, picking through the outer periphery of rubble. Miller's face, like the others, was sober, nearly luminescent in the fading light—a host of floating wraiths moving among the storm of debris, the buried dead.

How many dead no one as yet knew. So far none had been found. The good news was that the building had already been evacuated for the day. A skeleton crew of night workers had remained, from what Jeni could glean from snatches of conversation, but had been accounted for—bruised and bleeding, shaken but alive to return to their families. But all in all, they had been quite lucky.

Or forewarned, depending on how you accessed it.

Except for Agent Miller and Jeni, the other members of Miller's special unit had stayed behind in the little smoke-filled office above the sweatshop, Jeni a little surprised at this, surprised that of all the people Agent Miller had chosen to accompany him to the blast site, he'd picked her.

Surly uniforms kept tapping her arm, pulling her aside when Miller wasn't watching to head them off. "Ma'am, I'm going to have to ask you to stand behind the yellow police tape."

"It's okay, I'm with Agent Miller."

She'd have given anything for her old windbreaker with the big white ATF letters stenciled on the back; for its warmth if nothing else.

She kept sneezing, nose red with irritation, first assuming it was the fog off the bay, then realizing that, although the rapidly falling night was masking it, the air must still be choked with dust motes, clouds of swirling debris.

The members of San Diego's Search and Rescue were circling the building with wary apprehension, casting ominous glances at the gutted facade, as though fearful the whole remaining structure could come thundering down at any moment. Fog and night were thickening, a bone-chilling cold behind it, making a bad situation worse. Sirens wailed, mixed with human cries, a woman keening somewhere. Jeni felt her heart lurch. But not with sympathy. The ugly truth was, she had missed this: the excitement, the confusion, the mystery, even the tragedy. The truth was she had missed it more than she had ever admitted to herself.

Agent Miller came toward her out of misted rubble, stepping gingerly over twisted spiderwebs of concrete enforcing rods. His brow held a permanent crease.

Jeni could read his thoughts: How could this happen? The experts had swept the building thoroughly. What was it the bomb squad had said?—the place is clean, we guarantee it. Surely the building had remained under surveillance since yesterday afternoon's threat. How could he have gotten in, much less out again?

Her stomach gurgled insistently, oblivious to worldly matters. She hadn't eaten all day, sitting at that silly computer, trying to decipher its mysteries. The sensation had its irony. Professional law enforcement officers can't afford the luxury of empathy at a death scene. When you're hungry, you're hungry. Kelsie Merril, the only other female ATF agent she'd ever known, had once been seen absently munching a bagel in a crack house piled with bullet-riddled bodies.

Miller came toward her. "Sorry that took so long. Thanks for coming down. I think it's important you see this."

"It's all right, I'm glad you called."

He smiled gratitude. He looked haunted, and her heart went out to him. "Listen," he said, "I'm cold and hungry. Have you got time for a bite?"

She had time. She didn't want to go home. She was wide awake now.

He drove them to Sea Port Village, a restaurant called the Jolly Roger. A few short blocks from the blast site, the wind off the bay blew away all smells of death and debris.

The Jolly Roger was a tourist eatery with style: a view of the marina, yachts, and yawls rocking easily in their slips, masts lancing the starry sky, ringed by a rock jetty, the adjacent bay and the distant lights of the Coronado Bridge sparkling through the fog. Jeni had frequented it often, but not since Brian. Not since Molly's death.

After their waitress left, Miller sat staring solemnly into empty space, hands folded atop the polished mahogany table, glancing absently at the nautical decor: strands of marlins and fishnet, oak-framed paintings of ancient sailing vessels, fiberglass fish. Miller's mind clearly elsewhere. He sat unconsciously cracking the knuckles of his left hand.

"Any idea how the bomb experts could have missed it?"

Miller shook his head in genuine bewilderment. "They couldn't. They just don't miss, those guys. That detection equipment is extremely sophisticated, even without the dogs. Either this is a completely different kind of explosive device we're talking about or Handle got in there somehow after the experts left, got past the guards. I don't see how, and I don't see any other explanation. It just doesn't add up unless one of our own is pulling it off— one of the security personnel—and that's beyond all realistic conjecture, they're all monitored, every one of them." An edge to his voice. Jeni got the feeling Miller didn't relish being out of control, liked less being made a fool of.

Jeni watched him. "You'll get him."

Miller settled back, blew pent-up breath, blue Paul Newman eyes softening. "Now you're cheerleading me." He managed a smile for her. "Sorry. This thing has been a bitch. Exasperating from the get-go. The sound of that smug bastard's voice . . ."

Jeni sipped water, switched subjects. "The sweatshop setup is a great idea. How did you manage it?"

Miller shrugged. "We needed a covert hideout, and the sweatshop was already in place. It's run by a little sleazeball named Menendez who works for somebody who works for somebody who got his seed money from somewhere in the governor's office."

"Nice to know the state's condoning slave labor."

"It happens all over, Texas too, you should know that."

"Yes."

"Anyway, we showed up, told the sleazeball he could stay on at his salary, raised the salaries of the workers to above minimum wage, and carried out our little clandestine search for the bomber."

"And you found him."

"Handle found us. The computer winked on one day and there he was, bright with sarcasm."

"That must have been humiliating."

"Oh, he delights in embarrassing us, showing us how clumsy we are. And he's just about right. So far we have almost nothing on him. Including whether or not he's the real Solobomber." He smiled ruefully at her. "You know why they call him the Solobomber?"

"Because he works alone?"

Miller shook his head. "Because so far he's managed to set off three large explosions with a single target each. No one else was ever injured."

"So who's the target this time?"

"That we can't figure out. Yet. But there haven't been any casualties yet either. Apparently five minutes before the explosion someone set off the fire alarm and the skeleton crew got out."

Jeni mulled it over. "How much do you know about the guy in the yacht?"

"It's called a ketch, officially. He was Irving Bradford, publisher, owns over a thousand newspapers and television stations worldwide, including the *San Diego Union*. Billionaire. Third VIP killed by the Solobomber in three months. Speaking of exasperation, here's another bothersome statistic. Bradford was notoriously paranoid about bomb threats. His papers ran several articles on the bomber, one of his more notorious tabloids that refused to run the Solobomber's so-called manifesto."

"The one they ran in the *Times*? Something about creativity and individual rights?"

"That's it. Bradford was scrupulously suspicious of any and all packages that came to the paper's office, or to his home. He had both swept at least twice daily with a metal detector. And his car and his boat. We've talked to his right-hand man and private bomb expert, guy named Manuel. Apparently the boat was checked out thoroughly before Bradford went sailing off that evening. We're holding Manuel downtown but he looks to be clean."

Miller grimaced sourly. "Whatever Handle's using for an explosive, its not traceable with current technology. At least not so far."

"And the Statler Building?"

Miller shrugged. "Just an office building as far as I know, we're checking into it, of course. I think there's an electrical firm there, a shipping company, an architectural firm, stuff like that."

Jeni watched the man across the table with sympathy, remembering her days with the division. Miller had his work cut out for him. "How long have you been in San Diego, Paul?"

Miller seemed grateful for the switch in subjects. "About three months. We're one of three other special task forces assigned to the Solobomber case. One is in San Francisco, one in Santa Barbara, one in San Mateo, and the other here. The thing is, nobody's really certain he's even in California." He said it with that same exasperated air, expression flat, resolve laced with irony.

"Until now," Jeni filled in.

Miller shook his head. "Just because we've got some kook on the line who says his name is John Handle and is responsible for the bay bombing and—presumably—for this latest one doesn't mean he's our man. Maybe, but just as likely not. Maybe there are two bombers. Copycat serial killers exist, why not bombers? Hell, who knows." He reached for his margarita and took a good swallow, draining it. He signaled the waitress for another. Turned and looked at Jeni apologetically again. "Sorry, I don't usually drink this much, either."

Jeni smiled. "I've never heard an FBI agent apologize so much in the course of one evening. I've never heard an FBI agent apologize for anything, in fact."

Miller managed a rueful grin. "Is this the classic clash of FBI and ATF agents? I always thought that rivalry stuff between divisions was pretty silly. Like the army and the air force. We're all supposed to be on the same team, right?"

Jeni looked at her water glass ironically. "Sometimes people on the same team aren't even on the same team . . ."

Miller watched her. "So I understand. You've had quite a rough time of it, haven't you?"

Jeni assessed him a moment, head cocked. "I'm quite sure you know all about it by now, Agent Miller. My dossier would be easy to come by, and if Handle can get hold of it, certainly you can."

Miller accepted his second drink from the waitress, sipped at it, silent for a moment. "I wouldn't be doing my job if—"

"—if you didn't dig up the dirt on me?" Jeni finished flatly. She knew that was unfair, but the hurt and indignation of five years of accusations and denials had taken their toll on her decorum. For a moment she thought: Walk away, walk away from all this before it ends in disaster like the last time—

"Listen, Jeni, I didn't want to—"

"Just what does my file say, Agent Miller? I'd like to know."

Paul hesitated. "You joined the ATF right out of college. You were recruited by Brian Starbuck, whom you subsequently married. The two of you were quite a team. Then you went into hostage negotiations and there came Waco. Apparently some disagreement about the way you handled that."

Jeni fingered the stem of the glass reflectively. She hadn't spoken about it at length to anyone since Brian moved out. The last thing she wanted to do was unload on this perfect stranger. She wished now she'd ordered a drink. "It's a long story. A boring story."

"You were suspended from the Texas ATF pending investigation."

She gave him a caustic look. "If you can call a good-ol'-boy insider smear campaign an investigation, yes. They fired me. I appealed."

Paul frowned. "Look, we don't have to talk about it—"

"I had a run-in with a gun dealer once in the old days," she intoned coolly. "He was legally licensed and all, but I didn't like the looks of things. I asked him to surrender his business records to ATF's national tracing center. The guy turned them over, all right, smeared with dog shit."

Miller sighed.

"They say there's a computer bulletin board somewhere in Detroit that lists the names of the local agents of the Bureau of Alcohol, Tobacco and Firearms. It offers advice to anyone interested in detailed methods of harassing them."

Agent Miller held up surrendering palms. "I get the message. Everyone hates the ATF."

Jeni allowed a limp smile. "Not without cause."

Miller watched her. "Yet you stuck for a long time. Why?"

She shocked herself by reaching over and taking his drink from in front of him, taking a sip. She put it back immediately, sheepishly. "I'm sorry, God that was unforgivably gauche."

"Don't be silly, let me order you one—*waitress*!"

She started to stop him, but let it go. To hell with it, she was dying for a drink. "I stuck because people are people. I had friends in the department—good friends—and I had enemies. Yes, it has its share of chauvinist pigs but what organization or business doesn't? The truth is, I was generally well liked. At least . . . in the beginning."

Her drink came and she took a sip. And another.

A waiter was just coming with their food when Miller's pager went off. He pulled the plastic device no bigger than a cigarette pack from his belt, punched a button. Jeni watched him raptly. He was nodding. "Yeah, okay. Right."

Miller put the cellular away. "That was Hendricks at the office. Our friend is on the line again."

Jeni reached reflexively for her purse. "He wants to discuss the Statler Building?"

Miller was looking past her, through her.

"Paul? What's he saying?"

Miller studied her intently. "He says he'll no longer discuss anything without you present."

He threw bills beside their steaming plates, and they hurried to his car.

Chapter 8

Special Agent Jack Higgins was munching a toasted bagel when Jeni and Miller entered the office. Hendricks and the others were cool and collected in that detached way government cops have, as though mad bombers came into their lives as a matter of course. The Sprinter 9000 computer was lit up again (screen still blank), the man at the console turning as Miller and Jeni came through the door.

"He won't even talk to us," Higgins managed around a mouthful.

Miller pushed past him irritably. "He'll damn well talk to me!"

He gestured the man off the console chair and depressed a key on the computer. "Handle, this is Agent Miller. Would you like a body count on the Statler Building, or do you already have that information?"

The other agents turned in apparent surprise when the computer responded. "You should know better than that, Agent Miller. Do you think I'm so careless that I don't know who I've killed? There is no body count, and won't be. You should have stayed and finished your dinner at least. I wouldn't have minded the delay. I understand the food's quite good at the Jolly Roger."

Jeni's mouth fell open. How in hell did Handle know where they'd gone to dine?

"What do you want, Handle?" Miller sighed.

"I imagine Ms. Starbuck is famished. She hasn't eaten all day as I understand it. Right, Jeni? You are there, aren't you, Jeni?"

"She's here," Miller barked. "What is it you want?"

"What I want is for you to remove yourself from that computer console, Agent Miller, and let the lady sit down. The sooner you do that, the more time you'll have to head off the next detonation."

All eyes turned quickly to Agent Miller. Jeni saw a tick starting in the muscles of his left jawline. He was grinding his teeth silently. Finally, he rolled back the swivel chair, stood, and gestured for her.

Jeni sat. "Yes," to the blank screen. "I'm here, Handle. What is it you want to discuss?"

"Discuss? Oh, many things, many things, all in due course. How are you feeling tonight, Jeni? A little tired, a little hungry?"

"A little of both, yes."

"Sorry about the interrupted dinner. You haven't eaten all day, have you, my dear?"

And how in hell had he known that!

"You were wondering, upon ordering, who would be paying for it, am I right? You or Agent Miller. He's tall, isn't he, our Agent Miller? Would you say handsome?"

"What do you want with me, Handle?"

"Those blue, movie-star eyes. And you can call me John if that's more convenient. Is that more convenient, Jeni?"

"What do you want from me, John?"

"Well, now. What do I want? Some answers, firstly."

"*You* want answers?" Jeni glanced at Miller next to her.

"Why didn't you head off the Statler bombing, Jeni? You had plenty of time."

Jeni experienced a distant heat. "Why didn't *I*? Or why didn't the Bureau?"

The computer chuckled. "Oh, Jeni. Let's not depend on Agent Miller. He never feels the least responsible for anything. Trust me, I know. You, on the other hand . . ."

Heart quickening, Jeni replied, "Me, on the other hand, what?"

"You're somewhat of an expert on guilt. Your daughter, for example . . ."

Miller cursed softly, started toward the console. Jeni held him off with an upraised hand. "What exactly is it your require of me, Mr. Handle?"

"John."

"How do I figure in all this? What do you want? I'd like to go home and rest."

"And so you shall. Just another moment of your indulgence, please. How good are you with math, Jeni?"

"Passing."

"Oh, don't be modest. You made top honors in college. How good are you at calculating distances? I myself have a real talent for it. For instance. Given your endurance, your top speed, the distance between the sweatshop and the site of the next explosion, I calculate you should be able to reach the structure a full sixty seconds before the timer goes off."

At this last, the room sprang into action again, Miller pointing, Hendricks and the rest already leaping to phones, out the door. Jeni felt her heartbeat go from quickening to a painful gallop. Somehow she'd foreseen this.

"Of course I'm factoring in your present mental and physical state, your exhaustion from an excruciating day, your rendezvous with Miller and company, your lethargy this morning, your ongoing disappointment at losing the race . . ."

Christ, the guy is psychic!

Jeni started to say something when Agent Miller stepped in. "Listen, Handle, you can just knock off the shit now because if you're even half as all-seeing as you pretend to be, you surely know my department would never involve a civilian in this kind of madness."

There was pregnant silence from the computer.

Jeni had the momentary sensation they'd lost him. She looked to Miller, who was staring stony-faced at the blank screen.

"Agent Miller, I was conversing with Ms. Starbuck. Do you mind?"

"You'll converse with me, or no one, is that clear, Handle?"

Silence. Then: "I believe we've already had this discussion."

"Is that clear, Handle?"

"Ms. Starbuck?"

"She isn't available," Miller barked, losing his cool.

"You still have your Sprinter 9000 Walkman head-phones?"

"Yes," Jeni blurted before Miller could interrupt.

"Please tune the dial to 880 A.M. I've requested an Elvis tune that's one of your favorites."

Miller pushed Jeni aside gently, firmly. "Listen, Handle—"

"The Piedmont Apartments on State Street, Jeni. Fifteen minutes. You should make it just under the wire, if you begin your run immediately."

"You'll talk to *me*," Miller repeated vehemently, "or no one! Do you understand!"

But the computer was silent, and everyone still in the room knew it would stay that way again for a while.

Jeni was looking at her watch. Miller caught the motion. "What do you think you're doing?" he demanded.

Jeni stared at him. "As you said, I'm still a civilian. I intend to try for it."

He gave her an appalled look, then turned away. "Out of the question."

Jeni followed. "Look, the guy obviously isn't bluffing. Look at the Statler Building!"

Miller was fishing for another invisible cigarette. "We've got the address, the bomb squad boys are already on it."

"He doesn't want the bomb squad, he wants me."

Miller perched stiffly on the couch. "Well, he's not going to get you."

"Paul, I know that area, I can make it in under fifteen minutes."

Miller was out of patience, even with her. "What the hell are you talking about, Jeni? Let the pros handle it! What are you trying to do!"

"I'm trying to save lives!"

"By running straight into a blast! What're you going to do when you get there—assuming you get there on time. You don't even know where the bomb is, much less anything about dismantling a delicate explosive device. Talk sense!"

She kept glancing askance at the door. "I don't think there is a bomb there."

Miller squinted at her. "You just said the guy isn't bluffing—"

"This isn't about exploding another bomb. This is about trust. Or something. He wants to see if I'll do it."

"Well, he'll be sadly disappointed. I'm not turning this

office into a command headquarters for a lunatic. And I'm not endangering the life of innocent civilians."

Wounded at the reference, Jeni nevertheless kept at it. "Innocent civilians are already in danger, Paul."

"No! End of story!"

She eyed him. "You can't stop me."

"Jeni, it isn't the Piedmont Apartments. He knows we'll have that swarming with police immediately. He's trying to communicate with you over your earphones, exclude us, can't you see that?"

"Of course I can see that! So what? It's what he wants, and so far, Paul, he's gotten exactly what he wants. If you're afraid for me, have me followed at a distance." She was checking her watch again.

When she looked up she could see that Miller was at least considering it now. She decided it was time to fire all her cannons. "You can tune into my headset frequency right here from the command post, keep me in range all the time. Paul, we're not giving in to him, we're playing along for now. I'm going to do this. I can always chicken out at the last second."

"Assuming he's telling the truth about the 'last second.' " Miller kept slapping absently at his empty pockets. Jeni grabbed a pack of Marlboros from a nearby coffee table and stuck one in his mouth. He took it out, stared at it as if contemplating its contents. He heaved a sigh. "At least wait until we can be sure we've got your frequency."

Jeni held up the watch hand. "There isn't time! I need to go *now*!"

Miller fitted the smoke between his lips, patted for a light. "I don't like this, Jeni! I don't like going on record for it. And I like even less that it's you involved!"

She felt a small thrill in her stomach at this last. She

pulled the earphones and radio from her purse, silently grateful she'd worn flats tonight instead of heels. She'd have given anything for her trusty Reeboks.

At the door she said, "No more than one black-and-white. And keep them at least a block away. This guy has eyes in the back of his head."

Miller, not looking at her, sat stiffly on the couch, digging for matches, body rigid with impotent frustration.

Jeni started through the door and Miller was suddenly up and coming to her. "Hey!"

She turned back.

"Just . . . be careful for chrissake," he told her softly.

"I'm a pro, remember? I won't lose your job for you."

"Screw that," Miller said.

Jeni smiled. Turned. Began her run.

She knew exactly where she was going.

The Piedmont Apartments were near her neighborhood. She'd looked into them right after the breakup, considered a small efficiency one-bedroom; but they didn't accept pets and she would not part with Pierre Cardin, even though Brian had offered to take him. A sweet gesture considering Brian hated the cat.

Jeni jogged evenly down the courthouse lawn, finding her rhythm, turned left on Prescott, and hit the sidewalk paralleling the Pacific Coast Highway. She ran, with light evening traffic, in smooth, even strides, conserving energy for the sprint, ignoring the odd looks from passersby at this strange jogger in a beige sweater and flats. She checked the luminous dial of her watch. She'd lost nearly a minute sparring with Miller. But she knew shortcuts, backyards, and alleyways from her time with the agency, things that would trim seconds, maybe minutes, off her time, places Handle couldn't know of. She should be able to reach the Piedmont apartment complex in under ten minutes easily, even without the sprint. If she hadn't known that, she wouldn't have attempted this. At least she didn't think she would have.

After the first block she remembered to flick on the radio at her belt, adjust her headphones.

"Heartbreak Hotel" was just ending. Courtesy—she assumed—of a call-in request from Handle. Not her favorite Presley vehicle, but up there near the top, an old, reliable standby.

"—and that was the King, going out under special request for Jeni. Hey, it's coming up on the eight o'clock hour here on KXOK 880 AM your station for San Diego's oldies! Hal Fairmont spinning the platters for you this foggy eve, where you'll hear more about the weather and the news—including the big explosion near Sea Port Village—from our own Web Stickler at the top of the hour! Right now, Pete at Center High would like to send this out to Julie . . . and if you can give me the name of the artist on this tune I've got two tickets to Sea World here in my hot little jock hands! Here we go then with 'Silhouettes' . . . third caller wins!"

"So what do you think, Jeni?" Handle's voice interrupted, startling with clarity, loud and uncomfortably personal in her ears. It threw off her rhythm for a second. The station sounds disappeared.

She was just rounding Third and Broadway, dodging around pedestrians, a group of teens hooting at the lady in the bouncy sweater, inching her way uptown to more secluded, less trafficked streets.

"Jeni? It's John. Can you hear me?"

"I can hear you," she puffed evenly.

"These new Sprinter 9000 Walkmans are a marvel, aren't they? First the telephone, then the cellular phone, fiber-optic computers, and now two-way radios. Isn't progress wonderful!"

"Yes, gives one such a feeling of privacy."

Handle laughed in her ears. "My point exactly! Oh, I think we're going to get along famously, Jeni! You're breaking up a bit. Adjust your gain knob. Do you have it exactly on 880 AM?"

Jeni turned another corner, found a blessedly empty alleyway, glanced down at the radio hooked to her belt. "Little hard to be sure, Mr. Handle, under the circumstances."

A sympathetic chuckle. "I appreciate that. And please call me John. You call him Paul, you can call me John. Would he be very jealous, do you think?"

"Agent Miller?" It was becoming difficult, running and talking, it was interfering with her timing. Was Handle aware of that? Of course he was. "Why on earth would he be?"

"Not Miller. Brian! Is he the jealous type, your ex?"

"We're divorced."

"But you still love him, do you not? After all, twelve years and a child. One expects *some* residual feeling."

Her throat tightened. She had to will herself to relax: she couldn't run with her throat seized up. She rounded a trash can, cleared the opposite end of the alley, and jogged up Grape Street. It was a moderately steep hill— would take its toll on her calf muscles but cut minutes off her time. If she didn't wear out.

She didn't think she would. She felt okay. Fine, actually. The cool evening air was clearing her head, giving her a second wind.

"How are you holding up? Your breathing sounds slightly irregular."

"Well, that's because I'm talking and running at the same time."

"Forgive me. Would you rather I rang off?"

No! Keep him talking! Miller is locked on, taping this!

"Not really. I like company."

"You didn't like the black girl's company much. How much did it cost you?"

She was nearing the crest of the hill, thighs burning. She was more tired than she'd thought. It had been a tough day despite the late arousal. "A lot. I hope you didn't have any bets down on me, John."

"I'm not a betting man. Thank you for calling me John. Will it set back your AIDS hospice terribly, your losing the race?"

"It won't help." She wavered an instant at Sloane and Fifth, then took the tougher of the two options up the steep Sloane hill, glancing at her watch. She was making good time.

"Perhaps I can make it up to you. I mean, I was indirectly responsible for your falling, I suppose."

"And how would you do that, John?"

Silence for a moment.

"John? Are you there?"

"You're a very smart cop, aren't you, Jeni? You don't push. But you keep me on the line. I did well in choosing you."

"Choosing me for what, John?"

"All in good time."

She breasted Sloane and pulled cold, grateful air into her lungs, calves relaxing, shin muscles taking over for a while on the downhill side. It was a little easier to breathe.

"How are the legs holding up?"

"I'm in good shape, John."

"Beautiful shape. A beautiful woman. It worked against you in the agency, of course. Especially a sexist outfit like the ATF. Bunch of moonshine hunting good old boys from the Southeast, am I right?"

Jeni didn't answer.

"Why do you suppose it's that way, Jeni? An organization that big?"

"It's that way because the generation of AFT officials who hired the current senior managers were men. Men hired for their knowledge of southern mores, their expertise in handling country bootleggers. Once these guys reached positions of authority, they kept right on hiring people like themselves, perpetuating the bad habits." She swallowed hard. He had her talking too much again. Conserve, *conserve*!

"So why on earth did a bright, pretty young woman like you stay with them? With your inquisitive mind you could have done anything."

"Not anything. I was trained as a Treasury agent. And anyway, I loved the ATF. It's basically a good agency."

"Really. And how do you justify something like the unmitigated disaster at Waco?"

"We—they—learned a lot from Waco."

"As I understand it, it was mostly a lack of training, even among the field commanders. They lost the element of surprise. Would you agree?"

"The biggest mistake was that the top two commanders took part in the assault. Their perspective was diluted. If they hadn't been so close in, they might have called it off when things went wrong, averted disaster. One of them rode a helicopter, the other actually took place in the raiding party entering the compound. That was a mistake. A costly one. But the agency's learned from it. It's a good organization." She took a deep breath. "I really can't keep conversing and running like this, John."

"And Brian Starbuck—your ex—does he concur with all this?"

"Brian wasn't at Waco."

"That's not what I asked you, Jeni. Is Brian also sympathetic to the ATF? Or is it his contention that some of the disgruntled good old boys—the overly zealous patriot types that don't tolerate snitches—might be somehow responsible for the, ah . . . accident? The one that killed your child . . ."

Jeni received the stab of pain above her heart without breaking stride. Her breathing was labored now. She was still making good time but she was wearing down rapidly. There would be little left for a sprint if that became necessary. She decided to try to switch tactics with him. "You're a very informed individual, John. Were you with the Bureau at one time, perhaps?"

"Uh-oh. Now you are pushing. However, I will tell you that we have many friends in common, though whether they would consider me a friend at this point—well, you know the old saying about strange bedfellows! You sound labored, Jeni. Maybe we should curtail this delightful conversation for the time being."

No! Don't lose him!

"Whatever you say. Of course, I was hoping you might be of some help once I reached the Piedmont Apartments." She barely got it out, the last words shaky.

"Did I say Piedmont Apartments?"

Here it came.

"Is there a change in plan, John?" A familiar stitch was beginning at her left side. Probably from being forced to gulp air while talking to him. If the pain grew worse, she'd have to slow.

"Let me see now . . . If you've cut across town to save time—as I assume you have, that's what I'd do, using the alleys and hills on Grape and Sloane—then you should be coming up on Trinity Street about now. Am I close?"

How in hell did he do it? "Pretty close."

"Good. Turn left on Trinity, please. And cut through that backyard. I'd like to shake that pesky patrol car behind us."

Jeni felt her legs falter, rhythm gone to hell. "That will take me away from the apartment complex, John."

He ignored her remark. "Don't worry about the 'Beware of Dog' sign on the fence. There's no dog in that backyard."

Could he somehow see her? How could he see her? She leapt the short fence braced on one arm without losing momentum.

"There's a glass greenhouse dead ahead, do you see it?"

"Yes."

"I want you to jog through it. Both doors are unlocked. Kindly don't stop to smell the roses."

Jeni cleared a neat, close-cropped yard, approached the greenhouse, pulled the wooden door open, and ran on, over damp cement floor, the musky odor of humus and growing things. It was dark inside, her only guide the rows of pale, whitewashed nursery shelves on either side. The door at the far end was unlocked as well. How had he known that?

"How're we doing?"

"I'm through the greenhouse," she gasped, wincing at the worsening pain in her side. *Go away! Go away!*

"Turn left at the end of the yard. There's a short alley. Go right. You should have lost the cops by now. At the end of the alley, turn left on Figuroa."

Jeni felt her heart leap.

Figuroa was her street.

Her legs made the turns obediently. "What are we doing, John?"

"Tell me, Jeni . . . did you put the cat out?"

She felt a flood of heat. *"No!"*

"Is that a rhetorical 'no' or an answering 'no'?"

She could see her street just ahead. It should have been lined with police cars by now if Miller was picking all this up. She saw only a rusty green Dodge, a nicely kept Volkswagen. The rest of the block was empty. Her heart thundered.

"Don't bother looking for cops, Jeni. Agent Miller is deaf at the moment. I switched band widths on him. He has no idea where you are."

She picked up speed with a burst of adrenaline. "Please don't do this, John!"

"It's already done, I fear."

Half a block farther she went into a dead sprint. No one could touch her at a dead sprint.

Her house was three blocks away. Pierre Cardin was probably lounging on the couch before the bookcase, thick, black tail swishing impatience, wondering why she hadn't returned for his evening meal.

"Please don't hurt my cat, John! He's all I've got!" One more block. She'd be inside the house in under a minute. Her shoes slapped echoes across the cement walk. Mrs. Tiller, frail and bent, looked up curiously from her white porch swing across the way.

"The cat's not all you've got, Jeni. You have your memories of Molly, your pictures and family albums. Of course it's foolish to pore night after night over Molly as a toddler, as a first grader, as a snowflake in the Christmas play—"

"Don't!"

"And you still have Brian. Just because he remarried

a woman with children of her own is no reason to think he—"

"I'm"—gasping—"I'm almost to the house! Where's the bomb? How do I deactivate it?"

Handle's voice was almost laconic with patience. "I'm impressed, Jeni. You'd risk your life for a common house cat and a few painful reminders of a lost life. That shows great heart. Not necessarily great judgment, but terrific scruples. I don't think you can make it, though, Jeni, I honestly don't."

If she cut across the Trumans' front yard, leapt their hedge, she could be on her own front porch in another ten seconds. "I can make it! Where's the bomb, you bastard!"

"Somewhere . . . in your living room . . ."

She could scoop up the cat, dive through the kitchen window in the back, leave behind Molly's pictures, the mementos . . .

"Good-bye, Jeni . . . for now."

"Handle, you son of a bitch!"

The hedge was just before her. She reached inside for a final burst of strength and vaulted the green shrubbery.

The blast caught her in midflight—a yellow ball of flaming heat and Hiroshima wind that blew her effortlessly back over the hedge again. She'd glimpsed both front windows billowing twin funnels of flame and broken glass, diamond bright against the night; the clapboard sides of the house seemed to bulge outward as in a cartoon.

She lit on her back in the Trumans' damp front yard, the hedge saving her from the worst of the flying glass and debris shooting above her head like cannon fire. The first eight inches of foliage atop the hedge were sheared away black, neat and even as garden sculpture.

Jeni lay on her back, chest heaving, limbs dead, all

strength gone, watching the first roiling pall of greasy smoke cover the stars. She bled from a dozen tiny cuts, a few pieces of glass still in her scalp, her cheek.

Her headphones, still miraculously in place, thumped rhythmically to a pre-rock Rosemary Clooney classic: "... *ain't gonna need this house no longer* ... *ain't gonna need this house no more* ..."

Chapter 9

She never lost consciousness through any of it.

She lay on crisp white hospital sheets, staring at the Armstrong suspended ceiling squares and thought: Amazing. I never lost consciousness, and I haven't had a moment's rest since I woke this morning.

Miller's patrol cars had descended on her—sirens blaring, lights wheeling—seconds after the blast had blown her back over the hedge. A thoughtful uniform had kept the other officers and converging crowd of curiosity seekers away until the medevac boys arrived with their shrieking klaxons and foldaway gurney. From then she was treated as delicately as a newborn, though she sensed (correctly, it turned out) she had no broken bones, only minor burns and cuts, a slight loss of hearing from the concussion, which would gradually come back. Nevertheless, they loaded her into the ambulance as though she might suddenly shatter, tore off into the night with her, sirens and lights blasting the dark ahead all the way to County General. She didn't really need but endured the too-tight plastic oxygen mask clamped over her face. She was astounded just to be alive.

All the way she lay pushing the thought of poor Pierre Cardin from her mind, knowing that in his own way Handle had managed to wipe away Molly in a way that the car explosion and a long parade of psychiatrists and drugs had never managed, to destroy those insignificant little reminders of her that had kept Jeni from wanting to blow her brains out long ago. Without those, the little hand-made valentines, the snapshots, the videos, Jeni wondered, how can I ever prove she existed except in my own mind? She knew she was slightly delirious, from hunger, from Klonopin on top of alcohol, from two solid days of surrealistic surprises, but at last, lying on a stretcher at the hospital as another intern checked her over, she found a tear tracing its way down her cheek.

"Hurt?" the intern asked matter-of-factly.

"No."

Why her? Why did Handle pick her to terrorize? No matter how many times she turned it over in her mind, it made no sense.

We have many friends in common . . .

A pretty candy striper checked on her twice before the doctor—a nice elderly man with calm gray eyes and grayer temples named Levy—got around to giving her the once-over, pressing gentle fingertips over every inch of her bruised but unscathed runner's body. He smiled reassuringly, popped a few cc's of antibiotics into her rump, checked her IV, and told her she was going to be fine.

Paul Miller came into her room as soon as allowed, his face so tight with concern, Jeni felt a wedge of guilt.

Miller smiled down, gripped her hand, could not seem to find words, just stood shaking his head. This case is going to kill him, she thought, if it doesn't kill me first. Too caring, not the type at all I'd expect to see in his position. Knowing this made her feel even sorrier for him—it was obvious he wouldn't last long.

"I'm sorry," she volunteered. He kept shaking his

head. "I never should have let you. It was my mistake." He winced at the sight of the bandage across her brow.

Jeni knew distant resentment, despite the guilt. If she were a man, they wouldn't be having this conversation, not this way. "I already told you. You couldn't have stopped me."

Miller grabbed the back of a straight chair, slid it beside her bed. "I was the one in command. I was responsible." His eyes kept drifting worriedly to her bandaged brow. "The bastard."

She fought conflicting emotions, flattered and angry. He kept ignoring the fact she was—had been—a professional. *You want it both ways . . .*

She told herself to shut up. She told Miller, "I've been lying here thinking, Why me? Why blow up my house? What's the point? If he'd wanted to kill me, all he had to do was wait until I cleared the hedge." She ruminated for a moment, then as an afterthought, "It isn't even my place, it's rented."

"We're looking for bomb fragments. We'll get him. You should rest now, Jeni, we can talk about this later, there's plenty of time."

But they both knew there was not plenty of time. And his solicitous air—though endearing—wasn't going to stop another bombing. "I'm fine," she insisted. "Did you manage to record our conversation?" That came out more critically than she'd meant it.

"Most of it. Why?" He peered at her closely, brow furrowing. "Did he say something you thought might be significant?"

Jeni smiled slightly. "He said we have many friends in common. That could mean anything."

"What do you think it means?"

Jeni shrugged. "An ex-agent, maybe?"

"Or someone who knows you personally."

Jeni shook her head. "No. Not personally. I get the feeling sometimes he's dying to let me in on his little game, but he doesn't dare. Not yet."

Miller assessed her quizzically. "You miss it, don't you?"

The business of being an agent, he meant. She looked at her hands. "I miss the sense of accomplishment. Of making a difference . . . those times when I actually did."

"It must be something more than that."

Jeni smiled wanly at his intuitiveness. "Okay. Sometimes I regret . . . quitting. I don't like unfinished business. I'm not a quitter."

"I'd never have guessed."

She snorted. "Paul, get me out of here. I know you can."

"Why? You need to rest, at least a night's worth. Let the doctors do their job."

"There's nothing wrong with me. I don't belong here taking up a hospital bed. I should be doing something useful."

"I've already loused things up once where you're concerned."

"Besides," she ignored, "your people made such a racket getting me here, there's bound to be reporters."

"I'll keep the reporters at bay."

But she pushed it until he got the drift. ". . . and if reporters can get to me, then Handle damn sure can."

Miller's face went tight. Jeni pressed her advantage.

"He knows I'm here, Paul. We're putting nothing over on him. This guy is very smart. And way ahead of us. Ahead of you, I mean," she added, feeling his resentment but unable to phrase it otherwise.

"Besides," she continued before he could object again, "I'm starving. We never got to finish dinner, remember?"

Miller watched her a moment, eyes unfathomable. He was not a man who liked to be pushed, and Handle was pushing as it was. Maybe she'd gone too far.

He patted for invisible smokes. "All right. I'll buy the idea you may not be entirely safe here. I'll buy you dinner too. But that's it. After dessert, we're going to tuck you away until we nail this psycho."

Jeni reached for the nurse's buzzer.

He caught at her hand. "Is that perfectly clear, Ms. Starbuck?"

"I heard you," she said, already reaching for her clothes.

Miller drove her to an out-of-the-way little Thai restaurant in Del Mar.

Jeni picked delicately at delicious, spicy *pa tai,* sipped gingerly at a tall glass of Thai iced tea, sweet and peanutty. She'd incurred a terrific thirst since the incident but was damned if she'd give in to another alcoholic drink. She wasn't about to sacrifice what little alertness she had.

She wrinkled her nose, sniffing at her wrist.

Miller finally grunted. "It's cordite. From the blast."

"Dear God, can *you* smell it?"

He smiled.

"I need a proper bath. All they did was sponge me at the hospital."

"How's the head?"

"Quit worrying about me."

"Jeni," he said evenly, "I know how you feel, but I can't run this operation on women's intuition. I'm sure you were a superb agent, but you're a civilian now. I can't in good faith continue putting you in harm's way like this. I may be head of this sector, but I still take orders from upstream."

"Look," she stated, spreading her hands atop the table, "it's simple. Get me reinstated."

His eyes told her he'd been expecting that one. "I don't have that kind of authority, even if I thought it was a good idea."

"Come on, Paul, how hard can it be?"

"It isn't that simple." He shifted in the bamboo chair, posture assertive.

She forked noodles. "The truth is, it's less a matter of worrying about me than about your status as operations head. Because of me, Handle's calling all the shots. You're out of control and you don't like it. I'm a burr in your side." A noodle dropped from her mouth. She stared at it incredulously. She'd been stuffing herself. She put down her fork slowly.

Miller watched her quietly, the picture of control. "Jeni, negotiating with a perp, whether he's a mad bomber or a hostage taker, is always subject to limited control, you know that. The idea is not to control the situation, the idea is to prevent a bad situation from getting worse. Now, I played it your way because you are obviously a pro, and because I thought there was reasonable cause for retaliation from Handle if I didn't. But the result was another bombing, in which only through pure luck no one was harmed."

Except for poor Pierre Cardin, she thought. "It wasn't pure luck! He didn't want me harmed."

"That's speculation, Jeni. I can't put speculation in my daily report."

"It's speculation from someone with twelve years' fieldwork. If Handle'd wanted me dead, I'd be dead. He knew I wouldn't make it in time, he never intended me to. Let's play along with him for now. It's our best offense. We can break this guy. And if he does turn out to be the Solobomber, think of the future lives saved!"

"I have to think about present lives too, Jeni."

"I'm not afraid of him, Paul."

"I know. But you should be. He should scare the shit out of you."

"He's just a guy with some dynamite. Maybe a little more educated than most, but he can be brought down."

Miller shook his head. "We'll get him, but not with you running interference for us. I can't play into his hands this way, Jeni. Now, that's final."

She felt a rising heat. This way he had of throwing up the Bureau wall.

She looked away. "Fine. Listen, if it's okay with you, I'd just as soon skip dessert, huh?"

"Jeni, come on."

She waved him off. "It's okay. I'd just like to be alone for a while."

Miller started to say something, gave it up, threw a bill on the table, and took her arm. Halfway out of the restaurant, she pulled the arm away from him politely.

Outside in cool, ocean-misted night, she felt foolish and stupid. Angrier than she should have been. Miller was just trying to hang on to his job, the way she'd tried to hang on to hers.

She walked silently beside him to the restaurant parking lot. It was a lovely night. A night to walk along the pale shore of the Silver Strand and listen to the slapping surf. The way she and Brian used to.

Miller drove her to the big Howard Johnson's in Hotel Circle, an area as conspicuous and brightly lit as the Vegas strip. An area for businesspeople and conventioneers. Hide her in plain sight, that was the idea. In this hustle and bustle she would make a difficult target if Handle came calling.

Not that she was afraid. There was a lot she didn't know about the bomber, but the one thing she felt certain of was his desire to keep her alive. At least for now. She could have slept alone in the park tonight. Handle didn't want her dead. Yet.

He wanted her for something else.

She sat in desultory fatigue in the garish lobby while Miller checked her in. He made some calls on his pager, presumably a security team to surround the building, then came back to where she sat next to the souvenir shop, its window displaying brightly colored T-shirts with San Diego logos. He nodded toward the shop. "Want to pick up some things in there? Toothbrush, whatever?"

She wouldn't meet his eyes. "I can come down for them later. What room am I in?"

Miller produced a key. "Five-sixteen." And he handed it to her.

She thanked him and rose to find the elevator banks. Miller was right by her side. "I can find it," Jeni sighed irritation, "you needn't bother."

"It's no bother. Let's get you safely tucked in."

They rode in silence within the chrome cubicle under a Muzak dirge nearly comical in its inaneness. Jeni watched the illuminated floor numerals wink by, thinking how calmly, how prosaically, the week had begun, and here she was in this strange elevator with this essential stranger, her house, her belongings, her carefully preserved memories, burned to the ground.

Miller waited dutifully beside the door to 516 while

she fitted the key, let herself in to darkness and fresh-smelling sheets.

He held her arm a moment at the threshold, and Jeni turned to him, heart hammering. But he was only making the way safe for her, turning on the light, checking the bedroom perfunctorily, flicking on the bathroom light, checking behind the shower curtain, behind the single closet door. He came back into the living room, found her waiting with folded arms. "I guess you're clean."

"Thank you, Agent Miller."

"Do you still have your Ruger?"

"Yes."

Miller nodded. "Good. Well, you can reach one of my men instantly on line three, just pick up the phone. If you need anything, call either them or the desk. Don't wander the halls, even if it's just to get ice, okay?"

"Sure."

"Is there anything I can get you from downstairs?"

She shook her head against the wall, weary to her bones. "I'll have it sent up."

"Okay. I'm in 522, six doors down."

"I feel so much safer now, Officer."

"Call line three or my number, 520, if you need something. Avoid calling the desk if you can."

"Yes sir. Anything else? I'm a little tired."

"I know you are. Keep your window locked and— oh hell, you know what you're doing." And he closed the door behind him and left her standing there in the antiseptic-smelling hotel room with the plastic key chain in her hand and the dark night ahead.

Exhausted, she found she still couldn't sleep, even approach it.

The bed was too hard, the sheets too rough, the whole

thing too damn *neat;* she missed her own rumpled sheets at home, she missed Pierre Cardin's motor beside her, purring her to sleep.

Jeni slid off the hotel bed, drew herself a very hot bath, and lay back in bubbles and lilac water provided by the hotel in tiny plastic bottles. She luxuriated, the tub longer than hers at home (*you don't have a home anymore, there is no home*), her toes just touching the immaculate porcelain lip. Her body melted gratefully, but if anything the hot water only woke her more.

In too short a time the bath became suffocatingly hot. She shrugged exasperation, stepped from the tub, wrapped a fluffy white hotel towel around her, sat on the edge of the bed, hands in her lap. There was a print of a sailboat on the wall, badly painted with a pallet knife in too-big impasto swatches and stomach-churning colors.

She sighed.

Against Miller's wishes, she reached for the Sprinter computer atop the nightstand and punched in the desk.

Miller came on the line. "Agent Miller."

"Oh, shit. I meant to dial the desk. I'm sorry."

"What were you after?" he asked, not chastisingly.

"Someone to break me out of here."

He said nothing.

"I was trying to get a drink, actually."

"I can do that for you."

"Look, it isn't necessary. I shouldn't be drinking any more anyway."

"Because you're in training, right?"

Because alcohol and pills don't mix.

"Sorry to bother you, Paul. Were you asleep?"

"No. I was hoping to find something on TV to take my mind off things. I haven't watched TV in months. Is it always this bad?"

"Always." She smiled. He had a nice voice, now that he was winding down. "Well. I'll let you go. I imagine you have reports to file, paperwork to catch up on."

"I have a quarter of Johnnie Walker Red in my briefcase that's begging to be opened."

"Is that standard issue for you FBI boys?"

"No, but I'm working on it. How about it? The ice machine's right between us."

She had absolutely no idea if he was married, though she hadn't noticed a ring. Funny she hadn't gotten around to asking that. "Thanks. Maybe another time."

"Okay."

"Good night, Paul."

She turned out the lights, lay back down in the towel, and stared at the ceiling. She was bone-weary, she should be sawing logs by now.

She turned to the nightstand computer again on impulse and punched numbers. "All right. But just a quick one. I've got to get some sleep."

"Be there in five."

She slid off the bed, flicked on the nightstand lamp, and reached for her rumpled clothes on the chair opposite.

They felt damp and soiled. The idea of slipping into them again repulsed her. She retucked the towel at her breast, still not fully acknowledging what she was doing, and went to look at herself in the bathroom mirror. She thought she looked old and tired.

But he won't think so.

She flicked at her hair once with an open palm and turned at his knock.

He came in barefoot, wearing trousers and T-shirt, his hair slicked back from his own shower. He proffered plastic hotel cups, plastic bucket of ice, the bottle, attempting not to notice her towel and what was beneath it.

Jeni held back the door for him. She tried to look casual, didn't feel it. Everything was beginning to feel eerily orchestrated, as though this had already happened, would happen again.

Miller unloaded his arms at her Formica hotel table, dropped ice into the cups. He poured amber liquid, handed her one.

Jeni sipped, felt the burn, looked about, and found only the one chair. She moved to the bed quickly, perched on the edge of the mattress, found that even with her legs pressed together, the towel rode up alarmingly.

Miller was pretending to be busy making his own drink.

Jeni took another swallow, then another, heart already well ahead of her mind.

Agent Miller turned, looked about, spotted the single chair. He sat, the chair making him lower than the bed so he had to look up at her, the ivory sweep of her thigh unavoidable from that angle. There was nothing she could do but perch there with the drink like a silly calendar girl.

A silence that was beginning to stretch too long left her wondering if this was such a hot idea. The thought of small talk seemed absurd; they'd already talked. They should be in bed. So to speak.

Jeni took another drink to cover it, felt the warmth spread from tummy to cheeks. In another moment she wouldn't care about awkward silences. Or if he was married. She hadn't drunk this much in years. Alarm bells clanged, faded.

She looked up to find him watching her intently. The day's hard lines seemed to have eased from his face. "You're lovely," he told her.

She was surprised how good it sounded. So good it hurt her chest.

Miller set down his cup. "I'm not good at this," he offered.

Jeni said nothing as he came to her. It was all going to happen anyway.

He took her glass from her trembling hand and placed it atop the round table. He bent and kissed her lightly, more lightly than she would have liked. She had to increase the pressure for both of them and that opened the way for him.

She moved to snap off the bedside lamp but couldn't reach it, and reaching farther felt graceless, so she sat silently—silent as stone—while he kissed her cheek, her neck, the hollow of her throat, the tan line at her breasts. She felt not the slightest urge to stop his hands taking the top of the towel, pulling aside the edges. She was abruptly proud she'd stayed in shape with all the running. "My God," Miller breathed.

She felt him kneel, heard the thunder of her own blood in her ears, heard herself suck back a gasp at his kiss down there. He kissed twice more, then deeper, probing, provoking sensitive tissue irritable from wanting. "The rhythm of sex and its attendant pleasure is based on irritation": she had read it somewhere.

He pressed deeper yet and the ceiling went pink before her eyes . . . then roiled in warm waves of ocher. He licked . . . and again, and swept her past the edge with sudden, nearly violent force, Jeni gripping his hair, bowed, holding him there, terrified of abandonment. Jaw thrust, teeth clenched, she finished against his mouth, the end an explosion of white through which, paradoxically, she glimpsed Brian's face.

He let her rest, limp . . . a cool waft of air-conditioning teasing her pounding breast, puckering her nipples under a sheen that covered her head to foot. She thought her harsh breathing embarrassingly loud but could not seem to quell it, body and mind bifurcated.

The mattress gave and his face was above hers. "It's been a long time," she began . . . but he covered all talk with his mouth. Her arms went lazily around him. His tongue offered the salty trace of her own musk, his kisses exquisitely light, nearly skillfully torturous, making her wonder how many times before he'd done this, in a place like this. It didn't matter. She was all through with waiting, wanting only his fucking. She reached between, pushed his hands impatiently aside, and adjusted him, let him into the heart of her and all the rest beyond. Once fitted, he was hers.

She gazed up now into guileless, a boy's, eyes, and that broke away all remaining fear. In command now, confident against his helpless lunges, she cupped his buttocks and led the dance for them, all the steps coming back now, familiar and new. When his pupils went wide at his approach, she nodded encouragement, smiled fiercely, and joined him. He emptied long and violently, Jeni holding him like a tender mother.

She had just drifted off when she felt the movement. She rolled over to see him pulling on his shirt, catching her eye with an apologetic look. "I didn't mean to wake you."

"Must you go?"

He reached for his trousers on the chair back. "I think it might be best."

At the door he turned. An awkward moment. Thank you? I'll call? Nothing at a time like this was ever right or enough.

As it turned out, he said just the right thing. "Just because making love to you was akin to a religious experience doesn't change anything, Jeni. About your joining the force and all." There was little conviction in his voice. Or maybe he was just tired.

She smiled. "I know."

He nodded. Closed the door gently behind him.

Jeni rolled back over, went back to sleep.

The tall man entered Jeni Starbuck's hotel room with a passkey he had surreptitiously lifted from a cleaning cart.

No one saw him. No one roamed the halls at this time of night except cleaning personnel, and they always seemed to have the odd habit of staring at the carpeted floor when someone approached, as if they preferred not to know the comings and goings of the guests. He had timed it just right. She was in the deep REM state now, as the tall man gingerly, and without sound, brought himself and the small black attaché noiselessly through the door and locked it behind him.

He stood in the deepest shadow beside the window and watched the face of the sleeping figure on the bed, watched until his eyes adjusted completely to the deeper dark of the bedroom, and until he was sure by the rapid movement beneath the shell of her lids, and the regularity of her breathing, that she was safely past wakefulness.

Then, again without sound, he carefully removed all his clothes, placing them, folded neatly, atop the black attaché on the rug beside the window. He bent, naked, to the case, extracted something from it that caught a crystal glare of moonlight. He padded quietly to the bed. Without looking at Jeni Starbuck's face further, he aspirated the syringe in his left hand, and—without swabbing—carefully sent the needle into one of the major veins of her right forearm, flung outward conveniently toward him over the mattress edge. He sent the plunger home, draining 10 cc's of clear liquid Demerol into Jeni Starbuck.

He stood, watched her face a moment, padded back—no longer concerned with silence—and replaced the syringe in the attaché. He came to the bathroom, and although he had a pressing urge to urinate, did not (the FBI can trace the tiniest splash of urine), checking instead the medicine cabinet, using a small piece of toilet tissue to mask fingerprints. He found within the cabinet what he sought: a small vial of green tablets. He smiled, replaced the vial, and closed the door.

He returned to her bedside, stood above her face, cool and unlined in slumber, dark mouth parted slightly like a baby's, her whispered inhalation the slightest rustle of sound, the thinnest thread between life and death. The man edged closer, penis long, big testes heavy, pubic hair sparse unlike the cranial hair. The man watched the woman's face intently . . . watched until it gained color, cheeks flushing. The man leaned close, careful not to touch her, not to let a single strand of loose pubic hair fall on or near the lovely face, the white pillow. To further prevent this, he cupped his testicles in his other palm.

The woman on the pillow breathed deeply, eyes moving more rapidly now, and twisted once on the bed. She sighed, licked her lips once, twisted more eagerly. The man smiled.

He moved back to the black attaché, removed a plastic-sheathed knife, a scalpel . . . removed also a small wedge of metal no bigger than the nail of his smallest finger. He knelt carefully on the bed, between the long, muscular legs, separating them with his hands, knelt and bent and began to labor over her.

The woman hissed, yelped in slumber, but did not rebuke him. The tall man worked quickly, expertly, pulling free a section of stitching from the pale thigh . . . inserting—with the shining scalpel—the tiny square of metal, reclosing and restitching with a deftness, the nearly bored confidence, of a professional.

Finished, cool and unsweating, he lifted the woman in his arms and carried her to the bathroom. There he lay her across the cold tile between toilet and tub, her right leg pressed to the edge of the sink.

When he had left, when he'd gone, having pulled the door gently shut behind him, exactly as it had been, it was as though he had not been there at all. Yet part of him remained.

Chapter 10

The hotel-provided alarm clock ripped her out of sleep at 7:00 A.M.

She didn't remember setting it, and it took her a good minute to orient herself once her eyes were open. When she did finally awaken, cold and cramped, it was across chill bathroom tile, between tub and sink. Her brain was thick with tenacious sleep, her tongue coppery. She immediately took a very hot shower, then a very cold one. She ordered a pot of extra-strong coffee from room service and dialed Las Flores Emergency, stayed on the line until she'd tracked down the young, cow-eyed intern.

"Those pain pills you gave me, do they have side effects?"

"Only the ones I mentioned, Mrs. Starbuck. You should expect to experience some drowsiness. If driving becomes a problem, you'll have to stay home, or cut back the dosage and endure the pain. Is the pain persisting?"

"What about sleepwalking, could the pills induce that?"

"Well . . . I suppose it's possible. Do you normally sleepwalk?"

"Not to my knowledge. I did last night. I woke up in the bathroom. I also slept away half the day."

"You need to cut back on the pills. Try breaking them in two, that's less than twenty milligrams."

"I must have hit my leg against the sink. I'm bleeding again, a little."

"Are any of the stitches open?"

"No, the stitches seem fine."

"Keep an eye on it. If the pain persists, or swelling increases, I want to see you. Any other side effects?"

Jeni hesitated. "Weird dreams . . ."

"What kind of dreams?"

Sexual dreams, wet dreams. "Just weird. It's nothing. Thank you, Doctor."

She found everything she needed in the hotel gift shop: T-shirt, running shorts, sunglasses, toilet articles. Everything but shoes. The memory of her Reeboks loomed more precious than gold.

She was coming out of the gift shop at 8:15, lugging the plastic handle of a gift bag with the Howard Johnson's logo, when the chrome elevator doors hissed open across the corridor and Paul Miller stepped out before her.

She smiled, the bag suddenly heavy in her hand. "Good morning."

"And to you. I thought we agreed you'd stay in your room until I came for you." He glanced at the bag.

"Just picking up some personal items. Have you eaten?"

Miller's eyes lingered on the bag a moment longer. "No. I rang your room . . ."

She took his arm, guided them toward the coffee shop. "Thought I'd run out on you? After last night? Didn't anyone ever tell you trust is the basis of a relationship?"

"I do trust you." He smiled sardonically. "As implicitly as I trust my men. That's why you're on the inside and they're guarding all three exits."

They pushed into breakfast smells and clinking utensils. "You really know how to sweet-talk a girl," she said.

Over coffee she appraised him. "So what are you going to do with me now? I can't live at the Hotel Circle Howard Johnson's for the rest of my life."

Agent Miller dug enthusiastically into two-minute poached eggs. "Becoming quite a nuisance, aren't you? We may have to have you put down."

Jeni nibbled butterless rye toast, the only thing she'd ordered. "Is that what the FBI does with unwanted baggage?"

He nodded at her unappetizing breakfast. "Dry toast. Boy, that looks delicious. Can I have the waiter bring you some brackish water?"

"I'm in training, remember? There's another benefit run in a few months."

"Just don't train yourself away to nothing, huh?" His pager went off. Miller retrieved it. "Yeah."

Jeni watched him expectantly.

". . . uh-huh, well tell him to bugger off, I'm having breakfast."

Jeni reached for her napkin, all appetite gone.

". . . all right. Give us ten minutes." Miller replaced the pager.

"Our boy?"

"Bastard's up with the cock's crow." He began to gulp his coffee, looked up to see Jeni fiddling with the gift shop bag.

She pulled out the bright, tourist T-shirt. "What do you think?" It proclaimed "San Diego Rocks!"

"Cute. Going somewhere?"

"I distinctly heard you say, 'Give *us* ten minutes.' "

Miller wiped his mouth patiently. "Rhetorical. You're staying put in your room today."

"Paul, we both know the likelihood of Handle demanding to talk with me again. What are you going to do if he starts making threats and I'm not there to assuage them?"

Miller stood, signaled their waiter. "All the more reason for you to stay in your room close to your phone in case I need you."

"Paul, you can't bully this guy . . ."

His look stopped her. You can't bully Agent Paul Miller either, she thought. "You're staying put," he said evenly. Then softened it with, "I'll call you later. For lunch." And added less curtly, "If you'd like."

Jeni watched him shrug into his suit jacket, grab the tab, and head for the register.

She stared after him, chewing her lip thoughtfully. There were other ways of getting around Agent Miller.

Back in her room, she sat pecking in angry frustration at the hotel-provided Sprinter 9000.

If Miller wouldn't let her come along on the case, she'd join the case her own way. She knew some of the access codes at the Washington Bureau from living with Brian. It had been a while, but she was pretty sure she could find her way through at least upper-layer government codes and prefixes. It was against the law, of course, she no longer being an official member of the ATF, but who was going to stop her?

As she had done in her Lubbock days, she typed in the first set of prefixes, moved the cursor over the proper icons, sat back and waited.

Computers had come a long way from her first days with the ATF. Her old Mac had taken several minutes just to boot up. The new Sprinters—gorged with gigabytes—moved at the speed of light. She was into the NCIC files in about five minutes. Or at the front door at least.

She moved the cursor to the ACTIVE icon, clicked in. She scrolled down the alphabetical file and sure enough found the name HANDLE, JOHN. She smiled. By the time she saw Paul Miller again, she'd know as much about the perp as he did, as anyone on the case.

She clicked on HANDLE, JOHN and waited while the computer clicked and whirred.

It was taking its time.

She might have to dig deeper into the files. That could be a problem. The active-file code prefixes were changed every year or so even to Bureau agents, just to keep everything nice and covert, keep the agents on their toes. All she had were the old codes. If she got blocked, she'd be forced to do an end run around the file, find some unscrupulous teenage hacker to help get her in, digging herself a deep illegal grave. But maybe it wouldn't come to that.

Her screen lit abruptly with a single line:

NO ACCESS

Shit. Then she would have to seek out a hacker. That could take all morning, and if her guess was right about Handle, she didn't have all morning. Miller would be calling in any minute now requesting her presence at that silly command post above the sweatshop. It was all so ridiculous. She should have gone in with him in the first place. For a man with a great body, he had an incredibly stubborn mind.

To put off the inevitable, Jeni typed in another code prefix, waited.

She got her answer almost immediately:

NO ACCESS

She sat back, puffed out weary breath. Could be very problematic. These damn Sprinters grew more sophisticated every day. By now they might have found a way to trace her activities back to the hotel, getting her in deep shit.

Still, she couldn't bear just sitting around the hotel room doing nothing all morning.

She moved the cursor up to the NET icon and clicked in. The screen went blank a moment, then lit with:

NO ACCESS

Jeni frowned. What the hell was this? Anyone could get on the damn Net. You just pushed a button and the hotel put it on your tab. There was nothing special about it, certainly nothing illegal. She moved the cursor back and clicked in again.

NO ACCESS

She cursed softly, hit the Help key and typed in: WHAT THE HELL DO YOU MEAN, NO ACCESS!

The Sprinter 9000 whirred.

WRONG APPROACH

She sat back, dumbfounded. Wrong approach? In all her years of dealing with home computer systems she had never encountered that particular phrase before. Was this machine one of the new models? Maybe she'd better update her Sprinter at home.

But you don't have a home . . .

She sighed exasperation, typed in: PLEASE EXPLAIN. The computer whirred.

FORGET THE BUREAU—THEY DON'T KNOW
WHICH END IS UP

She felt her heart leap. Handle.

She sat staring blankly at the screen, fingers frozen over the keyboard.

She had the strangest feeling the screen was laughing at her.

The computer whirred.

KINDLY HIT YOUR POUND KEY

Hand trembling, Jeni did as instructed.

The computer whirred, honked. The screen went black.

Then the console squawked. Beeped once. And Handle's voice was in her room. "Top of the morning, Jeni! Sleep well on those soft Howard Johnson mattresses?"

Jeni let out breath slowly, sat back, folded her arms. "How did you find me, John?"

"Do you really want to talk about that when Point Loma is about to go up in flames?"

Remain calm. Detached. First rule of the hostage negotiator.

Yes, but who was being held hostage here?

"Well, you're up and at it bright and early this morning, John."

"Speak for yourself, Jeni. I doubt that Agent Miller

would take kindly to what you're doing with that hotel computer. But why don't we ask him ourselves? I have him on the line."

Jeni started to say something, was cut off by Miller's indignant voice. "Jeni, are you there?"

"I'm here."

"Well," Handle chuckled companionably, "all together and cozylike! Isn't technology wonderful! Our little Jeni was attempting to communicate with the active NCIC files in Washington, Agent Miller. Smart lass. I think this girl's bucking for reinstatement. Why don't you comply?"

"You're full of shit," came Miller's voice.

"It's true, Paul." Jeni swallowed. "I don't know how he did it, but he's tapped into the system somehow."

"You sound well rested, Agent Miller," Handle spoke. "Did you sleep well last night?"

Jeni felt a pang. No. He couldn't know about that . . .

"I slept fine," Miller told him. "How about you, Handle? Destroying Mrs. Starbuck's home give you a good night's rest?"

Metallic chuckles. "I believe it's *Ms.* Starbuck, Agent . . . the lady is divorced. As for the house, what must be done, must be done. The place was hardly a showpiece. And you didn't own it anyway, am I correct, Jeni?"

Jeni hesitated a moment, feeling Miller's exasperation like an invisible wall of tension emanating from the screen. "That's right," she said.

"I do apologize for the minor cuts and bruises, but in all fairness, I warned that you wouldn't make it in time. In the future you might do well to heed me."

"There isn't going to be a future," Miller put in.

A metallic sigh. "Oh, Agent Miller, we're all growing

increasingly bored with your chauvinistic histrionics concerning Agent Starbuck. And it *will* be *Agent* Starbuck now, right? You will have her reinstated with the ATF."

"Ms. Starbuck is a civilian, Handle. What is it you want to talk about at so early an hour?"

There was a moment of silence from Jeni's computer. Then: "Well, for starters," the computer replied, "we shall commence with our arrangement of conversing only with Jeni Starbuck. Is that clear? I repeat, is that clear, Agent Miller? Stick your pompous agency nose in one more time and I ring off, and you can find the next detonation on your own."

Jeni waited, heart pounding, envisioning the look on Paul Miller's face.

"I'm waiting for an answer, Agent Miller."

"Request acknowledged," Miller muttered.

"Good. Are you still with us, Jeni? In good spirits this morning?"

Jeni spoke calmly, succinctly. It was a game of chess. "I'm grieving, John. You killed my cat."

"Yes, well we'll discuss your pussy another time. Speaking of which, I'd give serious thought as to whom I allow into my hotel room at night, if you take my meaning. Do you take my meaning, Ms. Starbuck?"

Flushed, jangled, she held herself in professional check. Now was the time to show Paul what a pro she could be. Handle was bluffing. He couldn't know about last night. He was just trying to get a rise out of Miller, goad him. He couldn't have known. He couldn't.

"Are you there, Jeni?"

"What's on this morning's agenda, John?"

"Ah yes, this morning. This morning's going to be

quite a little workout, I'm afraid. Did you get plenty of rest? Once you finally got to sleep, I mean."

"I'm well rested, John. What is it you require of me today?"

"So cooperative. Really, Agent Miller, I think you could learn a great deal from our Jeni. How familiar with the Point Loma district are you, dear heart?"

"Familiar enough to know it's a long sprint across town from here."

"So it is, so it is. Too far to jog in forty minutes, do you think?"

Jeni could hear background sounds of the command post room coming alive with movement. "Why don't you just tell us what it is you're trying to prove, John? Wouldn't that be simpler?"

Her computer was thoughtful for a second. "Yes. It would in fact be simpler. But I doubt it'd get my point across in exactly the right way. You're a smart lady, Jeni. Smarter, I think, than most of the men in that little room above the sweatshop. Smart enough to realize there's a purpose to all this, an ultimate answer. All the pieces have their places, you've only to put them together. Once you do that, the game will be over. And if you're very good—and very fast—you'll still be alive at the end. It is not insoluble, Jeni, remember that. But without you, it's quite hopeless. So tell me, are you a willing contestant?"

"You destroyed all my running clothes in the explosion, John."

"But surely you've bought new ones by now."

"I have no shoes. The stores aren't open yet."

"An occupational hazard. Because of the inconvenience— because of the cat—I'm going to give you an extra ten minutes to reach 1014 Weston Court, Point Loma, San Diego. The clock is now running, Jeni."

She was already inching toward the door. "I can't possibly cover half that distance in that amount of time," she assured the computer.

"Never say can't, Jeni. Agent Miller, are you still lurking about?"

"I'm here, Handle."

"You may, of course, feel free to dispatch all manner of patrol car to the above address; however, the former rules still apply, i.e., I see one black-and-white within a mile of Ms. Starbuck and I arrange for a second detonation elsewhere in the city. I'm willing to forgive your little indiscretion of yesterday—having Jeni tailed—but I only forgive once, is that clear? Is that perfectly clear, Agent Miller?"

"I hear you."

"Still have your Sprinter 9000 headphones, Jeni?"

"I have them, but—"

"Then I suggest you get moving. And here's a hint. Try Sixth Avenue. I believe you'll find it helpful."

Before Miller could say anything, Jeni fled through the door.

It was a beautiful new day. Fog- and smog-free, clear blue sky and the sharp—and to Jeni, refreshing—tang of ocean breeze in the air, pungent but invigorating. The kind of sky under which you could run forever. Given enough time.

Through her headphones, Handle proclaimed, "Well, you must admit it's a lovely morning! Hardly any fog off the bay today! Did you take Sixth Avenue as I suggested?"

Jeni, eyes on her watch, swung into an easy rhythm on a sidewalk already crowded with downtown business-men. There was no use hurrying, she couldn't possibly make it across town to Point Loma in the allotted time. There must be more to this. No sense in killing herself un-til she found out.

"Jeni, are you there?"

"Don't you know, John? Can't you see me?"

"Now really, Jeni. How could I do that? Do you think I have a TV camera on you? From where? Do you hear he-licopters in the air? Your Dr. Keegie might think you were becoming delusional again. Another 'psychotic break'?"

The sarcasm was not lost on her. "Dr. Keegie? One of the friends we have in common, John?"

"Now, now, that would be telling. Bedside manner is not the same thing as friendship, would you say? Agent Miller, for instance. I know it's been a long time for you. I'm not here to judge. I'm only looking out for your safety."

She rounded a corner, dodged around a vagrant hold-ing out his hand for change. She was just another morning jogger. "My safety, John? I'm with the FBI now, more or less, thanks to you."

"So were those poor souls at Waco."

She felt good, leg muscles responding well, even with-out the usual warm-up. It was a beautiful, scintillating day. More amazing still, she didn't miss the damn house, not at all. Only poor Pierre Cardin. Yes, it would have been a splendid day for a simple training run on any other occasion. She felt she could go for miles and miles and never get winded. Run right off the face of the earth. "I'll never make it to Point Loma in time, John. What's the drill? Why are we doing this?"

"Would you care for a little music? They were playing some pre-army Elvis earlier."

"Whose place are you destroying today?" She headed down Grant Lane, fresh and free as the wind. How is it she felt so alive today? Did last night have something to do with it?

"You don't really care, Jeni, so why are you asking?"

"Of course I care."

"Not really. Oh, you care, but there's nothing you can do about it, so why dwell on it? What's really on your mind is that newspaper magnate's boat. That and the Statler Building. Now, what in the world could a rich newspaperman's boat, a commercial building, and your darling little one-bedroom in Ocean Beach have in common?"

"Absolutely nothing if you're a madman."

Silence a moment.

Jeni rounded Sanchez Avenue, thinking perhaps she'd gone too far with him.

"Well, I may well be a madman. Yes, I've been considered that in my time. But a madman with a method. You were thinking about the other bomb sites, weren't you? The other victims. Tell me you weren't."

"Okay," she puffed. "So what? Who wouldn't be?"

"And Miller has nothing on either the ketch or the Statler Building, right? Just a pleasure boat and a refurbished downtown turn-of-the-century brickfront for yuppies."

"Well, I don't really know, John, I've hardly had time to check with City Hall for all the building's records. There might be something there. As for Irv Bradford, his papers printed naughty articles about you."

"About the Solobomber. Maybe I'm not the Solobomber, Jeni. What's your best guess?"

"My best guess is, I'll last longer on this run if I speak in short declarative sentences," she huffed, heading up a slight incline toward J Street.

Handle laughed in her earphones. "Jeni, you're a sheer delight. Are you anywhere near J Street yet?"

"I just hit it."

"How time does fly. Turn left on Central Avenue."

"That's the opposite direction of Point Loma, John."

"Okay, forget it. You're on your own, kiddo."

"All right, I'm turning, I'm turning."

She cut past an old-fashioned barbershop, one with a striped pole out front—a vanishing breed—and swung onto Central and a phalanx of tattoo parlors. "Lovely street," she said.

"Well, San Diego's still a seaport, and navy boys will be boys. How's your time?"

She glanced at her watch. "I have approximately thirty minutes to cover fifteen miles. But don't worry, I'm a great sprinter toward the end.

Handle laughed again. "And don't I know it! That wonderful dive over the hedge!"

"For all the good it did me."

"Graceful, though. Lovely. You're really a lovely woman, Jeni. Classically lovely, I'd have to say, a throw-back to a more thoughtful time. Your profile belongs on a cameo."

"Where are we going, John?"

"What's the matter? Don't like the present course of conversation?"

"I just don't see what my looks have to do with bombed-out buildings and boats."

"Don't be edgy, Jeni. Are you being edgy?"

"No."

"That sun-streaked hair of yours is so natural-looking, you'd never know it came out of a bottle. Brian always preferred blondes, didn't he? Of course now he's found himself a real blonde."

Jeni broke stride, slipped sideways awkwardly, and ran into an old man, knocking him over. "Oh—*Christ*!"

She skidded to a stop, turned back, bent to help him up.

"What's the matter?" in her ears.

She pulled the startled old gentleman to his feet, which were, thankfully, surprisingly strong. His glasses were knocked askew; Jeni straightened them. "I'm so sorry! Are you all right?"

"What happened, Jeni?" in her ears.

The old man was dusting himself off companionably. "No harm done! Haven't been swept off my feet by a pretty girl in years! I like your shoes. Is that a new jogging trend?"

Jeni looked down at her worn flats. "Not really. Are you sure you're not hurt?"

The old gentleman, dressed in a natty blue suit and felt fedora, winked at her. "Well, maybe we should go up to my apartment and look me over."

Jeni smiled. "You're all right." She patted his arm and trotted on.

"Maybe I'll run into you again tomorrow!" the old gentleman called. Jeni waved without looking.

"Jeni, what happened?"

"I knocked down an old man."

"I'm sorry. Was it something I said?"

"Why don't you go to hell, John?"

"Should I? Should I sign off now and leave the game?"

"Maybe that's not such a bad idea. I've about had it with your games."

"Perhaps that's because you think you're a player. You're not, you know."

"No? What then, pray?"

"Well, 'pawn' is such a cliché. Let's say you're my 'piece' for the moment, and I'm moving you. That's not to say you couldn't *become* a player under the right circumstances."

"And what circumstances would those be?"

"All in good time, Jeni. Patience was never one of your crowning virtues. Something we learned at Waco, yes?"

Jeni felt the flush. "Maybe I'll keep on running, John, run away from your damned game altogether!"

"Whatever you say, dear heart. But if we quit now, how will you get what you want?"

"What is it I want, John?"

"Why don't you tell me?"

"Why don't you shove it?"

"You wouldn't have won anyway, Jeni, so quit taking it out on me. And quit taking it out on yourself."

She felt fire through her veins, found herself sprinting unconsciously, teeth gritted.

"You're breathing too hard. Better slow down. Have you reached the end of Central yet?"

"Just about."

"When you do, stop."

She wobbled, slowed. "What?"

"When you reach the end of Central, you'll see a pair of big red doors on your left. Stop before you reach them."

"Stop? Why?"

"Because you'll never make it to Point Loma without help. So I'm giving you a little help. Be thankful for small favors, eh?"

She saw the corner coming, slowed to a lope, chest heaving. Her feet were already swollen from the awful flats, blisters starting at her heels. She kicked the shoes at the gutter.

There was a rumble to her left, a piercing clanging, and the big red doors split in the middle, flew back. An engine roared in front of her, then the shriek of a siren. A fire truck.

Jeni stepped back as the big green vehicle pulled out, cautious for the moment to avoid unwary traffic, but soon to screech recklessly down the avenue. As the rear chrome bumper flashed by, she suddenly found herself lurching forward, reaching up, grasping the nearest grab iron. Before she quite realized it, she'd swung herself up on the rear of the hook and ladder.

Of course. This was the only way to make it to Point Loma in the allotted time. Even the cops wouldn't slow them, they were headed for a fire.

How had he done it? How had Handle orchestrated this?

Jeni clung tight with both hands as the long, unwieldy truck leaned into the corner—felt her grip loosen and nearly went with it, nearly spilled—but eased back as the vehicle leveled on Central and she regained her center of gravity. Then she was just hanging on for dear life, hair flying, eyes jammed against the piercing wail of the siren as they dodged magically around traffic.

Even in all the noise and excitement, Handle's calm voice came through clearly. "I trust you are now careening down Central courtesy of the San Diego Fire Department, yes?"

"How did you time it so accurately?" she gasped. "If you don't mind my asking."

"It's fairly easy to start a fire. Even without matches."

She nodded into the howling wind. "Of course, I should have guessed. How many died in this one?"

"Oh, it was only a small explosion, an old warehouse basement. Nobody hurt. Though you can never be entirely sure about vagrants, can you? At any rate, it will certainly throw our friend Agent Miller off the scent."

"Very smart, John, very clever."

"I thought so."

The fire truck took another lurching turn, Jeni taking the stress across shoulders and thighs. She was certain only two wheels remained on the pavement. She clung tenaciously, knuckles blanched white on the silvery grab iron, legs braced against the right fender.

"Still with us, Jeni?"

"You won't believe this, but as a little girl I aspired to be a fireman."

"I'm delighted to be fulfilling your childhood dreams. Just a bit further now, then I'm going to have to ask quite a lot of you."

She felt a pang. "Such as what?"

"You should be coming over Sycamore about now, am I right?"

"Just about."

"At the bottom you should be able to see the smoke on Concord and Vance. It's an old gray building with—"

"I can see the smoke. There's already another fire truck there. And cops."

"Yes, cops. I don't think it's such a good idea they find you clinging to the back of a fire engine, do you?"

"So you want me to leap off while this thing is still in motion, break my neck, is that it?"

"Which side of the street is the other fire truck parked at?"

"It's . . ." She squinted into the wind. "The south side."

"Good. The only other fireplug is on the west side, off Culver. Your truck will have to slow at Vance to make the turn."

"It hasn't slowed much so far, and it's made several turns."

"That's a narrow street, have no fear."

"Easy for you to say."

"Not easy at all. I don't want to lose you, Jeni."

"That's comforting."

"Are you near the bottom of the hill yet?"

"Close. There are cops everywhere."

"That's all right, they won't be looking at the back of the fire engine. Get ready."

"This isn't going to work, John, we're going too fast!"

"You can do it. I picked you because I knew you could do it."

"Shit, John, I—"

"He has to slow before he makes that turn."

"Okay . . . okay, he's slowing a little now . . ."

"Are you on the left side of the truck or the right?"

"The right, facing the engine."

"Get over on the left, quick. You have to be on the left to roll with the inertia."

"Christ, I can't let go of this iron!"

"You have to get on the left end, Jeni."

"I can't do it!"

"Then you'll get seen. And you'll never reach the detonation site in time."

"Well, why don't you just stop the damn detonation!"

"Get over to the left side. Jeni? Jeni, can you hear me?"

"Just shut up a second, will you?" She was stretched spread-eagle across the back of the flying truck, clinging by her fingers to the right grab iron, reaching out with her other hand, her left fingers, to the other. Abruptly the truck swerved.

Jeni let go, slid, grabbed the opposite iron at the apex of the turn . . . saw a rush of green shrubbery, knew instinctively it was now or never, took a quick breath and let go . . .

She was thrown into space.

"Jeni?"

She hit the shrubs, bounced once on her back, rolled onto green lawn, legs raked with scratches, some of them bleeding. But nothing broken.

"Jeni?"

For a moment she considered not answering at all. Serve the bastard right. "I'm here."

"You made it off the truck?"

"I made it."

"Unseen?"

"Everyone's watching the fire."

"Perfect. There's an alleyway just over the next driveway to your right, the one with the stone lions flanking the drive. Take it."

She wobbled to her feet, ignoring the pain in her legs. "Would it be all right if I stopped long enough to get my breath?"

"Take all the time you want, dear heart. You have exactly five minutes until the big bang."

"Shit!" She took off running, limping.

She had to pass in front of a few curious neighbors emerging from stucco cottages, but everyone was too engrossed in the fire to pay her much mind. She made it through the alley and into another long, sun-swept street flanked with fifties-style homes, manicured lawns, looking around her at a neighborhood that was beginning to feel familiar. "Okay, okay . . . which way?"

"Are you on Ketchem Street?"

"I'm on Ketchem! Which way, dammit!"

"Turn left. It's the third house on the second block."

She glanced at her watch. Three minutes left. Plenty of time to get to the house. But what about dismantling the bomb? She began to search the street for the comforting sight of a bomb squad truck. The street was empty of all but civilian passenger cars.

Jeni loped between streets, legs on fire, headed down Ketchem and around the corner, heading to the third house. Something was plucking at the back of her mind . . . something about this neighborhood . . . something she should know but could not place . . .

"How we doing, Jeni?"

"I'm almost there. Where's the bomb?"

"Inside the house."

"*Where* inside the damn house!"

"I'll tell you what you need to know when you get there. Trust me."

She could see the house now ahead. White clapboard sides, shake-shingle roof, newly painted mailbox in front . . .

. . . newly painted mailbox . . .

. . . and the name: "The Starbucks."

She felt a stab in her chest. Oh Christ.

"Handle, you bastard!"

It was Brian's house.

"Handle, you son of a bitch! Where's the fucking bomb!"

Her earphones were silent.

"Handle!"

She was past the mailbox now, dashing up the lawn, torn legs forgotten. All time forgotten. She would not be blown back across any hedges this time . . . she would not let this bastard kill Brian. She would not. She leapt the front porch steps and yanked at the door handle. It was locked.

"Brian!"

She hammered with clenched fists, hammered until the pain was replaced with numbness and hammered still. *"Brian!"*

What if he wasn't home?

She glanced at the driveway, saw his Taurus sedan parked there. "Brian!"

She ran across the front of the house toward the back door. On her way, through a picture window, she saw a three-year-old child staring wide-eyed at her amid interior shadows.

Heart leaping, Jeni tore open the back gate, rushed through, leapt the back porch steps, and yanked hard on the door handle. Locked.

"Brian! Open the goddamn door!"

There was no movement from within. She made herself glance at her watch: a minute twenty seconds left . . .

Jeni leapt from the steps, rushed back through the gate, grabbed a wrought-iron deck chair she'd seen before, and threw it at the picture window where the child had been but had now disappeared.

The glass spiderwebbed but held stubbornly; the chair bounced back at her.

She grabbed it again, held on this time, swinging with all her strength. The window crashed inward in a rainbow of flying glass and splintered wood, showering the shag rug within. Jeni leapt through, past the jagged edges. *"Brian!"*

Footsteps on the staircase. The little boy was running upward in a panic, screaming for his mother.

Jeni charged about the living room, searching, searching, but everything was unfamiliar, the household of another woman, and they were all out of time. "Handle, where are you, you son of a bitch! I'm in the house!"

Her earphones were silent.

"What the hell?" Brian's voice. He was standing at the top of the darkened staircase with his wife, one little boy clinging to his legs, another peering around his mother's smooth hip. She wore a silken robe, Brian was dressed in pajamas, both looked rumpled, beyond startled. It took a moment for Jeni to see the gun in his hand.

She started up the stairs, hesitated, clung to the newel-post. "Brian, you've got to get out of here *now*!"

He just stood staring at her, no recognition in his eyes, though surely he knew her.

"Brian! Your house, there's a bomb!"

Her ex-husband started down, was halted by his wife's clawing hand. What was her name? Marcia? "Brian, wait . . . what are you doing?"

Jeni dashed up the stairs, face tight with panic, reached out for the closest child, who shrieked as if stabbed and withdrew behind his mother. Jeni reached behind her desperately, felt the other woman's strong arms on her shoulders. "What the hell do you think you're doing!"

Jeni looked up pleadingly into Brian's dazed eyes. "There's a bomb in the house! We've got to get the kids out of here! *Now!*"

"A bomb?"

What was the *matter* with these people? Was the concept of a bomb so hard to grasp! Hadn't they read the paper, seen the news on TV?

Jeni reached for the little boy, Darin was his name, wasn't it? "Darin, can you come with me, sweetheart?"

Darin clung to his mother's waist, Marcia pulling him behind her. "Get the hell away from my child! What in the world are you doing! Are you drunk? Brian? Is she drunk?"

Brian turned to Jeni. "Jeni, what's this all about?"

"I *told* you! There's a bomb in this house! Do I have to spell it out for you?"

She looked at her watch. No more time left. In fact . . . it was past time . . .

The Starbucks and their children stared balefully at her, the kids cringing terrified behind their parents. In that instant, Jeni saw a picture of herself—a wild woman, legs scratched and bleeding, smashing through the window, dashing hysterically upstairs, reaching like some insane thing for the children.

And in that instant she knew. There was no bomb.

And somewhere far from here, or maybe near—in a place only he knew—Handle was laughing . . .

"Mommy, what's that?" One of the kids was pointing over Jeni's shoulder, back down the stairs.

"What is it, honey?" Jeni asked, and Brian was moving past her.

She started after him, then faster when she spied the big hatbox on the dining room table. "Brian, don't!"

She spun on the stairs, looked desperately to Brian's wife. "Is that hatbox yours?"

The other woman shook her head.

Jeni ran—"Brian!"—grabbed his shoulder, tried to pull him back. The kids started wailing upstairs. "It's a *bomb!* Mommy, it's a *bomb*!"

Jeni shoved Brian aside—shoved him hard into the

wall—sprinted to the dining room table, saw, before she got there, that the hatbox was *moving*.

"Jeni, get the hell away from there!"

She approached the lurching hatbox as though in a trance.

The circular lid popped off, a furry, beleaguered head assessed her. Jeni said, "Shit," softly, watched Pierre Cardin in his immaculate black suit climb nimbly over the rim, perch imperiously at the table's edge. He appraised his mistress with almond eyes, mewling indignance.

Chapter 11

The cab would not come.

Jeni sat in Brian's wife's kitchen, staring at a wall clock, hands folded impotently in her lap, feeling inordinately large and clumsy, like the rest of her, awkward and out of place. She was listening to the muffled movements of Brian's wife and her children upstairs, thinking, What a stupid-looking clock (like something from Woolworth's): why would Brian marry a woman with such dreadful taste?

Brian moved about the nearby stove to make them coffee. He had spent an hour on the telephone in another room as Jeni sat, alone and frustrated with only Pierre to keep her company. Finally he summoned a cab (Jeni watching the revolving hands on the dreadful clock) and still it had not come. And she was certain Paul Miller would not come either, even in plain clothes, even in an unmarked car, nor would he send someone. That would only give it all away, leave her with much to explain. There seemed to be no other way to play this.

Marcia—the new wife—had appeared occasionally lurking at the periphery of vision, making an elaborate show of fussing with the dishes (such a *good* little wife), while clearly catching snatches of conversation. She'd finally disappeared upstairs, giggling children in tow.

Brian turned with a steaming cup, set it before Jeni, sat himself down across the table with that expectant expression she remembered from another life.

She avoided the expression by sipping from her mug. "Thanks."

Muffled noises from upstairs: Marcia and kids getting ready for church, no doubt, it was Sunday morning. Brian was probably supposed to be getting ready too, he had mentioned once his new wife's enthusiasm for the church. But he was down here in the kitchen instead, with this crazy woman who had once been his wife, and who had now come to destroy their picture window with a chair, traumatize their children with wild tales of bombs. Offer no clear explanation for any of this, or for the cat in the hatbox.

Brian glanced past her, and she knew his wife had appeared in the doorway behind her. Jeni could picture her and probably the kids, Marcia tense and stiff, dressed to the nines, the kids stifling giggles.

"Are you coming, Brian? We're going to be late for early service." Voice flat, eyes boring through the back of Jeni's head.

Trapped between the two, Brian's eyes found sanctity in the ugly wall clock. "You and the kids go along. I'll join you after the cab comes."

Jeni could feel the other woman's eyes bore into her back, feel, instinctively, when they were no longer there. Marcia and her kids departed, front door thudding with unapologetic finality.

Unexpectedly Brian turned on her, face stone. "Do you think I'm an *idiot*?"

"What?"

"Jeni, your goddamn house *exploded* two days ago! It was on five local channels not to mention CNN. I trace you to the hospice and suddenly you disappear. You haven't called in to the hospice, you missed your appointment with Dr. Keegie—"

"Dr. Keegie called here?"

Brian looked away. "He was concerned. He doesn't think you're being properly monitored, and I'm beginning to agree with him."

Jeni jumped to her feet angrily. "Since when are you and Dr. Keegie my keepers? I believe you have your own family to look after now, and as far as Dr. Keegie goes, I'm strictly a volunteer patient."

"Keep breaking plate-glass windows and I'm sure your status will change."

"We're divorced, Brian, you can't threaten me."

Brian sighed, backed off. "I'm not threatening you, Jeni. I'm concerned about you. I've been on the phone with the Bureau. I did some checking around. I know somehow or other you got yourself involved in the Solo-bomber case."

Of *course* Brian would know what she was up to if he wanted to know. He'd always been a better agent than she had. She felt her blood rising at his interference.

"I did *not* get myself involved, I was *brought in*!"

"By a mad bomber."

Jeni was silent.

Brian reached for her shoulder conciliatorily. "I know you've missed being an agent, Jeni, but you're not an agent anymore and you *won't be*. Your FBI connection— what's his name, Miller?—is using extremely poor judgment. And so are you . . ."

It hung in the air, incomplete. She knew him so well.

"What's the rest, Brian?"

"I'm sending you out of town. You can visit your

mother in Florida, the cat can stay here for the time being. You can call the hospice when you get there. Agent Miller will just have to catch his own bomber."

"And if I refuse to go? I suppose you'll have me locked away in a psychiatric hospital."

"If necessary."

"You have no right—"

"I have no choice, Jeni. I'm not the only one who found out what Miller is up to. If I don't protect you, you'll end up being arrested and held for interference with a government matter and possibly even face charges. You know all I want is the best for you . . ."

"Naturally." Sarcasm reddened her cheeks. She rubbed at them, infuriated and helpless, knowing Brian never made idle threats and that she'd somehow managed, with Handle's encouragement, to get in over her head.

He walked her to the front porch. It was easier to breathe out here. She gazed out at Brian's neighborhood, Brian's life. She felt disjointed, strangely out of sync with the world.

She looked up at a crisp sound of tires at the curb: the cab. Two figures were seated in the rear. She turned to Brian.

"I arranged for an escort, just in case you have second thoughts." After a long moment, he said, "Listen, I want you to know . . . whatever this is about, I never blamed you for Molly. I mean, I know I was driving, but I always got this crazy feeling you thought I blamed you somehow. Well, I didn't. I don't want you to think that."

Jeni watched the cloudless sky. "They'd been threatening us for months, Brian," she said. "All the way from Texas. I should have gotten out of the department long before I did. It's my fault, all of it. Let's don't bullshit each other anymore."

Brian looked down at his hands as if the idea had suddenly formed there in his palms. He shook his head slowly. "I should never have left you like that. Just walked out. I shouldn't have done that. I've spent nights regretting it."

And it fell on her then, as unprepared for as a heap of bricks. He didn't love his new wife. Brian was not in love with Marcia. Or the kids. Or this life in Point Loma. Not at all.

How could she have missed the signals? Poor Brian, suffering not only the guilt of leaving his first marriage but the failed burden of his second. It was in his eyes, his posture, his every gesture, now that her anger had ebbed for a moment, now that she could really see.

She felt abruptly light, weightless. She had the strange sensation she was looking down on all this as from above, dispassionately observing these two people on the front porch of this strange home in this strange neighborhood. She experienced an almost godlike desire to reach down, pick up the strangers, and place them back in another home, another time, where a little girl might run up suddenly, laughing, tug on their clothes, and demand to be taken to the beach. All it took was arranging the players properly. She need but reach out . . . Instead she looked down to find Pierre Cardin revolving her ankles, bent and cradled him. "Stupid cat," she murmured. And looking closer, for the first time since he'd emerged from the hatbox, saw a tiny something, a folded wedge, worked into his collar.

Surreptitiously she worked the slip of paper from the cat's collar, slid it casually into her suit pocket.

An impatient honk broke her reverie. The cab was waiting.

* * *

San Diego International is a small airport in contrast to the size of its city.

Pilots, traditionally, resent it: the dangerous approach which includes skimming downtown structures, the runway, which is necessarily short, the water all around and the milky fog it sometimes produces. Once landed, captain and crew can revel in one of the great vacation towns of the nation. Once landed.

Jeni Starbuck marched brusquely down the adobe-style terminal halls, one of Brian's plainclothes agents on either side of her, the one to her left (built like a linebacker) carrying her luggage (a suitcase Brian had apparently had them purchase and fill for her, considering her own meager wardrobe lay in cinders), their destination gate 10.

The terminal was moderately crowded. A girl—maybe twenty but street-weary and looking older—drifted into their path, a tornado of long, unkempt hair above drab, sun-bleached serape, a hand-sewn fringed shoulder bag. She offered the trio a grubby palm, the impassive air of defeat that precedes little expectation. "Change?"

Jeni was reaching for her purse when one of the flat-faced agents shouldered the long hair and grubby hand roughly aside. "Get a job, cunt."

Jeni resisted a heated urge to snap-kick his groin. She did not know these Neanderthals, did not recognize them as part of Brian's staff, could not imagine where he'd secured them. It would be a pleasure to make them look like assholes in front of their superiors. Suddenly she was looking forward to what she had to do.

Just past the gift shop, the southwestern tile motif of the ladies' room caught her eye as the girl in the serape

pushed through the door. Her attendants urged her on, but
Jeni balked. "I need to use the facilities."

The two agents exchanged looks. The one with the
suitcase reminded her, "There's bathrooms on the plane."

Jeni offered him dagger eyes. "I have to *pee*. Would
you like to come in with me and hold my hand?"

The other agent grunted at his partner. "No windows,
we checked it out."

"Thanks for the vote of trust, guys," hissed as she
yanked her luggage from the other man's hand, shouldered between them for the rest room door. The movement caused her breasts to brush the biggest man's
massive chest, eliciting a smile. He winked at his partner,
who shook his head, snorted a grin.

The lavatory seemed empty. Jeni stood waiting before
a bank of stainless sinks, checked her hair and lipstick,
then checked her face. Tight. Tight eyes, tight-lipped resentment making her older. This was wrong, even if
Brian's motives were pure. But at least being off on her
own might buy her the time to accomplish some things
without his scrutiny. All she had to do was dump these
two jokers.

She pulled the slip of paper she'd taken from Pierre
Cardin's collar out of her jacket and opened it, smoothed
it out atop the Formica sink counter. She frowned at the
serrated edges: a blueprint. Or a section of one. Someone
had torn it from a bigger piece. But what bigger piece, de-
tailing what structure?

She turned as long-haired serape girl emerged from
one of the stalls. Jeni watched the young woman—possibly
pretty beneath the grime—move to sink and hot water.
To Jeni's surprise, the long hair came away, tossed to
the counter, revealing dark, close-cropped curls. The girl

reached for the pink plastic soap dispenser, turned suddenly fearful violet tyes on Jeni, who had been staring subconsciously. "Are you a cop?"

Jeni genuflected, "No."

The violet eyes lidded with relief, concerned themselves with the mirror.

A runaway. The Midwest or back East. Maybe even a petty crime in there somewhere, maybe running from her pimp. The height, the weight. Close enough.

She approached the girl gently. "Could you use a little change?"

The soapy face turned, regarded her wearily. "No, I'm an eccentric millionaire, writing a book on homeless teens. Christ yes I could use change."

Jeni dug into her wallet, counted out three hundred-dollar bills, handed them across the steaming sink. The girl watched from the mirror, eyes widening . . . then narrowing with suspicion. Dripping lather, she looked at the bills, then to Jeni.

"For the wig," Jeni told her, "the shoulder bag, serape, and jeans. You get my dress, purse, the suitcase and everything in it. All you have to do is hang around in here for a while after I'm gone."

The soapy face watched her a moment. "You in trouble?"

"Yes."

The soapy face chewed a reflective lip, eyes on the money. She nodded. "Make it four hundred?"

She found round, amber-lensed sunglasses in the girl's shoulder bag, put them on as added precaution. She slipped right past the two lounging FBI agents. One of them, bent over a water cooler, wasn't even looking. Real pros. They'd have been laughed out of her old department.

She strode calmly, deliberately, to the Avis booth, passed it by, took the airport shuttle to a Howard Johnson's in Del Mar. All the way there she wore the Sprinter 9000 Walkman headphones, praying for some word from Handle. The phones were silent.

Once settled in her new motel room, she shunned the itchy wig, showered quickly, sat at the writing desk with CNN on the motel TV, and unfolded the slip of paper again, the blueprint. It showed a maze of corridors, halls, and cubicles, white relief on blue paper. There was no legend, or if there had been it had been hastily torn off. What was Handle trying to show her?

She sat at the desk a moment, then snatched up a piece of motel stationery and pen. She wrote:

1. Newspaper magnate—bay bombing
2. Statler Building—no apparent connection
3. My house in Ocean Beach—ditto above
4. Brian's house—false lead??

She stared at her list for a moment, then added at the bottom of the page:

Don't forget bombings in L.A. and San Fran

She sagged nude, hair damp, the making of the list more an act of tangible motion than necessity: she had the events memorized. She picked up the piece of blueprint again and looked at her list.

The Statler Building.

Quickly she dressed in the soiled serape and jeans, called Budget Rental, had a new Mustang delivered, paid for it with cash. Eventually they would trace it, but not for a while. She drove for a quick hamburger, then to a nearby Pic 'n' Save for cheap skirt, blouse, and running shoes. She put on these new clothes in the store changing room, dropped the soiled articles in the plastic-handled store bag with the Pic 'n' Save logo, purchased a bottle of amber-colored hair dye, dumped the store bag in a trash receptacle outside the building, and drove back to the motel.

She took off the new blouse, filled the motel sink, and in bra and panties set to dyeing her hair. Head wrapped in plastic, she switched to the local news while the dye set, and watched for anything pertinent. There was nothing of import.

She dried and combed out her hair sans makeup. The color—"tawny auburn"— was close enough to her original hair color to cause her to start when she saw herself in the mirror. This is how she must have looked to Brian the first time they met: freckled, fresh, naive. Then, peering closer, she saw the shadow of her auburn-haired daughter and turned away abruptly.

She considered cutting her hair off short, but decided against it. They would find her eventually, sooner if she remained in town, but remaining in town was what she needed to do. She flicked at her hair, eyes on the mirror, found herself experiencing a pang of pleasant anxiety, calling up old training memories, memories of things she'd missed.

She had stepped over a line, committed to something of significance. It had been some time. It felt both reckless and controlled, fearful and expectant. It felt alive.

She sat down in front of the TV, adrenaline fading to a comfortably nervous edge she would need. She began the four-hour wait for the city to wrap itself in dark and fog. As it began, she switched on lights, went to each of the four motel windows, and began twisting shut the venetian blinds. She felt ready, confident but professional-wary. Back in the loop.

Across the street in a dark rental sedan, cigarette smoke threading the stars, the tall man watched patiently as the last motel window shuttered black.

Chapter 12

Under cover of dark, undulant evening mist, Jeni drove the rental car to Alameda Street, braked across from the Statler Building's disemboweled husk, and sat watching the silent streets.

There were no working streetlights here, all having succumbed to the blast and not yet repaired. The block surrounding the building itself was ringed by a high, temporary fence of hastily erected plywood sheets to discourage thieves, curious kids, and anyone foolish enough to tramp about the shell of an office building gutted by a terrible blast, the weakened superstructure, staircases, and floors of which were an invitation to sudden, plunging death.

Atop the plywood fence a necklace of red work lights had been arranged, extending the perimeter of the site, each with its own ruby-misted halo. Laced between lampposts in front of these, a yellow police tape warned off all but official personnel. Jeni waited within the Mustang until she was sure the dark streets were empty, then—Ruger weighting her purse—hurried across fog-dampened street to the fence, heels clicking wetly, black macadam reflecting her inverted, fun-house-mirror self.

Slipping under the police tape, she followed the plywood fence half a block to a makeshift guard shack, old shield case ready to display. Her pretext would be that she needed to check on official records, ATF stuff the guard would know nothing about. If he didn't phone in somewhere for clearance, she'd be home free.

But surprisingly the guard shack was empty, and the entrance door—though affixed with a lock—ajar.

Jeni entered cautiously, stepping around heaps of battlefield mortar and debris only just begun to be cleared by workers. Was there a late-shift cleanup team at work tonight?

She consulted the scrap of blueprint quickly, turning it over slowly in her hand, angling it this way and that. It was going to be guesswork, at least in the beginning. More of Handle's damned games.

She pocketed the schematic, approached the open maw of the building under a dirty-rag sky churning with moisture, all stars obscured. She found a series of planks tracing the worst of the debris and mud, treacherous with dew. She stepped upon them, craning about for workmen. To her right a ghostly bulk hunkered wetly, the tractor tread cab of a wrecking crane, its lattice tower jutting indomitably skyward, narrowing as it climbed to a tip shrouded by mist. From this tip a wrist-thick steel cable plummeted back to muddy earth, anchored by the ponderous iron wrecking ball hung now just above the debris, at rest and silent with terrible power.

Within the site proper, the high whitewashed fence provided a deeper sense of isolation, a foreboding island from the rest of the world. The fence and the northeast facade of the building masked or muted distant traffic noises. Jeni navigated the uneven planks, some of them teetering frightfully, stepped with reverence amid shadows haunted by the lingering aura of so many so nearly extinguished.

At the penumbra of moon-filtered shadow that would plunge her into the building's black cavity, she paused, heart pounding. Everything from this point on—tangled and foreboding as a jungle—emanated the opaque thrill of death. One false step . . .

She produced—sufficiently away now from prying eyes—a drugstore penlight, sent its weak yellow cone into the void, motes dancing before deeper shadows impenetrable. She dragged in ragged breath, put stalling behind her, urged her feet ahead, and entered Hell.

Silence, like heavy brocade, hung within the remains of a once-Deco foyer, modern angles now gone insane— silence except for occasional breeze-rifled flutters of hanging debris, tattered wallpaper. Pink intestines of cotton candy insulation caught the flashlight's beam, bulging obscenely from canted walls, ceilings that had lost their level. She traversed vertiginous walkways askew with shadows to a series of glass-shattered offices, long free of daylight, warmth, or electrical heating, ruined halls jealously trapping cold that chilled all the way to the bone.

Jeni stepped across blackened, pockmarked carpeting to a partial corridor flanked by a spiderweb of ruptured pipes, threaded cables and wiring. The reek of flooring newly exposed to dripping water and smelling of just cured concrete held a rich musk akin to dog shit. In those areas where no ceilings remained, up and up through a forest of steel beams, she perceived another roiling gray ceiling that was the sky, the starless night. Distant city lights pulsed the fog translucent, a dirty ocher.

She fumbled out the blueprint, let the cone of light play across it. She *might* be in the area indicated in the schematic.

She pushed through a half-collapsed office archway and found herself in a hurricane of dust-layered debris—

bits of couch and desk, snowbanks of shredded Berber
carpeting, a red naked I-beam exposed like a gaping
tooth. It was—had been—an executive's suite, now less
habitable than a ghetto flat. Her shoe crunched something. Jeni stepped back reflexively, glanced down.
Someone's wife and kids, dust-coated but unperturbed
under perpetual vacation sun, smiled up to her from a
shattered silver frame jammed amid the flotsam. She
played the beam over the happy faces, the boy proudly
sporting a Band-Aid at his temple, grinning youthful confidence, as though having survived the surrounding horror with only this little scratch.

She swept the light around the office, looking for she
knew not what; file drawers, she supposed. She found
only chaos. She stepped back out into the hall, crossed
carefully to the next office—gingerly as a rock climber—
stepped over a mangled green Eames chair onto carpet
black as pitch. On the far side of the room she found a
still-upright file chest, started toward it—

—found herself plummeting abruptly, stomach in her
throat, scream stuck there. Not black carpeting at all, just
black, floorless shadow. She fell . . .

. . . seemed to fall a long time . . . longer than could be
possible, long enough to give her mind time to reflect on
broken bones, ruptured flesh. Landed hard, abruptly, on
something and something else, collapsible and soft
enough to break the impact . . . furniture? She bounced
high in darkness, rolled, and saw, upside down, the strobing arc of the flashlight spinning away from her across
dense shadow . . . soon to be lost in gloom and rat blackness. Panicked, all pain instantly forgotten, she plunged
desperately after the slim security of the rolling cone, any
light more precious now than air, its absence promising a
black disoriented despair too terrible to conceive.

She clutched the penlight, struggled to her knees . . . found herself in the dripping catacombs of a subbasement. Her jaw ached terribly. Injured in the fall? And then she was surprised to find the real cause—her teeth jammed tight in a suppressed urge to scream, scream hysterically and unabashedly for help. She was afraid. Very.

She reached down deep, dredging up department-enforced training, agency calm. She must remain in control. Must marshal her thoughts. The first being a way up and out again, to the foggy night, the clean air . . .

Jeni searched the dusty floor quickly with the thin beam, cursing its ineffectualness. She half expected the meager light to fall in the next moment across the waxen face of a cadaver, the snarling muzzle of vermin.

She found and reclaimed her purse, rose to her full height on shaking legs. *Breathe deep, long even breaths, find your composure.*

And she saw that the flashlight's beam had discovered— to her immediate left (south?)—walls smooth and upright and as undamaged as though newly poured. Curious.

The floor beneath her, too, was barely buckled from the blast. She started forward, amazed, played the light about, consumed more by this super-enforced basement than by thoughts of escape. The beam led her to a steel door set evenly in the heavily reinforced wall. A large, powerfully thick door of immutable gray steel.

She twisted an unlocked brass knob, pushed inward, grunting, and found herself in a twenty-by-thirty cement alcove, the spear of light angling off tiers of pine pallets stacked neatly ceilingward. Each pallet held rows of new-looking cardboard boxes.

Searls Corporation, the flashlight revealed, and Jeni reached out to touch the red cursive company logo on the box nearest her. The pasteboard was crisp, wholly dry, no rain or fog making its way here. She swept the beam upward, found only boxes and more boxes, stacked evenly, methodically, to a ceiling braced with massive crossbeams oozing viscous icing mortar, durable as a war bunker. The place was like . . . well, a bomb shelter.

She set the flashlight atop a box, angled it for a work light, pulled down and pried off the lid of one of the boxes. Inside lay a bright nest of popcorn Styrofoam packing. She swept the top layer aside, dug down, brushed hard metal. She extracted a metal sheet.

It gleamed dully, eight-by-ten copper plating no thicker than a penny and road-mapped with highways of circuitry stripes: a computer board. She dug deeper, found more sheets amid the popcorn, a dozen in all. At the bottom of the box she withdrew a single, folded packing form with the Searls Corporation logo. She held the light close, found a listing of the boxes' contents, dates, paragraphs of legalese, a half dozen signatures. She frowned in the tiny enclosure, murmured, "Hmph."

In distant night, a rattled cough rumbled, vibrating down the smooth cement closure to Jeni's shoes . . . a bus or truck's growling motor on the street outside, bringing her back to her present predicament. She still needed to get out.

She combed the subbasement carefully with the beam, shaking her head. Whey go to such strenuous lengths to reinforce the Statler Building's basement, then fill it with warehouse products? Earthquake protection? But why pallets of computer boards here, in a building the city records listed as leased to life insurance, architectural, and graphic arts companies? Was this what Paul meant by shipping goods?

And why, she mused, swinging the yellow beam back

to the heavy steel door's brass knob, why leave such a carefully protected room unlocked?

She tucked the shipping slip in her pocket and retraced her steps to the outer corridor just as the growling motor sounded above her again, seeming closer this time. She picked her way through fallen beams, wafting firefly motes caught in the narrow beam.

She found herself assailed by a sudden sensation of swooping vulnerability, like someone afloat in a dark sea, unprotected from things below. The cone of light fell upon the twisted wreckage of a circular staircase. She stepped forward. At the same moment the wall beside her exploded in a shock of flying debris. The scream was torn from her lips.

Face afire with stinging concussion, hearing diminished to a low ring, Jeni found herself upside down again, still miraculously clutching the flashlight, upside down and staring at outside night, the smell of it and freshly powdered concrete pouring over her through the new six-foot hole in the wall.

Bleeding from tiny slivers, some still embedded in her arms, her hair, she struggled up again. She could not comprehend how she survived so near a blast, let alone what triggered it. Something she'd stepped on, like a Claymore? But Claymore mines were filled with steel shrapnel—she should be dead now, shredded.

She turned left as a violent explosion of concrete shook the air—looked up, glimpsed the blurred gray sphere of the wrecking ball trailing white dust like an earthbound comet . . . saw the thick steel cable supporting it only briefly as the ball *shooshed* back and out of sight again. Back to complete the arc that would send it crashing toward her again. Beyond the gaping hole, the whining growl of the tractor cab vibrated to her: not a bus she'd heard before, not a truck.

She spun, darted toward a gleaming length of handrail through the jungle of debris . . . the wrecking ball flashing back explosively, her world rocked, the earth-jarring thud of a howitzer lifting her, stinging particles raining, urging her toward a berserk staircase.

She vaulted, tripping over blocks of fractured mortar, gained the sagging metal stairs, leapt footfalls ringing. The flashlight's beam leading, Jeni climbed, spiraling. Faster, shoes hammering, faster than the thunderous ball could follow, fast as her muscular runner's legs could carry her . . . up and up . . .

. . . up until up ended at a sagging fire door. Through which she plunged, breathless, to find herself abruptly outdoors again, fresh, fog-thick air sweet.

Outdoors but five stories aboveground, in the middle of a sheared-away office building's west facade. Whose tenuous floors could crumble away abruptly with the next step . . .

Think! Use your training!

From here—so very high and lonely under ocean breezes—there would be nothing below this time to cushion her dizzy fall, only hard, unforgiving earth. She looked down . . .

A dim carpet of muddy-brown, sky-reflecting puddles, a train yard of planks, workman's silent tools, a courtyard of phosphorous debris . . . all so very far below. No help there, and none up here, when next the great steel ball came rushing.

Another grinding clanking. She craned, looking south, spied the tractor treads and cab, green and metallic, a distant toy. She ripped the Ruger from her purse, crouched still-armed on the edge of ruin, braced for recoil, and fired.

The first round whined ineffectually off the cab's re-inforced top as anticipated. She had fired only as a warning, could not really see whatever lurked within the cab's dark window below. As if in answer, the crane growled resentment, swiveled magically, drew back, the great steel ball climbing to her level. Ready to deliver the next blow, swat her like a fly from the broken wall.

I will not die up here . . . not alone up here in the dark and debris . . .

Jeni fired again perfunctorily, shoved the useless gun in her belt, looked about desperately for an avenue of retreat.

She gripped a twisted I-beam, saw with a strange calmness the huge gray ball tracing a luminous path toward her . . . saw that it was off course, would pass well below her. She decided to cling there where she was, poised at eternity, legs braced for the shock from below.

She cried out when the ball struck, ripped away brick and steel half a story below, the vibration reaching her teeth, knocking her sideways and forward, fingers tearing from steel flanges. She plummeted outward into blackness . . . realizing too late they didn't have to actually hit her to shake her loose . . .

She clawed out, flailing, found dubious purchase, found herself hanging, one-handed, from the naked flange. Grunting, kicking, she found better purchase with the other hand, hung there a moment getting her breath.

Not for long, though, the strain terrible, shoulders already going numb. Kicking, rowing, she built momentum, caught a heel, hauled herself up . . . got an arm around the beam in a death lock and rested again. Behind her unguarded back, she imagined the great sphere thundering back . . .

Bright spots danced before her eyes, the swooping dip of vertigo like a roller-coaster plummet; she fought back vomit. I'm disoriented, she thought, dizzy . . . just give me a moment . . .

Yet she must stand, must get out of here. Where was the ball?

She found her knees, crouched doggy style, regained her feet shakily, using a length of broken pipe for balance. She realized, clinging there stuporously, it was not she but the building itself that was swaying, that they were *moving* giddily through the night as though urged by a giant hand.

Panic blossomed. *The building's coming down! They've knocked the goddamn building from under me!*

She could not move, clung paralyzed. She heard— *felt*—a deep grinding, a laborious *giving in* as from the earth's farthest bowels. Adrenaline found her legs, sent her leaping, arms wide, thighs bunched like a dancer in flight, saw the next twisted staircase, and flung herself that way. Behind her, her perch gave way with a sigh, then a chorus of metallic groans. The world vibrated, slamming her side to side in the narrow stairwell, slamming screams from her, the sound dashed away by the louder thunder of the collapsing facade. A subsiding rumble . . . and she was running upward again, a roiling plume of dust chasing her, the gently rocking remains of the Statler's east wing beneath her feet . . . thinking: Never make it, never make it, never make it—

And again found clean night air. Not at the sixth or even seventh level—at the torn-away front of the ninth . . . so high, so far away now from distant earth, the crane's cab looked too ludicrously small to possibly do her harm, the plywood-ringed city block reduced to the angles and lines of the blue schematic in her pocket.

Yet even so the crane's revolving boom rose higher. So, too—once lifted on silent hydraulics to her level—would the behemoth gray ball.

Jeni turned there at the narrow edge, craned behind her at a black complex of twisted wreckage that was the remaining hulk of the building. Through a morass of nightmare angles, broken fixtures, the far wall stood upright and solid, clean-faced as it had been since its contractors first imagined it. The blast had not penetrated here, even most of the windows remained unbroken, sensibly in place. A ruby safety light beckoned. If she could pick her way through the jungle of rubble to these untouched offices and hallways—

That's the way they want you to go. Stay one step ahead of the enemy by doing the opposite of what he anticipates . . .

She fought indecision, chest working like a bellows. Echoing up to her, the grinding ring of the cab's winch raised the pendulous ball skyward, greedy for renewed havoc.

She scanned the stars above.

And in them—against them—found the faint threads of hope . . .

She stepped gingerly onto buckled plywood, arms wide for balance, heading gradually upward again over ruined flooring.

She reached a naked beam, stepped out on it unhesitatingly, trusting instinct, concentrating on the tips of her shoes, only the shoes, not the awful blackness below, placing one foot concertedly before the other . . . one before the other . . . before the other . . . and she *had* to look up, had to see where the infernal ball was . . . and in doing so, glimpsed her destination—

—which was nothing. The steel simply ended, became a blank fork where it joined the corner of a converging beam. There was nothing up here, no retreat, just skeletal red steel and chill San Diego night. Intuition had failed her. *No!*

A gust of wind flattened her hair from behind, pressed her clothing to her back in passing.

A spasm took her spine—it had not been a gust, but the mammoth ball swishing past, inches from her back. She was open and vulnerable out here on a tightrope of steel, no place to go but down.

Arms flung wide, she reached the far end, sank in careful slow-motion relief to her knees, wrapping her legs securely about the flanges where the beams met, gripping them with both hands the way a child grips a dental chair. Below, just to her right, the green toy cab came chugging, pacing her, lining up for the kill, the crane already revolving for the next—the final—swing. An unmoving target, she could not be missed. They would take her and the edge of the building out at the same time.

She looked up, eyes slitted, straining. Yes. A black I-beam, nearly invisible against the night, might be within reach . . .

Jeni balanced, took a clean breath, stood slowly . . . reached up with exhausted fingers and grasped the cool metal. She began to climb. What she sought swung lazily on ocean breezes not twenty feet above her head.

Below, the cab rumbled triumph, produced a grinding of gears that sent the great ball rising to meet her. She ignored it, climbing, hand over hand . . .

Ten feet later she froze against the cool metal, drained of all strength. She could move not another inch.

An ominous swishing sound, like the wings of a great beast. She turned her throbbing head and beheld her destiny.

The crane arm—level with her again—whipped around, the great ball rushing after it. The globe of steel loomed large, larger . . . soon to blot out the sky.

Jeni closed her eyes, awaited a death she could not imagine.

A brilliant flash illuminated the shells of her lids pink. She opened them to find the ball jerked back as if swatted, the crane's boom lit with a blue luminescence. A belch of ozone found her, the reek of burning insulation. A crackle of electricity arced the undulant sky, turning roiling moisture to solid, flickering mounds of cotton.

Untouched—alive—Jeni looked up.

From above, stretched just past the ninth floor, the threads of black high-tension cables ensnared the crane's tip as she'd intended. Severed on impact, the wires showered sparks, writhed and jumped like manic serpents, sending untold rivers of current down the crane's widening lattice boom to fill the metal cab with greenish, flickering death. So intent on ensnaring the fly, the spider had tangled with an alien web.

She watched the now inert ball, dancing with St. Elmo's fire . . .

Chapter 13

The tall man was not pleased.

Things were not going exactly to his liking, not moving at the projected pace.

The plan had become more convoluted than expected, requiring many more hours at the computer, requiring, in fact, another computer altogether. Not the little laptop that had served him so well until now, but one of the big industrial-strength giants they sold only in high-end electronic stores. Something nearer the level of the mammoth console he'd manned at Bureau headquarters in Washington, plumbed the depths of the agency's NCIC records with.

He could not simply buy outright such formidable power. Instead he had to laboriously cobble it together from various local high-end stores, a time-wasting prospect that necessitated the risk of his being out and seen, prompting another disguise or two. But the game could not be played without the proper equipment, especially when the opposition was itself so well armed.

Once the delicate equipment was in place, there was yet more labor involved before he could even switch on the power. The entire room (Mrs. Grindle's bedroom) had to be sheathed in lead and other special materials to help block out radio waves both coming in and going out.

This, coupled with the insulations he lined the new computer with, should prevent the enemy from tracing him here, should make the old woman's cottage virtually impregnable . . . at least for the moment . . . at least until the enemy caught on, adjusting its own equipment, bandwidths, and discovered him. Then it would be time to choose another location. Until his work was completed.

For the moment, he was reasonably safe.

All morning he had been sitting at the little wooden desk, laboring over the sketchbook with pen and charcoal, trying to draw the elusive Figure.

As always, his attempts were in vain.

He could not manage the face. He could not find the eyes, the delicate nose, the just-right placement of the mouth. The floor about him was littered with crushed and wadded efforts. His fingers were blackened and red with charcoal and sanguine chalk. He was beginning to sweat, to feel the burning edge of rage building at his center. He couldn't do it, he just couldn't get it *right*!

He looked about himself. It was this damn room.

He was sick of the drab little cottage. Weary of repulsive wallpaper, filigreed curtains, tired smells, an old woman's memories. It was stifling. Who could create in such a vacuum?

Earlier, he'd made a trip to the local art store to secure fresh supplies. Several masters' prints had caught his eye and he'd selected a few, hung them about Mrs. Grindle's bedroom to replace the awful sun-faded Woolworth's prints previously darkening the florid walls. The most offensive of these was a ghastly portrait of the Savior (surrounded by rather too obviously metaphorical thornbushes) lightly rapping at a heavy wooden door one would suppose represented the entryway to man's faith, the figure's beatific brow lambent with pious perfection, artless technique. He had thrown the print in the trash.

At ArtCo on Rosecrans, he'd discovered three over-priced but serviceably crafted reproductions, with tolerable color saturation and minimum printer's errors. Firstly Manet's *Olympia*, a favorite since childhood and always a delight. *Olympia*, with its juxtaposition of well-known conventions and contemporary context, mixed with a clear message of titillation, had shocked visitors of the Salon des Refusé in 1863. "Manet has the distinction of being a danger," the critics had said. But Manet had shown them . . . Manet had had his revenge.

The tall man put aside his sketch pad, lay back on Mrs. Grindle's too-soft mattress, arms behind his head, gazing past the oak baseboard, smiling revenge on the gloomy little chamber, the print hung on the north wall to catch early morning light, greet him on awakening. Olympia, reclining across from him—unself-consciously nude atop her cream-colored bed before a coal-black handmaiden—gazed back with confident contempt, her flower, neckband, bracelet, and especially her dainty shoes underscoring her smug sensuality . . . debutante breasts proffered, left hand casually, deliberately masking a plump, imagined cunt. A reinterpretation of Titian's *Venus of Urbino*, Olympia is, quite unabashedly, a very contented slut.

Next to this, he'd arranged Gauguin's *Spirit of the Dead Watching*, another longtime favorite and the near mirror opposite of the Manet piece, its florid flat Tahitian-inspired colors redolent, its recumbent Nubian's full buttocks directing the eye nowhere but there . . . then teasing up and across the ebon back to find rest in the come-hither innocence of the black girl's provocative face, almond eyes peeking coyly behind demurely arranged fingers. Ankles crossed, ass elevated, she seemed—to the tall man—to be saying, "Take me . . . I'm yours if you dare . . ." yet confident he would not—the sinister figure in black, lurking beyond the yellow sea of her bed sheets, waiting, watching. It gave the tall man a strange thrill, this juxtaposition of the grim background figure guarding the supple nude girl . . . an uneasy heat which often prompted an erection.

Not himself without religion, the tall man had replaced Mrs. Grindle's lurid dime-store Savior with another Gauguin favorite, *The Yellow Christ*. Flat-faced and serene with none of the cheapjack rendition's saccharine slickness, this yellow Jesus looks down contentedly on a group of Breton peasant women sedate in their mourning, surrounded by idyllic flora, a purple ribbon of river. The tall man admired Gauguin, admired his conscious breaking of representational and historical conventions . . . his attempt to return to simpler, more primitive times. Not unlike the tall man himself. It would be immensely pleasant, he often surmised, to exist in a dreamworld of Gauguin colors.

The final print he never looked at.

Purchased years ago, kept always near (this time within Mrs. Grindle's closed, top bureau drawer, bedside), he never looked at it, never went near it, never let it stray far from where he slept.

This was the Matisse. This was *Portrait with Green Stripe*.

It depicts the face of a woman, described in a startling array of hues and broad, slashing strokes, broken—shattered—into separate swaths. The shadow which models the woman's form is garish green, splitting the

face into separate, schizophrenic hemispheres. Her hair
is an ominous inky purple, her dress blood-red—all colors employed in a deliberate and disturbing departure
from the natural palette of the Impressionists. The
woman's eyes—bead black as a crow's—just avoid the
viewer's . . . reflecting not so much disdain as a kind of
animal detachment, as though the woman lived in a
world of her own making . . . as though the viewer were
less than passive, did not exist at all.

Quite often, lying atop the late Mrs. Grindle's bed,
the tall man would gaze silently at the other paintings and
see only the stern woman with the broken green face.
Only her. At times—thus transfixed—he seemed to be
listening . . .

But lately his reverie was disturbed by a cloying, sickly
sweet odor emanating elsewhere within the cottage. He
knew exactly where, but had not yet solved the problem
of how to eliminate the putrescence.

Tonight, the odors were particularly pungent, exacer-
bated by thickening coastal fog, the air pressed close, the
smell below seeping through the floorboards of Mrs.
Grindle's old cottage. He had begun to think eliminating
the old woman so quickly had been a mistake.

Still, something must be done about the smell.

He left the bedroom, the lovely translucent flesh of
Olympia, the magnificent buttocks of the Nubian girl, and
headed for the hall. He had already checked the small
cobwebbed garage earlier for shovels, spades, had discovered nothing. Perhaps the cellar.

The tall man descended to the first floor, past the hall
closet, from which the odor nearly overwhelmed, to
the cellar stairs and below to darker, rat-scuttling depths.
A single dust-caked bulb hung suspended from a long

cord at the basement's center, feeble glow throwing grotesque shadows over the octopus arms of the ancient furnace, transformed it into a crouching beast. He found no shovels here, no rakes, nothing at all to dig with. Mrs. Grindle's cleanup boy down the street must bring his own tools. He did discover a fat black widow, perched imperiously in her corner web, leisurely sucking the juices from a roach, surrounded by dried beetle husks. The tall man watched intently for a length of time, seeming to forget why he'd come down here. He occasionally licked dry lips.

On his way back upstairs, a dull cream-colored gleam caught his eye from the west corner. He moved closer to investigate and found his salvation. He bent, smiling, to the coffin length of an old Kelvinator meat freezer unit half hidden under a pile of mildewed blankets. He raised the heavy lid on stuffy, airless dark, sealed tight God knew how many stale decades ago.

He rummaged on knees behind the massive unit, found a brittle length of electrical cord beneath a patina of dust and clinging webs, engaged it in the nearest socket. He turned the big dial on the freezer's porcelain side, grunted satisfaction as the unit rattled to life, threatened to vibrate to pieces, then settled to a deep, vibrant hum. He set the dial to twenty-eight degrees Fahrenheit, dusted his hands, and returned to the upstairs closet.

Mrs. Grindle, already more mummylike than her living counterpart, was somewhat difficult to extricate from her plastic shroud. All sharp-limbed and angular from days of greedily encroaching rigor, she refused to cooperate as the tall man strained down the hall, dragging her skinny ankles. Mrs. Grindle—soiled dress riding up flaccid thighs—protested with occasional indignant farts as the tall man craned away, *thwumping* her nodding, scolding head over each cellar step.

A short, round little woman, she made a nearly perfect fit within the freezer's rapidly cooling interior, though he was obliged to snap and bend her neck to obtain this.

Standing back, wiping his brow, one hand prepared to close the heavy lid on his work, the tall man was halted by a heart-freezing apparition.

Mrs. Grindle—sunken skull askew—was watching him.

Perhaps decades ago she, or Mr. Grindle, had installed translucent green blinds on the two narrow cellar windows level with the outside yard, probably to block spearing afternoon sun as Mrs. Grindle—or the maid—labored at washtub or iron. Now, under ocher streetlamp, these windows threw the faintest leprous glow across cellar floor, the porcelain edge of the freezer, bathing the corpse a diseased jade, bifurcating the parchment face into twin, luminous hemispheres. Turning the sunken orbs into the bead-black eyes of a crow. The Matisse come to life—or death.

Trembling spastically, the tall man staggered back, let the heavy lid fall from nerveless fingers—a vacuous thud—stumbled back white-faced across mildewed cement. He swiped blindly at the wood railing behind him, eyes riveted to the freezer. Swiped and finally clutched the railing, hung there drained of his soul.

He sank to worn wood steps, eyes feverish, fixed on the cool casket of freezer. Huddled there, arms wrapping his knees, he shook—an abandoned child—hypnotized by the thing in the corner. He remained frozen, unable to move either forward to unimagined dread or upward to the purifying air of the hall.

After a time, he began to rock gently to and fro on the cellar stairs, keening a low, childhood song.

Rock and nod ... rock and nod ... listening to what the gleaming length of freezer had to say.

Chapter 14

She slept dead-through until 11:00 A.M.

Wanting a long, soul-reviving bath, she settled for a quick, stinging shower from the motel's stingy spigot, toweled while phoning in for breakfast, a gourmet extravaganza of shrink-wrapped honey bun and acid coffee, doubtless provided by the next-door 7-Eleven.

She scanned the motel's directory under Computer Equipment for the Searls Corporation. She could not find the company listed. She dialed information, including that of outlying areas, and found no Searls Corporation listed anywhere in Southern California.

She dialed the largest computer supply company she could find in the area, or at least the one advertising such claim.

"Web World, may I help you?" An adolescent voice, threatening to crack.

"Yes, I think I've got a burned-out computer board, but I want to make sure it's replaced by one from the same manufacturer. Do you handle Searls Corporation products?"

"What was the name again?"

"S-E-A-R-L-S Corporation."

"Doesn't ring a bell. We carry all the top manufacturers. Is that domestic or foreign?"

"I really don't know."

"Searls, Searls . . . just a sec." A muffled sound as the mouthpiece was covered by palm or chest. "Danny? Searls Corporation?" A second, then: "No, ma'am, we don't carry that line."

"And you're the biggest in town, right?"

"Biggest in the state. Where'd you buy the computer?"

"It was a gift. Well, thanks for your time." Jeni hung up, chewing her lip, hand still on the receiver. Beside the phone lay the Sprinter Walkman, volume knob on, turned high. It had lain that way all night, though she didn't truly expect any message from Handle.

Her eyes caught the folded copy of the *San Diego Union* atop the covers, retrieved earlier from the plastic boxes in front of the 7-Eleven and as yet unread.

She picked up the morning edition, unfolded it, and scanned the headlines. Down near the bottom: "Crane worker dies in Statler Building accident."

Jeni's heart sank. She searched for a name.

"Marvin Peckman, of Kensington, thirty-two years old." Marvin, according to the paper, had been with Canfield Construction for eight years. Body discovered by firemen, identified later by police on the scene. That was it. The item was short.

Jeni closed the paper, thinking: IDs can be faked.

She thought a moment. Then reached over and pulled the laptop to her, crossed her legs on the edge of the bed, and began tapping at the keypad.

FBI NCIC HEADQUARTERS
ENTER

She had seen Brian use the NCIC dozens of times to locate a subject's name. The files held extensive lists of all current and past FBI agents, though not just anyone could tap into the files. She couldn't remember the code prefixes Brian used, but maybe she could get in by using the common route. She wanted to do some checking on her new friend Paul Miller all of a sudden. See if there were any connections to Handle he wasn't divulging.

The laptop clicked and beeped.

NO ACCESS

She had anticipated that.

She sat thinking a moment. She typed an inquiry directly to the J. Edgar Hoover Building on Pennsylvania in Washington. She tried the Criminal Division first. No one named Paul Miller was listed.

She canceled out, and tried the Intelligence Division. No Paul Miller.

Heart beating slightly faster, she tried the Inspection Division. Nothing.

Training Division. Still nothing.

Laboratory Division. Zip.

Information Division. Same.

Administrative Division. London Division. Public Affairs. Special Operations and Research. SOLO. SWAT. RICO. NAACP. CAT-COM. She even went down a complete list of all personnel in any way connected to the director. No Paul Miller.

She sat back on the bed blinking at the laptop.

Could the computer be dysfunctional somehow? Doubtful. The more logical answer was that Miller was in there somewhere, all right, in deep cover probably, just not accessible through traditional channels. She needed to get into the damn NCIC.

Or maybe she'd just pay the elusive Mr. Miller a call.

She went to the bureau, found the Ruger, jacked it back and saw the comforting glint of cartridge brass, slid the gun into her waistband, put her jacket on to cover it.

Chapter 15

Right from the get-go it didn't feel right.

The little blue clapboard annex behind the office building seemed even more quietly removed from the rest of the world than usual . . . *felt* that way as Jeni came up the narrow walk to the wooden steps, the wooden door.

Which stood ajar.

Opening easily under her fingers to the same empty concrete floor, but no attendant "custodian" with mop and pail . . . no movement, no sound, no nothing but the distant song of birds outside. She stood a moment listening. *I don't like this* . . . Beyond the second wooden door it got worse.

The sweatshop was there, but the legion of Hispanic workers had vanished. Taking, apparently, their sewing machines and appliquéd hats with them.

By now, Jeni was running, swearing lightly under her breath, up the stairs to Miller's stuffy little command room with its heavy pall of smoke, sleeve-rolled agents, and winking industrial Sprinter. All of which, of course, were gone as well . . .

She stood in the empty doorway, face as vacant as the little room.

Nothing. Not so much as a discarded cigarette butt. Neat. Tidy. A lingering of Lysol. Someone—or someones—had done a very commendable job of cleaning up.

"What the fuck," she heard herself breathe softly, more astonishment than epithet, something deep inside her seeming to drop away. "What in bloody hell?"

If she were going to become a part of this game—really a part of it—she needed a better computer—a console Sprinter 9000. If she could afford one. Her funds were limited.

She decided to go to the closest ATM, since there was a good chance that Brian had already staked out her bank, or even, she supposed, frozen her funds. That, however, could take several days; she needed to withdraw her money *now,* before she was cut off completely.

Jeni stood before the ATM, inserted her card, and typed her PIN code. The machine whirled.

WELCOME TO
FIRST AMERICAN SAVINGS
PRESS ONE:
WITHDRAW CASH
WITHDRAW SAVINGS
DEPOSIT
ASSISTANCE

Jeni pressed ASSISTANCE on the monitor window.
The screen went briefly dark, then relit with a green font.

JENI, THANK HEAVENS
YOU'RE BACK! YOU'VE NO
IDEA HOW BORED I'VE
BEEN WITHOUT YOU!

Jeni fell back in shock. Even here, Handle could get to her. What if *he'd* used the bank's computers to freeze her assets? As she thought this, the screen went blank for a moment, then the computer whirred and clicked and spit out twenty or so twenty-dollar bills.

I KNOW YOUR NEEDS.
NO ONE ELSE DOES.

Again, another pile of twenty-dollar bills, until, according to Jeni's count, she had two thousand dollars. Almost exactly the amount in her savings account.

The screen went dark. Behind Jeni a large woman in a bright blue suit stood patiently, shoving her sunglasses onto her disheveled hair. Jeni moved between her and the screen, uncertain how to end this communication with Handle.

She pressed ASSISTANCE once more.

KINDLY LOG IN YOUR PIN
ONCE MORE

Jeni obeyed. Behind her the blue-suited woman shifted, her patience growing thin.

PURCHASE MODEL 3112
SPRINTER.
USE PIN.
SEEK AND YE SHALL FIND.

Abruptly the screen went black and her ATM card appeared in the slot. Jeni took it and stepped back from the machine as the woman nosed in front of her. She looked around her. The fog had cleared. It was going to be another beautiful day.

Chapter 16

The tall man cruised the little motel twice, slowly, encircling the narrow block like a motorist seeking parking space—in reality sharply attentive for cops. Cops came in all shades and colors, you couldn't be too careful.

No cops today. He parked once more across from Jeni Starbuck's motel, sat awhile smoking—unfiltered Camels—checking his watch occasionally, eyes flicking to door 317. No one came in, no one came out. He hadn't supposed anyone would, but he was nothing if not cautious. The game was drawing to its logical conclusion . . . not a time for reckless haste.

The tall man left his car, arced the half-finished butt at the curb, crossed the street (light traffic at this hour of morning—all commuters at work), stepped across cracked asphalt and peeking weeds to the motel's sad facade. He rapped once lightly at a door in need of fresh paint. There was no answer, as he'd expected, and he immediately let himself in with a credit card.

The room smelled of Pine-Sol fighting irrepressible mildew, and—vaguely, near the bed—of the Starbuck woman. He paused long enough to look down at the rumpled, unmade sheets, at the length of her impression still there, picturing strong, supple frame, supine and slightly curved, pale legs long, calves muscular even at rest. He saw again the way she had lain in the motel room, breathing serene trustful sleep.

He found the "Do Not Disturb" sign on the bureau and hung it on the knob outside to prevent the cleaning lady entering unexpectedly.

He began a systematic search of the room.

He had to orchestrate this carefully, lifting, touching, smelling, but placing every object back in its original position to ensure against suspicious eyes, trained eyes. He even removed his shoes to prevent leaving heel marks.

As he went about his methodical business, he referred regularly to his watch, pausing intermittently, head cocked to outside noises, the sound of approaching tires. When this occurred—twice—he stood motionless and calm until the tires had either passed or stopped at the room next door.

Halfway through his inspection, there commenced a rhythmic banging against the south wall. The tall man, not pausing, listened quietly ... heard muffled voices, a woman's eager falsetto above urgently squeaking springs: "... *oh like that* ... *do like that!* ..."

A secretary and her employer, no doubt, on lunch hour break: it was that kind of place. The thumping sounds annoyed, masking other possible warnings, forcing him to work more quickly, though no less efficiently.

It took him exactly fifteen minutes to finish, precisely the window of time he'd anticipated. He anticipated everything. It was how he conducted his life.

He failed to find evidence of anyone else in the Starbuck woman's room, evidence that anyone other than he had rifled it. But they would come. Eventually.

The tall man nodded, smiling in the shadowed room. Fine. That was fine. He was enjoying the game. Could play it all day and night without sleep.

And this game—convoluted as it had become—was ending soon now. Soon.

Jeni drove through town away from the bank, down Pacific Highway past Sea Port Village where she glimpsed an unusual sight.

The massive San Diego Convention Center at water's edge was aglow with activity, people lined up at the huge entranceway, milling on the front steps, the streets overflowing with parked vehicles. Not unusual in itself, it was after all a major convention center. But for the first time she noticed the towering yellow banner stretched across the landward facade: "Comp Con II!—San Diego welcomes computer experts and novices from all over the country!"

She pulled down Anacapa, crossed the bumpy trolley tracks opposite the terraced tiers of the building, and nosed to the curb before the entryway in a red parking zone. An LED moving screen was running a continuous red electronic crawl above the main doorway: COME JOIN US IN THE AMAZING WORLD OF CYBERSPACE! COMPUTERS OF ALL MAKES FOR USE AND SALE! BARGAINS! CONTESTS! FUN! ADMISSION $12.00!

Jeni cut the engine, stepped through a crowd ranging from teens to the elderly, most clutching convention pamphlets and hardware magazines, and approached the ticket booth. She saw the Sold Out sign before she got there, marched up to the girl behind the window anyway. "Any chance someone will cancel before the evening's out?" Jeni smiled.

The ticket girl, a freckled teen with flaming hair and weary countenance, shook her head automatically. "Ma'am, you couldn't get in there with an ice pick. We were sold out in advance two days ago."

Jeni nodded, turned away—turned back. "Any advice on where I can buy a good computer?"

The girl shrugged.

Jeni hopped back down the steps to her car in time to find a pink ticket under her wipers.

She drove the rental through the Gas Lamp Quarter, down Broad Street, and past shop after closed electronic shop.

At Chandler, amid startled honks, she made an abrupt U, angled back down the street, and braked at the curb before a door displaying a white Open sign. It was the store she'd phoned earlier.

Inside, she quickly perused the latest array of Sprinter 9000 equipment, positioned strategically at the entryway, heaped ceilingward amid cardboard promotional stands that blocked all other views. Day-Glo cursive extolled the virtues of the Sprinter 9000, *the most important piece of electronics in your home*—the copy slanted to make you feel slightly inferior, grievously outmoded for not yet owning one, especially under such ridiculously simple financial terms.

Jeni made a few layman's inquiries to a slickly efficient young salesclerk in business suit and earring, was assured a child could learn the rudiments of a new Sprinter in a few hours. The eager clerk was flush with enthusiasm and the confidence of a burgeoning field.

"Ma'am, in the next two years you're going to find a Sprinter 9000 in every home, and not just this country, all over the world. Networking. That's where it's at. People won't even drive into work anymore—some already don't—everything will be done with the touch of a button. Everyone is going to be linked to the computer, and the computer of choice is the Sprinter."

The young man's earnest pitch was radiant with manufacturer's jargon, technical facts and claims irrefutable.

"And that's just the beginning, ma'am. See" (*sotto voce* with sly contempt) "IBM has this lame Home Director stuff they use on the Aptiva PCS. Compaq has their own line. The idea is the computer becomes a central console to control and link household appliances. Home automation." He gave a derisive snort. "Hardware's already antiquated. Sprinter's already replacing the TV and telephone as we know it. Also books, libraries, movie theaters, the whole concept of interactivity between individuals, between man and machine. You'll become autonomous. You know what that means?"

"Too well," Jeni told him.

"You'll never have to leave your house, ma'am. Never."

"And this is a desirable notion?"

The young man appraised her blankly. "Ma'am," spoken with an oracle's wisdom, "it's the future. You don't want to live in the past, do you?"

Jeni avoided that one by nodding at a tower of gleaming merchandise. "Whatever happened to good old Apple?"

The young clerk grinned rehearsed pleasure. "Want my personal opinion, ma'am? This time next Christmas, you won't see a piece of hard- or software in this store without the Sprinter logo on it. Sprinter rules."

And, as if that were her cue to not argue the foregone, the boy let smiling silence do the rest of his selling for him.

Delivery was out of the question. Jeni took the heavy components back to the motel room and one by one carried them in. It took almost two hours for her to set up the Sprinter, and even then she wasn't certain she'd used it to the best of its capabilities. It would have to do.

When she finally got it up and running, she keyed in her PIN. Immediately the screen sprang to life.

PLEASE HIT YOUR POUND KEY

She pressed the pound key and Handle's voice filled the small room.

"I was wrong when I referred to you as a pawn, Jeni Starbuck. You have just promoted yourself to player. You should be aglow with self-congratulations."

"What happened to Paul Miller?"

A soft chuckle. "Are you asking me?"

"You're the one with all the answers."

The voice hesitated. "Well, at the risk of hurting your feelings, my dear, perhaps he's just avoiding you. Wasn't exactly professional in his dealings with you, now was he?"

"In other words, you're not telling."

Now a full-out laugh. "You know me well, Jeni. Too well? Better than your own husband, I think. And I'm still awaiting a thank-you for not disposing of your miserable cat."

"Thanks. Why'd you spare Pierre Cardin?"

"What point to his death?"

"What point to any of your deaths?"

Silence, during which she was certain she'd lost him.

"There is a, shall we say, natural order to things. Once disrupted, that order needs restoring. I do my best to correct my mistakes, just as you do. Molly, for instance. Obviously it suited no one's purpose to have her die, and yet die she did. From that came your suicide attempt, your hospitalization, your divorce, Brian's new marriage. Mistakes all. Life can become a chain of them. I feel duty-bound to break the chain upon occasion."

"And how long is your own chain, John?"

"Longer than yours, dear heart, but of course I'm older. What was it Dickens said? 'You forge the chain in life that you will wear in death.' I fear the hereafter shall be no picnic for me, having welded my own dubious links rather early on."

Jeni sensed a shift in his usual sardonic tone. A sorrow?

"I'm sorry, John."

"Truly? Well. Then I suppose it would be insensitive to mention that you were almost rejected by the ATF because your empathy scores on the psychological testing were too high. Not a desirable trait in a government agent, but then you had the drive and curiosity to make up for it, didn't you?"

"What's the next step, John?"

"Now that you're a real player, that decision lies with you. I've given you the tools you need to seek your answers, but in fact you are quite beyond my control, always have been. Start at the beginning. The rest will follow. Remember what you've learned. *Everything is significant!*"

"What do you—"

"Time to learn to fly, Jeni. I have the utmost faith. Until we meet again . . ."

A static *blip* and the room was silent once more.

Begin at the beginning . . .

She glanced down and saw her list lying beside the computer.

1. Newspaper magnate—bay bombing

The beginning had begun.

Chapter 17

Jeni strode up the wide curving front walk flanked with Malibu lights and hibiscus to gleaming Maxfield Parrish columns, an enormous double door with lion-headed knockers glowering brassily. She tapped once, heard distant, melodic chimes.

She waited, serenaded by crickets. Streetlamps glowed from palm-lined curbs—a lovely street in an old, well-kept neighborhood—but dark beyond the sodium halo, deep shadows stretching everywhere. Deep shadows, deep silence.

She stepped up to the front double doors, decorated with insert stained-glass windows and ornate carving, and pressed the doorbell.

Inside the house she could hear the echoing chimes. She waited a moment, listening for movement. There was none.

Twice more she tried the bell, listening. Nothing.

She stood looking at the door, frowning, then, on a hunch, took hold of one golden doorknob and turned. The door clicked and swung open.

Of course. She was expected. But not by Mrs. Bradford.

She stepped through the door into an elegant darkened foyer, Victorian in style, as was the rest of the house. She listened again, this time not certain exactly what she was supposed to hear, but the house seemed empty, silent as a grave. To her right was a spiral staircase.

If Bradford had a home office, it was almost certainly on the second floor.

If Bradford had a home office, he almost certainly had a computer.

Jeni climbed the serpentine staircase of sparkling scrolled alabaster, crimson carpet, cupids gamboling at opposing newels. At the second floor, Jeni peered through open doors down endless paneled hallways beneath gargantuan diamond chandeliers, hall tables heaped with zinnia, cleome, nasturtium, bachelor buttons, walls decorated with original oil paintings.

Before a set of towering double doors graced by curling gold handles, inlaid gold trim, she pushed into a warm, spacious library, replete with fireplace, ceiling-to-floor books, brass sliding ladder, a rich mahogany desk and red leather chair. Heavy brocade kept back the night. Logs burned brightly in the fireplace. Alone in the warm, flickering room, Jeni regarded the desk with its Sprinter 9000, glowing softly in the dark. She approached it cautiously, reading the words on the screen.

WHY IS A RAVEN LIKE A WRITING DESK?

A quote from Carroll: *Alice in Wonderland*. The riddle with no answer the Mad Hatter had presented Alice.

She smiled. Handle was the Mad Hatter and she was Alice. Did that mean she was dreaming?

Some dream, she thought, more like a nightmare.

Everything is significant . . .

It's a test. He'll give clues, but you have to put it together yourself.

Writing desk.

Writing. Letters . . .

Correspondence.

She sat in Bradford's maroon tufted leather swivel chair, surprised to find it actually fit her. Bradford must not have been a tall man. Her fingers flew across the keys as she searched his document files, looking for something, anything that might provide a motive for murder. There were hundreds of files labeled in cryptic computer code; it would take a week to read them all.

A name caught her eye.

SPRBM.DOC

SPR. Sprinter? Worth a look.

She brought up the file in an instant, scrolled down rapidly.

Her eyes were directed immediately to the heading: conservative black Helvetica bold:

THE HOUSE COMMITTEE
ON NATIONAL SECURITY
Official Business

June 16, 1995

Dear Irv:

    I just wanted to write a brief follow-up note after the banquet to thank you again for your generous donation. I don't have to tell you what your selfless contribution means to the leaders of this great country—to the cause—and what it will eventually mean to every American, though God willing, they shall never be privy to the details.

Thanks to your generosity, the NCIC—and thus the country itself—are one step closer to regaining the kind of national security this great land has enjoyed since its inception by our forefathers. Through you, and other philanthropic visionaries like you, we will, God willing, triumph in this terrible war of technological attrition.

Cyber terrorism is, as you know, very real and very much here. In the twenty-six years since our Defense Department created the Internet as a means of maintaining vital communications needs in case of nuclear war, that very system has proven to work against us, becoming the weakest link in our nation's defense.

Supervisor Ress of the FBI's computer crime squad is not optimistic about the risks. As our society becomes increasingly more computer reliant, it simultaneously becomes computer vulnerable. Even moderately skilled hackers have shown their ability to crack some of our most vitally protected systems. Now the heart of national security, the FBI's NCIC, is itself at risk. I don't have to tell you the catastrophic implications should that great matrix of files be tampered with.

As Duane Andrews, executive vice-president of SAIC, says: "A terrorist state that doesn't have the technology can hire the technology."

The Defense Information Systems Agency has estimated over 250,000 attacks by hackers on Pentagon unclassified systems in 1995 alone.

Nearly 160,000 of those hackers succeeded in entering our systems. The potential consequences are that the Pentagon may not be able to generate, deploy, and sustain forces during a major regional conflict in the event of information war attacks on support functions controlled by networked computers.

Our military has, of course, been keenly aware of these threats for some time. For seven years now a defense-sponsored panel representing leaders in the telecommunications industry, law enforcement, national security, and the military has been meeting in secret, privately sharing information. The outlook is harrowing. Only two years ago the NSIE (National Security Information Exchange) blocked a security leak that could have wiped out the New York Stock Exchange's computer trading records.

Since 1990, as I have informed you, NATO's "Lathe Gambit"—code name for the panel of InfoWar experts—has been meeting every six to nine months to discuss new problems in this ongoing war, comparing notes and resolving legal conflicts when pursuing hackers across national borders. Their job has been effective, though not 100 percent so.

I don't think I need enumerate further at this juncture. Drastic times call for drastic measures. And with "The Solution" we may at last have achieved the kind of weapon needed to win this war. Your contribution in the form of monies lent our organization has gone far to—

Jeni jerked as the room went suddenly black. The electric fireplace winked out.

The printer hummed to a stop, its green function light winking out.

She stood in darkness, trying to remember where she'd put her purse and the silvery Ruger handgun within it.

Hands outstretched, still gripping the pages, she blind-walked the circumference of the big desk, knees colliding painfully with the red leather chair, moved around, sweeping the desktop, finally brushing into the soft leather and brass buckle of her purse. She jammed her hand inside, rummaged, and withdrew the gun. She began, still quite blind, inching her way toward what she hoped was the direction of the door.

She brushed a wall . . . swept down it a few feet, fingers trailing over a switch. She flicked it a few times for good measure to no avail: the room remained black.

She inched along, gun at port. Halted, breath held. Was that a muffled noise from below?

She hesitated. Silence.

Jeni shuffled along the wall, feeling ahead with her free hand, found molding, then the first of the high library double doors. She pushed outward into hallway gloom.

Less dark here, some light filtering through the high moonswept windows at either end of the long hall. The staircase was left, if she remembered correctly.

She froze. More muffled sounds from below. A scuffling?

A premonition of doom plucked at her—the cop's sixth sense. There was death in this house.

She inched along, gun held high.

She slowed. Voices now, muted and indistinct. Male voices. Below, in the living room or foyer.

She crept to the head of the winding staircase, paused at the gamboling cupid newel. She cocked her head. Two distinct voices, it appeared, one slightly more basso than the other. Arguing about something, modulated with hurried movement. Jeni felt blood pulsing behind her ears.

She took a first tentative step down the stairs . . . then

another . . . another, the voices rising in volume as she descended.

". . . *the hel! were you doing here anyway!*"

"*What the hell do you* think *I was doing?*"

Jeni stepped down . . . down—

—gasped as the house lights flared suddenly on. She froze, gun rigid, pressed herself flat against the balustrade. She peered downward, craning, chest knocking.

On the bottom level, between living room and foyer, a middle-aged woman lay stretched supine across rumpled throw and marble floor, thick red liquid pooling lazily behind gray head. Eyes open, arms flung in an outward shrug, she seemed to be acknowledging some private irony—life's final joke: death. Paul Miller stood above her, shaking his head, .38 Special aimed downward past his thigh. Behind him, muttering nearly inaudibly, someone stalked back and forth in restless shadow.

Miller hunkered, cocked his head, reached out and closed the corpse's eyes. "Nice shot. Clean. She didn't suffer."

"Gee, that's a comfort. What the hell are you doing?"

"Closing the victim's eyes. What's it to you?"

"Agent Miller, the sentimentalist. Better quit screwing around there. Where does this put us, by the way?"

Miller straightened, shouldered his weapon beneath his jacket, studied the woman. "It puts us with the last of the surviving Bradfords dead at our feet."

"Thank Christ. Old biddy. What's the latest from upstream?" The shadow came into chandelier glow and Jeni felt her teeth clench back a hiss. Brian stood beside Agent Miller, reholstering his own weapon.

"Same old game: get Handle."

Brian snorted, paced around the corpse. "And your people are no closer to that than before, right?"

"We're closer. We're always closer."

"Sure you are." Another snort. Then Brian turned on his heel.

Miller swiveled. "Where the hell do you think you're going?"

"Back to my wife and kids. I'll let you tidy up."

"The hell you will."

"Look, Miller, I got my orders, you got yours. Get one of your elite team to clean up the nice marble floor. Just be sure you get all the blood. Or is this one supposed to look like a suicide? Have a nice day."

"Starbuck—"

Brian turned wearily at the door.

"Fuck you."

Brian smirked. "Fuck *you*." And left.

Jeni closed her eyes a moment on the stairs, gripped the rail until the stairway stopped swaying.

In a moment she was backing up slowly again to the second floor, gun before her rigidly now, eyes bright with fear and anger, back, back up the richly carpeted stairs.

She paused in the endless hall to wait out another wave of vertigo. She was trembling.

At the library door she paused again, craned. Were those footsteps on the staircase behind her?

She pushed quickly in, found no inner lock on the twin doors, scoured the room hurriedly: no other doors. Only the windows.

Definitely footfalls in the hallway now.

She rushed to the line of brocade curtains, swept the first aside, unlatched the window, and eased up the pane silently. She gazed straight down into deep-shadowed night. Deep shadow and a pale ghost of trellis.

She remembered, too late, the letter still glowing on the computer screen. The library door was opening.

She barely had time to slip over the sill . . . reach down for the first flimsy wooden rung . . .

Chapter 18

All the downstairs doors were locked, as she'd expected.

But by now she was getting used to breaking into places again, the old training becoming more and more familiar, more and more handy. Anyway, she'd already pulled a B&E on this place once this week, it was familiar territory.

She slid neatly through an upstairs window graced by ghastly puce bedroom drapes, slipped past an ugly teak bureau, and padded—shoes off—to the two slumbering figures lying atop the shadowed bed. She placed the muzzle of the Ruger against Brian's temple and leaned close to whisper. "Just keep your mouth shut and come with me."

Brian opened his eyes, then wider, started when he saw Jeni's shadowed face haloed by moonlight. He glimpsed the silvery gun from the corner of his eye, frowned anger, opened his mouth, then shut it as the muzzle pressed harder.

Silent, Brian peeled back the sheet, stole a look at Marcia's peacefully snoring form, and slid off the mattress. He was naked.

Jeni gestured with the gun toward the bedroom door. When Brian nodded at the closet, mouthed, "Robe?" Jeni shook her head, snapped her gun wrist emphatically at the hall.

It was cool outside, as California nights typically are.

Jeni marched him through the side garden, down flagstone steps to the quivering rectangle of pool, pushing the muzzle into his bare back. Halfway there he turned to her calmly. "Jeni, this is ridiculous."

"My sentiments exactly. Move your ass."

They strode down the length of dark water to the deep end, where Brian turned.

"Get in."

"Jeni, what the hell are you—"

She lowered the gun to his shriveled penis. Brian slipped into the water.

"In the middle. Start treading."

Brian pushed from the pool edge, began to dog-paddle, facing her. Jeni squatted comfortably atop the tile lip, legs crossed, Indian style, gun trained on his bobbing form. "Now then. Without the bullshit. What's going on?"

Before he could open his mouth, she added, "I was at the Bradford mansion tonight."

Brian's Adam's apple bobbed once, she noted with some satisfaction. "Jeni, let me explain . . ."

"That's what we're here for. Take your time."

"I can do it better on dry land."

"You can do it faster right there."

He nodded acquiescence. "All right," voice strained with effort. "Obviously you haven't been told the whole truth."

"Obviously. How long have you been working with Miller?"

Brian shook his head. "I'm not, in the strictest sense. He has his bosses, I have mine. He's legitimate FBI. We're both working to get Handle."

"But it's so top secret, you can't tell even an ex-ATF agent. Even your ex-wife."

"That's about the size of it."

"Bureau bullshit." She shook her head in disgust. "Which one of you killed Mrs. Bradford?"

"Neither. She was dead when we got there. Handle got to her."

"Uh-huh. Says you. Which brings me to my next question: what brought *you* there?"

"You did."

Jeni nodded. "You've been using me to get to Handle. I figured that. Through the computer, right?"

Brian nodded. "Your bank PIN code."

Jeni grunted affirmatively. "You and Handle have been playing yourself against each other through me. I see."

"No, you don't see. Jeni, let me out of here, this is tiring."

"That's the idea."

"There's a lot you need to know. I can't possibly get through it all treading water."

"Cuts down on the lying, though."

"No more lies."

"Yeah, sure."

"What's the need now? The cat's out."

"I've heard that one before. Think we'll just swim here a while longer."

Brian paddled, visibly trembling in the night breeze despite the exercise.

"You should keep your pool heated, lover."

"Jeni, I have documentation to back up everything I tell you."

"At headquarters, of course."

"That's right."

"What else you got there? Sawed-off shotgun? Box of dumdums?"

"I'm not asking you to trust me anymore, Jeni. Only to listen. One more time. What do you say?"

"I'm thinking about it. By the way, aren't you interested in knowing?"

"Knowing what?"

"Which of you is the better fuck."

Brian licked his lips. "If we keep talking, Marcia and the kids will wake up. You don't want that."

"Don't I? We could compare notes with Marcia while we're on the subject of getting screwed. Maybe make up a foursome."

"Let me come out, Jeni. I need to tell this as much as you need to hear it. I can't promise it's not going to make things more dangerous for you. It will. I've tried to protect you from that. But in a way, I'm glad it's out in the open finally. I hated the lying part." Gasping a little now as he tread water, his lips turning blue from the cold.

She watched him passively. "Yeah. I bet you did."

"Please. I'm cramping."

After a moment, she motioned toward the edge with the muzzle. Brian swam to her.

He left a note for Marcia—he'd been called away to late night duty, something he claimed she was accustomed to. Jeni believed him, having once been accustomed to it herself.

With Jeni following, Brian's car led the way to his command post, a tiny ocean cottage a few blocks from the beach, nondescript and dark. Brian opened the front door with a key, led her through the foyer and into a parlor where files were scattered on all surfaces and several computers kept silent vigil. A single bed stood unmade in one corner.

She motioned him into a chair with her gun hand, sitting opposite. He stared at her for a moment, squinting.

"You changed your hair."

"How nice of you to notice."

"You look—younger."

"Let's cut to the chase, Brian. Show me what you've got. Now."

He pulled out drawers, unfolded maps, drew books and charts from under the bed. The place was a command center, he explained. He'd been here every day since his return from China.

Jeni sat on the edge of the bed, gun in her lap, and let him explain.

"Okay. I know a lot has been kept from you. I know you're filled with resentment, but Jeni, you must believe me when I tell you it was done for your own good."

Jeni rolled her eyes. "Without the birdseed, Brian."

Brian paced a moment, then sat back on the edge of the computer desk, facing her resolutely. "First of all: China. Yes, I was over there. But it wasn't to act as liaison between us and Chinese manufacturers of illegal Michael Jackson CDs. I was checking up on the Communists, all right—on them, the Russians, the Iranians, the Japanese—anyone capable of computer manufacturing. It's all part of a new program—a massive program—to secure cyberspace.

"Paul Miller, myself, and a handful of others scattered across the nation are part of an emergency response task force, directed by the FBI and based in the Justice Department. Its purpose is to manage any terrorist incident involving an attack in cyberspace. It's called the Cyber Security Assurance Group. We function as both an emergency response team and an investigative body. We address and respond to any collapse of the National Information Infrastructure, all the country's vital computer systems including banking, transportation, telecommunications, what have you. The CIA is right in there with us. Jerry Smith is heading up their end of it, he's CIA general counsel."

"I know Jerry Smith."

"I know you do. Well, to quote Jerry: 'If we have a Solobomber who decides to launch an attack with a PC instead of a bomb, there will be a great deal of damage.' Attorney General Janet Reno, acting under a classified presidential directive, is chair of one of the panels for this thing, which includes, in addition to FBI and CIA directors, cabinet secretaries from Treasury, Commerce, Transportation, and Energy."

Jeni sighed. "Your point?"

"Let me set the stage, there's a lot to assimilate. This has been one tough cookie to negotiate and set up. The commission faces almost insurmountable obstacles in balancing government interagency turf battles as well as dealing with industry and the private sector on this thing. The latter opposes Internet regulation."

"What's the answer, Brian? And what's it got to do with me, Irv and Miranda Bradford, and John Handle?"

Brian glanced askance at the big Sprinter 9000 beside him. "Japan's Nippon Telephone and Telegraph is already selling data-scrambling chips here that make the stuff allowed for export by the Clinton administration look about as protective as a peashooter. Foreign software makers can sell products here and abroad that are much more powerful than American companies are allowed to export. If American preeminence in the computer industry is undercut, other nations will certainly gain the advantage, both economic and military. Unfortunately the administration's response to date has been to backpedal. It allows U.S. companies to sell powerful encryption products abroad, but on the condition they leave decoding keys where we can get at them with a court order."

"So?"

"So what foreign business or government wants a product that lets the U.S. government eavesdrop on them? Both American companies and American computer users are stuck in the same dilemma. It's a security catch-22.

"Now. Our group believes the answer lies in more and better encryption. Don't prevent businesses and individuals from protecting themselves. We now know that defending against hackers takes precedence over eavesdropping on their conversations. Particularly when terrorists can buy all the foreign encryption tools they need to hide from our government. Better encryption, that's the solution. You understand encryption, right?"

Her look told him.

"Sorry. I'm used to dealing with idiots. Well, since it's exactly like the combination on a gym locker, the more numbers on the lock, the longer it takes someone without the combination to get in. Computer encryption is made up of bits, each bit doubling the number of combinations a thief or hacker would need to break in."

Jeni nodded patience. "Again, your point?"

Brian held her eyes levelly, replied softly, "John Handle invented the process."

Jeni jerked.

"That's right. Your buddy on the Walkman. The Solobomber himself. He's former FBI, defected. I should know. I recruited him."

"Defected to who, the Chinese?"

"To himself."

Jeni, still holding the gun, sat back on the bed. "I don't get it."

Brian paced the little room. "Well, you're not alone. The FBI and CIA have been trying—unsuccessfully—to outmaneuver and second-guess John Handle for weeks. He was once the most brilliant mind in Washington, head of the NCIC. Now he seems to *be* the NCIC."

"How did he manage that?"

Brian shrugged. "Broke in, killed the guard, recalibrated and scrambled the entire subsystem. Now no one can get in but John Handle. John Handle controls the cyberspace portion of the nation. Which is directly connected to a rather large part of the world in general. His power at this point in time is, well . . . just about unlimited."

"He's mad?"

"As a March hare. Delusional."

"And his plan?"

"To protect his baby, his child. This incredibly complex system he helped create." Brian smiled ruefully, held up thumb and forefinger about an inch apart. "The crucial part of which is about this big . . ."

Jeni frowned. "A chip. This is about a chip?"

"A very new, very powerful microchip." Brian made a disgusted face. "Security. Clandestine control. Shit. It never works for long. It always, eventually, unravels. Always will."

Jeni motioned impatiently with the gun. "Tell me about the chip."

Brian sighed. "Quite simply, Washington needed an efficient way to keep tabs on the increasing number of nuclear terrorists, individuals and/or organizations, most of which are on the other side of the world. The answer, of course, lies within the problem itself. The computer. We took our lead from Time Warner, Turner, AT&T, all the other corporate giants that are merging daily in our workaday world. We bent the rules a little—cheated on an antitrust law here, ignored a couple of international treaties there. Bought and sold, stepped on a few toes. And pretty soon what did we have? The biggest, most complex and far-reaching corporate merger in modern history. So big the major shareholders don't even know what they're holding. A corporate giant that dwarfs the likes of IBM and Microsoft. A computer manufacturer that—for all intents and purposes—rules the communications ends of the planet . . . which, today, is the same as ruling the planet, period."

Jeni nodded. "The Sprinter Corporation."

"Listen, Bill Gates did it and no one even raised a brow. No one hollered 'antitrust!' Well, a few did. But anybody who didn't want to be left behind climbed aboard. Everybody bought Windows 95. If that's not a monopoly I don't know what one looks like."

"You're saying that every computer manufactured in the world now is a Sprinter 9000."

"In essence. There are a few that go by foreign names. The Sony people were very hard to deal with. But we produced the vital parts right here in Silicon Valley. If you wanted the best, wanted to play ball, you dealt with us. Japan may rule the automobile industry, but when it comes to computer chips, we bow to no one. We make the best. The best and eventually the cheapest. What self-respecting terrorist could resist? In fact, what choice do they have? Control what the terrorists buy, and you control the terrorists. At least in theory."

"So now you've got the whole world buying the Sprinter 9000, what next?"

"Next is the chip. And this is where Handle's genius

came in. He invented—microprocessed—an amazing piece of technology. Something small enough to fit atop your fingernail, but powerful enough to connect the world. It amounts to a digitally compressed two-way audio-video transmitter/receiver. For the moment, called M-PEG 4. And here's the genius part—once installed, it can't be got to without tearing apart and wrecking the motherboard. And even if you manage to get to it, the chip burns up, self-destructs the moment it's tampered with. Ergo: no one can copy the chip. It's foolproof. That was Handle's genius. An amazing telecommunications chip that could not be replicated in the marketplace. America finally held the edge against terrorism."

Jeni chewed her lip. "And the uplink is with FBI headquarters, of course. Anyone who purchases a Sprinter 9000, plugs it in, can be monitored by the Bureau. The ultimate wiretap."

"Exactly. Even the most amateur of terrorists use the computer. Or at the very least the phone, which, thanks to fiber optics, is now the same thing. Pick up a phone, turn on a computer or television anywhere in the world now—try to communicate in any mode short of shouting at the top of your lungs—and the FBI knows about it, knows who you are and what you're up to, even if you do it in another language, even if you use code. We have computers that can break codes even before they're invented, codes tougher than the Navajo Indian codes we used to get past Japanese decoders during World War II."

Jeni stood, tucking the gun in her waistband. "That's not genius, it's Orwellian."

Brian made a rueful sound. "Big Brother is here. The system works. Better than even we dreamed. If I told you how many acts of terrorism this thing has already squelched you'd be staggered. It's war, Jeni. The dirtiest war. The way you win it is to fight dirtier than the other guy."

Jeni got up from the bed, began to pace.

Brian watched her. "You think I'm making this up? I'm not."

"I'm having a credulity problem with this megamerger of yours. How can that many major players in the corporate world keep their mouths shut, allow your little anti-terrorist scheme to remain covert?"

"Sprinter's a legitimate business merger, Jeni. In fact, it's somewhat organic. IBM and Westinghouse may be a shareholder now, may be replaced by RCA and Time Warner tomorrow . . . exactly the way the average corporations are bought and sold. The political part is known to only an elite handful, all government agents. They control the muscle end, not the dollars and cents."

"Sort of like the Mafia used to control Vegas?" Jeni paced, arms folded. "Only something clearly went wrong. Someone apparently suffered a moral dilemma, a First Amendment crisis of faith, yes? Our pal Handle, it turns out, is a patriot. Surprise."

Brian looked disgusted. "Patriot. That's what he'd have you believe. Handle, the self-appointed moralist. His posture being that you can't take what is essentially a military tool and place it in the hands of ordinary civilians—even if those civilians aren't aware of what these new computers contain. It's morally corrupt, governmentally irresponsible. Like Iran-contra, Watergate."

"Isn't it? Morally corrupt?"

"You were an ATF agent long enough to know the necessity of military and government secrecy. Handle's full of shit. There's nothing moral about a psychopath like him. He isn't concerned about the rights and privacy of the average American. He's a murderous psychopath with paranoid delusions. Besides, the government has more important things to do than eavesdrop on the local citizenry."

"Yes, but they *could* eavesdrop if they so chose. Monitor anyone at any time. In their beds, on their toilets . . ."

"You sound like Handle."

"Why, because I'm capable of seeing his point? I didn't say I agreed with it. But you have to admit, potentially at least, this puts an end to privacy as we know it."

He looked doubtful. "The system employs only highly trained government agents seeking to tap into terrorist activities. We're not interested in crack raids or spying on illicit couples."

"But you *could* spy on illicit couples. That's Handle's point."

Brian shrugged. "I suppose that's his warped little narrow-minded position, yes."

Jeni nodded. "Okay. So Handle defected from the FBI, became the Solobomber, and took out his frustration on innocent people, the very ones he claims were being abused, that it?"

Brian held up his palms. "Not exactly. In all fairness, I wouldn't say the word 'innocent' applies anywhere in this thing. It rarely does where war is concerned."

"Irv Bradford, for instance? He donated money to your cause. Helped finance the research for the project. The Solution, I believe it was called."

Brian nodded over his cup. "You read our letter to Bradford."

"In Bradford's library, courtesy of Mr. Handle. You knew I was upstairs in the study?"

"Yes."

"Why did Handle kill Miranda Bradford?"

Brian made a nonplussed gesture. "Security risk? She

had access to her late husband's files. Maybe he thought we'd gotten to her first. Or maybe just to tease us, who knows? He loves his little games."

"If this genius chip is in all the computers, why can't you trace him through any department store Sprinter at the local mall?"

"Because it isn't in *all* the computers yet. We only just started shipments of the M-PEG 4 models. Complete saturation will take more than a year. But yes, we do have Sprinters containing the chip. Trouble is, Handle has found some way to jam us at his end. He is the genius, after all."

"And the Statler Building was the drop point for the motherboards. Packaged under a phony company logo called the Searls Corporation, but manufactured in Washington. How'm I doin'?"

"Supposed to be top secret. Handle found out, probably through his control of the NCIC."

"And he tried to blow it up. Destroying your plan."

"But not the boards. We anticipated that one, had the things stocked in an enforced bunker."

Jeni paced, assimilating with the computer in her head. "Still some unanswered questions. Why did he send me to the blast site? Why give me the blueprint? Why did he send me chasing all over town on those breakneck runs? Where does Jeni Starbuck fit into this thing?"

Brian settled on the edge of the desk, poured more coffee. "We're not sure. Could be any number of reasons when you're dealing with an unhinged mind. Handle and I worked very closely together during the initial concepts for the chip. He was the technical genius, I was the idea man, the instigator, I ran all the legal interference, talked it up with the White House. Neither of us got the credit we deserved. I was even turned down for a promotion. But at least I understood why this thing had to remain strictly clandestine in order to work. Handle . . . well, Handle was not what you'd call a wholly rational individual to begin with . . ." He stopped for a second, hesitating guiltily. "He used to stare at that picture of you and Molly I had on my desk. He'd ask me questions about you, about Molly. I didn't think much about it at the time. He's a very cordial guy when he wants to be . . ."

Jeni gave him a level look. "If he's that much of a psycho, why the hell did the FBI hire him in the first place?"

Brian smiled wryly. "He broke our code with a home computer he built himself. We wanted him on our side."

"But now the genius is out of the bottle."

Brian grunted. "We'll catch him, it's only a matter of time. He's only one guy, feverishly trying to block his signal from us. We have a whole team working day and night to break his code. Once we do that, we move in."

"And what? Kill the guy who created your monster for you?"

"I should think institutionalization would be a more humane sentence." Brian drained his cup.

Jeni sat quietly, staring at the gun in her lap. "I don't know. He doesn't sound crazy over a pair of headphones. He does crazy things, but there's a kind of sincerity to his voice. He doesn't *sound* mad."

"How does a madman sound?"

She thought about it. "Handle sounds . . . betrayed. Almost sad."

"You're breaking my heart." He set down his coffee, turned back to her. "So. What do we do now?"

Jeni looked at her gun. "I'm not leaving town, so you and your fed friends can just forget that one. I'm in it now, Brian, up to my ears. Handle knows that even if you jokers don't."

Brian nodded. "I agree. And I don't see why we can't work together on this thing . . . if you're willing to comply."

"Define 'comply.' "

"Okay. For now we pretend this conversation never took place. You sit tight here for the time being. I doubt Handle'd be stupid enough to try anything here, now that he knows you've tapped him. He probably won't use the computer again. But if he should, I'll keep him on the line until you can get a trace. *Do not* try to contact him via your bank PIN code! Attempting to contact him again will only foul up our wiretap. We need him to call you, not the other way around. And please, don't go out again. I can bring you anything you need. If Handle calls, talk to him, but don't push him. Don't try to outsmart him, you can't. Just give us time to verify the trace. We're getting closer every minute. When this thing is over, I'm going to make sure you get the credit I didn't. I can't imagine the Treasury not reinstating you."

"I'm not the type to sit tight and do nothing. You should know that of all people."

"I know it. But it's our best bet for catching this guy." He nodded at her gun. "Or you can shoot me with that thing, I suppose."

She appeared to think it over. In fact, her mind was already made up. "All right." She placed the gun on the nightstand beside her. "I'll hang here for a while. For a *while*. At least until we see what his next move is."

Brian nodded. "Fair enough."

She looked at him levelly. "That doesn't mean trust you, Brian. I wouldn't think twice about using that gun if I thought you were lying to me."

He looked about. "Well." He stuck his hands in his pockets. "For what it's worth, I'm sorry about all the lies.

One thing we did have during the marriage was the truth between us. I hated violating that. Detested it."

Jeni leaned back against the headboard, watching him. "Yeah. I'll bet."

He watched her a moment. "So. We're agreed, then? You'll stay here, lie low?"

"I'll try."

He nodded. "Okay. Anything I can do for you?"

"Like what?"

He watched her. She was stretched long and curving across the bed. "Magazines? Food? Books?"

"Yeah, bring me some Defoe. *Robinson Crusoe*."

Brian smiled. Walked to the door and opened it. "I'll be in touch, then."

She waited until she heard the sound of his departing car, then left the bed and settled herself before the computer.

Chapter 19

The tall man was on the move again.

He'd had to leave old Mrs. Grindle's place. They were closing in on him there.

Despite all the precautionary measures, all the lead shielding around the computer's mainframe, every possible scrambling and misdirecting of signal he could conjure, they had eventually cracked his code, isolated that location. It would only be a matter of days before he would be paid a very quiet, very stealthy and exacting visit. No sirens in the night. No warning. Just a light rap at the door one afternoon while he was lying contentedly abed, perhaps watching the Gauguin across from him, or the comely Manet—Olympia with her plump inviting breasts and enigmatic smile—while the yellow Christ looked on uncritically above the tall man's headboard.

Yes, they'd come. And they would nullify him.

He would be no more, vanish from the face of the earth. They would leave no trace or record. It was the area of expertise in which they excelled.

If it was a private group—one hired by the CIA, a Mafia faction perhaps—they would kill him very slowly with great skill and greater pleasure, employing a cattle prod perhaps in his anus, or the slow removal of his sack, making him chew, then swallow his own testicles before they disemboweled him, then stole a few hundred dollars to make it look like one of the ever-growing number of satanic rituals.

They had all kinds of ways, the CIA, the FBI, and the tall man knew them too well. That was the problem with the government ways, they never changed. Therefore becoming predictable, easily got around. So it was time to lie low for a while. Put some distance between himself and their cyber bloodhounds.

He left the old woman's home and hit the streets.

It was okay. It was fine. He still had a few more days before all the pieces were in place.

It was at this juncture the turning point occurred in his life.

Something so remarkable, so incredibly serendipitous, he could only put it down to fate, a concept he ordinarily held little truck with.

This event, however, could be compared only to a religious experience, a crisis of faith.

He found the little girl. He found Molly.

He'd been wandering aimlessly the flora pathways of Balboa Park one sunny afternoon, playing the role of the lonely artist, sketch pad and easel in tow, pausing at this fountain or that koi pond to paint the various lovely parkscapes, the patrons, the kids gamboling the gardens before the wide, wooden arboretum, the lovers lounging manicured lawns. In reality, he'd been laboring under a patina of sweat with sanguine chalk and three-ply Bristol, quietly, stubbornly sketching the memory of the elusive Figure.

Page after page had been slashed at with heavy, broad strokes, only to be clawed and wadded and finally tossed at a concrete trash container. It was hopeless. He would never be able to draw her. He could never get past the face.

It was his guilt, of course.

The day was beginning to grow late and he'd nearly had his fill of sparkling fountains, sidewalk jugglers, aerospace buildings, Imax theaters, art museums, and frustrated sketches. Packing his paraphernalia, he prepared to leave, go back to his motel, and watch the endless parade of Sprinter commercials on TV. He found some relief in their irony. *"Sprinter! It's taking over the world!"* Would that they knew.

He was rounding a filigreed passageway (the park's architecture a Spanish moderne motif of a past turn-of-the-century world's fair), heading for his car . . . when she appeared . . .

Abruptly. Just suddenly *there*. Beautiful, dark-eyed, more lovely than memory.

Molly.

Older, of course, than the last picture he'd seen of her (taken just weeks before the car accident) but undeniably Molly. There could be no other.

The tall man froze there in the archway, heart jolting, staring at the wan, lovely creature ahead of him . . . careful to step back into shadow so as not to be seen. She was well guarded, of course, that was to be expected. There were several dark suits around her, close but not obviously so except to the trained eye—but guarding her nonetheless.

Clumsy. He could spot them in a snowstorm. He could smell them. Clumsy and irresponsible, allowing her out in plain sight like this for him to discover. Yet there she was, slim and beautiful and not eight yards in front of him.

The tall man stood staring enraptured, soaking her in, every line, every gentle curve of jaw and cheekbone. Molly. Not dead at all . . .

A momentary thrill of terror. Could it possibly be a trick of the light? He had to be certain . . .

He stepped closer, daring exposure. But no, it was the child, all right . . . the dark searching eyes, the waterfall of auburn curls, the slim (now adolescent) body. He could throw the sketch pad and chalk away. She was here.

Lonely, alienated, fearful, as was to be expected. But here.

The tall man felt his fingers tighten on the weapon in his suit pocket.

He'd found her. Fate had led him to her. He'd found her and he'd see to it she was taken from them.

He'd take care of little Molly.

Then he'd see to the mother . . .

Chapter 20

She punched in her bank PIN code, ignoring Brian's warning.

The screen remained blank. Obviously Handle wasn't going to respond to that. The question was, what would he respond to?

Another game.

She thought about it for a moment, then typed in her maiden name: JENNIFER LOUISE HARRIS.

Immediately her fifth-grade report card was duplicated on the screen, including Mrs. Jansen's comments that "Jeni is not working up to her full potential."

She laughed out loud. "Very funny . . ."

Okay, Handle, I get the message. My full potential.

She typed in her Social Security number.

The screen went dark, then brought up what looked to be an official document. Jeni peered at it in surprise.

PSYCHIATRIC RECORD—JENNIFER STARBUCK
DR. R. L. KEGGIE, M.D.
DIAGNOSIS—DEPRESSION

Patient is a white, 33-year-old female with no history of psychiatric admissions before July 1996, when

patient's daughter died and patient attempted suicide.
(See notation.)
After two weeks on the psych ward at V.A. Hospital,
patient is released to the care of her husband with in-
structions to visit my office every two weeks.

RELEASE PRESCRIPTIONS:
Klonopin—10 mg at bedtime
Fenfluramine—40 mg daily
Resperidal—3/day for three weeks

*Prognosis: Good. Patient's husband is very support-
ive and patient is cooperative.*

   Jeni stared at the computer screen with irritation. Handle's way of showing he knew far more about her than she
did about him? She pressed Erase and the screen went
blank again. She typed in angrily:

               YOU CAN DISH IT OUT BUT
                 YOU CAN'T TAKE IT!

   Abruptly the screen lit with another document almost
identical in form with the first, but longer, more detailed.
Jeni read with astonishment.

PSYCHIATRIC RECORD—JOHN HANDLE
DR. R. L. KEEGIE, M.D.
DIAGNOSIS—SCHIZO-AFFECTIVE DISORDER
WITH PARANOIA

Caucasian 44-year-old patient has a lifelong history
of institutionalization, starting at age 10 when his
mother committed suicide with a gun in front of him
and he attempted same. I.Q. tested at age 15 indicated
genius level 186, with talent in the areas of art and

music. Plays six instruments, although has refused to play since reaching adulthood. Personality charts show psychosis with paranoid delusions and auditory hallucinations, all controlled with drugs at the present time.

Recently released from private psychiatric institution into the care of Brian Starbuck on a temporary basis for government experiment; must take medications as ordered. Seen weekly here. All blood tests indicate normal levels, health seems good. Despite some persistent flight of ideas, patient is cooperative, congenial, and well versed in many subjects. Speech somewhat stilted, but could be effect of medication.

RELEASE PRESCRIPTIONS:
Stelazine—2 twice daily
Depakote—1 gram daily
Trazodone—50 mg daily
Zoloft—50 mg q morning

Prognosis for recovery is poor; however, patient may continue to function if he is compliant with prescribed meds.

Jeni tried to slow her breath, heart pounding, stomach lurching with vertigo, as if she'd just stepped off the edge of a cliff. *Brian had Handle released from a psycho ward? How could he? Or was this another one of Handle's games?*

"Handle, speak to me," she said out loud.

The response came with startling, heart-jarring speed:

BRIAN LIES.
YOU MUST LEAVE THE COTTAGE.
WHEN THEY FIND WHAT THEY
WANT FROM YOU,

YOU'RE TO BE TERMINATED.
LEAVE.
YOU CAN BEAT THEM.
THE POWER IS WITHIN YOU.

Jeni typed, hit the wrong key, cursed, fumbled out an-
other message: WHAT POWER? WHY DO THEY
WANT ME? I WANT ANSWERS NOW OR I DON'T
LEAVE.

A moment's pause.

Then:

TOO LATE

Jeni blinked.

She typed: EXPLAIN.

SOMEONE IN THE HOUSE

Scalp crawling, she whirled about at the figure behind
her—found only shadows.

Outside her window the Point Loma foghorn moaned
once.

She typed: NO MORE GAMES!

I REGISTER
MOVEMENT IN HOUSE
BOTTOM FLOOR

Jeni craned around. She sat absolutely still, head
cocked. She heard nothing. She typed: BULLSHIT. NOT
PLAYING.

COMING UPSTAIRS NOW.
GET OUT!

The computer screen went dark.

Jeni typed in her PIN code furiously. "Son of a bitch."

The screen remained blank. The house lights went abruptly out.

Somewhere in the old cottage a board creaked. This is where I came in, she thought absently.

She pushed away from the computer desk, faced the half-opened door, peered into shadow. "Brian?"

No sound.

Academy training urged her hand to her old shoulder holster, found empty air. She peered blindly about the little room, naked as a woman in shark-infested waters. The Ruger was atop the bureau, wasn't it? Or had she put it on the nightstand? Shit.

Creaking sounds on the upstairs hall now. Footfalls.

Jeni silently nudged off her shoes, padded to the bureau on tiptoes, swept the top with splayed fingers, knocking over a bottle of something with a musical clink. She winced, froze. Listened. Moved to the nightstand, found the Ruger, hefted it, and turned toward the door.

She waited patiently, giving her slowly contracting retinas time to acclimate to the gloom. She found the room suffused with dim moonlight from the southeast window—enough to be seen by. She was still exposed, if only in silhouette. She padded quickly over, drew the shade silently. Darker now, but not absolute. Moot anyway, for someone using night-vision goggles or infrared gun sights . . .

She turned with the Ruger, paused . . . sure she'd detected movement from the bedroom door.

She noticed the sound of her own harsh breathing, got it under control, distinctly heard footsteps entering the room now.

"Brian?" On her lips, stopped in time. It could be anyone. It could be Handle.

She waited until she heard the footfalls again, then started silently toward the northwest wall and the closet, matching the soft thumps. She could see no figure, but also did not feel she herself was seen.

The footsteps halted, and she with them, breath held in her throat, gun at high port. Very, very slowly she thumbed off the safety without making the normally audible click.

The gun is empty.

She'd taken out the clip earlier to ensure not harming Brian; failed to reload.

There were two full clips in her purse, but whoever was in the room now was between her and the computer desk. She stood in impotent darkness, silently cursing herself.

Noise now. Someone poking about the desktop. A rattle of papers . . .

Then a sudden spear of yellowish glow—a penlight, probably—followed by a scrabbling sound of more rifled papers. She glimpsed a dark-gloved hand.

She used the sound of shuffling papers to mask her movements, began backing cautiously to the door . . . if she could find the door.

Just before she located the molding, she heard a piece of paper rustle to the floor. She craned back and saw the narrow beam of light sweep downward across the desk legs . . . to the carpet . . . across a throw rug, to find the dislodged papers. The beam fell across her discarded shoes.

Jeni slipped quickly out the door into the hall without looking back.

Every muscle ached to run. She fast-walked instead, as silently as possible down the darkened hall. She was still mostly blind, though moonlit windows afforded some vision: dark lumps of end tables, rectangular ghosts of framed pictures. She had no idea how many other intruders—if any—were in the house.

She hugged the wall, feeling ahead with her free hand, still clutching the empty weapon, ready to employ the hard metal butt if necessary. Or—if the lights flared suddenly on again—to bluff with it.

She swept invisible floral wallpaper with her free hand, wide fanning strokes until her fingers brushed the banister and she found the newel. She gathered herself, then stretched out a leg blindly . . . found the lip of the first step. She started down, inching in braille, searching with her toes; the old stairs creaked protest, pinching her face into winces.

She stopped. Listened. She could hear nothing from upstairs now. But had the man in the bedroom heard her creaking the stairs? She'd heard him, earlier. She listened, straining, head cocked, decided to try another step.

Before her toe could find the stair, she heard another creaking sound, *below* her.

Someone on the way up.

That meant at least two of them in the house, perhaps more. She felt tightening in her solar plexus, leg muscles already bunching to run.

Her mind raced with options. Call out *"Freeze!"*? Aim the gun downward and bluff her way past? But that would leave her exposed from the back, and she knew the guy upstairs had a light.

Another creaking from below, closer. The old stairs were proving as dependable as sonar. Another creak . . . she could feel the vibration through her bare feet this time. A heavy step, a big man . . . nearly to her . . .

Carefully, silently, she nudged herself away from the banister, sidestepping soundlessly to the opposite wall . . . found it without making noise, pressed herself flat into it, as flat as she could make herself.

If the man coming up to her was using the rail, he *might* brush past her without making contact. Unless, of course, he already knew she was there, was watching her right now through infrared lenses.

Jeni froze against the wall, breathing through her teeth. Another creak, loud. Another just below her. And now his odor . . . cigar or cigarette smoke-permeating clothing, a whiff of aftershave.

Right beside her now—she could hear *his* breathing, easy, confident . . . moving past now . . . *creak, creak* . . . and on up the stairs. She held rigid, waiting to be well clear of earshot.

She glanced below. A dull pool of moonlight bathed the front hall. If there were more of them down there guarding the foyer, she'd never make it to the front door.

The back door? They'd have that covered too. Depending on how many of them there were. Depending on *who* they were.

Brian lies.

She started down carefully again—froze. Whispering from below.

More of them, then. At least two.

She felt a sudden pressing urgency, a nearly precognitive sense of foreboding. She began descending the stairs rapidly, silently, listening—head tilted—for the whispering sounds.

She achieved the bottom step without incident, turned right, faltered uncertainly (*this seems wrong*), turned left, and made her way toward what she was fairly sure was the kitchen. If she could quietly pry up a kitchen window—

She collided abruptly with human flesh, elicited a male grunt of surprise. "Jennings?"—a deep raspy whisper.

Jeni grunted an answer, but it didn't work; flailing hands brushed her shoulders. "Hey . . . *hey*!" Strong fingers pressed into the flesh of her upper arms.

Jeni feinted, pulling back as if struggling helplessly, crouched abruptly low, and struck up hard with her knee, felt squashed genitals, a vibrating cry of pain echoing the narrow room. The steel fingers let go. She ran.

—felt something grip her right ankle, bring her down hard, crashing to unyielding, musty carpet. She cushioned the brunt with the heels of her hands, but forehead and chin smacked thin carpeting and hard wood beneath; magenta fireworks erupted behind her lids. Distantly she realized something was clawing across her legs now, working its way up her back spiderlike to pin her.

She rolled under an elephantine torso, recognized the hard jab of a service revolver under suit coat, dug automatically for it, dropping the useless Ruger. She felt beefy hands clamp on her own, wrestling her for the weapon. She held firm, but lost leverage under his weight, her assailant using the advantage to roll atop, force the air from her diaphragm. She prevented the muzzle from finding her stomach but could find no air for her lungs. Amid conjoined gasping, the purple spots blossomed again. A moment more, and they'd precede the consuming numbness of unconsciousness.

She dropped that tactic, let go the revolver, swept the rug quickly with her left hand, brushed the Ruger. She gripped it, swung blindly, savagely, at a waft of garlic-laced breath.

The metal grip vibrated off jaw or cheekbone—another painful grunt, and the heavy weight left her. She rolled automatically, gasping raw air, winced convulsively at two rapid reports nearby, saw the attendant flares of light, robbing what little night vision she'd gained.

She found her feet, ran blind serpentine lurches toward the kitchen, heard a third report behind her, an insect buzz past her ear.

A suddenly explosion of white—

—followed instantly by sharp pain and a red numbness sweeping outward from her soul. *I've been shot!* She felt the hard floor against her back again . . . *this is how it ends.*

Dark.

. . . someone was cursing somewhere . . .

She caught: "No shooting! Stop shooting in the *goddamn dark*!"

A warm tingling spread rapidly from her spine, an insistent headache descending. She had not been shot. She had run headlong into a wall.

She pushed up amid the sound of scuffling shoes. "It's a woman!" "Well, stop the goddamn firing!"

She couldn't seem to rise above sitting, body lagging behind urging brain, a phantom weight pulling her back to the hard, smelly carpet. She held it at bay with her elbows, watching the colored light show within her skull, waiting for it to pass, equilibrium to return.

"Somebody put the frigging lights back on!" "Peterson, is that you?" "Shut up, you dumb bastard!" "She's right here somewhere!"

She perceived two milky slivers in the distance, reckoned they were kitchen windows, lit by exterior streetlight. She shoved up in vertiginous slow motion, wavered, fell . . . lucked into a wall for support. She squinted. The two milky slivers merged, became a single window. She limped toward it.

"Hey!"

Someone grabbed her from behind.

She feinted left, doubled, jabbed back with her elbow. An old trick but he wasn't buying it. Trained agents—they *must* be. The grip tightened, found her throat.

She struggled, air gone again. Twisted, dancing with him, he matching every step, every evasive maneuver. "I got her!"

Jeni flailed wildly, faking a helpless attempt to wrest free. Her aggressor planted his feet firmly against the wild lunges, left himself flat-footed. As she'd intended.

His attention fixed on her upper torso, she brought her naked heel down into his instep with all her remaining strength. He howled pain, and she could breathe again.

But he retained a bulldog grip with one hand as she dodged away. She used the rebound to drive her fist toward an invisible face, missed, grazed bearded cheek, but felt the sharp edge of her elbow connect squarely with his teeth, loosening them inward. He let go. *"Mutherfukker!"*

She dived for the kitchen door.

In there, she found enhanced visibility: a ring of amber windows illuminated with outside sodium glow. Everything here was deep, elongated shadows, the pale glint of chrome fixtures. She scrabbled for the nearest window, endurance gone, operating on fumes now.

A dun figure bounded from behind a hulking edge of refrigerator. She glimpsed the silvery arc of a nickel-plated Colt.

She dropped to her knees, quick as Pierre Cardin, received the teeth-jarring collision of knees against her ribs, rose quickly again on sinewy runner's legs, and cartwheeled the figure over her shoulders in a graceful arc. The shiny Colt went off with a flare of white thunder, but only reflexively. Before the heavy figure had struck

linoleum she attained the kitchen counter, was tugging up
the window.

—halfway up—imaginary slugs tearing into her
back—when the lights came back on, washing everything
white.

She squinted past painful glare, saw one blurred figure
sprawled on the floor, another lurching through the door,
white shirt streaming, mouth mangled, gun raised.

A third figure coalesced from behind the one whose
teeth she'd loosened. This one, calm with controlled patience, clamped a hand on the other man's weapon, forced
it down ... stepped in front of him, weaponless, and
became—in the watery pinpoint of her pupils—Paul
Miller.

"All right, all right. Everyone chill. Jennings, put your
piece away."

Jeni squatted in the kitchen sink, glad to discover the
wetness at her thighs and butt was tap water, not blood.
One hand still hefted the sill.

"I've got people out on the lawn, Jeni. Come down off
the sink."

Jeni stayed put, abruptly aware she was gripping someone's service revolver, not remembering picking it up.
She held it before her. "Want my best guess, Paul? My
guess is you've got squat out on the lawn. And if I put
this piece down, you'll blow me right out this kitchen
window."

Miller may have repressed a smile. He looked old, she
thought. Deep circles under his eyes, as though he hadn't
slept.

He put his hands on his hips, reached out once without
looking to hold one of his advancing men back, then replaced the hand on his hip calmly, not taking his eyes off

Jeni. He looked her up and down. "What happened to your shoes?"

"Upstairs with your man with the penlight. Did you find what you were looking for on the desk?"

Miller shrugged. "Haven't found squat yet, actually."

Jeni smiled, held the gun. "Sure you haven't."

Miller gestured. "Your knee's bleeding a little."

She didn't need to look. "From old stitches. When I went over the hedge, remember? Damn thing keeps weeping. Going to be a problem at the next marathon."

Miller nodded. "Yeah, I'd have it looked at. Want to tell me what you're doing here tonight? Or do you prefer sitting there soaking in that sink?"

She glanced up as two more agents entered the rapidly cramping kitchen. "Tell you what, Paul, you show me yours and I'll show you mine."

Miller did smile now.

Then turned to the man with the bloody mouth. "Jesus, Ted, you look like shit. She sucker-punch you?"

"Lucky hit," from the big man, wiping his chin, glaring at Jeni.

Miller shook his head, appraised the others crowding the kitchen, six of them altogether. "Whole goddamn squad can't stop one little ex-ATF agent. Christ. I'm getting too old for this shit."

He reached across the counter, snagged a paper towel from its under-cabinet dispenser, handed it to the big man. "Wipe your mouth before the A.G. sees you like that."

Miller turned to the others. "All right, you fellas clear out. Take a smoke."

The group looked at each other. Jeni thought she recognized one of them from the little command post above the sweatshop, couldn't remember his name.

"Clear out where?" one of them offered sullenly.

Miller's tone sharpened. "I really don't give a shit, Phil. Go get a drink, go fondle your girlfriend. Do something. You've done such a magnificent job here."

The man Jeni thought was named Jennings said, "You going to stay here alone with her?"

Miller rolled his eyes. "I think I can handle it, Carl. You boys get lost now."

And the group retreated, grumbling.

Miller pulled out an antique kitchen chair and sat sighing at a round table with checkered oilcloth top. He began fishing for invisible cigarettes.

"Why don't you carry gum or lollipops like everybody else?" Jeni asked from her perch.

Miller patted his pockets. "Those damn things just make me want to smoke all the more. The idea is to quit."

"It isn't working."

He grunted concurrence. "*You're* working, on the other hand. Been a very busy ex-agent. Want to talk about it?"

"With whom? With whom am I talking, 'Agent Miller'?"

"You know damn well with whom you're talking."

"Do I? According to Handle I'm to be terminated. A succinct little phrase."

"How did you know Handle was transmitting here?"

"How did *you* know? And while we're at it, thanks for calling and leaving your forwarding address."

"Don't get smart with me, Jeni, you're supposed to be out of town, remember?"

"Yes. Your idea or Brian's? Of course, according to Handle, Brian lies anyway. Who else is lying in this little game, Paul?"

Miller looked puzzled. "What about Brian?"

"Let's cut to the chase, Paul. I saw the two of you

standing over Miranda Bradford's body at the mansion. Heard you too. Afterwards, Brian and I had a nice chat. I know all about the Cyber Security Assurance Group and your work for the National Information Infrastructure. I know about Jerry Smith and the CIA's part in this thing."

Miller watched her, poker-faced. "That's interesting. What else do you know?"

Jeni slid cautiously from the wet sink, gun still trained on Miller. She leaned against the counter. She was pretty sure he couldn't see her exhaustion, her vibrating legs. "I know about the microchip."

Miller's cheek twitched imperceptibly.

"I know John Handle invented it for spying on foreign and domestic terrorist groups as part of his work for the bureau's NCIC sector. I know all about the Sprinter Corporation, the phony Searls Corporation and its shareholders . . . guys like newspaper magnate Irv Bradford, who contributed funds to the cause and who Handle is less than kindly disposed to. Shall I go on?"

Miller nodded. "By all means."

"I know what M-PEG 4 is and what it's meant to do. How employing it in every computer and thus in the hands of every citizen undermines the constitutional rights of those citizens, and I know that our friend Handle is not kindly disposed to that as well. I know you guys can't find him and stop him from blowing people up because he's a genius and keeps switching wavelengths on you, but I already knew that.

"I know your people nearly got me killed at the Statler Building, chasing me all over hell because your brilliant guy with the crane thought I was Handle. I know that John Handle is the brains behind this whole antiterrorist scheme and that you're fucked without him. And I know that Paul Miller is about as good at lying as he is in bed."

Miller raised a brow. "I'll take that as a compliment." He puffed out his cheeks acquiescently. "Well. You know a lot. And the source of this avalanche of hitherto privileged information is your ex-husband, Brian Starbuck?"

"Engendered under duress."

"From?"

"Having his nuts blown away in the family swimming pool. I told you, I overheard the two of you at the Bradford mansion."

"Brian brought you here? To use the computer to contact Handle?"

She thought about it. "Brian doesn't know about that part."

Miller stood now, began pacing the kitchen in his customary way. "Let me get this straight, Jeni. Brian Starbuck told you he arranged with the Bureau to assign him this cottage as a command post. To help trace and get a location fix on John Handle the Solobomber, is that correct?"

"It was a recently vacated crack house post according to Brian, but yes, that's about it."

Miller paced.

"I'm waiting."

"Exactly how much do you know about your ex-husband?"

She frowned.

He finally stopped pacing and leaned, arms folded, against the table edge. "I have been in constant contact with Charlie Beakman since my operation here in San Diego began. I know intimately everyone assigned to and connected with the Solobomber task force. Brian Starbuck is not among them."

She felt a familiar stab. "Are you saying you're not

working with Brian on this thing? I told you, I *saw* the two of you at the Bradford place."

"Brian's been trying to get with the task force for months. In fact, he's become a constant pain in the ass. Why do you think the Bureau sent him on that little vacation to China? Brian's not even supposed to be aware of our operation here. Unfortunately he's got internal connections and a Sprinter 9000 of his own. He can monitor Handle from his own location right along with the rest of us."

Her eyes narrowed. "You're saying he's not even *part* of the operation?"

Miller nodded. "That's right. I've done a lot of covering up for him. Like that night he showed up at the mansion after Handle killed Mrs. Bradford. He's a bit of a wild card. He knows—like you—too much about the facts. The Bureau would like him put out to pasture permanently. If they knew how much of a nuisance he really is, they would."

"Then why don't they?"

"Because I—my staff and I—cover for him. He's a good agent and an old friend. I'm damned if I'll let them retire him prematurely over a temporary setback incurred while doing his job. We've all suffered a little fatigue in this business, you should know that."

Jeni watched him calmly. "You're telling me the same kind of crap about Brian that he said about you."

Miller shrugged. "Maybe. Brian will say anything to be a part of this thing, keep his hand in his work. He's carrying around a lot of anger about losing this latest chance at promotion. Helping solve the Solobomber case could get it for him."

Jeni hesitated, thinking about her own headlong drive

to get involved, to be a part of something again. She could readily imagine Brian—any agent—doing the same.

Miller spoke gently. "I'm sorry, Jeni, I know you've both been through hell and this is just one more piece of bad news. All I can say is that, officially at least, Brian Starbuck is not part of this stakeout. The last I heard, in fact, Brian hadn't completed his mandatory leave of absence from the Bureau. Technically, he's not even supposed to be carrying a shield."

"What are you talking about?"

Miller studied her sympathetically, shook his head. "Jesus. They didn't even consult you."

"About?"

"Brian's been on leave for the past seven months, following his discharge in September."

She regarded him blankly. "Discharge from what?"

"From Veteran's General. Brian suffered a breakdown shortly after his second marriage. Apparently he assumed full responsibility for what happened. Took on all the attendant guilt with it."

"Guilt over the divorce?"

"Over Molly's death."

She felt a welling heat.

"The Bureau's had him under observation for months now. I can't believe no one informed you. I mean that's *cold,* ex-wife or not."

"Assuming I believe all this, what you're saying is, China was just to get him out from under your feet."

Miller sighed. "As I said, a kind of working therapy. He did okay for a couple of weeks, as an unofficial associate liaison. The Bureau thought the vacation might do him good—they could supply him a walk-through job that wasn't, strictly speaking, governmental. It didn't work out quite so well in the end. He overstepped, bungled a couple of small deals, no great damage. But the front office put him on a plane back here to California to resume convalescing. Marcia—his wife—has been wonderful, they tell me. And the kids have helped . . ."

Jeni found herself grinding her teeth. "Are you telling me Brian lied about his part with the Cyber Security Group? Are you saying he isn't really a part of the National Information Infrastructure, the—"

"There is no Cyber Security Assurance Group. I believe I have heard of the National Information Infrastructure, but Brian is certainly in no way connected with it. There is no antiterrorist campaign implemented by the government. There is no magical computer chip invented by John Handle. The Sprinter Corporation is a legal private enterprise, albeit an enormous one, but it certainly is not part of some massive government conspiracy. I mean, think how . . . outlandish that sounds. As for M-PEG 4, I have no idea what in hell that is. And as far as Jerry Smith's and the CIA's involvement, well, I have Jerry's home phone number, you can call him right now if you care to verify. Are you all right? You look pale."

She realized her knuckles were gripping the counter edge. "I'm fine, thanks." She regarded Miller evenly. "You smug sons of bitches. You're all so goddamn adroit at lying, aren't you? Part of the training, right? Built-in. Why should I believe you? Why should I believe any of this?"

"Would you like the number of Brian's doctor? It's classified, but I assumed they had at least informed you." He shook his head. "Jesus, the unfeeling bureaucratic pricks."

He moved toward her and she raised the gun rigidly. "Your phone numbers could be horseshit. I know the depths of deceit within the agency, at which stratum, and exactly how deep. I was with Treasury, remember?"

"Then you also know that we don't rat on our own. Or lie to them."

"But I'm not one of your own, am I, Paul? I'm the outsider. Just like Handle. It's me Handle communicates with, not you, not Brian, not Jerry Smith. He may be nutty as last week's fruitcake but I'm the one he's linked with, for whatever reason."

"Part of his game, to confuse us, throw us off. He knows we're close to cracking his code. You're a spanner in the works, a monkey wrench to complicate operations. Only it isn't working. Yes, we've had to watch out for you—include you at his insistence—but it hasn't slowed us down. You have no idea the number of brilliant minds working on this 'round the clock, Jeni. We're only hours now from locating him, stopping him."

"Stopping him from what? Blowing someone else up, or going to the *Times* with the cover-up? The truth is, you're still no closer now than you ever were to figuring out how he does it, how he manages to blow up buildings, people, without ever seemingly being there to set the charge. How he manages to walk through walls like a ghost, then detonate explosives with razor timing."

"We know how he does it. He sets them off by some form of remote control from a safe distance. Not terribly imaginative. Just cowardly."

"That doesn't explain how he gets the explosive planted in the first place. He's got the whole town terrified, locked up, and you stand around flat-footed."

"We'll know how he plants them when we catch him. And there is no secret government cover-up, Jeni. No magic computer chip. It's a madman's delusion. Don't let him suck you in like this."

"No? I let you suck me in pretty good. Of course, I was doing most of the sucking, as I recall."

"That had nothing to do with this. Don't demean a personal moment that holds great meaning for me."

She snorted, pushed away from the counter, still holding the weapon. She began pacing back and forth in front of Miller. "Why doesn't he go to the tabloids if he wants to expose this thing? Why this protracted game, this circuitous route using me as messenger boy? He's not a stupid man, what's he *doing*?"

"Getting us to chase our collective tails is what he's doing. You included."

She shook her head. "I don't buy it. It's not that simple."

Miller sighed. "Jeni, I need to see the computer."

She looked up at him . . . looked down at the gun in her hand. To show him the computer would be an act of betrayal. But to whom? Miller was here now, he'd find it eventually anyway. "That's how you knew to come here tonight, right? Brian's computer. You were monitoring Handle on it."

"Monitoring you. Your bank PIN code. I'm assuming that was Handle's idea, yes?"

"Yes."

Miller nodded. "Smart. He's been patching through the bank's computer system, overriding them, rerouting their circuitry to accommodate his own transmissions." He smiled ruefully. "The one path through cyberspace that was right under our noses."

"You never checked to see if he was using bank computers? That's hard to believe."

"We checked, but without enthusiasm. Trying to hack into bank systems is very difficult now. They keep changing their modems, constantly updating the personal identification number codes to protect their customers and themselves. Experienced hackers used to rip them off in the past. Only the genius-level pros attempt it now."

"But clearly Handle is a genius. You should have considered that."

"We considered it, we just didn't stay on top of it. It was such an obvious ploy it went right past us. Handle's terrific at hiding in plain sight. And we have limited manpower."

"But it was me you were monitoring?"

"Yes. Handle can transmit to you in relative anonymity from where he's hiding, via your bank's PIN code—he can do this and still block his signal from us. But when you transmit to him via your own computer, you make yourself and Handle vulnerable to our spotters. We picked up your signal tonight, traced you here."

"I gave away Handle's hiding place, then."

Miller looked chagrined. "Well, theoretically. But he's more than aware of the dangers. He'll cover his tracks, switch locations again. We believe he does it all the time. Anyway, he certainly won't be using the PIN code method of contacting you in the future."

"Then why bother with Brian's computer?"

"Routine. It may tell us something, who knows?"

Jeni mulled it over. But it was too late anyway. "All right. It's upstairs." She lowered the gun slowly.

On the way, Miller stooped to the cottage floor, retrieved something gleaming from the old carpet, and tossed it to Jeni. "Isn't this yours?"

She caught the discarded Ruger one-handed.

Upstairs, Miller checked over Brian's Sprinter carefully, running practiced fingers over the chassis, the monitor, over and under it, trailing fingertips down the wires and cables to the wall. He even got under the desk at one point and scrutinized the base, craning up through spiderwebs.

Finally, he switched the computer on, pulled the chair back for Jeni, gesturing. "Punch in your PIN code."

Jeni sat. Thought about it a moment, did as he asked.

The screen remained blank.

Miller nodded anticipation. "Like I said, he knows we're onto him now. I'm afraid your days of conversing with Mr. Handle are at an end. Doesn't matter. We'll have him within twenty-four hours."

"You sound very certain."

"When Handle answered your transmission he took a big risk. Even if he's left the immediate vicinity, we can nail the general area. He allowed himself to become very exposed this time, a dangerous move for him."

"He must have wanted to communicate with me pretty badly."

Miller grunted. He put a tentative hand on her shoulder. "You look tired. Have you been eating?"

"What about me, Paul? What are the Bureau's plans for me?"

Miller wandered to the bedroom window, peered out the curtain at darkened streets. "Technically they could put you in lockup. You're considered that much a security risk. A lot of people would be a lot less nervous if you were."

"I just moved you another inch closer to capturing Handle, according to your own admission."

He turned from the window. "Don't get cocky. Handle loves that." He smiled wryly, shook his head. "You are, Jennifer Starbuck, one enormous pain in the ass."

"You're not answering my question. What are you going to do with me?"

"I have this little problem. I'm very fond of you. I feel

responsible for you. You're a danger to me, yet I'm afraid for you. I'm a little afraid *of* you, too . . ."

Jeni returned the wry look. "Sounds like you're describing Handle."

Miller snorted. "Except that no matter how frustrating or enlightening, no matter how fascinating or infuriating, I never—right in the middle of it—have the least desire to make love to John Handle."

Jeni turned away from the perfect blue eyes. "Let's keep it technical, huh?"

"I think the thing that's going to hurt the most when this whole mess is over is the fact that I've lost your trust," he said.

She stared at the keypad before her. "Yeah, well, trust is a funny thing. Not exactly an abundant commodity these days in the best of situations."

Miller leaned against the window. "Frustrating, though, that we never really got the chance to have our private situation . . . not a normal one, anyway."

Jeni shrugged. "What's normal?"

"Having candlelight dinner with you at an open-air Hawaiian restaurant, walking in the surf afterwards . . . that sounds normal to me right now."

"Normal or therapeutic? You need a break from this. Any dinner would do, any beach."

"Maybe. But not any girl."

"Then where do we go from here?"

He pushed away from the sill. "Well, I should put you in safekeeping. The side of me that cares for you wants you under guard. The official side of me knows you're probably more valuable to the effort by staying here in this cottage. There's a chance, however remote, Handle will call again. And knowing you're a lady who loves chances, my guess is you'd prefer the latter."

"What about Brian?"

He patted the invisible smokes again. "Brian." He sighed. "I don't know. Christ, we're so close to ending this case, I can feel it. I hate to blow the whistle on a fellow agent at this late date, but he's gone way beyond ethics with this little freelance setup here. If the A.G. got wind of his private little command post it could be both our jobs."

"Or you could receive considerable kudos if his little command post helps capture Handle. Both you and Brian could gain by that." She cocked her head at him. "Sure you're not concerned that Brian might be upstaging you on this one? Bucking for a promotion of your own, perhaps?"

Miller shot her a level look. "Thanks. I've been busting my ass to keep the two of you out of considerable heat for just that selfish reason."

She shrugged.

"Okay. For tonight let's keep you here. Any chance at Handle at all is worth something. Just remember, this is a psycho we're dealing with." He moved to the desk, picked up the phone beside the computer, listened for a moment, hung up. "This is working. Here's my number." He handed her a card. "Anything gets weird, call. I'll have one of the team circle the block once an hour just to play safe. We can't use local cops—Handle's tapped into all their bands. But we'll keep a close eye on you, never fear."

"And if I hear from Brian?"

Miller looked tired, stopped patting for cigarettes and ran a hand through his hair. "Play along for now. Keep quiet about me, about tonight's raid. I'll deal with Brian when the time comes, but for now this is probably the best place for you. Is there anything you need?"

I need a hug from Coral, Jeni thought, from the little AIDS girl. But she's dead. "No. I'm fine."

"You've got food here?"

"Brian says there's food in the fridge downstairs."

"Okay." Miller straightened the cuffs of his coat in an elaborate stall. He looked nervous and bushed.

"What's the matter?"

"The matter. The matter is I'm very tired right now and want very much to kiss you. And I'm too fogbound at present to know if the moment is right. If you'd even want it."

She watched him. "Afraid of rejection?"

"Terrified."

Jeni pushed up, regarded him solemnly. "Why are men obsessed with solving all the world's problems simultaneously? You analyze the shit out of everything, then quake before intuition. It must be a dreadful way to exist. Why can't you just work through the moment?"

Miller puffed weary breath. "We're a whole other sex, I guess." He stretched, groaned. "And when you get to be my age, the moments grow increasingly finite."

She chewed her lip a moment as if considering something. Then moved to the bedroom door and opened it for him. "Go get some rest, you look like hell. I'm going to draw myself a scalding-hot bath and do the same."

He nodded, moved to the door. "Sounds very logical and prudent. You should be an agent."

At the last moment, he turned to her. "You're very strong, aren't you? Stronger than I knew."

She crossed her arms. "Strong enough."

He watched her thoughtfully. "Maybe stronger than all of us . . ."

Then waved once at the air and let himself out.

Chapter 21

The tall man waited for nightfall this time.

Not from necessity. The best-conceived crimes are oft performed during daylight's brightest hours. The awaiting of eventide, though, is inbred in us. The West Plains Indians had waited for nightfall before attacking, to mask their movements. Or so the movies had taught us.

The tall man's preference, however, lay in opposing tactics—not to mask, but to *blend*. Crime was more compatible with confusion, discordant movement. Crowds. He was a gregarious soul by nature.

Yet tonight's mission—the final, unrelated mission before the Big Bang—involved a kidnapping, and that could only be orchestrated in the wee hours, when the girl's guardians were minimally posted, the tall man's escape route cloaked by friendly shadow.

He stood in dewy, fresh-cut grass before the faux Roman columns of the imposing structure that sequestered her, and stared up at the softly glowing windows of her prison.

"Faux" was the operant word here. Someone had gone to a lot of trouble to imitate ancient Roman architecture . . . a kind of cross-purpose irony, since the Romans themselves had gone out of their way to imitate and steal from just about everyone else. These towering columns before him, he noted smugly, had been borrowed from the Doric, Ionic, and Corinthian. The famous Roman arches were taken from the Etruscans.

The tall man consulted the luminous dial of his watch. Nearly time now. He pulled his suit jacket closer under cool San Diego night. He waited. Waiting and patience were the spearheads of his operation. He returned his gaze to the building.

Probably an early-1930s erection. At least some semblance of craftsmanship had remained in those days before the war. His eyes scanned the veneered concrete. Not genuine Roman marble here, but cheaper brick, tile, pebbles, stucco, and plaster instead. Still, someone had tried. At least it lacked the ghastly geometry of Art Deco that had spread like a cancer after the World's Fair. And you couldn't beat good old concrete. The Romans themselves had run rampant with it, using this essentially cheap, adaptable material to develop everything from aqueducts to triumphal arches to the mammoth domes of the Pantheon.

Movement now at the main entrance broke his reverie. The tall man stepped back under tangled shadows of acacia.

A thin parade of dark suits filed out under ocean breeze to descend steps as high as the Capitol Building, following a curving glow of alabaster path to sodium-lit parking lot. Half an hour later, another parade, this time the umber uniforms of second-echelon guards. Silence then.

Which meant all but the one remaining security guard had departed the child's wing. The tall man made his move.

Entry was almost embarrassingly simple.

He strode silent halls through pools of evenly spaced light, not bothering to mask crisp footfalls of leather on marble, sounds a Roman governor might have made.

This single guard, a portly muscular man in his fifties, was caught himself off guard, though not totally by surprise. The tall man, ever the chameleon, looked the part— one of the remaining staff left behind to do paperwork or check on things. He held himself with that kind of confidence, approached the single, beefy guard with officious smiles, banishing all suspicion. Confidence and an easy, deliberate gait can work miracles, the tall man had learned long ago. Appear as though you belong somewhere, and so you will.

To the extent that he was able to pause leisurely in the child's doorway, look in upon her and engage the unsuspecting guard ("Harris, Ben," according to his black plastic lapel plate) in after-hour conversation, offering him a cigarette.

Guard Harris hesitated, clearly torn. "We're not really supposed to smoke in here."

The tall man grinned, shook out a Camel. "Come on, Ben, your secret's safe with me."

The guard accepted the smoke with grateful, even trembling fingers, inhaled deeply, blew blue fumes at the tall man beside him. "Sorry, what did you say your name was? I don't think I've seen you on the regular staff."

"Smith. Dick Smith. How much do you suppose she weighs?"

Guard Ben knotted slow-witted brows a moment, then craned around to look past marble doorway at the girl in the next room. "Her? Oh . . . sixty, seventy pounds maybe. Got a good solid frame on her."

"Yes. She's been well cared for."

"Well," Ben puffed modestly, "I can't take credit for that. We got other people see to that. I just walk my beat and signal upstairs if anything looks funny."

"Signal, Ben?"

"On my pager. It's a two-way. One of the new Sprinters."

"Ah, Sprinter! Exemplary corporation."

Ben the guard snorted. "You kidding? Wish I had stock in that baby! You ever watch the stock reports, Dick? Dow Jones averages?"

"Ben, in truth, I rarely have the time these days."

"Well, I can tell you that the Sprinter Corporation is way off the chart. Beating the hell out of the competition."

"That a fact?"

Guard Ben leaned close in conspiratorial tones, as though the deep, empty halls held invisible ears. "Listen, you ask me, the whole thing's a government monopoly."

The tall man feigned riveted interest. "You don't say. And how's that, Ben?"

"Hey, when was the last time you saw a corporation grow that fast? I mean, in the space of just two years, Sprinter's cornered the entire computer market. I know you're just a layman, Dick, but you ask me, this was a government deal from the get-go. Oh, yeah. Just like Iran-contra. Just like Waco. Know what I think Uncle Sam's up to?"

"Enlighten me, Ben."

Leaning close, the reek of tobacco enveloping the tall man, Ben muttered, "I think they're trying to corner the world market on these fancy new computers. Buy up all the little guys until the monopoly is complete."

"To what end, Ben?"

"To what end? To the *money* end, pal! Hey, it's just like the whole gasoline thing. You think the government doesn't control the world oil cartels? Way I heard it, gas is so plentiful you couldn't *give* the stuff away, the truth be known."

"That a fact?"

"Oh, yeah. Just like the Jews controlling the diamond

industry. They say the diamonds are so thick in certain parts of Africa you can literally pick 'em off the ground, trip over 'em. Course, you got to know where to look. But it's a scam, oh yeah. Everything's a scam in this country now. Been that way since they killed Kennedy."

"Well, you've certainly done your research, Ben."

"Bet your ass I research. Got to these days." Guard Ben nodded toward the next room. "Wouldn't surprise me if that little sweetheart in there is part of some bureaucrat's conspiracy."

"You think?"

"Hey, it goes all the way to the top. It's everywhere. They're omnipresent. You know what that means?"

"I believe I do, Ben. Tell me, you look like a man of veracity. What do you suppose the odds would be on spiriting away a little jewel like that in the next room?"

"Spiriting?"

"Stealing her, Ben. From the very people who stole her in the first place. I mean look at her. You can't treat a delicate young thing like that with the contempt of a damned commodity. What do you suppose the chances are of two fellows—two urbane connoisseurs like ourselves—removing her from this marble tomb? My bet is there are people who would pay much for her release. More than enough to make you rich, Ben, keep those fallen arches from falling further. What do you say?"

Guard Ben squinted. "Man, you serious?"

The tall man glanced furtively down both ends of the empty corridor. "Not a soul in sight, Ben. We could get her into my car within three minutes, no one the wiser. Green Chevy, parked right at the curb. I've got it all timed out. I excel in the area of things well timed. We could carry her together. You know, just in case she became unwieldy. What do you say, Ben! Partners in crime?"

Ben—face twisted strangely—was already reaching within his jacket for the pager.

The tall man—smiling anticipation—was there seconds before him, ice pick in hand.

He had come to regard the ice pick as a favored weapon, ever since the incident at the Bureau's NCIC headquarters.

Since that time, he'd learned to use it more adroitly.

He had Molly in the car in under three minutes with hardly a struggle. She said nothing and didn't appear to recognize him. She rode cooperatively against the backseat, streetlamps washing her bland, lovely brow, though it was impossible to speculate on what they might have done to her. Never mind. Soon she would be safe in her new home.

The tall man smiled satisfaction. Now it was the mother's turn . . .

Chapter 22

A shock of explosion awakened her, vaulting her upright, the concussion still rolling through her.

She sat stiffly within the little cottage bed, legs tangled in sheets, listening. The rumbling faded, became a growing, sibilant whisper, then the uneven musical timpani of rain across the eaves. Not an explosion. Thunder.

The cottage bedroom flickered with strobic flashes.

Jeni looked to the blinds to shut out the lightning, found the pale walls awash in rainbows of coruscating color. But not from the window. From the flashing computer atop the desk.

Bleary-eyed she stumbled toward it, trailing sheets.

She swept stray curls behind her ears and settled before the blinking, multicolored screen. It had come on again of its own accord. Was Handle attempting to signal her? If so he had failed; it was the thunder that had awakened her.

Abruptly the screen went blank again, the room swallowed in darkness.

Jeni sat blinking. "John? Is that you?"

She pressed a key marked: VOLUME. "John? Are you transmitting?"

The screen lit with letters:

WHY ARE YOU STILL IN THE
HOUSE?

Jeni dug cobwebs from her eyes. "John, can you see me? Is that how you knew someone was in the house tonight? Can you see and hear me from your location?"

THEY'RE ONTO ME—
BE HERE IN A FEW HOURS.
CAN'T USE AUDIO FREQUENCY
ANYMORE. YOU MUST GET OUT
OF HOUSE.

"John, listen to me. Paul Miller was here. He says Brian is—"

MILLER IS FULL OF SHIT.
THEY ALL ARE. STAY IN THE
HOUSE AND YOU WILL DIE.

"John, I need to ask you some questions."

POOR LITTLE JENI.
MILLER IS SO TALL, SO HANDSOME.
THOSE PERFECT BLUE EYES—
YET YOU STILL HAVE THESE
FEELINGS FOR BRIAN. SUCH
A BOTHERSOME CONFLICT OF
INTERESTS—AND WHO'S
TELLING THE TRUTH?
POOR JENI.

"You tell me the truth, John. Is there a government conspiracy as Brian said? Is Paul covering for him? Is the

Sprinter Corporation involved in illegal activity? Is there a secret antiterrorist operation involving computers?"

> WISH THERE WAS TIME FOR
> THIS—YOU ONLY HAVE A
> SHORT WHILE TO LIVE.
> DO NOT SACRIFICE
> MOLLY'S LIFE
> IN VAIN.

Jeni looked at the last words, stunned. "John. Do you know who killed Molly?"

> WHY DON'T YOU ASK THE
> FBI? IT'S ALL IN THEIR
> SECRET NCIC FILES.

"You've blocked the files, John. No one can get to them but you."

Silence from the Springer 9000. Then:

> STAND BY

The computer screen flashed red twice. Then blue. Then deep magenta letters bathed Jeni's face.

> FBI NCIC FILES
> FOR OFFICIAL USE ONLY!

Jeni held her breath.

> PLEASE PRESS YOUR
> POUND KEY

Jeni pressed the key.

The screen lit with a blue menu. She moved the cursor to the FILE icon.

ALPHABETICAL LISTING
OF ALL CURRENT FBI
PERSONNEL

"Who am I looking for? John? *I don't know his name.*"

YES YOU DO

She scrolled down the list of names, squinting in frustration, trying to make the connection. Names she knew, names she didn't know. When the cursor reached one name she knew, it froze.

Starbuck, Brian.

"No!" she said aloud.

STARBUCK, BRIAN
AGE: 38
HEIGHT: 6'1"
HAIR: BROWN
EYES: BROWN
ADDRESS: POINT LOMA,
SAN DIEGO

Jeni blinked.

A dull pain began at her sternum, fanned slowly outward.

The screen, as if in response to her cry, went abruptly blank.

"John! John, what the hell's going on! This can't be right. What are you trying to do to me? Goddamn it, John, *answer* me. Brian did not kill Molly. Brian did not kill his own daughter!"

The screen was silent.

"John, I am not leaving this house until you talk to me. I know you like me. Or feel sorry for me, or something, otherwise you wouldn't have kept me alive this long. What is it you're keeping me alive for, John? What is it you want from me? Talk to me, damn you!"

THE POWER IS
WITHIN YOU

"Why do you keep *saying* that! Just tell me the truth, no more riddles. Was Brian responsible somehow for Molly's death? Just tell me, I won't breathe a word of it, you have my promise."

MOLLY LIVES

Jeni stared at the screen, throat dry.

The screen went black. Then bloomed with a color photo of Jeni, Brian, and Molly smiling under summer skies, dressed in nautical attire. Coronado Bay, summer 1987.

The screen, like a slide projector, switched abruptly to a new picture: Brian and Paul Miller grinning companionably between a string of trout, a woodland thicket behind them. Jeni had never seen the picture before.

Black screen, then: a picture-postcard view of Washington, D.C., from the air.

Black screen, then: a ground-level view of the Washington Monument.

Blank, then: a squat, ugly corner building in Washington, which Jeni recognized as FBI headquarters.

Blank, then: A grainy black-and-white photo of a low-ceilinged room, flanked by rows of computer banks. A

small legend centered at screen bottom: NCIC HEAD-
QUARTERS: OFFICIAL USE ONLY.

Blank screen, then: a figure sprawled beside a swivel
chair before a console of computer screens. The figure's
clothes were drenched with red, though the surrounding
floor was perfectly neat, even fresh-waxed. Next to the
figure lay a common household ice pick.

Blank screen, then: A close-up of Brian Starbuck's
grinning face, a series of red numbers and abbreviations
below his official FBI passport photo.

"What are you doing?"

Jeni turned with a yelp at the voice behind her. Brian
stood in the doorway, hair matted to his forehead, rain-
water dripping from his clothing, a quizzical look on his
face. Behind Jeni, the computer beeped once and went
dead.

Outside, past the window, a low roll of thunder traced
the neighborhood in diminishing echoes.

"Brian? What—you're soaked."

He came toward her. "Is that Handle on the computer?"

She swiveled quickly, felt a surge of relief at the blank
screen, checked to make sure the machine was switched
off. "I was just fooling around. Trying some stuff." She
turned and forced a smile.

He stood over her, gazing at the screen silently. Rain-
water plopped on the keys. Jeni smelled the sweet odor of
just-wet streets from his jacket. "What are you doing up
so late, Brian? You're soaked through."

He turned to her, seemed to study her eyes a moment.
Then looked down at himself, began shrugging out of the
wet coat. "Storm caught me between the car and the
house. Had some late night paperwork to catch up on at
the office. Thought I'd swing by and check on you. Saw
your light. What's the matter, can't sleep?"

"It's this house. It got so close with humidity, even with the open window. I feel like a prisoner."

"So you killed time playing with the Sprinter. Could be dangerous."

She slid off the chair, moved quickly past the bureau, eyes on the nightstand beside the bed, the Ruger resting there. She continued past it to the bathroom. "I just get so bored. Would you like a towel? How about a drink?"

He was staring at the screen, back to her. She was thinking: How long had he been standing there in the doorway?

He finally turned. "A drink sounds good. Any food in the place? Something to make a sandwich with? I missed dinner."

Coming back out of the bathroom, she glanced at the Ruger but didn't make a move toward it. She tossed him a bathroom towel. "Is there a working refrigerator around here?"

"I think so, downstairs." He rubbed his hair dry. "Come on, let's investigate. You don't look sleepy anyway." And he smiled at last, hair a mop, and peeled off his wet jacket.

Jeni took it from him, hung it on a chair back, returning his smile.

Not feeling it. Not feeling the least relieved as they descended to downstairs darkness through the warning growls of the storm.

She hadn't visited the kitchen since her vigil in the cottage had begun.

Together, they found a working stove, an old brass kettle, two boxes of Lipton tea bags amid cobwebbed cupboards, and an overworked refrigerator containing half a carton of coagulated milk and a box of stale black donuts. A bottle of Johnnie Walker Black rested on the counter.

Brian sniffed the donuts, winced. "Anything in the lower fridge?"

Jeni was stooped low, foraging in metal bins. "Here's a loaf of bread . . . looks unopened." She pulled apart plastic, sniffed a slice. "Smells okay. I could make us sandwiches if we could find something to put between the bread." She looked up at him hopefully. "Maybe we should just go out . . ."

Brian was reaching deep into the fridge. "In this weather? Ugh. Here's a jar of mayo that looks decent." He checked the inside door, flipped up plastic lids. "Hey, a pack of Kraft cheese slices! Now all we need's some meat."

Jeni straightened, shook her head. "That's it. Not even a can of Spam."

"I was sure Beaky said there was plenty of meat in the freezer." He pulled open the freezer unit, found only ice-encrusted trays.

Jeni looked about, spied the basement door. "Maybe the freezer's in the basement."

Brian followed her gaze. "This place has a basement?"

"Looks like it. Shall I check?"

"All right." He turned to the counter. "I'll see to our drinks."

Halfway down the cellar steps the house rocked with another ear-splitting jolt of thunder she felt through the soles of her shoes. The lights flickered . . . dimmed . . . came up again. Jeni slowed on the scarred steps, imaged—remembering the Statler Building—being trapped down here amid musty cobwebs and darkness. She had a penlight in her purse upstairs, should have brought it.

She stepped onto chill concrete floor, gazed about under the dull illumination of a single dust-encrusted bulb:

deep, stretching shadows, a labyrinth of debris and discarded keepsakes. Either the occupants had just moved and left their cellar junk to the FBI, or the house was on loan. Probably the Bureau had paid them for a Disney World vacation. Whoever the owners were, they must be fairly elderly, some of the piles of antique lamps and sewing machines and trunks looked turn-of-the-century.

Another guttural roll of thunder.

Jeni could hear the drum of rain increase in volume above her. It was going to be a good Southern California soaker. They needed the rain, she mused absently, moving across cracked concrete amid pools of shadow; the hills and arroyos were yellowing, a potential fire hazard, something Southlanders had come to live with.

"How we doing down there!" his voice just audible from above.

"Mildew and spiders!" she hollered back. "No freezer yet!"

A stutter of lightning revealed a series of greenish, ground-level windows ringing the cellar walls. She could squeeze through one of them, be out into the storm, safely away from here in minutes.

But you're safe right here, Jeni.

Right. She believed in nothing anymore. In no one. The weight of it a mountain on her back.

The windows lit brilliantly, followed by an A-bomb shock of thunder that left her gasping. The lights flickered . . . flickered . . . Winked out.

She stood in blackness. "Shit! Not *again*!"

She heard rustling above her. "Hold on! I'll find the fuse box!"

She stood impotently in opaque void, dark as a well bottom. She was beginning to feel like one of those mole rats on the *National Geographic*.

She knew growing unease. How cavalierly civilized man regarded everyday miracles like the incandescent bulb . . . how abruptly lost he was in its absence. How much its slave.

A finger of window lighting threw ocher shards at her. She glimpsed a dull length of white—a porcelain gleam in one corner of the cellar—before blackness snatched it away again. "Brian! I think I've found the meat freezer!"

She inched forward squinting, guessing at directions, awaiting the next aerial flash from outside. When it came she was ready. Yes, definitely a long, casket-sized freezer unit of some kind just over there in the corner. She wished she had the damned penlight.

She blind-walked, hands outstretched, trusting the image still etched on her retina.

The window lit brightly, followed by attendant thunder. The swaying bulb blinked on again. *"Hooray!"* from upstairs.

Jeni approached the gleaming length of freezer, heard now the rhythmic chug of its motor. A good sign.

She found the latch quickly, tugged up the heavy lid with a grunt.

The bulb flickered again, dimming the cellar to deep shadow. Even so, Mrs. Grindle—a grinning mummy now—beckoned livid and green from her frost-lined coffin.

Jeni started—the lid slipped from nerveless fingers, thumped shut. The bulb dimmed to black again and she was alone with the thing in the freezer.

An arrhythmic pounding behind her. She whirled.

Under strobic flashes, she beheld Brian leaping the cellar steps, eyes lit demonic with yellow lightning. He clutched a bright length of ice pick.

The Ruger, fully loaded—cleaned and ready—lay atop the bedroom bureau. Two long stories above her.

Chapter 23

"Freeze!" she cried reflexively.

Footfalls advanced on her . . . hesitated.

"Just stay where you are, Brian, I've got a Ruger trained on you!"

"Jeni?"

Rain sheeted loudly against the windows behind her. If she could reach them in the darkness . . .

"Jeni, what the hell are you doing?"

"Just stay put, Brian! I've seen the old woman. I know all about the guard at NCIC headquarters. Handle showed me everything on the computer, ice pick included. Now, I want you to put the pick on the floor. Now! Do it!"

"Fine. All right. There."

"I want to hear it rolling toward me."

"On its way." A metallic tumbling sound.

Jeni knelt, swept the floor blindly before her, located the wooden handle. "Now your service revolver . . ."

"Jeni, you know an agent never surrenders his—"

"Now!"

She heard metal sliding across concrete until it brushed her fingers. She breathed-in relief, straightened, broke the weapon, and checked the wheel with her fingertips. Full, except for the empty safety chamber. She snapped it shut. "Guess what, Brian? I was bluffing. Now I want you to raise your hands and back up very slowly to the stairs . . . you may use one hand to reach behind you and feel for the wooden banister. Do it now!"

"Jeni, calm down—"

"Do it now, damn you, or I'll blow your lying ass away!"

Footfalls advanced on her.

"Goddamn it, Brian, I'm not bluffing this time! I'm sick to death of screwing around in the dark with you agency assholes!"

The footfalls stopped somewhere in the abyss ahead of her. "Okay. Easy now. Let's talk about this. What's this about an old woman?"

"You know goddamn well what. You've been using her house as a private command post. Apparently she didn't take to the idea. So you put her on ice. Nice. Now, I want to hear the sound of you backing up."

Silence.

A match flared, Brian's face became a livid Mardi Gras mask.

"Stay back! Move to the stairs!"

He ignored her, came forward across gray concrete, the match head throwing grotesque shadows.

"I mean it, Brian!"

He nodded amid billowing shapes. "Then I guess you're just going to have to shoot me, Jeni." He moved past her. Jeni jumped aside, stiff-armed. Brian stopped before the pale length of the freezer unit. He unlatched the lid, hefted it. "Jesus . . ."

He craned to Jeni. "Who is she?"

"Don't play dumb with me, asshole!"

Brian sighed, turned to the corpse again, finally thumped the lid shut—winced pain, shaking the match from his fingers. The cellar plunged into familiar darkness.

"Jeni, listen to me—"

There was a sound of footsteps on the stairs.

In blackness, Jeni felt Brian move close. He whispered, "Just stand easy, now . . ."

Footfalls descended evenly, deliberately, to the basement floor. Paused.

Jeni stepped back, gun hand swiveling back and forth between Brian's voice and the sound on the stairs.

"I'm an FBI agent," Brian threatened officiously. "There are weapons trained on you. Stand where you are!"

More movement from the stairs. A rattling sound, soft cursing, then the cellar bulb came flaring on again. Paul Miller stood at the foot of the stairs, hand inside the metal circuit breaker box adjacent the banister. He held his service Colt before him.

Brian drew relieved breath, muttered something derisive.

Miller snorted, nodded at Jeni. "Some FBI agent. Looks like she took your gun from you."

Brian dusted his sleeves distractedly. "Couldn't stay away from her for five minutes, that it, Miller?"

Miller came across damp concrete, held out his hand to Jeni. "I'll take that, thank you . . ."

Jeni hesitated . . . backed away, gun leveled. "What's . . . going on?"

Miller glanced at Brian. Brian glanced back.

Jeni stepped back another foot, eyes on both of them. "Oh, this is great! The *two* of you! Fine! What are you going to do, kill *me* now?"

Miller ignored her, came around the side of the freezer. "What have we here?"

Brian lifted the lid for him one-handed. "Our friend left us another present."

Miller bent close, examined the frozen face. Nodded. "May I present Mrs. Agatha Grindle. Age, eighty-three. Late of Ocean Beach, California. Probable cause of death: suffocation."

Jeni clutched her gun. "Who is she?"

"I told you. Been looking for her for the past week . . . her and her meat freezer. They've been missing from her Ocean Beach cottage since the fourteenth. Handle's last hiding place before his present location."

"Which is where?" she demanded.

Miller shrugged. "We're still looking."

Jeni took the lid from his hand and slammed it shut. She steadied the gun, leaned against the unit between the freezer and the two agents. She assessed them levelly. "You're in it together, aren't you? You've been working on it together from the beginning."

Miller shouldered his weapon, gave Brian a jaundiced look. "Not exactly together. Your ex here tread well past the line of professional discretion. Most of the time I've been covering his sorry ass from the A.G." Miller produced a penlight from his coat, swept the cellar floor with it.

Something caught the corner of Jeni's eye. Still holding the weapon, she knelt before the freezer, reached behind one of the porcelain legs, pulled at something attached to it by a length of elastic string. She held it up to the dusty bulb: a small tag like those used for airport luggage. She handed it to Brian. "Read it."

"Brinkman Movers—San Diego's Finest. Move anywhere, in town or out."

"Look here at the cellar floor," Miller called, then directed his light downward at their feet. "Trail of scuff marks from here to the stairs. He had the old woman moved here, all right. Sometime when the place was unoccupied."

Jeni turned to her ex. "Why'd you come running downstairs at me a few minutes ago brandishing an ice pick?"

Brian dusted his hands absently. "I heard you drop the lid. I called out, but the storm masked it."

"Why the pick?"

"I was cleaning out the refrigerator freezer, making us some drinks, remember?"

Miller made a speculative sound. "Having drinks. How cozy."

Brian ignored him. "Besides, I had the service revolver under my jacket. Use your training, Jeni."

She felt a familiar rising heat. She was the third wheel again. Day late and a dollar short. She'd been used. Just how much and in what way, not yet completely clear to her. But she felt certain the news would get worse.

Brian slipped the mover's tag into a plastic bag, turned to Jeni. "How long ago did you speak with Handle?" he demanded.

Jeni considered.

Miller turned to her, tone in league with Brian. "Jeni, this is not the time to be protecting your psycho pen pal. Please answer him. How long since you spoke with him over the upstairs computer?"

She felt another flush of anger, felt like drilling them both. She turned to Brian coldly. "I was talking with him when you walked in tonight out of the rain. Or he was talking with me, anyway."

Miller nodded. "No audio, right? He knows we've picked up his audio frequency. He should be in custody any minute now."

Miller pulled a two-way from his pocket, punched a key. "Echo-Fox-Four. Yeah, Miller here. We've found the old lady. Right. At SAC Starbuck's Offsite. The mover's address tag matches. How goes it on your end? Good. Stay in touch."

He pocketed the radio, looked up to find himself under Jeni's icy glare. "Easy. I know you're angry, but—"

"Angry? You used me! All this time you've been in constant contact with each other. Sharing information. All *kinds* of information, no doubt. Swapping snappy stories about the stupid 'split tail' from San Diego? Oh sorry, they don't call female agents that in California, do they? They call them 'skirts,' or is it 'breast-feds'? Sorry, fellas, I'm a little out of the loop here, not up to speed with current Bureau jargon."

Brian stepped toward her cautiously. "It hasn't been like that, Jeni."

"No? How has it been, Brian? I'm dying to hear the next lie."

Miller turned from examining the floor. "Not everything's been a lie, Jeni."

"Really, Paul! How gratifying. Give me one isolated incident of veracity. I'm *dying* to hear it. In fact, I'm probably *dying* period, right?"

"We're not lying now," Brian told her. "If you don't trust Paul or me, you can contact the A.G. personally. I'll give you the private phone number."

Jeni snorted. "And the A.G. is *beyond* lying, of course!" She shook her head caustically. "In it together from the beginning. Christ, you make some pair." She tucked the gun in her waistband.

Miller endured the gibe patiently. "What are you accusing us of, Jeni? Cheating? It takes two to cheat, as I recall . . ."

Brian shot him a warning look. "Knock that off, Paul." Then to Jeni: "Before you start taking potshots, try to remember something. Yes, there's been untruths on the Bureau's part. But it was done to protect not only you but the lives of everyone in this city, perhaps the entire nation."

Jeni waved him off. "Save your patriotic paeans for the uninitiated masses, Special Agent in Charge Starbuck. Just level with me about one thing. Did you or did you not do hospital time for a nervous breakdown? Or is that bullshit too?"

Brian nodded. "I did some fatigue time at Veteran's, yes. I wouldn't exactly describe it as a breakdown. The Bureau thought the rest would do me good. After Molly's death, I tried to keep myself occupied, keep my mind off it. I went a little overboard with late hour work, burning the candle at both ends."

He paced around the freezer's scuff marks, hands on his hips. "Anyway, it turned out to be a fortuitous event where Handle was concerned. We put my hospital stay and China vacation in the pipeline, knowing Handle would pick it up. Meanwhile, I began working covert on the case as soon as I was released. It was the perfect cover." He looked slightly chagrined. "Or so we thought."

She turned to Miller. "And the Sprinter Corporation, the cover-up, computer conspiracy, the magic chip?"

Miller hesitated, ran a hand through his hair.

"Oh for chrissake," Brian groaned, "tell her, Paul! She's been lied to enough, goddamn it! And what has it accomplished? What has it gained you besides confusion? Quit being a company man for one minute of your life and talk to the woman!"

Miller blew out indecisive breath, turned a tight circle, wrestling with it. "Okay. But goddamn it, Jeni, I did what I was trained to do as a federal agent. A special agent in charge under extremely clandestine conditions. Brian had no right leaking that kind of sensitive information. It's a

privilege to carry this shield, dammit! A privilege your ex
forgot on occasion. When you're given classified information, you keep it classified. You tell no one." He
looked at Jeni. "Not even someone you love. Information
like that can get you killed."

Brian made a face. "Not any less efficiently than the
way you people were killing her!"

Miller ignored him. "Jeni, you simply can't imagine
the repercussions . . . the enormity of this thing. The importance of discretion where this project is concerned is
incalculable, absolutely vital. It makes the secrecy surrounding the Manhattan Project look like kindergarten
stuff. The Stealth fighter pales beside this. Everything
pales beside this. This is global. Monstrous."

She watched him coolly. " 'Monstrous' is the word."
She looked at each of them. "So Paul covers for Brian
when he's out of line, and Brian covers for Paul to protect
the project. Swell. Did you also cut your fingers and share
blood under a full moon?"

Miller's face grew tight. "Innocent little Jeni, on the
other hand—pure as the driven snow—never lied once
during her term with the ATF, right?"

"I said, lay off her," Brian warned.

Miller glared at him. "Hey, *pal*! You ran out on her after she lost her only child, left her flat right in the middle
of her most vulnerable time! Where do you get this
holier-than-thou shit?"

Brian looked as though he might actually hit Miller,
but Miller gave him his back, turned to Jeni. "As for who
was sleeping with whom, as far as I'm concerned that's
still a private matter. I'd appreciate it if it ceased to be
a topic of public conversation." He regarded both of
them. "I'm ashamed of nothing I did. Your own con-
sciences are . . . well, your own."

Brian made a rueful grunt. "The succinctly pious Agent Miller."

Jeni found herself suddenly weary to her bones, weary of all of it. Who were these guys? "Whose idea was it to get me out of town?"

Brian shrugged. "More or less a joint effort, I guess. Paul was concerned you'd stumble onto the truth sooner or later, I was afraid for your safety." He caught Miller's glare. "And yes, to be fair, vice versa."

Jeni turned to her ex. "I'm curious. What was the impetus to start telling me the truth, Brian? You surely realized the jeopardy you were placing your career in. And we *all* know how important your career is to you."

Brian considered, finally threw up his hands. "I hate lying. How's that?"

"Not good."

"All right, how's this, then—the lying was working against us, becoming so convoluted we couldn't keep our own stories straight. You were a real ringer, Jeni. A danger to the operation, but a valuable asset in connecting with Handle. But for all that, we were flagrantly breaking the law by involving a civilian with clandestine work. So off you went."

Jeni nodded ruefully. "Off I went."

"When that didn't work, when we found you weren't going to cooperate with the idea of leaving town, I began an immediate campaign to get you reinstated, make you part of the team. Trouble was, I couldn't get anyone to back me." He looked askance at Miller.

"Washington thought your civilian status more prudent," Miller told her. "They didn't want to rock the boat, risk losing your magical bond with Handle. I agreed."

"And Brian, you were a legitimate part of the operation from the first?"

Brian nodded. "Paul and I both command our own posts. Miller is SAC of his squad. I work rogue out of this cottage and the house in Point Loma. My cover is semi-retired FBI agent. Officially, I'm even deeper cover than Miller. His team doesn't know I'm on the case. As the theory goes, the less people know, the less chance it gets to Handle." He smiled wryly. "As the theory goes."

Jeni nodded. "But Mr. Handle is a wild card. Has *he* ever been truthful about anything to your collective knowledge?"

Miller regarded the meat freezer. "The truth from a psychopath is like the horizon that keeps receding the closer you get. The problem with being a wacko is most of the time you don't know yourself what the truth is, much less reality. Half-truths can be the most dangerous kind of all."

Jeni looked behind her. "But you think he killed the NCIC guard? And the old woman here in the freezer?"

"We know he did the guard, and probably the old lady. We're guessing he posed as a renter, knocked off the owner, and set up shop in her cottage with his computer. Used every ounce of his genius to shield his frequency from us while he set about wiring the city. He got to you—got around us—through your bank PIN code. Then when he found out we were onto that, he cut out. But not before having the freezer shipped here."

"To make Brian look like a psycho? That's pretty far out."

Brian smiled. "Yeah? You bought it, didn't you? Never underestimate Handle's ability to fuck with the human psyche."

Jeni pushed away from the freezer with an uncon-vinced air. "I don't know. I don't know about you two." She turned. "Little too pat, Handle leaving that mover's tag there to be so conveniently found. How do I know one of you didn't put it there?"

The two agents smiled ruefully. "You're missing the point," Brian told her. "Of course it was meant to be found! Handle never sets up an elaborate joke unless he's sure he knows the victim will get it."

She thought about it, considering, mind racing. Internally she felt stalled, hesitant—part of her still reluctant.

She decided to surrender to the urge. She was tired of all the lies. Tired period. "He told me Molly's alive."

Brian looked up sharply. "That's crap. He's mad, Jennifer."

"Is he?"

Brian's tone was brittle with anger. "Our daughter's dead, Jeni. I was there."

"You were unconscious for a time after the accident. Her body was burned beyond—"

He whirled emphatically. "Molly's dead, Jeni! Dead! Goddamn it, I'm not going to let this lunatic hurt you further! You've been hurt enough! By all of us!"

She turned away, paced back to the white length of freezer, gazed at it absently. She leaned against the porcelain edge, aware of the softening patter of the rain above. The storm was passing. She felt strangely detached, removed. Everything passes . . . everything passes . . . time is only a dimension . . . nothing is real . . .

She couldn't believe she'd ever allowed these men to touch her. She couldn't believe she wasn't more angry about it now. Only strangely numb. The whole thing was already beginning to assume the gauzy aspects of a dream. Yet it had happened. And Paul, at least, seemed genuinely regretful. Even Brian appeared sincere.

Sincere. Latin extract?

Yet something in life had to hold sincerity and meaning;

something had to stand for truth, cohesion, else what was the point?

Maybe there is no point, kiddo . . . how do you explain little AIDS-ridden Coral? How do you explain Molly?

"How far upstream does it go? To the White House?"

Brian cut Miller off before he could answer. "I'm not going to lie to you anymore, Jeni. So I'm just not going to answer that question for the moment. I suspect you'll know the answer before the night is out. If you survive." He sighed. "If any of us do."

She looked up with alarm. "Survive?"

Miller stepped in. "We have reason to believe Handle's up to something big. And that it's going to happen very soon. It might involve all of San Diego, maybe even parts of San Juan Capistrano and L.A., we're not certain yet."

"He has that kind of power?"

"Claims he does. We have to assume the worst. Unless we get to him first."

She felt deep, inner chill. "He's got the entire *county* wired? And no one's detected the detonation devices yet? How can that be possible? What have you people been doing?"

Brian's pager went off. "Yeah?" He listened, nodded, looked abruptly shocked. "Now? All of us? Even her?" He listened. "All right." He put the pager away, looked at Miller. "He wants to see us. All of us."

Miller balked. "Jeni too?"

"Jeni too. Now."

Jeni looked from one to the other of them. "Who's 'he'?"

Brian gestured. "Come on. It's high time you experienced the whole operation."

Miller was consulting his watch. "In the next hour or so, it won't make any difference anyway."

Brian held out his hand to his ex-wife. "Mind if I have that back? I'd as soon the director of the FBI didn't know someone took my piece from me."

Jeni genuflected. "The director? He's here in San Diego?"

Brian grunted. "*Everyone's* here in San Diego."

They headed upstairs, Brian shouldering his weapon. "Where?" Jeni wanted to know. "The central command center?"

Miller nodded. "You could call it that."

Brian grinned mirthlessly as they headed to his car through shifting curtains of rain. "You'll get a boot out of this, Agent Starbuck," he told her. "Welcome to the real world."

They headed down Pacific Highway toward the Embarcadero, Miller at the wheel of his Plymouth, Brian beside him.

Jeni, in the back, watched neon-streaked blacktop through the warbled smear of her window. The storm was shifting, not giving up after all. They headed through light downtown traffic, toward the bay, the diamond tips of spreader lights becoming visible as they approached, reflecting the dark waters of the channel, the marinas. Soon she made out the lazily rocking shapes of ships, rich men's schooners, two-masted ketches and yawls. "Is this where you put me in cement overshoes and dump me in the bay?"

Brian grunted behind thwacking wipers. "This is where you get a free pass to cyberland, Agent Starbuck. Some would say it's the equivalent of drowning."

The bright facade of the San Diego Convention Center swam into view down the avenue, its big yellow "Comp Con II!" sign still fluttering above the entrance, the

constant mill of people still present. To her surprise, the
Plymouth slowed past the trolley tracks, pulled before
the curb and the big red LED electric crawl: WELCOME
COMPUTER CONVENTIONEERS! Miller cut the engine. The
two men turned to her from the front seat.

Jeni blinked. "This is the command center? A convention for cyber dweebs?"

Brian climbed out on his side. "A little respect, please.
These dweebs are the best chance we've got of nailing the
ubiquitous Mr. Handle."

Miller came around the side of the door, opened her
side for her. "Just play dumb now, Jeni. You're with us.
We'll do the talking." He reached into his jacket and
handed her a yellow ribbon attached to a white card pro-
claiming: "Cyber Convention Official." "Pin that to your
blouse."

As they turned toward the crowded entrance the ground
shook beneath them concussively, a knocking echo rolling
in from the east. A simultaneous "Oooo" welled from the
crowd on the convention steps, all eyes turned eastward
momentarily, followed by nervous laughter.

"Thunder," Brian muttered.

Miller exchanged a brief look with him.

Then, guiding Jeni, they stepped past the girl in the
ticket booth imperiously and marched directly through
the convention doors past the young guard, who nodded
in recognition at their yellow tags.

Inside, they crossed a narrow, crowded foyer filled
with milling conventioneers, then pushed past another
stationed guard through two large swinging doors into the
main convention room. The sight was impressive.

The entire first floor of the center—a building the size
of a football field—was packed elbow-to-elbow with
conventioneers, young people and old, tall and short, of

every race and creed, all seated at dozens of tables before hundreds of brightly lit computer screens, fingers busily tapping at keyboards, clicking mouses, downing cup after cup of Coke or coffee. At rough guess, Jeni estimated somewhere in the neighborhood of three thousand computers and their attendant operators.

She walked with Miller and Brian across the main floor to a short flight of stairs where they climbed to the first-level mezzanine for an overview. She had an instant's déjà vu: that first moment in the little sweatshop, Hispanic women bent before their sewing machines . . . that sensation squared to infinity as she paused at the polished brass rail and gazed down at the concerted heads of the operators, each before a winking screen.

A drifting blue haze traced the ceiling, despite numerous "No Smoking" signs posted on support columns between operators' tables: Jeni got the sense rules were low-priority just now, so intent were the officials on reaching their objective. And there were officials everywhere, walking casually amid the tables, smiling convivially, dressed in suits not unlike many of the conventioneers. But she could spot an agent anywhere.

She shook her head in bewilderment at the endless rows of blue and green monitor screens. "All these people are working for the government? All trying to break Handle's code?"

Miller leaned for a moment against the rail beside her, gazed down, expression as awed as her own. "They work for us, all right. It's just that most of them don't know it."

She looked askance at him.

Miller nodded at the scene below. "The convention is real. It was planned months ago by the San Diego Cyber Society as part of their annual event. We just sort of commandeered it."

Brian joined them on Jeni's other side of the rail. "We talked to the heads of the convention, explained, without going into detail, that this was an emergency government operation, that we needed as many talented computer minds as we could get in as short a time as possible. The convention was the answer."

Miller concurred. "We got the sponsors to hold a little contest. Each of the conventioneers was given a list of Handle's possible code prefixes, then challenged to break them. Of course, they've no knowledge of anything about John Handle, to them it's just a fun convention game."

"What's the prize?" Jeni asked.

"Three thousand dollars and a free subscription to *Cyber Monthly*," Brian said. "As you can see, we had no trouble getting volunteers. Very competitive, these cyber dweebs."

She looked down at the multitudes. "Three thousand dollars for helping save the world. Who are these people, where do they come from?"

"From all over the country," Miller told her. "From every walk of life. There are amateur housewives down there and seasoned hackers. Some of the latter have jail records. Some of them—the best ones—have skipped parole. They don't know we know, but we know. And no uniform is going to yank them away from those screens until we say so. Some of our 'conventioneers' were even recruited from jail officially."

Abruptly the building shuddered lightly under their feet. The overhead lights flickered momentarily, then regained their original brightness. The rows of computer screens— each attached to its individual surge suppressor—remained unaffected. A thousand hands stopped typing momentarily, looked up . . . then, as the ceiling lights expanded again, resumed tapping simultaneously, focused as Las Vegas gamblers before one-armed bandits. Brian turned stone-faced to Miller. "Thunder?"

Paul Miller gestured toward the hall. "Maybe a small quake. Come. His Majesty summons . . ."

They led Jeni down the richly carpeted hall past a series of oak-paneled double doors to a smaller, innocuous door boasting a "Janitorial Supplies" plaque. Miller knocked once, and—with another sense of impending déjà vu—Jeni allowed herself to be ushered through the little gray door.

It opened into a spacious conference room, trimmed in mahogany paneling, highly polished oak desk, framed photos of sepia-toned cityscapes of an earlier, bygone San Diego.

Jeni recognized him immediately from pictures she had seen of him.

"Welcome, Agents Miller and Starbuck," the silver-haired, impeccably dressed figure stated softly. "And welcome, too, Agent Jeni Starbuck. It is my pleasure to reinstate you to the ATF." He reached for her and took her hand. "I am FBI Director Sanford Manners. I don't believe we've met, but I'm quite impressed with your reputation."

Jeni shook his hand, which was cold and soft. "As I am with yours."

Sanford motioned them into their seats, offering Jeni the one closest to him.

"I'll get right to the point, since we haven't much time," he said, his voice showing no strain, as if he were entertaining in his garden rather than trying to prevent a terrorist from taking over the city. "We created John Handle, Jeni. *We,* not the CIA. We groomed him, set him up with the opportunity to let his genius shine. And he created an antiterrorist strategy that is so pure in its genius that it rivals the best of Edison's work. It is, quite simply, the most advanced weapon for both domestic and international security of this century. Don't ever forget that. Don't let the fact that Handle betrayed us, that he is a psychopath and put both the achievement and the country in danger, detract from its initial importance. It would have been—it *will be*—the FBI's finest contribution to this nation and its people. It runs as deep as the very foundation of democracy and freedom."

Jeni cleared her throat. "Sir, if I might . . . John Handle was a psychopath before the Bureau 'discovered' him."

Manners nodded. "Yes, and we take full responsibility for that. We should have monitored him more closely. We were caught up in the excitement. It was a mistake and we're paying for it now." Manners ground his teeth, making his left cheek dent. "Geniuses are supposed to be eccentric. We made our share of mistakes. Mistakes we will rectify." He looked at her levelly. "Because we can't afford to lose this one, Jeni, this incredible instrument of defense. Not today, not in a world ruled by the computer. And we can't afford to lose the months and years of carefully orchestrated covert glue that has held it together. Secrecy, Jeni, despite what the common citizen may believe, is not an evil concept. It is, properly used, an invaluable tool. This country has been *run* by covert operations since before World War II."

"I'm aware of that, sir."

Manners nodded. "I know you are. And our friend John Handle knows it too. Why he has chosen you as his latest obsession I cannot know, nor do I frankly care." He glanced at his watch. "Whatever the case, in less than thirty minutes, that red phone on the table beside you is going to beep. John Handle is going to be on the other end." He looked levelly at her. "And you, Jeni Starbuck, are going to pick it up."

Jeni stared at the small red phone. "He wants to talk to me?"

"He does and he will. Because you are going to cooperate with this prick and we are going to get our antiterrorist program back on-line. You will please acknowledge the order, Jeni."

She appraised him. "Order?"

"You're one of us again, Jeni, remember?" He smiled. "Are you bucking for a promotion already?"

Jeni shook her head. "I'm not bargaining, sir. I don't want the post back."

"All right, what is it you do want? Name it. A new house in the country? A stable? Cars?"

Jeni stared at him, incredulous.

"I can arrange them for you, Jeni."

She looked down at her lap. She was experiencing that caved-in feeling again, that nearly out-of-body sensation. What on earth was she doing at the San Diego Convention Center talking to this strange man? . . . this legend, this leader of the country's most powerful organization, a man more myopic than her grandfather? "What I'd like . . . as a civilian, as a woman . . . is just simply to be asked. Instead of told. To be recognized, feel that my opinion matters. That's all I'd like."

"Very well. I'm asking you, Jeni. Help us."

"And if I refuse?"

"But you won't."

"But if I do, you'll go ahead and order me anyway, correct?"

"Yes, that's correct." He smiled, not a nice smile, and leaned down to the table, his shadow falling over her. "Do not underestimate the extent to which I can make a life truly miserable, Jeni. Yes, even a civilian life. It's easier than you can imagine."

Jeni held his gaze. "Not at all, sir, I can imagine it quite well."

Manners's smile widened, exposing perfectly shaped, perfectly white incisors. "I do hope, in this case, I shan't have to." And he reached between them and covered her hand with his own briefly before Jeni pulled it back. It was the temperature of marble, his hand.

Manners was watching the board again, back to her. "As soon as this thing is over, I'm sure we can find sufficient funds within the Bureau for some kind of vacation, or whatever else it is you need. But for now, for the country, and the sake of your child, you will cooperate, yes?"

Jeni's eyes jerked to him. "My child? You know about Molly?"

"I do."

"Handle told you he has Molly?"

"Your husband told me."

Jeni sagged. "Ex-husband. And it could all be lies. I'm the one that told Brian."

Manners shrugged. "Nevertheless, a risk worth taking, I'm sure you'll agree."

Jeni lifted her eyes slowly, a light dawning. Was that an ace she just felt being dealt?

Manners watched her impassively.

"Well. Looks like Mr. Handle has got me exactly where you want me."

"Interpret however you wish, Jeni. I know personally I'd find it impossible not to seek out any possibility my own child was still alive, no matter how remote."

Yes, she thought, I'm sure you're counting on that. "What is it I'm to say to Handle?"

Manners turned confidently, aglow now that he had

her. "The ball's in his court. I assume he has some kind of compromise in mind, some order of clemency in trade for information. We grant him immunity, he promises not to blow anyone else up, that sort of rubbish. We'll agree, of course."

Then go back on your word, she thought.

Manners was studying the blank board, muttering to the room. "We're going to get the bastard this time . . . we're going to get him and he's going to pay. But first he's going to finish his work for us."

Jeni found herself gazing at a small outdated Apple computer across the room atop an oak credenza. "For an agency attempting to catch a cyber genius, you're somewhat outmoded, sir. Why no Sprinter computer?"

Manners was about to speak when the red phone purred.

Jeni looked at her watch, then at Manners. "It's early."

The director pointed. "Never mind, it's him. Pick it up. And Jeni—"

She hesitated.

"—the country is counting on you."

She watched Manners a second, turned to the insistent phone, and lifted the receiver. "Hello, John."

Chapter 24

"Good evening, Jeni. Our distinguished Director Manners is treating you well, I trust?"

"What can I do for you tonight, John?"

Manners came close, but not too, as if resisting the temptation to listen in.

"Oh, you've already done it, Jeni my dear. You've gotten yourself well clear of that wretched cottage. Now I can press the button."

Jeni and Manners made eye contact. "Why would you want to do that, John? It's just an old cottage in Mission Valley. The roof leaks."

Handle chuckled. "It's a bit more than that, Jeni. You're perfectly safe, then? Director Manners is being a gentleman despite his love/hate *idée fixe* with the opposite sex?"

"Can we end it now, John? Is it almost over? I'd really like to get back to my life now."

"Yes, I know you miss the clinic. I was sorry to hear about the little girl. Coral, was it?"

Jeni leaned back. "As a matter of fact I've decided to retire from my job at the clinic."

There was no response.

Director Manners started forward, frowning. Jeni tilted the mouthpiece. "John?"

"Retire? You started Project Future as I recall."

"With the help of friends. People who have more stamina . . . more sincerity than I."

"Sounds as though you're learning about yourself, Jeni. That's good. That's very good indeed."

Manners was glowering at Jeni, a tight *ask him what he wants*! expression on his face.

"So what's the agenda, John? Any more errands you need run tonight?"

"Not for the moment, dear. For the moment just sit back with your amiable host there and enjoy the show. And remember, the power is within you."

"How could I forget, John? Are you hanging up now?"

"Must be about my business. Takes all my attention to orchestrate the show."

She looked up at Manners. "The show, John?"

"My one regret was that it wasn't possible to arrange this around the Fourth of July. You can see the irony there, yes? But I fear Director Manners and company are closing in fast. *Au revoir,* sweet Jeni . . ."

The phone went dead.

"He hung up." And Jeni did the same.

Director Manners opened his mouth to say something . . . and a distant *boom* vibrated the room slightly. Ice tinkled in the conference room water pitcher. Thunder again?

Whatever Director was about to say, he seemed to have forgotten for the moment.

The conference room door flew open. A squat, bespectacled man, dripping perspiration, burst in, red face pinched with anxiety. He clutched a sheaf of papers. He looked dubiously at Jeni.

"She's one of us," Manners told him. "What is it?"

"He's starting!" the little red-faced man gulped, wiping sweat from his eyes. He held up one sheet, traced a line with a shaky finger. "This just in from the north side. The Aerospace Museum at Balboa Park is in flames. And just now there was an explosion aboard one of the yachts at the Mission Bay marina. It set half the slips afire. No casualties reported yet."

Manners was reaching for the briefing papers when his pager went off. He caught it. "Yes?" He nodded, cheek swollen again from grinding teeth. "Shit."

He snapped off the pager, returned it to his jacket. He looked more affronted than nervous. "Fire department. The mayor's office just—"

Another distant explosion cut him off.

For a moment time seemed to hang suspended, all three occupants of the room staring wordlessly at each other.

Then Jeni was bolting for the door.

On the mezzanine balcony she was nearly knocked over by Paul Miller racing for the stairs. Jeni followed him.

Miller charged down the balcony steps, Jeni leaping to catch up. "Paul?"

On the convention floor, Miller shoved aside a startled hacker brusquely, began tapping savagely at his keypad. The computer screen went blank . . . blinked into focus; a news anchorwoman materialized. She was facing the camera with professional bravado, though clearly rattled, the Channel 7 logo superimposed at lower screen left. A continuous crawl trailed below her: LIVE FROM THE CHANNEL 7 NEWSROOM. ". . . and the report is official now," the anchorwoman intoned evenly, "the mayor's office in downtown San Diego has apparently suffered a major explosion. Mayor Wenkam and family are away on vacation, and no injuries are yet reported. This is the second such explosion within the hour to have hit the city. Our correspondent Debbie Wallace is at the scene with . . . one moment please . . ." She looked off-camera, eyes askance, expression a professional veneer masking dread. "... uh ... this just in ... another explosion has occurred in the El Cajon section of the city, three miles southeast of—"

She was cut off by a rocking concussion in or near the studio. Overhead klieg lights swayed crazily, the desk jumping before her. She screamed. People ran before the camera, blocking the view. Someone yelled "Cut!" Something heavy fell off-camera, followed by another scream. The picture began to decay into snow.

Miller jabbed the keypad, punched in another number, switching channels. The screen blanked, lit with another anchor seated behind a super of the Channel 2 logo, a white-haired, elderly gentleman. "—and reports coming in from all over San Diego now that the city is apparently under some kind of terrorist siege, not unlike the type of explosion that occurred at the Statler Building just a week ago. We here at Channel 2 have only scattered information, complete details of which will be made available to our viewers just as soon as ..."

Miller straightened from the screen, turned to Jeni, who was ignoring the news programs. She was gazing past his shoulder, eyes rapidly sweeping the rows of convention tables.

Her expression was abruptly revelatory, mouth agape. "They're all Apples and IBMs," she murmured softly. "There isn't a Sprinter computer in the building!"

She turned, stunned, to Miller. "How are you going to catch him without a Sprinter, Paul? These computers are all outdated. Why aren't you using the same machine Handle is?"

Miller licked his lips, swallowed. He glanced at Brian coming up behind them.

Jeni turned to her ex. "Brian? What's going on? Why

were no Sprinter 9000 computers allowed in the convention building?"

An explosion just next door. An earthquake force shook the building. People screamed. A light fixture fell, exploded.

Dust roiled across the convention floor. Contestants leapt from their chairs. Someone yelled "Bomb!" Screens winked out. A stampede started for the southeast exit sign.

Jeni stood stolidly regarding the two agents. Her eyes were hard as stone. "You sons of bitches . . ." She took an unconscious step backward. "It wasn't a spy chip at all."

Brian started toward her but she yanked away viciously, eyes blazing now. A crowd of panicked hackers pushed past them, between them, nearly knocking Jeni over in their headlong flight to the crowded exit doors.

She gripped the edge of a table, regarded the two agents venomously, head reeling despite the sudden revelation. "You didn't create a chip to spy on terrorists. You created a chip to *destroy* them! The chip *itself* is an explosive!"

She sank down trembling on the table edge, dozens of terrified conventioneers sweeping past them, emptying the building. "Oh Jesus . . . what have you people done?"

Miller stepped toward her, was halted by her expression. "It wasn't supposed to happen like this, Jeni, you must believe that. It was only in the experimental stages. We never got the official go-ahead to ship the armed computers."

She watched him dizzily, throat tight with disbelief. "No? Then how the hell is Handle destroying half the city right now! There's an explosive device in every Sprinter 9000 in San Diego, isn't there? And a Sprinter 9000 in half the homes in this city! Not to mention yachts. Not to mention laptops in hospitals, libraries. The goddamn things are *everywhere, even the hospice!* And you lunatics have *armed* them! Dear Christ, were you *mad*?"

Brian cracked anxious knuckles. "It was only a theory, Jeni—"

"Brian! The goddamn atom bomb was only a theory!"

"It was intended strictly as a backup measure, a last-minute thing Handle came up with. No one really thought it would work. It—"

"How many of the damn things can *explode,* Brian!"

He regarded her with haunted eyes. "We . . . we're not certain how many are actually armed. Over a hundred were manufactured for the test. We're lacking hard data on how many of that group made it into the Sprinter test program . . . and how many of those machines were accidentally shipped out."

She almost laughed. "Accidentally!"

Brian swallowed thickly, looked away.

Jeni regarded her ex-husband coolly. "But Handle knows, right? Handle knows it to the letter! And just twenty of the damn things could turn San Diego into Hiroshima." She sighed, pressed trembling fingers into tightly slitted eyes. "And Handle's hidden in a basement somewhere with his finger on the button." She lifted her head, looked around the convention room. "The only reason we're not dead ourselves is because you cowardly shits made sure there were no Sprinters inside this command headquarters." She shook her head. "Christ, no wonder it's taken so long to trace him!"

Miller approached her cautiously. "It wasn't only that, Jeni. Yes, we can trace Handle's signal more easily on a Sprinter, but he can trace us too, keep switching wavelengths on us. The theory was that we could stay hidden from him by using the older equipment. The problem is, obviously, it takes a lot longer."

Jeni watched him sadly. "You and your damn theories."

And Miller, as exhausted as the rest of them, lost it, finally. "We were trying to protect the *nation,* goddamn it! You think that's a cakewalk, Jennifer? We're trying to keep the American people safe in their homes with their loved ones in a world that's shrunken to the size of a twenty-inch *screen.* You still think it's about guns and bombs? It's about computers! It's about Web sites! It's about *communication*!"

Jeni nodded wry irony. "Communication. Right. Why just spy on the enemy when you can blow his ass up while you're at it? Hi, we're America—you're history!" She did laugh now, nearly giddy with overload. "This is fucking priceless! You people have gone *beyond* Fifth Amendment infringement. You're beyond the rights of *humanity*! Who the hell did you think you were, *Christ Almighty*?"

Miller and Brian were looking beyond her.

Jeni turned to see Director Manners threading his way patiently through the surging crowd, pushing panicked bodies from his path like a farmer parting wheat. Like Moses parting the sea, Jeni mused dolefully. He moved calmly, confidently, through the stampede. "We're going to code red immediately!" he shouted. "Paul, contact Jamison now!"

"What the hell is code red?" Jeni demanded.

As Miller exited obediently, Brian turned to her wearily, nearly colliding with a straggler rushing past. "It's a directive, an order to San Diego Edison. Cut all power in the city. Handle may be a genius with a computer, but he can't run one without electricity. No power, no explosions."

"And no way to *trace* him anymore!" Jeni shouted, a hacker knocking into her, jarring her teeth. "Dammit,

Brian, you can't just arbitrarily shut down the city's power. What about the hospitals? What about the airports?"

Another rocking concussion beyond the building. Brian grabbed a table edge for support. Plaster snowed down from creaking ceiling fixtures. "They've been warned in advance. An emergency drill, they were told. Most of them have automatic backup generators and batteries."

Jeni sneered. "*Most* of them! Is that going to help some surgeon in the middle of a heart operation? Some poor air traffic control guy landing a 747? That airport's dangerous enough when it's lit."

Brian swallowed. Manners stepped between, intervening with practiced aplomb. "We're doing what needs to be done, Jeni. Kindly join the spirit of the program or I'm going to have to ask Agent Starbuck to escort you from the command center." He put a warm hand on her shoulder. "I believe you promised full cooperation."

Jeni snapped away as if bit. "Get your hand off me, you effete prick! You want sexual harassment troubles? I'll ram them so far up your ass you won't be shitting platitudes for a week!"

Manners withdrew his hand delicately, yielding an amused reptilian smile. "Well. A woman of spirit. How ever did we lose her to the ATF, Brian?"

Music boomed suddenly over the convention room's P.A. system. "Heartbreak Hotel."

Everyone turned.

Hundreds of computer screens were scrambling simultaneously, warbling and filling with snow. Then, magically, they all cleared at once. A black-and-white image of a glossy-haired young man making love to his guitar formed on every computer screen on the convention floor.

"Welllllll, since my baby left me—" amid adolescent screams of orgasmic bobby-soxers.

Manners squinted perplexed at the multitude of mirrored images. "What the hell is this?"

Jeni smiled secretively. *"The Ed Sullivan Show,"* she told him. "Circa 1956."

Brian turned to her. "Handle?"

Jeni held the faint smile. "He's watching everything we do, hearing everything we say."

Manners snorted at the screens, turned an imperious heel, and began picking his way back through litter and spilled coffee. "I suggest we await the results of code red in the conference room. There's fresh coffee." He turned at the staircase. "Agent Starbuck?"

Brian and Jeni were staring mesmerized at the nearest computer screen. Jeni shook her head in awe at the screaming teenagers. "Look at him," she murmured, nodding toward the gyrating singer. "He has them completely in his power."

"Agent Starbuck!"

She turned then with Brian, following the stiffly impatient director up the stairs.

The conference door burst open again, Jeni sloshing coffee at the intrusion.

The little red-faced bespectacled man stood there in damp shirt, sleeves rolled, clutching a fresh sheaf of papers over which he dripped anxious sweat. "It isn't working!"

Manners was pouring Coffeemate in his cup. He turned almost casually to the beet-faced courier. "Sit down, Simmons, you'll have a heart attack."

"No thank you, sir."

"Precisely how is it not working?"

The little man shuffled papers. "We've got power out all over the county, including Del Mar and National City. So far there have been two detonations in Chula Vista, one in National City, a small blast in San Ysidro near the border, another near the Fashion Valley Mall off I-8." He shuffled to a new page. "The latest one was in West Mission Bay near Sea World." He looked up, swallowing. "The city is in a panic. All the highways jammed. Everyone's trying to leave town at once. The local police are in gridlock. It's worse than a seven-point quake, sir. There's no way to contain—"

"Simmons!"

The little man gaped, chest heaving.

"Thank you. That will suffice. The convention's carpet is being leased to us, kindly stop dripping on it."

Manners stirred, sipped his coffee confidently, made a pleased expression. "The situation *will* be contained. We anticipated a certain degree of public panic. We have the situation under control." He pushed a chair toward the little man with his shoe. "Sit. And know solace."

Simmons ignored the chair. "But, sir, he continues to detonate the Sprinters!" He glanced askance at Jeni, as if fearful—even at this late hour—of divulging secrets. "He's overridden the power supply somehow. I know it sounds impossible, but he's done it. The Sprinter 9000s require too much juice to operate on battery power alone, yet he's detonating them. Sir, families . . . innocent people—"

Director Manners drew himself to full height, glowering over the cringing courier. "That will do, Agent Simmons. Please return to your field office and continue monitoring incoming reports. I want to know every detail. Is that clear?"

Agent Simmons, dripping profusely, gave Brian and Jeni a hopeless look, then hurried from the room.

"Agent Starbuck, will you be kind enough to shut the door, please?"

Brian stared at the director, face wan, lifeless.

Manners finished adding another dash of creamer. "The door, please, Brian."

Brian closed the door.

Director Manners moved to the oak table, pulled back a chair, sipping. "Well, it seems we have a new problem."

A distant blast shook the room; Manners's coffee sloshed scalding across hand and cuff. He did not—Jeni noticed—even wince.

He set down the cup carefully and began patting the back of his hand delicately with a clean white hanky pulled from the pocket of his immaculate suit.

Jeni turned to the window and a view of the blackened city, scattered portions billowing with ghostly glow, plumes of yellow-orange light curling skyward. There must have been over two dozen small fires in the area by now. The scream of sirens, even here behind thick mortar, was still so strident you had to talk inordinately loud to be heard.

Few of the frantic fire trucks were doing any good, unable to reach their destinations. Every highway, every service road, as far as she could see was bumper-to-bumper with wide-eyed, terrified civilians, yelling and honking and screaming animatedly at one another.

The poor uninitiated fools, Jeni thought. They must think it's the day of judgment, come at last. Gabriel has sounded his horn . . .

She turned quietly to Manners, started to say something, was halted by the sight of his burned hand. It was scalded red. But more than that it was shaking, nearly imperceptibly, like the early stages of Parkinson's. The tick in his cheek was more pronounced.

He's scared, Jeni realized. Deep down he's more terrified than any of us.

"Is there any way he could use the phone system, sir?"
she asked him.

Manners shook his head. "Negative. We've shut down
Pacific Bell as well as the electric. Handle must have divined some method of transmission completely beyond
our scope. Our best experts can't figure out how he's doing it." His left cheek bulged, twitched.

Jeni returned her gaze to the outside fires.

A sense of hopelessness hung in the room that the director's calm facade was doing nothing to dispel.

Brian, head in arms, jerked up suddenly, eyes lit with
inspiration. "The cellular towers! Could he be using
mountain cell sites to transmit to the chip somehow?"

Again Manners shook his head. "We thought of that
days ago. They've all been shut down. Everything electric
and wireless that falls under San Diego jurisdiction is under our control." He grimaced, pressing back internal frustration. "The bastard is *beating* the system somehow!"

Jeni laughed once mirthlessly.

The two men turned to her, startled.

"The bastard," she intoned drily, "has won. I hardly
think, after this cataclysm, the project will remain *covert*
in even the most remotely meaningful sense. And without
secrecy, you don't have an antiterrorist weapon. Or am I
wrong about that too?"

Manners avoided her eyes, picked up his coffee with a
trembling hand, steadying it with the other.

Brian put his head down again. Another distant explosion vibrated the oak conference table.

Jeni left the cool pane of the window, moved to the credenza for more coffee. She poured slowly, eyes unable
to avoid drifting back to the picture window, the chaos

without. The air was so thick with smoke now it looked as though a deep fog had descended over the beleaguered city. Yet even in this hour of catastrophe there was beauty to be found: the roiling smoke made the pale stanchions girding the mighty Coronado Bay Bridge glow with ethereal loveliness.

Coronado. Where it seemed only yesterday, she and Brian and little Molly walked laughing in sunset surf . . .

Jeni gasped. The Styrofoam cup slipped from her fingers.

She rushed back to the window, straining to see past the bridge at the thin finger of island across the bay. There was too much greasy smoke to make out Coronado itself. Still, it had to be the answer! She whirled to the men. "He's not in San Diego!"

Manners turned. Brian jerked his head up expectantly, eyes red.

Jeni could barely contain herself. "He's not on San Diego power—electric, phone, *or* cellular! He's right there across the bay! He's on the island!"

Manners held his enthusiasm in check. "Why do you think—"

"Coronado seceded from the mainland years ago. It's a completely self-contained city. With its own power supply. Can't you see, it's the only answer!"

Brian leapt up, nodding. "She's right! They have their own city council over there, their own government, everything. If there's a cellular tower on that island, Handle could be using it to boomerang across the bay to the San Diego Sprinters."

Manners watched them a moment.

Then he rose, turned to the door, opened it, and shouted down the hall. "Simmons! We need a map of Coronado Island. Now! Something that shows all the power grids, including any cellular sites. In the conference room, ASAP!"

He turned back to the others, face impassive. "I think this has already been done. As I recall, there are no cellular sites on Coronado." He began a hopeful pacing. "Still, I suppose it won't hurt to check."

The map took over twenty minutes to be carried by runner from the county courthouse, the streets still hopelessly snarled with traffic.

They spread the diagram across the conference table and began attacking it.

They found nothing.

Brian straightened at length, sighing frustration. "The only cellular phone tower is within the navy compound at the end of the island, and Handle sure as hell doesn't have access to that. He's good, but not that good."

Miller muttered a defeated "Shit," slouched heavily in a chair, reaching wearily for his coffee.

Brian continued to scroll down the map's legend with a finger. He shook his head. "Nothing, nothing . . ."

Manners ground his teeth, cheek trembling. Jeni had the sensation he was about to erupt from within.

"Don't you think," she addressed him carefully, "under the circumstances, we could have the city's power turned back on? Code red obviously isn't working."

Manners turned her a cold shoulder. "We'll proceed with SOP until I deem otherwise."

Jeni stared at the darkened cityscape, seething.

Miller sat up abruptly. "Wait a minute! I was over in Coronado just last week. I could swear I saw some phone or TV aerials on top of one of the big new resort hotels." He grabbed at the map, pulled it over. In a moment he jabbed a finger at the paper. "There! The Belmont Arms, right on the beach. That's the place, I'm sure of it."

"They might be merely TV cable equipment," Manners countered.

"Well, if it's a chance, I think we should check it out," Brian insisted. He gave the conveniently near phone a longing look that wasn't lost on the director.

Manners considered, started for the door . . . turned, muttered, "The hell with it," and grabbed up the receiver. "Peterson, please. Yes. Pete! Director Manners. Cut code red. Yes. And I need you to check on a building for me. The—" He turned to Miller.

"Belmont Arms."

"—the Belmont Arms in Coronado. Find out if there are any cellular sites constructed on their roof. Right." He hung up, turned to the group. "Well, if Mr. Handle was listening in on that little conversation, we're dead meat."

Five minutes later the phone purred. Brian snagged it. He nodded, smiled, hung up, and turned to the others brightly. "The Belmont has a cellular site! Company called InterWeb. It was installed on their main tower roof just six weeks ago, practically brand-new."

Miller smiled. "Smart bastard."

Everyone pressed close to the map again. Brian nodded. "That has to be where he's transmitting from. Everything else within a fifty-mile radius has been checked and covered."

Manners gestured toward the red phone. "Get Coronado Naval Base on the horn. I know Admiral Hendry over there. He can get a team of navy SEALS ready for—"

"No!" Jeni stepped in front of Brian, clamped her hand over the receiver. "No calls to Coronado direct. It's too dangerous."

Miller nodded. "She's right. This has to be a surprise

assault if we're going to catch the bastard, prevent him from slipping away again, setting up shop elsewhere."

"There *is* nowhere else," Manners argued. "We have both towns covered now."

"That's what you thought before," Brian told him.

Manners made a sour face. "All right, choppers, then. We send a helicopter from the naval base to—"

Miller was waving him off. "He'd hear a chopper before it left its pad. Besides . . ." He glanced askance sheepishly at Jeni, ". . . we have reason to believe some of the navy's newer fleet may already have installed the converted Sprinters. It would take hours to disconnect them from a chopper console."

Manners looked appalled. "The air force has the secret Sprinters?"

Miller shrugged. "It's a possibility. We're not sure how many were actually shipped, or to whom, that NCIC info and Handle's in control of that. But we know the navy was on the list for new equipment. I don't think it would be prudent to use airpower under the present circumstances."

Manners groaned. "Christ . . ."

"Yes," Jeni noted coolly, "whatever we do, let's not blow our own people out of the sky."

Manners glared at her. "How do we get to him, then?"

Brian was studying the map. "Okay, the air is out. That leaves ground-level access, of which there are only two connecting points to the island. One across the Silver Strand—which is presently grille-to-grille with hysterical civilians, including shoulders and access roads—the other is the Coronado Bay Bridge, which is equally jammed from end to end. You couldn't blast through that gridlock with an A-1 tank."

"What about the bay ferry?" Miller offered. "That's only a ten-minute trip."

Brian shook his head. "Might be quiet enough, but without lights, in this smoke, a channel crossing would be suicide, and Handle is sure to spot the lights, even be expecting them."

"How about private aircraft? A civilian Cessna?"

"No," from Brian, "they carry computers now too. Besides, the civilian airports are as jammed as the roads."

Miller rolled his eyes. "Christ, we've tied our own hands!"

Manners, patience and nerve finally fried, slammed a fist across the map. "Well, goddamn it, there must be a way to get to the bastard!"

"There is," Jeni told him calmly. "The same way we got the map here. A runner . . ."

Everyone looked at her.

She was already pulling off her purse, stretching calf muscles against the table. "Me."

The men stared quietly a moment.

"You Bureau assholes lucked out again. I've run that bridge in the last two marathons. I know it inside and out."

Manners looked unconvinced.

Jeni, all business, pulled the Ruger from her purse, checked it carefully. "All right, here's the way we're doing it. I want no one following me, no one trying to monitor me through headphones or anything else. Nothing to connect me in the least way to Handle, tip him off. You fellas just sit tight here in your little room and pretend to be flummoxed. If I see anybody jogging behind me on the bridge I stop running, is that clear?"

"You can't, Jeni—" Miller began.

"Don't tell me I can't anymore!" Jeni snapped. "You're the ones who *can't*! I do what's necessary!"

She reached around, unsnapped her skirt, and threw it on the oak table. She wore a black legless leotard beneath, long legs tanned and muscular. There was a small bandage across her left kneecap. Brian nodded. "What about your war wound?"

Jeni shrugged, accepting the map from him, tucking it into her waistband. "Only hurts when I run."

The group turned to find little red-faced Agent Simmons standing in the doorway, clutching a fresh sheaf of papers, startled eyes fixed on Jeni.

"What is it, Simmons?" the director demanded. "How long have you been lurking there?"

"I . . . well, I was bringing some potentially good news, sir . . ."

Manners sighed impatience. "What does 'potential' mean?"

The little man wiped sweat from his brow, consulted his papers. "Well, the weather bureau assures us there's a major storm off the Baja peninsula, heading rapidly for downtown San Diego. That means another, even bigger front within the next hour, lots of rain, a break for the firefighters . . ."

The little man looked up again at Jeni's long, tapering legs. ". . . but not such a break for someone attempting to cross the bridge on foot."

Brian spat an invective. "That's it! Forget it, Jeni. You're not going to attempt that bridge in a gale. You could get blown right over the rail. There's no protective pedestrian fence on that structure."

Jeni snorted, folding her skirt neatly. "Shut up, Brian."

Manners regarded her with mixed hope and pessimism. "You honestly think you can jog that long bridge in this dark and smoke? Dodge through all that tangle of snarled traffic? There's bound to be trucks stalled there, big trucks, blocking your path. You sincerely think you can make it?"

Jeni shoved the gun into her waistband after the map, took a final swig of coffee, handed him the empty cup. "Are you serious, Mister Director? Handle probably set it up this way from the beginning."

She turned her back on the men in the room and headed out the door.

Chapter 25

By the time she'd trotted down Grape Street (an even, measured canter) and approached her objective, the area was completely devoid of pedestrians. Though certainly not traffic. Cars, trucks, vehicles of every make and kind sat bumper-to-bumper in eerie silence before and over the great curving blue arc of the Coronado Bridge.

The entire bridge—indeed, all highways and roads leading to it—had become so hopelessly gridlocked from Highway 8, through downtown, over Pacific Highway, and throughout all service and secondary roads and streets that the drivers, their families and pets, had abandoned their vehicles and headed out of town on foot. One massive biblical exodus from the city to the promised solitude of desert hills and arroyos beyond. Jeni could already spot the flickering specks of small campfires in the surrounding mountains, imagine fearful faces huddled around them against the terrors of the night, the chill rain, prowling coyotes and pumas. It conjured TV images of fleeing Bosnian refugees.

The bridge itself, usually a gracefully engineered arc of blue steel and gleaming columns, had transformed into a narrow ribbon of junkyard vehicles, many of them smashed and battered, auto alarms wailing mournfully,

some with engines still running, exhaust billowing waste-
fully to join the already eye-searing blanket of fire smoke.

And dark. Everything was cloaked in dark, roiling
haze. Only occasional puffs of wind and rain, staggered
with lightning flashes, revealed the entire nightmare sce-
nario. Like the Statler Building aftermath—like Oklahoma and Waco—this was another vision from Dante's
Hell. Ethereal and grim, etched in flickering, chiaroscuro
shades of somber gray and black.

She could follow the footpath to the right of the traffic
lanes, but even this was blocked here and there by canted
automobiles, vans, and trucks. The flight from the island
had been conducted without goal or purpose, despite
a pathetic attempt at order from police bullhorns and
buzzing choppers. Once begun, it snowballed quickly
into a hysterical dash to freedom, led by a panicked, unprepared populace—supposedly trained for earthquake
emergency—whose familiar world of family dinners and
primetime TV was suddenly exploding all around them.

Jeni jogged evenly, craned to the troubled sky. Above
the wail of car alarms, the beat of choppers and drone of
emergency firefighter aircraft echoed over the city. Since
no fire trucks could reach the mounting scenes of disaster,
the water droppers were all the city had to fight the growing conflagration with. Dipping and buzzing like insects,
gathering their tanks of seawater from the bay and nearby
ocean, the planes and choppers zigzagged dangerously
close to each other through the thickening fog and smoke,
San Diego's only hope of quenching the spreading flames.
If the fires—and there were over thirty individual ones
now—spread to nearby, sunbaked hills, not only would
the entire town be engulfed, but the flames could spread
down the coast to Mexico, and upward, presumably, all
the way to L.A. before they were contained. It could easily

evolve into the worst fire catastrophe in the nation's history. Were it not for the recent early rains, this would no doubt have already been a foregone conclusion.

Jeni neared the opening of the bridge thinking about the wind.

She almost wished she'd gotten away before sweaty little Simmons arrived with his forecast. She had enough to think about—traffic and flames and the upcoming altercation with Handle—without worrying about being blown off the damn bridge.

There was still a shifting curtain of moisture over the city, a gathering series of ever stronger gusts coming off the ocean . . . gusts that would increase in velocity as she approached the apex of the bridge.

She jogged past the first girder, marking the bridge's mouth, and glanced down automatically at her watch. Almost exactly midnight. That meant, if she could maintain this pace, she should be able to reach the other side, jog onto the island itself, somewhere around twenty past the hour. The record, set by the whippet-thin black girl who had beaten her in the marathon, was twenty minutes, forty-two seconds. Of course, that had been in bright daylight, perfect visibility, moderate wind, and no greasy fire smoke to choke on.

Even so, consciously or otherwise, Jeni felt herself picking up her pace.

It's your chance . . . your second chance . . . to beat the record.

She pushed aside the thought, slowed again to a measured gait. This wasn't about winning a damn race. This was about hunting down a madman. Halting a disaster.

Being a useful agent again?

Yes, perhaps that too. Nothing wrong with feeling a little useful again.

And the possibility of seeing Molly again?

She pushed that thought aside too.

It wasn't even a consideration. Molly was dead. She could feel it in her heart, would know in her heart if it were otherwise. If Handle or Director Manners thought the clinging hope of a desperate mother finding her daughter alive was incentive for this dash, they were sorely mistaken. She wasn't that naive, for all the blunders she'd made since this thing began.

No, this wasn't about hope and the renewal of a life. This was about death. It was about the chance to see Handle again—one more time—without the makeup and disguises. It was about obliterating him and stopping the madness. It was about starting her own life again.

Well . . . you seem to have it all figured out . . .

She did feel a strange inner peace, despite the mild lance of pain up her left leg.

Her knee. It was probably beginning to weep again slightly. She'd meant to get back to the hospital, have it checked; there just hadn't been time. Probably a stray bone fragment that cow-eyed intern had somehow missed. What was his name? He'd been so nervous asking her for that date. No matter. She'd have the knee looked at when this was over with. Meanwhile, it didn't hurt that much . . . a constant reminder of every footfall, every shock of pressure up her leg, but she'd known worse, she'd known far worse. She could hack it. For the moment.

She was, in fact, feeling pretty good, hardly even breaking a sweat yet. Thank the cool night breezes for that, despite the occasional billowing warmth from distant fires, the intermittent lungful of noxious smoke and fumes. She even felt good enough to pick up the pace a bit.

The darkened hulk of a Plymouth wrecked against the

guardrail blocked her path, its headlights still on, spearing twin beams of smoke and fog. She dodged around it expertly, was past it and back on the path with hardly a beat missed. There would doubtless be more such obstacles ahead, the entire bridge was a study in panicked flight. She only prayed there were no major pileups, that she would not have to stop and physically crawl over wreckage. That *would* cost her time.

And she felt she was making very good time, better than expected. True, the wind was heavier now, but pressing mostly from the west—her left flank—not in front where she would be fighting it. She felt more than strong enough to compensate for the present gusts. Unless the gale hit . . .

Maybe you really could break the black girl's record . . .

She couldn't suppress an inward smile at her insistent ego. One more irony to add to the growing mountain of them: her breaking the decathlon record with no one around to see it. Wouldn't that be a hoot? Handle would appreciate that one.

She felt good, confident. She hadn't been in this kind of physical shape since the last race. And the idea *was* to stop Handle as soon as possible, right? Perhaps she should pick up her pace a bit. She wasn't winded yet, not in the least. What difference did it make if she beat the record *and* subdued Handle? As long as she did her job she could win an Olympic medal, for all anyone cared. And the sooner Handle was dispensed with, the better for all concerned.

Jeni licked her lips, warming to the idea. She began to push herself measuredly . . .

She was just a few clicks away from an actual sprint when the white-hot blast knocked her over backward.

She lit on rump and elbows, head slamming the left

front door of a jade Taurus. She was thinking—before everything went black—*He's blowing up the bridge!*

She awoke knowing everything, eyes jerking immediately to her watch.

She hadn't been out more than half a minute. Still plenty of time to break that record. If she could move . . .

She pushed up, a thin ribbon of warmth running in her eye, and found her wobbly legs. They steadied quickly. She felt no broken bones, no serious scrapes or abrasions except for a small cut somewhere in her scalp where her head had made contact with the Taurus.

The bridge spanned ahead of her as before, vanishing in the mist. She resumed an even, steady trot, realized now it had not been the bridge but a yellow Honda canted against the center lane that had exploded.

Of course. Sprinter laptops were standard executive fare these days. There was even talk of installing them directly into the vehicles, like CD and tape decks.

Fanned by the heat of the disintegrating Honda, she jogged on, pressing back an insistently plucking headache. She ignored it. She had lost only moments.

But a race—any kind of race—can be lost in moments.

She pushed herself harder, trying to make up for the lost seconds, hugging the guardrail, beyond which existed only dark, roiling smoke and a hundred-foot drop to unforgiving salt water. Another blast like the one just experienced could easily blow her off the bridge. On the other hand, if she happened too close to another computer-installed vehicle—if Handle set it off—she'd perish in a wall of flame, fried alive. She preferred the dizzy drop to water.

This isn't a race, it's a fucking obstacle course! An arcade game!

Yes, the old Pac-Man. No, Ms. Pac-Man . . . she was the yellow blinking ball chasing through the maze, the cars the blue meanies ready to gobble her.

Could Handle see her somehow? Deliberately detonating vehicles as she approached? Or was he even aware she was on the bridge? About a quarter of the way across the bridge in fact, approaching the middle. The wind was picking up . . .

She faltered, nearly fell . . .

Pain was rocketing her left leg. She looked down in the gloom, saw the pale skin below her knee streaming black blood. The old running wound. Had the stitches popped when she fell?

The pain was increasing with every shocking jar of her shoe. She could just tolerate it. But if it accelerated, she'd have to slow, maybe stop; the race would be over and Handle would win again . . .

She gritted her teeth, dug in, purposely pushed harder, approaching a sprint.

A mistake. The pain increased, lanced right up through her thigh, threatening to topple her.

She eased back into an easy lope. *Okay, okay . . . take it easy, you can do this, don't let him beat you this early into the game. You still have plenty of time.*

She glanced at her watch. Yes, a good fifteen minutes before the . . .

Before the what? Before losing to the black girl's record?

But that isn't what the race is about, Jeni.

She shook her head in midstride, grateful as a fresh curtain of cooling rain washed her from the west, washed away her thoughts. Her face had been burning hot. She must be more tired than she'd thought. It had been a long

night. Handle's cryptic messages . . . Brian and his ice
pick . . . Mrs. Grindle's parchment skull grinning from the
freezer . . . Paul Miller, the arrogant Director Manners.
And now this lunatic midnight marathon, this gauntlet of
exploding automobiles and lashing rain, the black waters
of the bay waiting down there for her to make the slightest
miscalculation, stray too near the rail . . .

You must have been nuts, kiddo, this is suicide . . .

Through the pall of smoke, a small, whitish blur was
coming up on her right . . . a rectangular sign affixed to one
of the support columns. As she approached she could make
out indistinct blue lettering, some of it in caps. It looked
like a sign for pedestrians, not motorists. She squinted, arrested for some reason by the idea of reading the sign.

She cried out abruptly. A lone gust, harsher nearly
than the exploding car, caught her unawares, driving a
stinging wall of rain before it. Warm rain, not cool like
before—warm rain from the gulf. The Baja Hurricane
had arrived.

She slewed sideways under the gusts, shoes slipping on
wet cement, grasped frantically for the elusive rail, missed
it, felt herself tipping, tipping . . .

. . . lashed out with both arms as her hip skidded
over the side, glimpsed a black, sparkling abyss far below. Her fingers brushed a dark girder, caught with
taloned nails, held.

She'd read somewhere that, beyond a certain height,
hitting water could be akin to striking concrete . . . the human body explodes like jelly . . .

She maneuvered her rump back over the railing to level
pavement, slid to solid ground, exhaustion claiming all
further movement. Unbidden, her head fell back against
the support beam. She found herself looking up at

the white rectangular metal sign posted to the girder, the blue lettering: "San Diego Suicide Prevention Line— 619-856-0298."

Jeni pressed her throbbing head to the cool beam for a moment, filling her heaving lungs, a smile tracing haggard features. Suicide. She'd heard the bridge was a favorite choice of those seeking self-destruction. She laughed weakly. Here she was, with all she could do just to survive exploding cars and sledgehammer winds, and this damn sign reminds her not to willingly cast herself over the rail. Something vaguely humorous about that. Handle would love it. She could almost hear his familiar metallic chuckle.

She allowed herself another moment's respite, then shoved to her feet.

The instant she placed her full weight on the left foot, the pain nearly undid her again.

She pressed down gingerly, hissing, digging her nails into the flesh around the oozing knee to distract the pain. She was beginning to bleed like a pig. This would never do. Why in hell did she have to *fall* during that damn marathon? She would have beaten that bitch!

You fell, princess, because the ketch blew up in the bay . . . and Handle detonated the ketch. You can thank him for this.

Yes, she could thank Handle for a lot.

She put out her foot again, testing tentatively. The pain shot upward, eliciting another gasp, but only as far as the calf this time. She took a step, wincing, thought perhaps she could endure another, then another, biting back the pain.

Come on! You can't walk *the rest of the way!*

One step at a time, that was the way. She walked faster . . .

faster . . . forced herself finally into a slow lope, lips pressed
in a flat, bloodless line. The pain retreated a millimeter. Better. A little better.

She glanced at her watch.

Quit looking at the damn watch!

But she couldn't seem to help herself.

Her head jerked up, startled. The sky at the far end of
the bridge was filling abruptly with dancing white light.
Lightning, pulsing behind the dark curtain of smoke? But
as she drew nearer she could see that the lingering brightness held a uniformity. A definite shape began to take
form through the glowing smoke and mist. It was the big
Diamond Vision TV screen set above the bank building
on the island side of the bridge, the one that had announced the winner of the AIDS race between ad crawls
for the Sprinter 9000. Why in God's name was it func-
tioning now with no one here to see the ads? A short circuit of some kind?

A fresh gust blew the smoke eastward. Jeni craned,
squinting upward at the towering screen. Her heart
skipped.

"WELCOME TO THE JOHN HANDLE
ANNUAL RACE FOR AIDS KIDS!"

Jeni shrieked involuntarily as a big Chrysler town car
exploded directly in her path.

Blinded, night vision gone, she threw herself flat, skidded painfully across rough pavement, tearing the knee
wound wider, leaving a thin sanguine trail. Shrapnel and
flame tore above her head in a yellow fireball. She felt a
pressing heat across her back, smelled the pungent odor
of her own singed hair, imagined herself afire.

But she was not afire. Or if she had been, the strengthening downpour quickly quenched it.

She rolled left, got to her knees, and hobbled away from the flaming wreckage. Two more seconds delay and she would have jogged right into the blast. Had Handle anticipated that, timed it?

She leaned against an abandoned RV, gasping gasoline-saturated air. She gripped her knee, willing back fresh ice picks of pain. She couldn't seem to get her breath properly, the gasoline stench suffocating. Nausea rose to greet her, chased by coppery bile. She jammed her eyes tight and fought the welling urge to vomit. Her greatest fear was passing out, falling into the spreading flames. Every dizzy lungful demanded she sit down . . . lie back on the cool concrete, let the warm rain cover her like a blanket . . . rest . . . just rest . . .

And never get up again . . .

She jerked awake. Found herself on all fours staring at her haggard reflection in a muddy puddle.

She forced herself upright, stood swaying shakily, the driving storm hammering her back now. Despite the gusting rain, the entire bridge smelled like the inside of a refinery. It kept blowing curls in her face. Should have cut them long ago, her mind wandered . . . sprinters don't have long hair. Vanity. Brian had always like her long blond hair. Used to run his fingers through it . . . softly . . .

She snapped her head up, saw a river of gasoline-driven flame funneling toward her. She staggered away, supported by the door of the RV. Pinpoints of orderly winking lights marched in reflection across the gleaming concrete. A hallucination? She looked up.

The letters on the big sign had shifted, melted, were forming another image. In a moment she recognized the familiar outline of a new Sprinter 9000. Ad copy appeared beside it.

"THE NEW SPRINTER 9000!
COMMUNICATE WITH THE WORLD!
ZAP! — AND YOU'RE THERE!"

As she watched, the ad copy faded. The picture of the computer seemed to glow red. Then exploded in a shower of diamond-white lights.

Jeni regarded the big electronic sign with a wan smile. Handle was having his little joke.

The screen began to form images again, lights coalescing. They winked into a patchwork pattern that became an enormous clock. It read: 12:13.

Jeni swallowed. Jesus. The bastard was timing her.

She pushed off again with a will.

Ten agonizing minutes later, she'd crested the hump and was loping awkwardly downhill toward the island below, the effort shifting from aching calf muscles to her shins. Some of the pain in her knee was relieved.

Well, she needn't worry about checking her watch anymore. She had the time right in front of her, three stories high.

She ran, glancing about herself on the final lonely mile of the bridge. She had the strangest feeling she was being watched by crowds of people . . .

"Hey! You've got to see this!"

It was Agent Jamison from down the hall, calling excitedly from the conference room door. Director Manners exchanged looks with Agents Miller and Starbuck, then the three of them joined Jamison on the mezzanine balcony. Jamison pointed over the brass rail. "Take a look!"

Below, on the convention floor, empty now of any trace of hackers and conventioneers save the remaining flotsam of their litter, every unmanned computer screen was brightly lit and flickering with images. Gone was *The Ed Sullivan Show,* the screaming bevy of teenagers. The screens all displayed an identical image: an aerial view of the Coronado Bridge, the twisted parade of stalled vehicles crushed together like an endless steel centipede, some gutted and charred, some still billowing flame, some wailing with alarm systems. And, hugging the bridge guardrail, a lone runner with streaming auburn curls loped toward the entrance to the island ... loped steadily if shakily downhill toward the big Diamond Vision screen that marked the finish line. And the screen was lit with the image of an immense clock.

"Jesus," Brian breathed, "he knows. The bastard knows. He probably knew all the time. We should never have made those phone calls."

Paul Miller shook his head. "He would have known anyway, the brilliant prick. Christ, how the hell did he manage to rig a camera on that bridge?"

Agent Jamison grunted beside them. "He didn't rig it. That's an existing Highway Patrol video cam to monitor traffic and potential fliers."

"Fliers?" from Director Manners.

"Suicides," Jamison told him. "Handle's merely tapped into the camera's system. The way he taps into every other goddamn piece of electronics in town." Jamison leaned over the rail, shouted down at a man moving among the rows of unmanned computers. "Kline! Put one of those screens on a local channel! Let's see if we can get a news broadcast!"

The man below saluted with a wave, moved to the nearest console, tapped the keypad. The screen winked and stayed focused on the image of the bridge. Jamison shook his head.

"Christ, he's got all the stations blocked—got our runner on every channel in this city . . . maybe on every channel as far up the coast as San Luis Obispo. All of L.A. knows about this."

As they watched, the big diamond screen lit with another "commercial" of an exploding Sprinter 9000.

Manners's face burned. "That's it! We put navy choppers in the air *now*! I want that high-rise surrounded!"

He turned stiffly toward the conference room—not ready for Brian's arm, which jerked him abruptly around. "No!"

Manners, apparently unused to being touched, much less manhandled, stepped back in mild dismay, looked upon Brian Starbuck as one discovering a maggot beneath a rock.

"We're not doing a damn thing until my wife reaches that island and does what she was assigned to do!"

Manners regarded him with humored patience. "Wife, Agent Starbuck? Correct me here, please, but it was my understanding you and the young woman were divorced."

Brian held the other man's unctuous gaze. "You're staying off that phone, sir, until we hear from Jeni."

Manners smiled slowly, both men aware Brian's career could end with a flick of the director's finger. Manners turned to Paul Miller with arched brow as if soliciting his opinion.

"He hasn't hurt her yet, sir," Miller concurred, "and he's had plenty of chances. Blunder in now and he might do anything. I think the prudent thing would be to play along a bit longer."

"But we *have* been playing along, Paul. And he's continued to make a mockery of both us and the project. You *are* cognizant of the repercussions—the irreparable damage to the Bureau—should the deepest inner workings of the nation's top covert project become a lead-in for the fall prime-time lineup?"

"I've considered them, sir. But this isn't prime time. And any disgruntled employee or hacker seeking publicity could patch into that signal on the big screen. It's no big trick to edit an existing commercial, rig a quick CGI effect, and show Sprinter 9000s exploding all over the place. It doesn't mean the public is going to make the connection, relate those images to a secret government project. What little public is even watching television at this hour. I vote we bide our time, let the Starbuck woman have her chance."

Manners studied him a moment, turned back to Brian. "And if we're wrong, Agent Starbuck? If he's targeting the girl right now? He has a camera on her this very moment. Do you really think he'll allow her access? Let her simply waltz through the front doors of that high-rise, ride the elevator to whatever suite he's occupying, and apprehend him unchallenged? After months of precisely choreographed planning, allow himself to be undone by a single woman with a small handgun?"

Brian took an unsteady breath, spoke quietly. "I don't know, sir. All I know is, he hasn't harmed my ex-wife in the least way so far, not a hair on her head. And he's had ample opportunity. Yes, I could be wrong . . ."

"But you're willing to chance it."

Brian glanced at Paul Miller. "I think, sir, that sometimes in life you just have to go on intuition. Sir."

Manners appraised them both. "Intuition." He glanced over the rail at the flickering screens, Jeni's small form dodging doggedly between cars, hair flying in the mounting wind. She was limping badly. But holding pace.

Manners turned from the rail. "Very well. For the present we play it her way."

He approached the conference room. "For the present . . ."

It was all downhill from here. Literally.

From this point to the finish line—the big cement abutments that marked the end of the bridge—the pavement sloped gracefully downward, the wind at her back. Under normal circumstances she'd have a fifty-fifty crack at the black girl's record.

But these are hardly normal circumstances.

And she'd have to start her sprint now.

And there could be no more exploding vehicles, no more sudden blasts of tropical wind . . . no more sudden surprises from her bleeding kneecap.

Jeni glanced down. The bleeding had stopped, the pressure off that part of her leg, now that muscle groups had shifted tension from uphill pull to downhill braking. She was beginning to feel other, minor cuts and bruises on her arms, her head, her back . . . but that was a good sign, that meant the pain in her leg was easing, no longer masking them.

She glanced up at the big diamond screen. Five minutes to beat the best time ever.

Yes . . . and use up all the remaining strength you'll need to subdue Handle.

She felt a glowing warmth of adrenaline at sight of the finish line through the wisping smoke.

To hell with it. She'd given everything she had to everyone but herself. She deserved this, goddamn it. She dug in her heels and began her sprint.

Long legs pumping, heart racing, breath coming in short but careful measured gasps, Jeni Starbuck did what Jeni Starbuck did best. She ran. Full out. Top speed. With everything she had.

It was easier than she'd have guessed.

At top speed, all the muscles ached, the cuts and bruises disappeared. A small spike began in her knee, threatened to climb higher, then eased and finally melted away. She was past all pain now . . . she was airborne . . .

She ran smiling.

Wind whipping her hair. Not storm wind, but wind of her own making, created with the inertia of her own body, her own endurance. Maybe she couldn't outshoot some of the others on the range, maybe she was not the best female ATF agent that ever came down the pike, maybe when it came to marriage and relationships she was just another statistic . . . but by God she could run.

And the faster she ran, the quicker it went. The easier it got.

Her heart might be ready to burst within her chest for all she knew, but for now she was one with the wind, for now unstoppable. Nothing could touch her in a sprint—not Handle, not anyone. She grinned fiercely into the wind and soared.

Twenty yards from the finish line she knew she was going to make it.

More than make it, she was going to bust the record. The big Diamond Vision clock hand revolved slowly, even it couldn't catch her.

Fifteen yards from the finish line, a big, dark green trailer loomed into view, parked sideways on the median.

It wasn't really in her way—she wouldn't even have to break stride to get around it—but something about its great, silent hulk unsettled her. If Handle was going to play his final hand, here's where he'd do it, within the hard steel shell of this long, dirty green trailer.

She could almost see the Sprinter computer waiting inside its darkened windows on a kitchen counter, a living room table. Waiting. Waiting.

She glanced up at the clock. Forty-five seconds.

She reached down deep and pulled out all the stops. Top-end now, all muscles straining, no going back . . . do or die . . .

Yes . . . do or die . . .

She approached the right front bumper of the trailer.

She passed it, came alongside the silent green doors. She cast a glance through darkened windows. The pavement began to tremble beneath her feet. *No!*—

Only the wind, a final jesting gust. She passed the rear bumper of the trailer without incident. Nothing blew up. The night remained silent.

The finish abutment was before her, then past her.

She glanced up breathlessly at the big screen. The clock was gone, replaced by bright flashing letters, all caps.

"A NEW WORLD RECORD! JENNIFER STARBUCK—
WINNER BY TWO POINT THREE SECONDS!
CONGRATULATIONS!"

Somewhere—it must have been deep in her mind—there was great cheering.

Chapter 26

She knew exactly where he'd be.

The Belmont Arms was a series of three cylindrical new age high-rises casting their twenty-first-century reflections over timeless bay waters. In the garden, some of the towering palms walk-side had yet-wrapped fronds, the workmen and gardeners still completing their jobs. In the foyer the smell of new paint permeated. Everything was new; high-tech glass and gleaming metal, spartan without being austere, ordered without being officious.

She rode the bank of shiny brass elevators to the top floor of suites, stepped off in a dimly lit hallway, glanced right, then left, spotted the sliver of light beneath the door at the far end of the plush corridor, and—Ruger in hand—walked purposefully toward it, unafraid and ready. She was hardly limping.

Jeni opened the door and found John Handle.

He was seated at a massive burl wood desk in deep shadow, framed by a magnificent twenty-story-picture-window vista of his burning city. There was a Sprinter 9000 humming softly before him.

His face and upper chest were swathed in shadow. Nevertheless she sensed him smiling.

Handle spoke first. "Well. And so it ends."

Jeni shut the suite door softly, a perfectly aligned,

slightly pneumatic sound. She held the gun before her, stepped into the spacious room.

She couldn't see much, but enough to tell it was an expensive room, well appointed. But then she didn't need to see much. Just enough.

She stepped into pale rectangular glow from the picture window, skin crawling with gelatinous reflections from the wide, dripping pane. She moved in just far enough to be certain Handle could discern the silvery glint of the gun; then, straight-arming it at him, she stopped, legs slightly apart, and spoke. "Kindly take your hands off the computer keys, Mr. Handle. Or I shall be obliged to blow you to kingdom come."

Handle—hands not moving from the keypad—chuckled his familiar chuckle. "Oh, I think not, dear Jeni. Not with so many questions still unanswered. I didn't bring you this far to leave you in the dark at journey's end."

"You didn't bring me anywhere, John. I brought myself. Step by step."

Another appreciative chuckle. "Indeed you did. I may have dropped the clues, but you divined them . . . divined them admirably, far better than those miserable peers of yours. Sorry this whole thing had to become so tediously protracted. I had to wait until they finished constructing this tubular sepulcher—the rooftop cell site, you know. Without it, I couldn't locate and detonate the last of the computers."

"And have you, John?"

"Have I what, dear?"

"Detonated the last of them? And if so, why are your hands still on those keys?"

Handle shifted in his swivel chair, did not remove his hands from the pad. "All destroyed, my lovely Jeni, all but two. One of those is right here under my fingers. As keenly appreciative as I am of your talents with firearms, I don't believe even you could put a bullet through my skull before I flick my left pinky and rid this lovely island of the top level of floors of this Cyclopean nightmare." He craned around disapprovingly. "Who do you suppose occupies these monstrosities anyway? Surely not the locals. I mean, look at this floor, for instance." He waved a disgusted hand. "A little Frank Lloyd Wright there, a little Walter Gropius Pan Am Building there, a bit of Mies van der Rohe here. Did you see the parking lot? It's the goddamn Kennedy Airport. Saarinen is turning over in his grave. What a sad little miasma."

The gun was already becoming heavy in her outstretched arms, his voice like a lulling metronome—her exhaustion catching up rapidly, now the chase was done. "And the other computer?"

Handle squeaked his chair. "Ah, the other one. The other one is of no immediate threat to anyone. It isn't even a computer, in fact, not yet. It's the last remaining microchip. It cannot be detonated without some minor adjustments to its circuitry. More importantly, it cannot be replicated, not without me. Need I say they would kill for it? I have it well hidden."

"Why are you holding on to the last chip, John? Why not just destroy it?"

That seemed to give Handle pause. "Why. Why. Let me see if I can explain it before your friends from the convention center descend upon us with wildly thrashing helicopters. How did you enjoy our friends, by the way, our resplendent Director Manners? Quite the snappy dresser, isn't he?"

"Let's stick to the subject, please, no more games."

"But Director Manners is the subject. Did you find the meeting edifying?"

"No. I didn't."

"You see, it was never really about antiterrorism, Jeni, it was about money. Greed. It always seems to be about that, doesn't it? But it was *supposed* to be—when I was signed on board—it was *supposed* to be about spying. It was supposed to be—like Reagan's Star Wars—a protective device, something we would eventually *share* with the enemy. The idea being that if everybody's instantly traceable, there can be no more point to spying, yes? That's how it was intended to go. That's how they promised me it would go. In the right hands, the right leaders, it could still go that way. So I burned all my papers and left the secret of the chip in the chip itself. And I hid it very well."

"Too well for anyone to find, apparently."

"Someone will find it, Jeni. Someday. Someone like you. I have great faith."

She chewed her lip thoughtfully. "So. The federal government and private enterprise were in bed together, is that it? Not all that unusual, John, or even illegal. Private enterprise funded the home front during World War II, won the war in fact, according to some."

"But not a war of this size, my darling. And not without first consulting those paying for it, namely the American people. The consortium that put together the Sprinter 9000 empire broke every antitrust law on the books. Approached free enterprise with the delicacy of the Mafia. You can't virtually eliminate the competition while simultaneously manufacturing the complete monopoly of a new computer industry unless you do. And that, my dear, defies constitutional rights. But what else is new? Would you like to sit? Can I get you something to drink?"

"I don't really think we have the time, John."

"Oh, the choppers won't be here for a few more minutes. They'll give you your shot with the madman. You're their golden girl now. They'll make a media darling out of you when this thing's over, after twisting the facts, of course, manufacturing the usual disinformation. I can see their little wheels turning already. Have a seat. You haven't even asked me about Molly yet."

"My daughter is dead, John."

Handle watched her. "Is she? Well. Perhaps she is. There have been many victims in this pathetic little drama, I fear."

"Molly wasn't a victim of this, John. This is your mess, kindly don't drag her into it."

Handle sat back now, one hand remaining on the keys. "Jeni . . . my trusting Jeni. Molly, your lovely daughter, was the biggest victim of all. And, I'm very much afraid, the first."

She felt her heart hitch. "What are you talking about?"

"I'm talking about the man who killed your little girl. Me."

"You killed Molly?"

"We all killed Molly, Jeni. Me, Brian, the Bureau . . . Brian was carrying the prototype Sprinter in his car trunk. I warned him it was unstable."

Jeni reeled back. "Brian . . . poor Brian . . ."

"His guilt must be overwhelming. More so than yours, Jeni, for he knows the truth."

"But your invention killed her! And the investors! And what did you kill the old woman with?"

Handle sighed. "As I said before, Jeni, I did that which I was compelled to do. The old woman died because I needed her apartment. I needed her apartment to buy myself time, to figure out the codes, to track down the armed computers your friends so cavalierly sent out into an unsuspecting world. One life to save thousands. And I killed her because she wanted to die. She was half dead already, of loneliness. I took no pleasure in it. I'm not the soulless beast they'd have me be, Jeni."

"And the NCIC guard?"

"Regrettable. He wasn't supposed to be there. And I needed to get to those files. I reconfigured one of the major banks' computers to send five hundred thousand dollars to his widow's account."

"Which makes everything quite all right, I suppose."

"I didn't say that. I regretted all the killings. But I told you it was necessary to break the chain, to rectify the mistakes. Some innocents have lost their lives, it's true, but you're assuming that life is preferable to death. That is not an assumption I make."

"You are one crazy son of a bitch, John."

"Am I? Oh yes, because I talk to my dead mother. I see. And what does that make a woman who converses incessantly with her dead daughter? Every day. Same time, same cemetery. A little obsessive there, aren't we, Jeni?"

"Shut up, you lunatic prick!" and she leveled the gun swiftly.

"Oh, I really don't think so. Not until you've heard it all. You think you're the only one that's suffered from Molly's death? Sweetie, you don't know the half of it." He turned, squeaking the swivel chair, gazed out the window behind him at the dying fires. The storm was turning the tide. The town would survive. "I never saw little Molly in the flesh. But I saw snapshots, the ones in Brian's wallet, the ones on your dresser. A beautiful child. A hauntingly beautiful child. I couldn't seem to get her out of my mind."

He turned back to her. "I was a pretty good sketch artist, did you know? Oh, but you've seen my work, in Dr. Keegie's office, yes?"

"The charcoal of Keegie."

"Easy to capture a face like that. So little emotion to get in the way." He sighed. "But I could never quite capture Molly's spirit, not on paper. It was too . . . ethereal. Like an angel's. I tried, though. Oh, you can't know how I tried. Over and over I drew her. All to no avail." He looked down at the keypad. "You want to know about guilt? Sweetie, I eat it for breakfast. Or it eats me." He closed his eyes a moment. "That face. That lovely, angel's face . . ." He opened his eyes. "So much like her mother's . . ."

"Stop this."

Handle sighed. "Brian, of course, blamed himself. Blamed himself terribly, but—because of the project's top secret status—could never tell you about it." He smiled sadly at the woman with the gun. "That's what ended the marriage, Jeni. Brian didn't hate you for Molly, he hated himself. Couldn't live with it. Ended up at Veteran's blubbering like a baby."

Jeni pressed back tears. ". . . Jesus . . . Jesus . . ."

"So you see, kiddo? You can take some of that weighty guilt from your lovely shoulders and throw it this way. Throw it Brian's way too. He didn't abandon you, Jeni. He abandoned himself. All in the name of a safer USA. Just a couple of guys trying to do their job. Until the assholes took over. Get you a chair now? Right there beside you . . ."

Jeni, blinded by tears, fumbled out, found the chair back, scooted it over, and sat heavily.

"Sorry, fresh out of Kleenex. Where were we? Oh yes. That brings us to Agent Miller. Another nice dope just doing his job. Just like all of us. Right up to the point where he was so far in he couldn't find a way out. I also like to believe there were altruistic motives for your two lovers sticking with this insanity. Manners was close to retirement.

If Brian or Paul could get in there, maybe they could diffuse the thing, or at least approach it with less megalomania. It was I, by the way—not Miller—who placed that initial Sprinter in your lovely Ocean Beach roach nest."

"Why deliver a computer to me? Were you planning to kill me?"

"No. Only your past. You needed to leave the pictures, the memories. I forced the issue."

Jeni sat hunched forward, barely aware of the gun in her hand. "Why, John? Why me? Why in hell put *me* through all this? What did I ever do to you!"

"I loved you, Jeni . . ."

Jeni looked up in shock.

Handle smiled gently. "It's this kinship I've always felt with you. You were to me the ideal mother, one who would not only die for her child but live for her. My mother couldn't live for me, and I couldn't live without her. Kinship. We're a lot alike you and I, Jeni. Oh, yes we are. And I wouldn't have put it past Manners and his thugs to get rid of you. You were dangerously close to Brian and Brian was dangerously unstable. The best way I could protect you was to put you out in plain sight, make sure everyone knew you were involved, an apparent vital link to me. Then, too, I felt great blame for Molly . . ."

Jeni watched him. "The whole truth, John, and nothing but?"

"Mostly. And of course your involvement confounded the other side. I let it slip—oh so surreptitiously—that there was a strong chance I might have hidden the final chip in your apartment. So you see, no matter where you were shunted about, they weren't about to knock you off until they were sure you didn't have the big prize. They had much invested in it, as you can imagine."

Jeni shook her head, Ruger forgotten. "Money. Money and greed . . ."

"Makes the world go 'round, as the song says."

"It's nightmarish."

"But the nightmare is over. It's time to wake up."

When she looked up, Handle was standing. His face was partially lit now from the side. He was younger than she would have supposed. But the hollow eyes held a weary wisdom. She motioned with the Ruger. "Sit."

Handle smiled, walked past her. "And be blown to smithereens? No thank you. I don't intend to linger in this Gothic mausoleum any longer than necessary. My story is told. And my trusty launch awaits dockside. There's room for two, if you're so inclined . . ."

"Don't make me shoot you, John!" She swiveled as he headed for the door.

Handle chuckled. "That, my darling Jeni, is something you'd have done long before now. By the by, the Sprinter's hard drive is locked . . . the machine on that desk will self-detonate in six minutes. There's no way to reverse it."

Jeni whirled to the desk anxiously . . . whirled back in time to see Handle disappearing through the door. She leapt after him.

Through warm, steady rain, they came down a short grassy hill to one of several small docks near the ferry landing.

They crossed booming planks past slapping pilings, to a sleek powerboat rocking gently beside the jetty. Handle turned to Jeni, held out his hand. "Ladies first!"

She still had the ridiculous gun on him. "John, you know I can't just let you sail away down the bay."

"It's a ChrisCraft, dear, not a sailboat, and you aren't

letting me escape, you're coming with me." He took her hand.

Jeni let him guide her into the craft.

Handle twisted the key, the twin inboards catching with a throaty burble. He turned and looked toward the cityscape across the bay. "Looks as though the rain's got most of the fires under control." He winked. "I'm nothing if not a master of timing!"

Jeni sat on the cushion beside him. "Was the weather part of your plan too, John?"

Handle smiled. "I'll never tell, Jeni dear." He set the throttle to neutral and turned to her. "Scoot over behind the wheel, will you? I shan't be a moment." He climbed from the lazily rocking craft back to the dock, began to unleash them from their cleat.

Jeni was watching the glowing city, the blanket of stars beyond it just becoming visible now through the thinning smoke, when she felt the rope flop heavily behind her into the boat's stern. She turned to find Handle grinning at her from the dock.

"Farewell, darling Jeni. In another lifetime, I'd have found the nerve to kiss you good-bye."

She felt her heart jump. "What are you doing?"

"Little unfinished business back at the high-rise. Nothing to concern you." He pointed outward. "Follow that necklace of lights to the east. That's the *Star of India* moored at the Embarcadero. Use her spreaders to guide you. You can reach Sea Port Village and a phone from there."

Jeni fumbled with the gun, got it up. "Get back in the boat, John. Now."

Handle's expression shifted like passing storm clouds. "I'm sorry, Jeni, for everything. There's just not enough time to tell you how truly sorry I am." He smiled. "It's such an . . . ineffectual word anyway."

"In the boat, I mean it!"

"I know." He held up his hand. Then he bent, drew a card from his coat, and handed it to her. "You can walk to this address from Sea Port Village. The place is doubtless crawling with cops by now. Still, I highly recommend it."

Jeni appraised handwritten numbers.

"The middle part, Jeni. The part you missed. And once you've found the middle, it's time you let the beginning go."

"I don't understand."

"You will. I have great faith." He consulted his watch. "In just under two minutes this entire portion of the jetty will be a fireball." He looked at her. "Allow me this single favor, Jeni of the sunny smile. Allow me what's left of my somewhat tarnished dignity. The state has such . . . sterile methods of retribution. And I abhor needles. Farewell." He turned, strode up the path toward the high-rise.

She could go after him, but there was no more time for that. Or she could shoot him in the back, of course.

At the top of the grassy hill he turned. "Remember. The power is within you!"

And he was lost in the darkness and smoke before the towering building.

Two minutes later, safe at the center of the slapping bay, she heard, then felt, the tremendous heat of the explosion behind her. Trailing comets of debris rained plopping and hissing about the surging boat. She did not turn around to watch.

One hour later she was limping the weed-choked front walk of a little Ocean Beach cottage. Her knee was hurting again, but not intolerably.

The place was indeed crawling with police, so she

didn't really need to check Handle's hand-scrawled address, but checked it anyway.

A uniform barred her way at the front door, its molding bathed in strobing blue lights from two parked black-and-whites at the curb. "It's okay," Jeni told him dismissively, "Special Agent Starbuck, ATF."

"Can I see some ID, please, ma'am?"

"You can call FBI Director Manners at the convention center," and that seemed to shut him up.

On the staircase she found a cigar-puffing homicide detective in khaki raincoat and squeaking rubbers coming down. "Starbuck, ATF, what have we got?"

The lieutenant looked her up and down once, then turned on the stairs with her. "Come on, I'll show you. What's the ATF's interest, the old lady dealing drugs?"

"The Grindle woman, right?" from Jeni, wincing at the ancient steps.

"Yeah, that's the name. This is her house. But she ain't here. The old lady is—"

"I know about the meat freezer, Lieutenant."

In the bedroom they found Handle's computer still turned on and humming.

The lieutenant puffed on his foul-smelling cigar and used it to gesture at the walls. "Fucking art gallery."

Jeni approached *The Yellow Christ* above the bed slowly . . .

She stared quietly a moment, then turned to the bronzed nude on the wall opposite: Gauguin's *Spirit of the Dead Watching*.

"I like that one." The lieutenant blew smoke. "Nice ass. And the figure skulking back there behind the bed reminds me of my mother." He croaked a phlegmy laugh.

Jeni turned toward the corner beside the bureau.

She was reaching out when a uniform nearby called to

her. "Sorry, ma'am, got a hands-off order on that one. It's the real McCoy."

Jeni stood transfixed before the original oil. Not a student of the visual arts, she nonetheless recognized the piece from infrequent visits to the Balboa Park museum. It was Edvard Munch's *Puberty*, circa 1894, though she could not know this. She could see, though, that the young girl pictured—wide-eyed and naked on pale sheets, throwing unabashed teenage loneliness and vulnerability at the viewer—shared the bold, flat simplified use of form and color with the Gauguin opposite. Jeni would discover later, digging through musty, familiar Coronado library stacks, that the image was one of the painter's masterpieces, considered by critics a kind of visual paradigm for humanity in crisis. Munch, she would learn, was an artist obsessed with melancholy, due to the early death of both his mother and sister from tuberculosis.

That aside, there was no mystery at all who the girl in the painting was meant to represent. It was Molly.

The adolescent Molly, the Molly that would have been: the middle part Handle had promised. His gift to her: the Molly she never got to know.

MOLLY LIVES

And it was true. Would always live in her heart, belonged there, safe and warm. Belonged there, not in her head. She was too much in Jeni's head.

The later part, of course, was Jeni herself—same questing eyes, same full, eager mouth. The beginning part—the child—she knew too well. Must now—according to Handle—learn to let go . . .

"Some crazy son of a bitch stole her right out of the art

museum in the park. Walked right in, bold as brass, and hauled her away in his car. Knocked the damned guard senseless."

"But didn't kill him?"

"The guard? Naw. Clipped him a good one, though. The lab boys still can't identify the weapon."

"An ice pick," Jeni told the lieutenant, still watching the painting.

"Scuse me?"

"Look for the blunt end of an ice pick, the handle. Look for the handle."

Five minutes later, limping down a lightly misted front walk, she buckled under familiar pain, pressed nails into her knee, wincing.

"You okay, ma'am?" a uniform obliged.

"I'm fine. Old injury."

The officer, young and stylish in his plastic-covered patrol cap and leather jacket, went back to his notebook. "Bleeding a little. You ought to have that knee looked into."

Lightning lit the north sky a sly, electric smile. Jeni looked up, eyes bright.

And suddenly knew exactly where the last computer chip was hidden.

Epilogue

The cow-eyed intern at Las Flores Emergency pointed with his pinky at the nearly indiscernible smudge on her X ray.

"See it? Right here. Smaller than your little nail."

Jeni, still in johnny smock, eased from the cold metal table and joined the young man at the illuminated plastic screen. The cow-eyed intern squinted. "See? Right there. Must have missed it the first time. Probably a piece of gravel, or maybe even a tiny bit of chipped bone."

Jeni watched quietly behind his shoulder.

"Navy surgeon. Top grades at Annapolis."

"The power is within you."

She was trying to place the time and location. It could only have been that first night in the hotel, after she and Paul Miller had made love. Handle had come calling after Miller left . . . come into her dreams. Two men had invaded her that night . . .

"Be damned," the young intern was saying, squinting closer, "looks for all the world like a computer microchip."

He turned to Jeni. "I can take it out right now if you like, only requires a local."

Jeni slipped into her blouse. "No rush," she told him. "Not an emergency, is it?"

"Well, no. It'll keep till you're ready. But it has to be a burden carrying that thing around inside you."

"Yes. It is a burden."

The intern jotted antibiotic prescriptions. "Well, you give me a call when you want to be free of it."

She took the slip of paper, smiled from the office door. "Thanks. I'll give it careful consideration."

She found Brian waiting for her in Point Loma, on the cemetery cliff before Molly's grave.

He was standing, head lowered, in front of the stone, back to her, hair rifled by early morning ocean breeze.

A lovely morning. Clear and blue. All traces of smoke—some from still-dwindling fires—leveled to a flat line above flatter sea, just off the lighthouse point. Excepting small patches of smudged, fire-blacked blocks, you'd never know there had been a conflagration the preceding night. Traffic still jammed the highways and service roads, but traffic returning, not fleeing. Everything about the day bespoke a new beginning for the city.

As Jeni approached, she saw, from the edge of Brian's jacket, a marbled tail swish once in the breeze. As her ex turned to recognize her, she found Pierre Cardin curled contentedly in his arms. "Good morning," Brian offered. He seemed guarded. For the first time since she'd known him, unsure of himself.

"And a good morning it is," Jeni replied, reaching out for the plump, black and white flanks. She smiled. "Hello, you stupid cat. You've gained weight." Pierre came into her arms and she rubbed the flat, luxurious head, sending him into closed-eye ecstasy. To Brian she said, "Thank you for baby-sitting."

Brian shrugged, breeze flapping his jacket lapels. "Not a problem. I think the kids were really growing attached to him." He nodded at her fresh dressing. "How's the knee?"

"The knee is under safekeeping. For the moment." Jeni cradled her cat, looked down at her daughter's grave.

Brian shifted uncomfortably. "Would . . . you like to be alone with her?"

And Jeni found herself shaking her head emphatically, a little surprised at herself. "No. No, that's okay, I'm not staying. Just came to say good-bye." She smiled wistfully, looked out to the brassy expanse of sea. "It's just a stone, after all . . ." Which also surprised her. "And not a very pretty one at that . . ."

After a moment she turned to find Brian watching her intently. "Did you have trouble getting here?"

She shook her head. "I know all the secret routes."

"I mean . . . after last night's . . . telecast. I thought perhaps people recognized you, gave you trouble. Is that why you're leaving town?"

She smoothed Pierre's flank. "Partly. I don't think Pierre Cardin is ready for instant stardom. And God knows I'm not. A little vacation sounds apropos."

"Any place special?"

"I've been thinking about Santa Barbara. I like the West Coast. I could stay with Mother in Florida, I suppose, but I'm not really ready for that either."

Brian shuffled. He seemed very nervous. "They still haven't found his body, you know."

She said nothing.

"You actually saw him die in the explosion, is that right?"

"I saw him walk into the building," Jeni lied. And the sensation of lying was peculiarly familiar. Handle, in the end, had made liars of them all.

Brian shrugged, looked out to sea. "Well, that kind of concussion obliterates just about everything, I guess."

Jeni nodded. "In any case, it's up to someone else to look for Mr. Handle now. I'm moving on."

And when she looked over, he was still watching her keenly. "Yes. You are."

After a minute, hunched against cool ocean breeze, Pierre clutched to her for warmth, Jeni said, "Well."

"Will you do something for me, Jeni?"

"What is it?"

"Will you write to me? I may have a new address, I'll let you know. But will you stay in touch, please? I'd appreciate it. There's still things I'd like to tell you. When the time is right. If you're interested, that is."

She nodded. "Yes. I'll do that, Brian."

As she was walking back to her car, to her astonishment, Pierre Cardin leapt abruptly from her arms and loped back to Brian, began circling his legs.

Brian scooped him up apologetically. "It's nothing. He smells the kids."

He came toward Jeni, held the cat out to her, but she waved her hand. "No, you keep him. If you don't mind, that is."

He held the cat, watching her. "Breaking all ties?"

She shrugged. "Pierre was never much for traveling. And if the kids really like him . . ."

Brian stroked the broad head. "Well, you know what they say. If you deliberately leave a thing behind, it means you want to return someday."

She came toward him, bent and kissed the cat's flat head, turned—turned back and kissed her ex-husband lightly on the cheek. "See you, then."

And walked with the wind to her car.

*   *   *

Fat Frieda, always in motion, was like trying to nail Jell-O to a tree.

Jeni, trailing breathless in her wake, was finally obliged to grab a thick, trunk-sized arm and haul the perturbed face about. "Frieda, have you been listening to a word I've said? I'm *leaving*! Quitting the clinic. I just came by to get my things."

The mountainous black woman, arms loaded with laundry, appeared more annoyed at the interruption than the news itself. "I heard you. Mind if I get this load into the wash now?"

Jeni threw up her hands. "Fine! Just thought you might like to say good-bye!"

Frieda turned passively. "Good-bye."

"I'm leaving you in charge!" Jeni called after the mountain on legs.

"Like hell you are, girl! I'll keep a lookout till the new director gets here, but you ain't stickin' me with all that paper shit."

She turned imperiously at the laundry room door, and now Jeni could see the clouds of disapproval on the broad, black brow. "You got to fill out some papers of yer own 'fore you go totin' off."

Jeni sighed. Frieda was not going to make this a clean break. "Just mail them to me."

"Un-uh, no way, girl. You just park your pretty blond butt there till I get them forms. It's the clinic rules. Hell, you made the damned rules, it's your clinic."

"Frieda—"

"What you want, chile, you always underfoot!" A bright-eyed boy of six or seven was blocking the door with a catcher's mitt bigger than himself. To Frieda he demanded, "You wanta play catch?"

"Shoot! I don' know nuthin' 'bout no baseball. Get outta

my way now, scoot! And don't be throwin' that ball in this here clinic." She pointed out the window behind Jeni. "Go out yonder on the new field and play wit yerself."

Jeni turned, surprised, found a freshly graded acre of land on what had once been a dump behind the clinic's shabby rear facade. A crew was pouring white lime boundary markers. "What's this?"

Frieda backed through the door. "New joggin' track. Almost finished." She gave Jeni a knowing look. "Private donation. Don't suppose you'd know nuthin' 'bout it." And she disappeared through the door.

The boy, tossing his new baseball high—high enough to put out a ceiling light—sauntered confidently Jeni's way. He stood before her, deliberately tossing the ball before her face, daring her to catch it. When she refused, sat down in one of the rickety folding chairs instead, he stuck the ball in the gigantic glove and regarded her with a cheek huge with pretend tobacco, probably Double Bubble. "I got HIV," he announced defiantly.

Jeni nodded. "Yes."

"That's AIDS. You know what AIDS is?"

"Yes, I do."

The boy nodded, gum revolving. "Ain't gonna kill me, though. I'm gonna beat it. Know why?"

"Why?"

" 'Cause I can beat anybody. You play baseball?"

"I'm afraid not."

"How about just catch?"

"Baseball's really not my sport."

The boy began tossing the ball ceilingward again. If he missed once it would land squarely atop Jeni's head. "You ever had AIDS?"

"No."

"Well, it ain't gonna beat me. Nothin' ever beats me."

When Frieda returned, this time with an armful of papers, she found Jeni nodding at the boy's retreating back. "New recruit?"

"Just yesterday. Fill all them forms out in triplicate. And don't fudge or I'll be after your pretty white ass."

Jeni was watching the boy. He was still tossing the ball, moving through the clinic, trying to probe someone into a game. "Looks healthy enough."

Frieda turned on her heel. "Yeah, don't they all?"

When she came back into the waiting room a few minutes later, Frieda was surprised to find it empty. She glanced out the window to see Jeni heading toward the parking lot, clutching the papers. "Didn't even say good-bye," the black woman muttered. She shook her head once.

"Excuse me . . ."

She turned to find a tall, handsome man in a sports jacket standing politely behind her.

"Jesus! Who you, Paul Newman!"

"Could you tell me where to find Ms. Jeni Starbuck, please?"

"Could I tell who?"

"My name is Paul Miller. I'm a friend."

"Uh-huh. You look like a cop, Mr. Paul Newman."

Miller smiled at such imposing defiance. "Well, whatever I am, this is a social call."

Frieda turned to the window. Jeni had stopped for a moment before the parking lot to gaze at the new field and track area. As she lingered there, the little boy with the big glove came sauntering up behind, tossing the everpresent ball. Jeni turned to him.

"Well, Ms. Jeni busy right at the moment," Frieda informed the blue-eyed man. "Y'all just have to come back."

Miller held his smile, turned, looked behind him, draped his jacket over his elbow, and sat patiently in one of the rickety folding chairs. "Thanks. I'll wait."

Frieda shrugged. "Suit yerself"—hefted the woven laundry basket, glancing at the window.

Outside in early afternoon glare, the kid with the big glove was pointing adamantly at the newly graded track. Jeni, arms on her hips, was shaking her head, explaining something. The boy, confident with defiance, tossed the big glove and ball to the grass and jabbed a thumb at the track arrogantly.

Jeni made a defiant gesture at him, kicked off her high heels impulsively, and, stocking-foot, loped after the kid's skinny legs, which were already flashing across the new blacktop.

As Frieda watched, heavy basket comfortable in her massive arms, the blond-haired woman gained quickly on the boy, was soon pacing him. As they started down the track together, the child picked up steam, began to run in earnest, hair flying. Jeni held pace, but had to stretch her long legs to do so.

If the boy kept urging ahead like that, she'd soon be forced to sprint.